REVENGE
OF ROME

SIMON SCARROW

EAGLES·OF·THE·EMPIRE

REVENGE OF ROME

HEADLINE

First published in 2024 by
HEADLINE PUBLISHING GROUP LIMITED

1

Cataloguing in Publication Data is available from the British Library

Hardback ISBN 978 1 4722 8717 5
Waterstones exclusive ISBN 978 1 0354 2694 2
Trade paperback ISBN 978 1 4722 8718 2

Typeset in Bembo by CC Book Production

Printed and bound in Great Britain by Clays Ltd, Elcograf S.p.A.

Headline's policy is to use papers that are natural, renewable and recyclable products
and made from wood grown in well-managed forests and other controlled sources. The
logging and manufacturing processes are expected to conform to the environmental
regulations of the country of origin.

HEADLINE PUBLISHING GROUP LIMITED
An Hachette UK Company
Carmelite House
50 Victoria Embankment
London EC4Y 0DZ

The authorized representative in the EEA is Hachette Ireland,
8 Castlecourt Centre, Dublin 15, D15 XTP3, Ireland
(email: info@hbgi.ie)

www.headline.co.uk
www.hachette.co.uk

Pour mes bons amis
Yannick, Véronique, Solène and Évrard Vermorel

Merci pour tous les bons moments!

BRITANNIA:
REBEL TERRITORY AD 61

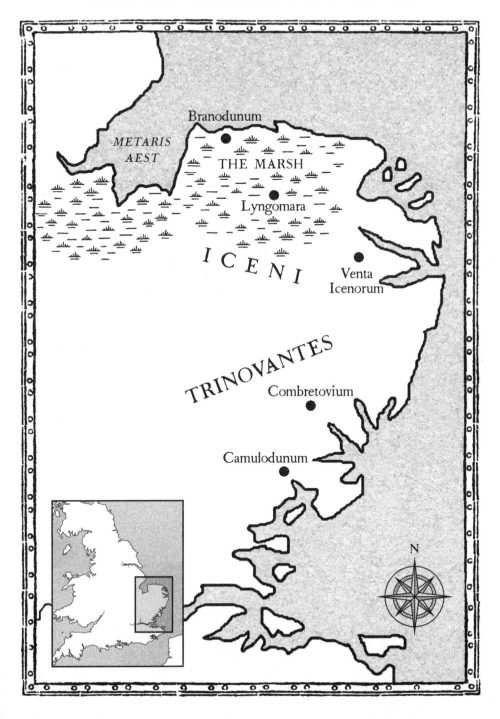

Branodunum

METARIS AEST

THE MARSH

Lyngomara

I C E N I

Venta
Icenorum

TRINOVANTES

Combretovium

Camulodunum

N

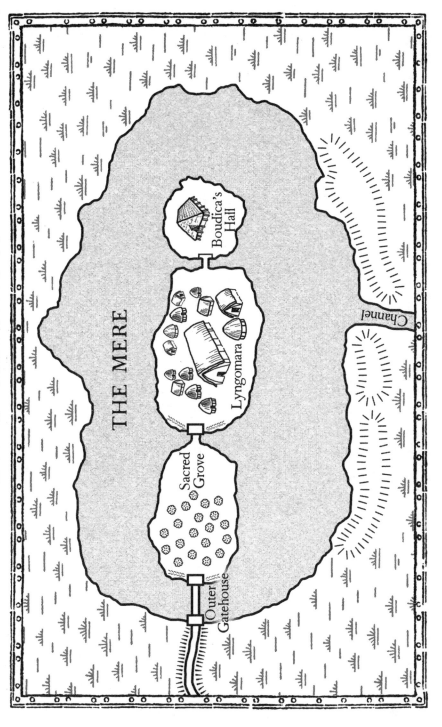

LYNGOMARA AD61

THE MERE

Boudica's Hall

Lyngomara

Channel

Sacred Grove

Outer Gatehouse

CHAIN OF COMMAND

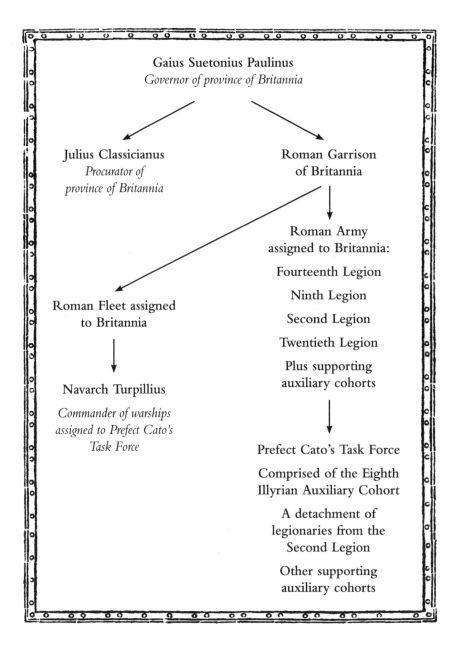

Gaius Suetonius Paulinus
Governor of province of Britannia

Julius Classicianus
*Procurator of
province of Britannia*

Roman Garrison
of Britannia

Roman Army
assigned to Britannia:

Fourteenth Legion

Ninth Legion

Second Legion

Twentieth Legion

Plus supporting
auxiliary cohorts

Roman Fleet assigned
to Britannia

Navarch Turpillius

*Commander of warships
assigned to Prefect Cato's
Task Force*

Prefect Cato's Task Force

Comprised of the Eighth
Illyrian Auxiliary Cohort

A detachment of
legionaries from the
Second Legion

Other supporting
auxiliary cohorts

CAST LIST

Roman army of Britannia

Prefect Cato, commander of the Eighth Illyrian Auxiliary Cohort

Gaius Suetonius Paulinus, governor of the Roman province of Britannia

Prefect Thrasyllus, commander of the Tenth Gallic Auxiliary Cohort

Centurion Tubero, commander of the Eighth Cohort's cavalry contingent

Centurion Galerius, senior centurion of the Eighth Cohort

Centurion Macro, legionary veteran and second in command to Prefect Cato

Tribune Helvius, the governor's chief of staff

Agricola, tribune on the governor's staff

Phrygenus, surgeon of the Eighth Cohort

Trebonius, Cato's manservant

Prefect Quadrillus, prefect of a cavalry cohort

Julius Classicianus, procurator sent from Rome to report on the situation in Britannia

Centurion Torcino, commander of the legionary cohort attached to Cato's task force

Prefect Fulminus, prefect of an infantry cohort

Navarch Turpillius, commander of a naval squadron of the fleet based in Britannia
Legionary Gaius Bullo
Polyclitus

Roman civilians

Claudia Acte, lover of Prefect Cato and former exiled mistress of Nero
Petronella, wife of Macro
Lucius, son of Cato
Titus Besodius, captain of the *Minerva*, an entrepreneur with an eye for adventure

Britons

Boudica, Queen of the Iceni, the proud leader of those cruelly oppressed by Rome
Syphodubnus, a noble of the Iceni and adviser to Boudica
Bardea and *Merida*, daughters of Boudica
Tasciovanus, chief of the settlement at Combretovium
Vellocatus, Tasciovanus's son
Bladocus, chief of Boudica's Druids
Ganomenus, chief of the settlement at Branodunum
Hardrin, his grandson
Garamagnus, a brigand
Varibagnus, commander of Boudica's bodyguard
Pernocatus, a hunter

In Rome

Emperor Nero
Poppae Sabina, Nero's mistress
Burrus, commander of the Praetorian Guard
Seneca, a smooth-tongued senator

CHAPTER ONE

Britannia, AD 61

The Iceni queen looked over the battlefield below her with a mixture of horror and despair. Across the slope, tens of thousands of her warriors were being forced back by the Romans. In the centre, a great wedge of legionaries was carving its way through the heart of her faltering army. The auxiliary troops were advancing on the flanks as well, all the while forcing the rebels back towards the vast arc of wagons and carts drawn up along the crest of the hill. The families of the warriors and the other camp followers had been expecting to witness the complete destruction of the Roman army of Governor Suetonius, but their earlier conviction of imminent victory and triumphant cheering had long since succumbed to a growing sense of anxiety and silence.

Four times the rebel army had charged across the stream at the foot of the slope and up the far side to assault the far smaller force of Romans drawn up with dense woods covering their flanks. Each attack had been met with a hail of javelins, ballista bolts and other missiles before the two sides closed in hand-to-hand combat. After a bloody rebuff, the rebels withdrew across the stream to reassemble for the next effort, leaving their dead strewn across the slope in front of the Roman line. The enemy had filled the gaps in their ranks, retrieved serviceable javelins from the battlefield and prepared to hold their ground again. Although

1

their reserves were being steadily depleted, the Romans' line had been broken only once during the day, and even then they had swiftly dealt with the threat, re-formed ranks and driven Boudica's warriors off.

Now the fourth attack had resulted in disaster. The rebel warriors had been in poor spirits as they were herded back into their warbands by their chieftains. With so many of their comrades lying dead on the opposite slope, and the wounded crying out for help, their earlier courage and confidence had ebbed away. This time, the Romans, as if sensing their loss of nerve, had pursued them down the slope, across the stream and up the far side.

The rain that had begun some hours before was now a downpour, and frequent bursts of lightning illuminated the battlefield, freezing the combatants in silvery gloom for an instant. An instant was enough for Queen Boudica to grasp the ghastly truth. Her army was not only beaten, but in danger of annihilation. Already the right flank was being pressed back on the wagons and carts of the baggage train and the spectators crowded on top were scrambling to get down and escape. Their cries of panic could be heard even above the din of battle.

The tip of the Roman wedge was aimed at the centre of the rebel line and steadily drawing closer to Boudica and her entourage, who were mostly mounted on chariots to better observe the battle. Her two daughters, Bardea and Merida, stood on a nearby chariot, equally aghast as they beheld the unravelling catastrophe. One of Boudica's closest advisers, Syphodubnus, approached and gripped the rim of the side panel above the wheel.

'The battle is lost,' he said, just loudly enough for his words to reach her. 'You must leave while there is still time to escape.'

Boudica looked down on him with a bitter expression. 'I cannot leave. I will not abandon my people. I will not betray them.'

'There is nothing left to betray here. We have lost. But the rebellion continues as long as you live. If you die here today, or are taken captive, all hope of driving the Romans from our lands dies with you. Is that what you wish for?'

It was a clumsy attempt at emotional blackmail, but there was sense to his words. The rebels had already proved that the Romans could be defeated. Their Ninth Legion had been cut to pieces in an ambush, the veterans at the Roman settlement of Camulodunum had been overwhelmed, and the towns of Londinium and Verulamium had been razed to the ground, their inhabitants slaughtered. Tribes across the island would take great encouragement from the example set by Boudica and her followers. But would the crushing defeat unfolding now unnerve them? Would their will to resist crumble away? The rebels had come within reach of driving the Roman invaders from Britannia. The spirit of rebellion must endure, she resolved. And for it to endure, the leaders who had inspired so many thousands to follow them and take up arms against Rome must survive to continue the fight.

'Boudica!' Her adviser shook the side panel. 'You must leave. Now!'

She drew a breath and steadied her resolve, then nodded. 'Very well.'

Syphodubnus did not wait for further instructions, but turned and ran over to the captain of the royal bodyguard, drawn from the finest warriors of the Iceni. He was standing with his men in front of their horse-holders and mounts. The adviser thrust his arm towards the wagons blocking the way behind Boudica and her entourage. 'Clear those away!'

The captain hesitated, glancing towards his queen.

'Boudica has ordered this,' Syphodubnus snapped. 'Do it!'

The captain cupped a hand to his mouth to bellow the order, then he and his men surged towards the nearest wagon, already abandoned by its owner. Taking hold of the yoke, several warriors braced their feet and hauled the front pair of wheels round before their comrades heaved the wagon free of the mud. The captain threw all his strength into helping to shift the heavy vehicle as he called out to his men, 'Come on, lads. Move this bastard!'

For a few beats the wagon was still, then it began to move fractionally, ploughing through the sodden ground, then gathering pace until the bodyguards had moved alongside the next wagon in the line. They rushed to repeat the process with the second wagon as Boudica stared at the approaching Romans, no more than fifty paces away. The rebels were being forced back towards her and were threatening to entangle themselves with her entourage. She turned to her charioteer. 'Turn us round and make for the gap!'

The charioteer called out to the two horses either side of the yoke and the vehicle began to turn away from the battle and trundle up the slope. The other chariots followed suit, and the loose formation moved towards the widening gap being created by the bodyguards. As her chariot approached the opening, Boudica ordered the driver to halt and waved the rest on. One by one, in the slashing rain, they rumbled past and made their way down the far side of the hill.

Her adviser came hurrying over.

'What are you waiting for, my queen? Go! For Andraste's sake, go!'

Boudica was torn between the desire to escape while she still could and the sense of honour that called on her to remain with her army and share its fate. That fate was all too clear now. The right flank was being crushed against the line of wagons, the men packed so closely together that they could not move or use their weapons. They were dying at the hands of auxiliary soldiers whose short swords excelled in such confines. As the rebels were cut down, their enemies climbed across the dead to get at those still living, who were now letting out piteous wails.

4

Closer to, those at the rear of the crumbling rebel line had spotted the movement of Boudica's command party, and as they fled through the gap in the wagons, a series of angry cries spread through the ranks.

'Boudica's running!'

'We are betrayed! Gods have mercy on us!'

The words cut through her heart like a blade. There was little chance of escape for those who remained, and the Romans would show no mercy to any rebel caught in the vice between the Roman line and the tightly packed vehicles of the rebel baggage train. So much Roman blood had been spilled during the rebellion that their thirst to avenge the earlier defeats and the massacres of so many Roman soldiers and civilians would not be easily satisfied.

As word of Boudica's abandonment carried through the rebel ranks, a howl of despair rose up and she felt it in every part of her being. It felt like the end of the great cause, which had united tribespeople who had been bitter enemies before the Romans came. All the while, hope, then confidence, had grown that the invaders would be hurled back into the sea and the peoples of Britannia would be free again. Memories of the laughter and joy that had accompanied the swelling ranks of the rebel army as it marched from victory to victory now rang hollow, as the first taste of crushing defeat filled her with its bitter fruit.

She turned away from the dreadful scene and ordered the charioteer to continue through the gap. The other vehicles were waiting a short distance down the slope, and as she got closer, she could see the numbed expressions of her closest followers as the rain fell like shafts of steel from the dark clouds smothering the landscape. On either side, across the slope and beyond, streamed the camp followers. They had left their wagons and their loot behind and were fleeing for their lives. They needed to get as far from the battlefield as possible before finding somewhere to hide from an enemy that would hunt them down and slaughter those deemed to have had anything to do with the rebellion. Amongst them were those warriors who had managed to scale the baggage train and escape the slaughter on the battlefield. Those still on the far side of the wagons were doomed.

The ground, already churned up by the wagons and carts that had been hauled up to the ridge the day before, was slick with mud as the rain turned the slope into a quagmire. The ponies strained to pull their burdens downhill. The chariots, so nimble and swift on firm ground, were now clumsy dead weights that lurched and slid alarmingly. The going was not much better for the mounted bodyguards who followed the slow procession. Most of them dismounted to lead their horses carefully down the slope rather than risk a fall that could cripple a mount and its rider.

Boudica and her remaining followers glanced back continuously for the first sign that the Romans had broken through and were coming after them. She knew they would expend every effort to capture her. The Roman governor would want to have her bound in chains and forced to march behind him as he paraded through Rome in triumph when the defeat of the rebellion was celebrated in the imperial capital. She had long since resolved never to let that happen. Even as the rebels had gone from victory to victory, she had made a pact with her two daughters that none of them would be taken alive. If necessary, they would assist each other to die if the rebellion failed and they were in danger of being captured. They had sworn never to become trophies of the accursed Romans and their emperor, Nero.

When they reached the foot of the slope, the even ground made the going easier. As the bodyguards remounted, their captain turned to Boudica for orders. It was a critical moment. Should they head north, working their way round the thinly spread Roman forts, and join the northern tribes that had not yet been conquered? The fugitives could throw themselves on the mercy of Queen Cartimandua of the Brigantes. Might Boudica sway her into taking up arms and renewing the rebellion? She considered this briefly, then discounted the idea. It would entail crossing enemy-held territory with no guarantee of success at the end and every chance of suffering betrayal. There was no point in heading south. That had been the centre of the Romans' power before the rebellion, and they were sure to consolidate their control over that part of the province after today's sweeping victory.

That left the east. Two days' march away, three at the most, lay a vast sprawl of low-lying land and marshes that stretched towards the sea and far into the territory of the Iceni. She knew the area well and was aware of how easy it would be to conceal herself and her followers there and continue the resistance to the invaders. There was no better place to recover, regroup and rebuild her army while carrying out hit-and-run attacks on Roman villas and forts, and on patrols sent to look for the rebels. The ponderous Roman legions would be bogged down if they attempted to enter the marshes. And the memory of the fate that had befallen Varus and his three legions when they had blundered into equally difficult terrain lingered in the minds of Roman commanders. They would be wary of sending their best soldiers into any traps that Boudica might set for them. They had suffered heavy losses already and they would be hard pressed to restore order as it was.

East then, Boudica decided. She raised her hand and pointed in the direction of her tribal homeland. 'That way.'

The charioteer flicked his reins and called out to his ponies, and her chariot lurched into motion. One by one the others followed, and the bodyguards formed up into a loose column to cover their rear. Behind, the sounds of battle faded and the desolate shouts of the rebel army died away. Around them trudged the camp followers, looking up anxiously as they became aware of the passing chariots and mounted men. Some stared at Boudica with undisguised hostility, over the disaster she had led them to.

7

Most regarded her with fear and shame as the scale of their shared defeat under her leadership became apparent. Only a handful raised a muted cheer and urged her to continue the fight. Boudica acknowledged the latter with a nod and a brief wave of her hand.

They had covered around two miles when they saw the dark mass of a forest ahead. Boudica indicated a track that led in the direction of the trees, and the column angled towards it. One of the ponies pulling her daughters' chariot had gone lame and had slowed the small group down. A moment later there was a cry of alarm from behind. Gripping the side of the chariot with one hand, she raised the other to shield her eyes from the rain while she scanned the landscape. Then she saw movement on a low ridge off to one side as a line of horsemen crested it and began to swarm down the slope, heading in their direction. She turned to her daughters on the chariot behind her.

'With me. Now!' she ordered, and the pair hurried across to clamber up to join her. The younger, Merida, moved stiffly, and Boudica could feel the girl trembling as she put her arm around her. 'They won't take us. Remember what we have agreed.'

Merida looked at her with an expression of infinite sadness, her despair emphasised by the drenched locks of hair plastered to her head and over the shoulders of her tunic. She tapped the haft of the dagger hanging at her waist. 'I'll do it. If I have to. If I can't, then . . .'

Boudica hugged her. 'If you can't, then I'll make it as quick and painless as I can, my child. Before Bardea and I join you.'

A chariot pulled up alongside her and Syphodubnus snapped an order to the charioteer. 'Get them into the forest! Do it!'

The chariot rumbled away as Syphodubnus shouted orders to turn and deal with their pursuers. The captain of the bodyguard was already marshalling his men. They were equally adept at fighting on horseback or on foot, armed with swords. The Iceni tribe's battle standards depicted a blue horse on a white background – with good reason, for they were among the finest horsemen of Britannia and more than equal to any mounted force the Romans could field against them.

Boudica watched as the bodyguards, some four hundred strong, approached the Romans at a steady walk. The enemy were distracted, running down the fugitives from the battlefield, slaughtering warriors, the elderly, women and children with neither pity nor discrimination as they sated their bloodlust. The commander responded too late to the danger, and as the brassy trumpet notes pierced the hiss of the rain to sound the recall, Boudica's bodyguards broke into a canter. Those fleeing the Romans did their best to get out of the way, but even so, several were trampled by their own side. The enemy cavalry were still rallying to their standard when the Iceni captain gave the order to charge. The rebel horsemen smashed into the disordered ranks of the auxiliaries, thrusting their lances and using the superior weight of their mounts to barge the Romans aside, knocking some from their saddles. Others were run through and slumped over or swayed as they tried to get clear of the fighting. The Roman commander had managed to rally no more than fifty of his men and they were quickly surrounded.

A grim smile formed on Boudica's face as she watched the enemy whittled down by her warriors. It was the smallest of compensations for the great calamity of the day, but it felt good to see the careless arrogance of the Roman cavalrymen punished. A small group of auxiliaries gathered about their standard attempted to fight their way free, surging through the Iceni horsemen. One by one they were cut down. Only three of them broke the Iceni line, and then only for a moment, before they were chased down by the fresher mounts and killed.

The captain of the bodyguard allowed his men a brief respite to finish off the Roman wounded and loot the enemy bodies before he formed the band up and rode back to join the chariots. Soon the column reached the edge of the forest and followed the track as it wound its way through the trees. At least the hard-fought nature of the battle had left the enemy in no shape to continue the pursuit for any distance. In addition, it would be dusk soon, and they would be foolish to blunder into the forest, where they could be ambushed by the survivors of Boudica's army.

Even though their people had suffered a great defeat, her bodyguards were flushed with their small triumph over the auxiliary cavalry, and some of them brandished the heads they had taken as trophies in keeping with Celtic warrior tradition. As Boudica watched them exchange boasts about their deeds in the brief fight with the Roman cavalry, a poignant memory of her childhood came to her. She had witnessed the same high spirits from Iceni warriors returning from raids against rival tribes. They had hung the heads of their enemies from the lintels of their huts and made offerings to the gods by throwing their armour and weapons into the river before feasting through the night in celebration of their victory.

Those days were gone. There would be no triumphant return to the Iceni capital for the warriors of her bodyguard. The Romans would be sure to burn to the ground every Iceni settlement they could locate, once they had slaughtered every living thing therein, down to the last dog and goat. That was how they set an example to others of the fate that befell those who defied Rome. Boudica and the survivors of her army, along with those who remained in the Iceni settlements, would have to abandon their homes and hide in the marshes. Theirs would be a dangerous existence full of hardships, but there was no alternative if they were to survive and keep the flame of rebellion alive. It would be many years before they could build an army powerful enough to face the legions in battle once again.

The captain of the bodyguard rode forward until he was alongside Boudica's chariot. He carried the captured standard of the Roman cavalry unit in his hand and grinned as he held it aloft.

'My queen! For you.'

Boudica regarded the auxiliary standard with acute hatred for a moment. She had seen the enemy's standards up close many times when attending ceremonies in Londinium, and before that when she had fought alongside the Romans when they had been allies of the Iceni. That was before the rebellion had been ignited by the outrages perpetrated against the tribe. She felt a familiar surge of rage in her veins as she recalled the rape of her daughters and her own flogging at the hands of the Roman procurator. Only after taking a deep breath was she calm enough to give the captain her orders. She was tempted to keep the standard to use alongside the gilded eagle captured when the rebels had ambushed the Ninth Legion soon after the revolt had broken out. But the legion's eagle was prize enough, and she thought of a better use for the auxiliary standard.

'Leave that planted in the ground at the edge of the forest, where the Romans will find it easily. Tell your men to pile some of the enemy heads they have taken at the bottom of the standard. I want the Romans to know that even though the battle is lost, the rebellion is far from over, and this is what they will face when they come after us. We will fight them from the depths of every forest, from every marsh and under cover of night. Every man they send after us will live in fear of traps and ambushes. We will wear them down as we strike at them from the shadows. This we will do, I swear before Andraste. We are the Iceni, the greatest warriors of our island, and we shall not rest from avenging our fallen while a single one of us draws breath and can continue the fight!'

She sensed a movement at her shoulder and turned to see her younger daughter slumping onto the bed of the chariot with a groan. Boudica crouched beside her.

11

'Merida! What's happened?'

'My leg.' The younger woman eased the folds of her cloak aside to reveal a bloodied slash in the cloth of her breeches and a gaping wound beneath. A surge of dread gripped Boudica's heart. 'How?'

'My own fault.' Merida smiled weakly. 'I had ordered our charioteer to go down the slope to encourage our warriors. I didn't see the Roman javelin until it was too late and . . .' She gestured helplessly at the wound.

Boudica had drawn her own dagger and was hurriedly cutting a strip of cloth from the bottom of her cloak.

'Get her breeches off,' she instructed Bardea. As the wound was exposed, Boudica had to suppress a gasp as she saw the extent of the damage and the amount of blood welling from the torn flesh. 'Hold her.'

She worked quickly to attach the makeshift dressing before tying her daughter's leather headband round her thigh above the wound. Merida gasped in pain.

'I'm sorry.' Boudica cupped her cheek. 'We must stop the bleeding. Now lie down.' She turned to Bardea. 'Keep that tight.'

'Yes, Mother.'

As Boudica rose to her feet and prepared to order the charioteer to move off, she noticed the blood covering her hands. Her daughter's blood. She blanched in horror, then wiped it off on her cloak. 'Get us out of here. Go!'

CHAPTER TWO

Rome, late summer

The din from the banqueting hall of the imperial palace was dimly audible in the private audience chamber in the squat tower overlooking the heart of the Forum. Several slaves entered bearing small trays of delicacies and silver jugs of chilled wine that glistened with condensation after being fetched from the ice room in the deepest cellar of the palace. Under the guidance of a steward they set them down on the tables between the opulent dining couches and a dais on which rested a preposterously ornate couch, its frame decorated with gold leaf. On it was laid a large mattress, packed with the finest wool. The steward pushed a slave aside in order to arrange the emperor's bolsters himself. Aligning them precisely, he scrutinised the silk covers minutely, brushing away any unsightly blemishes, then stood back to review the chamber's remaining furnishings and the layout of the refreshments.

'That couch on the far right,' he called out. 'Bring the front end round a little.'

The nearest slaves bent to edge the heavy piece round, then back a little, on the steward's orders, until he judged the angle to be right.

'Stop. That's it.' He waved them back and examined the setting carefully. Nero was very particular, and inclined to rage at any slight imperfection in furniture, serving dishes and seating arrangements. The emperor frequently complained that such failings distracted him from his creative endeavours and unsettled his concentration on matters of state. A finely tuned intellect and artistic sensibility such as he claimed for himself was an intricate and delicate affair. He could not afford to compromise his endeavours through the anguish that attended the slightest perception of disorder in his surroundings. Stuff and nonsense, the steward reflected. He had served under two previous emperors, the crusty lecher Tiberius and the serially cuckolded fool Claudius, before the latter's adopted son had gained the throne at the tender age of sixteen. Any hope that the youth's immaturity would be cast aside as the demands of running the Empire forced him to grow up had not yet been realised. Nero exhibited the same petulance and impatience as before and was content to act on the prompting of the last senior adviser to flatter him before making a decision.

The steward occasionally wondered if any other empire or kingdom would tolerate such a ruler. Truth be told, he wondered why Rome tolerated Nero at all. In the six years of his reign he had not evinced any of the qualities one would expect of the ruler of the world's greatest empire. Perhaps that was because there were no effective constraints on his behaviour; he was too powerful to care about what he did, and those around him were too frightened to risk losing influence by offering even the mildest of criticism. The emperor took their bare-faced flattery at face value. How had such an individual come to be trusted with such great responsibilities? The gods must be mad, or unremittingly mischievous, to impose such a ruler on Rome.

The steward checked himself. It was not for him to second-guess the will of Jupiter and his divine court. Matters of statecraft were far above his quotidian concerns, and yet he could not help a discreet sigh as he considered his master's limitations. He wondered if his train of thought was duplicated by servants in similar positions in other empires. Was another steward, at the same moment, in far-flung Parthia, agonising about preparing a chamber for an equally unworthy ruler?

Further consideration of the inequities in the attribution of power ceased as the door to the chamber creaked open. A Praetorian in a white tunic ducked in and nodded over his shoulder. 'They're coming!'

'Out!' the steward ordered the slaves. 'Be quick about it.'

The staff hurried out, leaving through a silk curtain that covered a service entrance to the modest audience chamber where Nero chose to confer with his most trusted advisers. The steward plucked the curtain into neat folds before he stepped to one side and lowered his head so that his gaze would not accidentally meet that of a member of the emperor's retinue – or, gods forbid, the eyes of Nero himself. The latter would be a breach of etiquette for which there would be harsh consequences.

With further creaking from the hinges, the main doors to the chamber were opened by two Praetorians who stood to attention on either side as voices echoed along the corridor beyond. The higher-pitched tones of Nero talking garrulously were accompanied by the obsequious praise and laughter of his companions. The young emperor paused at the threshold and removed his arm from the shoulder of the strikingly attractive woman who had accompanied him from the banquet hall. Poppaea was several years older than Nero but behaved as if she was younger by the same margin. She ran the tip of her tongue along her lips lasciviously before she giggled.

'Don't be too long talking with these old men. I'll be waiting for you.' She reached up to kiss Nero, then withdrew at the last moment to tantalise him and pinched Nero on the backside before running off down the corridor, laughing.

The emperor stared after her with an adoring expression and blew a kiss.

15

'How lucky I am to have such a devoted partner to share in my labours.'

Some of the men around him exchanged cynical looks. Poppaea Sabina had been instrumental in persuading Nero to murder his mother and remove her as a rival for his affections. Before that, she had seduced and married one of his friends, Otho, as a means to position herself close enough to Nero to seduce him in turn. Now Otho had been sent away from Rome and she was making plans to divorce him and marry the emperor.

The emperor led the way into the audience chamber. His small party of advisers waited until he was comfortable on his raised couch before the grey-haired senator Seneca gave a discreet nod and they began to arrange themselves on their own couches.

The Praetorians quietly closed the doors and took up position behind Nero, where they could instantly intercede if the emperor was threatened. Three of the four previous rulers of the Empire, Claudius, Tiberius and Augustus, had almost certainly been poisoned, while Caligula had been murdered by a faction within the Praetorian Guard. No position within the Roman Empire was more dangerous than that of the men who ruled it.

The current commander of the guard, Burrus, was a few years younger than Seneca, but equally grey and made haggard by his years of service. Forever balancing the need to protect his master with ensuring that Nero never had any cause to doubt his loyalty was strain enough to exhaust any man. Moreover, he lacked the ready wit and smooth tongue of his colleague, who was ever able to defuse any suggestion of suspicion or disfavour with humour and outrageous flattery. Burrus needed time to weigh the impact of every word before he spoke, which made him come across as rather dull and boorish by comparison to the smooth-tongued Seneca. As a result, Nero only tolerated him, displaying none of the affection or respect that he accorded the senator. But each served the emperor's needs in their different ways. For the present.

16

Nero glanced at the steward and clicked his fingers. The steward hurried forward and poured some of the Falernian wine from the silver jug into a goblet. He took a sip and then carefully wiped the rim where his lips had been before setting the cup down.

'Now the food,' Nero commanded, hesitating before he pointed out some of his favourite pastries. 'That one. And the grapes – that small bunch there – and the tart.'

He watched closely as the steward tasted small amounts of each item, then waited a moment for any sign of an adverse reaction before he waved his hand towards the side of the chamber. 'Enough.'

As the steward backed away, head bowed, Nero picked up the pastry and took a bite, chewing and swallowing before he smiled at the others. 'Do join in, gentlemen.'

While they did so, Seneca addressed the purpose of the gathering. An imperial courier had arrived at the palace earlier in the evening with an urgent dispatch from the governor of Britannia. The sealed leather tube he had carried had made its way up through the hierarchy until it had been placed in the hands of Burrus, who had broken the seal, extracted the scroll and quickly read its contents before passing it on to Seneca. When he too had read it, the pair had approached Nero, lolling on a couch with his mistress, to pass on the news and request this private audience of the emperor's closest advisers to discuss their plans for the future of Britannia.

'Your imperial majesty,' Seneca began. 'While Suetonius and his forces have won a great victory, the situation in Britannia is hardly satisfactory.'

'Is it ever?' Nero sighed. 'That gods'-forsaken island of barbarians has been a thorn in our sides ever since that dotard Claudius gave the order to invade. One campaign after another, with every governor boasting that it will be the last before the island is finally under our control. And then there's Suetonius, off dealing with Druids at the arse end of the world, leaving the way

17

open for some damned woman and her band of animals to foment a rebellion. It's been a bloody disaster from start to finish. A waste of men and resources, Seneca. As you have often reminded us.'

Burrus stifled the urge to smile at the other adviser's discomfort. Seneca had been the guiding hand behind those in the Senate who had been questioning the wisdom of expanding the new province beyond its existing boundaries. Some had even raised the possibility of withdrawing from Britannia altogether, despite the loss of face that would cause the Roman Empire. The rebellion had put paid to that prospect for the foreseeable future. To withdraw now would turn the much-needed victory into a defeat. To the mob in Rome, and the Empire's enemies abroad, it would appear that Rome had won a battle but lost the war. Such humiliation could not be countenanced. Which was why Seneca now had to sway his young master into believing the opposite of what he had been steering him towards for some years. Far from abandoning Britannia, Rome was now obliged to commit herself to remaining there and completing the conquest of the island, whatever the cost and no matter how long it took.

'It was vital for the security of the province that Suetonius put an end to the Druidic cult, imperial majesty,' Seneca responded. 'It was something of a priority. And he achieved his goal.'

'Only by stripping the rest of the garrisons of their best men to fill out the ranks of the army he led against the Druids,' Nero countered, wagging the half-eaten pastry to emphasise his point. 'Suetonius was a fool. I expect better from my generals. He blundered into the campaign like a junior tribune on his first outing under arms. Why, even I would have done better than that.' He paused and frowned slightly before nodding to himself. As is often the case for such men, arrogance and ignorance trump wisdom on almost every occasion. 'Of course I would have done better than that. I am the emperor after all. Just one step away from divinity and the wisdom that goes with it. I would have made a tremendous general, it's true. I'd not have made the same mistake.'

'Naturally, imperial majesty,' Seneca continued in a mollifying tone. 'But Suetonius, unlike yourself, is only human. In the event, he has redeemed himself somewhat by defeating the rebels and crushing the uprising.'

'That remains to be seen,' said Nero. 'That woman – the one who led the barbarians. What was her name again? Bodicina . . . Bonducia . . .'

'Near enough.' Seneca gave a deferential nod as he corrected his master. 'Boudica.'

'Yes, Boudica. The report says that her body was not recovered from the battlefield. So she's still at large, and likely as not determined to continue her struggle against my soldiers with all the further losses that entails. No doubt Suetonius will be angling for some kind of public celebration to mark his victory. If so, he can think again. There'll be no triumph for him. No parade through the streets of the capital at the head of his trophies of war and whatever pitiful barbarian prisoners he has spared. His carelessness is what caused this mess. I've a mind to strip him of his position and send him into exile. He deserves no better.'

Seneca nodded and assumed a thoughtful expression. 'You are right, of course, imperial majesty. However, it might be worth considering how this plays out as far as the mob is concerned.'

'Which mob?' Nero retorted archly. 'The one in the street or the one in the Senate?'

Seneca allowed himself an amused chuckle. 'Does it matter which? The response of both has to be considered. I have no doubt that you are right about the rebellion continuing, particularly if this Boudica still lives to serve as its figurehead. But Suetonius, for all his faults, has provided Rome with a victory, and that can be used to distract both mobs from the reasons why such a battle was necessary in the first place. Victories tend to induce

19

the plebs' forgetfulness in such matters. That is to our advantage. If you choose to punish Suetonius, you will undermine the value of his victory in the eyes of your people. They will ask questions that frankly would best be avoided. It will make a bad situation look even worse. That is in no one's interests, imperial majesty.'

'Are you suggesting I reward him?' Nero scowled. 'I think not. What kind of precedent would that set? I'll have governors queuing up to provoke rebellions in order to put them down in the hope of garnering honours and public acclaim.'

Burrus sighed inwardly. This was the kind of hyperbole to which young men were prone, this particular young man most of all.

'Precisely, imperial majesty,' said Seneca. 'There can be no question of being seen to reward Suetonius while there is any chance of the rebellion flaring up again.'

Nero gave a snort of exasperation. 'Well, if I can't reward him and I can't punish him, what in the name of Jupiter's great big balls am I supposed to do with him?'

'Nothing.'

He frowned. 'Nothing? Oh, that's helpful.' He adopted a sneering ironic tone as he continued. 'Very helpful indeed, Seneca. Where would I be without your sage advice, I wonder? Have you reached that age when a man's wisdom begins to fail him? Perhaps I need to clear out my advisers and replace them with younger, more mentally agile minds.'

Seneca took the criticism impassively. 'It is always wise to have fresh minds consider a problem, imperial majesty. Just as it is wise to make judicious use of hard-won experience. I am honoured to make my knowledge of the arts and politics available to you, in the same way that my esteemed colleague Prefect Burrus is honoured to share his understanding of military affairs, to best guide your judgement and decisions.'

Burrus sat up stiffly as he silently cursed Seneca for drawing him into this exchange. He'd much rather sit it out and let the wiser man steer the emperor's thinking. But as Seneca had pointed out before, it was more effective to tackle Nero on two fronts and let him think he had got the better of one of them as he reached a decision. More often than not it was Burrus who got to play the weak link and suffer the consequent incremental erosion of his sense of pride.

Nero's attention switched to the commander of his guard for a moment before he turned his gaze back to Seneca. 'This is a political matter rather than a military one. What would be the purpose of doing nothing about Suetonius?'

'As you pointed out, you can't be seen to either reward him or punish him. I would advise you to leave the man where he is, far from the public gaze, and in time he will cease to be a problem. Provided that he suffers no more defeats. If he eventually manages to crush what is left of the rebellion and capture or eliminate Boudica, then you might want to offer him some kind of minor reward for the achievement. Enough to placate Suetonius, his faction in the Senate and the mob in the streets. I suggest that we tell the Senate and the people of Rome that a victory has been won and that Suetonius is working hard to restore peace to Britannia. That should keep them all satisfied for the present.'

As he considered Seneca's advice, Nero stroked the scant band of bristles that constituted the beard he was attempting to grow. 'I suppose so. But what chance has he got of putting an end to this revolt and getting Boudica in the bag?'

Seneca shrugged. 'Alas, imperial majesty, I am not a soldier. For advice on military affairs I humbly suggest you direct your question at someone who has the expertise I lack in such matters.'

Burrus shot a hostile look at Seneca as the latter lay back and helped himself to a small sprig of grapes.

'Burrus? What opinion does my most trusted soldier have to offer? Can Suetonius finish off these rebels? Or should I send a more competent replacement to complete the job?'

Burrus hurriedly composed a reply. 'Some might question why Suetonius was being replaced, imperial majesty. As Senator Seneca says, best to leave him where he is. As for his ability to restore order and end the rebellion, that's more complicated. I read his latest dispatch only moments before we convened this meeting—'

Nero motioned a wheel turning and Burrus nodded as he cut to the heart of the matter. 'The rebellion has already cost us most of the Ninth Legion, all the veterans in the reserves at Camulodunum and the auxiliaries and legionaries lost in the withdrawal from Londinium and Verulamium, as well as those who were casualties in the battle with Boudica's army. That's in addition to the men lost in the campaign to take Mona and destroy the Druids. What's left of the province's garrison is going to be thinly spread dealing with the brigands and pockets of fresh rebellion inspired by Boudica. Suetonius is going to need reinforcements. Plenty of 'em. And he's going to need time to impose order, rebuild the settlements and encourage merchants and settlers to return to Britannia.'

Nero sighed. 'Never ask an old soldier a simple question. I just want to know if it can be done. Well?'

Burrus took the plunge. 'Yes, sir. In my estimation, it can be done.'

'Estimation is not the degree of conviction I was looking for. Very well.' Nero thought for a moment, then nodded as he reached a decision. 'Suetonius stays where he is. We tell the people that he has won a great victory and has assured us that he will put an end to the rebellion once and for all and bring us the ringleaders in chains. We send him sufficient reinforcements to guarantee that those barbarians in Britannia can't spring another embarrassment on Rome. We also give him a free hand with respect to punitive action against those tribes who took part in the rebellion.' Nero's voice took on a cold tone. 'I don't want those scum to ever forget what happens to those who choose to defy Rome, to defy me. I want Boudica brought to me in chains. I want the lost eagle of the Ninth Legion recovered. If that means razing every last farmstead, slaughtering every last man, woman and child, then so be it. We'll send all that in a response to Suetonius. And I'll give him no more than two years to conclude this matter. If he fails to do it by then, he will incur my displeasure. It might be better for him if he didn't live long enough to do so.'

'Yes, imperial majesty,' Burrus responded, making mental notes about the redeployment of forces the emperor's orders would entail. Given the existing demands on the soldiers defending the vast length of the Empire's frontier, it was going to be tricky to reinforce Suetonius adequately. That would present the governor with difficulties. And not just him.

Burrus's thoughts shifted to the part of Suetonius's dispatch where he mentioned the force he had earmarked to hunt down Boudica and her surviving warriors. Whoever was given command of that column would be at the sharp end of things, pressured for results by the governor, who would be pressured by the emperor in turn. Burrus had read enough reports on Britannia to know how difficult the terrain was in the east of the province. Its dense forests and vast stretches of marsh and bog had scarcely been penetrated by Roman patrols. It was perfect for the kind of ambushes and hit-and-run attacks the Britons had adopted successfully in the past.

The officer on Boudica's trail was in for a hard time of it, and with very little prospect of garnering any glory. If he was successful, Suetonius would claim the credit. And if he failed? Then Suetonius would hold him accountable. In short, it was a question of survival and anonymity or death and dishonour.

'Sooner him than me,' Burrus muttered under his breath. 'Poor sod.'

CHAPTER THREE

Camulodunum

At that moment, the officer in question was sitting on a stool at his campaign desk as the rain drummed on the roof of the goatskin tent. A dull glimmer of light from an oil lamp hanging from a small stand provided the only illumination as Prefect Cato bent over the report he was preparing for Governor Suetonius on the reverse side of an outdated dispatch. When the rebels had burned down the governor's headquarters in Londinium, they had destroyed almost all the province's official records and stocks of writing materials. As a result, the governor, his staff and other officials and army officers were obliged to make do with whatever they could retrieve from the ruins of the towns and villas across the broad swathe of the region scourged by Boudica and her rebels. In time, fresh supplies would reach the army based in Londinium and be sent on to the various columns dealing with the remaining rebels.

Cato was obliged to use waxed tablets for most documents, but these were heavy and burdensome, and had the disadvantage of obliging him to write in a large hand. Today, however, he had been fortunate. One of his men had found some scrolls and writing implements in the ruins of one of the dwellings of Camulodunum. Whether they had been overlooked by the rebel looters or dismissed as having no value to illiterate tribesmen, he was grateful for the use of them.

Until the rain had begun to fall, that was. Some flaw in the stitching of the tent's seams had begun to admit water, which had started to drip onto the table so that Cato was obliged to hunch forward to prevent drops falling onto the scroll and making the ink run. He had considered moving his desk, but there were other leaks, and besides, he had almost completed the document. So he hurriedly concluded, lowered his quill and put the stopper in the inkpot, then held the scroll up to the light to read back over his words.

He had taken some care over the tone to ensure that he did not come across as too demanding. The governor was dealing with the most unenviable torrent of challenges as he attempted to address the breakdown of control across much of the province. Although Boudica and her army had been defeated, their earlier successes had inspired many others with the prospect of the imminent collapse of Roman authority, and bands of brigands were roving across the landscape terrorising Roman settlers and loyal tribespeople alike. The thinly spread Roman forces were struggling to restore order. As soon as they had chased off one lot of brigands, another band struck elsewhere. At the same time, the port facilities of Londinium had been destroyed, along with the bridge across the Tamesis, which greatly hampered communications within the southern half of the province as well as restricting the landing of supplies from Gaul. Not only had the army to be fed, but tens of thousands of civilians as well. Those who had escaped the rebels were now returning to the ruins of Verulamium and Londinium, and it would be many years before the survivors cleared away the rubble, rebuilt their homes and restored their businesses.

To this litany of problems burdening the governor, Cato was about to add another. He had been tasked by Suetonius with forming a column to hunt down Boudica and her remaining followers, who had most likely returned to their Iceni homeland.

In addition to destroying the remaining rebels and capturing Boudica, Cato had been ordered to recover the eagle standard of the Ninth Legion, captured by the rebels when they defeated the legion not long after the rebellion began. It was a daunting task. His own auxiliary unit, the Eighth Illyrian Cohort, was mostly comprised of infantry but with a large cavalry contingent. It had suffered heavy casualties in the battle against Boudica, in addition to those men lost in the earlier campaign against the Druids and their allies. Of the original strength of over eight hundred men, only a hundred and fifty infantry and fifty cavalry remained. Suetonius was wise enough to know that was far too few to risk in any headlong pursuit of the enemy into the marshes, and he had promised to send Cato reinforcements once the latter had set up his base at Camulodunum, ready to strike north into Iceni territory: a cohort from the Second Legion as well as sufficient auxiliary replacements to bring him up to full strength. None of the men had reached him yet, however, and his small command felt very exposed out in the middle of the land of the Trinovantes, the very first tribe to join Boudica's rebellion. The main focus of his report on the situation at Camulodunum was to stress the need for reinforcements and the other forces he had been promised without coming across as too concerned for the safety of himself and his men.

The report also covered the condition of the former veterans' colony that had been founded at Camulodunum. His orders had been to repair the colony's defences as far as possible so that it could serve as a secure base of operations. No thought seemed to have been given to the degree of damage he might expect to encounter – which, considering the state of Londinium, should have been anticipated. The truth was there were no defences to repair. Camulodunum had been the first Roman settlement to be attacked by Boudica and her followers, and in their rage, the enemy had been determined to destroy it as completely as possible. The rampart had been pitched into the outer ditch. Nearly every building within the defences had been burned to the ground, and all that remained besides the blackened ruins of the colony was the pediment and half-completed columns of the temple dedicated to the previous emperor, Claudius. The cohort had cleared the rubble away from the temple precinct and repaired the damage to the curtain wall in order to create a relatively secure camp while waiting for the reinforcements to arrive, but the air within the precinct still carried the acrid tang of the conflagration.

Distressing as the wider devastation was, it was the sight of the smoke-blackened temple that caused Cato the most grief. That was where the defenders of the colony had made their last stand when the outer defences fell, and where one of Cato's companions, Apollonius, had fallen. Cato felt a degree of guilt over the fact that he had never told the man that he counted him as a valued friend. Now it was too late. There also had died the adopted son of Cato's closest friend, Centurion Macro. Parvus was a mute whom Macro and his wife had taken on soon after Macro's return to Britannia to retire in Camulodunum. He had perished in the flames along with Cato's dog, a large, scarred brute who had been unswervingly loyal to those who had cared for him. At least the two of them had managed to save Macro's wife, as well as Cato's son and Claudia, the woman who had been Cato's lover ever since he had rescued her from brigands while he had been stationed in Sardinia some years before. Petronella, Lucius and Claudia had been put on a ship bound for Gaul just before the rebels took and destroyed Londinium.

Cato felt each loss keenly, but his grief was tempered by the mercy shown by the gods in sparing his old friend and comrade Macro, one of the handful taken prisoner by the rebels and the only one to escape before the enemy could sacrifice him to their god, Andraste. Cato smiled grimly. Macro was surely beloved of the gods of Rome, who seemed to use him for their personal amusement – putting him in the most dire of predicaments just to see what feat of courage and ingenuity he would deploy in order to escape death. Though to say his life was charmed would be an overstatement, since his mother had died in Londinium. She had refused to abandon the inn she owned in the heart of the town, and perished in the flames.

'So much death,' Cato muttered as he reflected on the tragic course of the rebellion. And there would be more to come before some semblance of order and authority was re-established in the Empire's newest province. Not least as a result of the punitive operation he had been tasked with. He sighed and used the last of the ink on the quill to print his name at the bottom of the report. Then he rolled it up, took out a leather tube from the box containing his writing materials and carefully inserted the document before placing the cap on the tube and setting it down on his desk.

He sat back and stretched his shoulders as he yawned and closed his eyes for a moment. Beyond the pattering of the rain falling on the tent he could faintly hear the noises of the camp: murmured discussions occasionally punctured by laughter or loud exchanges between comrades. Despite their isolated posting in the heart of what was still enemy territory, the men seemed to be in good spirits. This was most likely a consequence of having survived one of the most bitter and hard-fought battles Cato had ever experienced. There was always an element of rejoicing at such a thing, even as men grieved for the fallen. Sometimes the effect lasted for a long time. Even the rain of the last two days had not soured their mood noticeably. He smiled to himself. The weather was one thing they *were* prepared to grumble about. Every soldier in every army throughout history had that in common.

The sound of the tent flap being opened caused him to open his eyes, and he turned to see Macro enter. A head shorter than

Cato, the centurion was powerfully muscled. Even though he was in his early fifties and most of his hair was grey, he was still a force to be reckoned with. He eased the hood of his cape back and shook the drops from his fringe.

'Fucking weather. You'd think the bloody island would sink into the sea given the amount of rain that falls on it.'

'And yet you chose to retire here . . .'

Macro made a face. He had accepted land around Camulodunum when he took his discharge from the army, and settled into a house in the town along with his wife, Petronella. Now the house was a pile of sodden ashes, the farmland he had owned was devastated and the business he had owned with his mother in Londinium had gone. Macro had lost almost everything. When the rebellion began, he and the other reservists at the colony had been recalled to the army, and now he served under Cato once again as his second in command. It would be some years before he would save enough, or acquire sufficient loot, to be able to afford a second attempt at retirement. Fate could be hard to those least deserving of hardship, Cato mused. Certainly Macro deserved better after having served Rome for the best part of thirty years across the Empire, shedding much blood in the process.

'Retire?' Macro sniffed. 'That's behind me now. I'll probably still be in uniform when I die of old age, the way things are going.'

'Somehow I find it hard to imagine you dying of old age. You were born to die in battle, or from overindulgence in wine.'

'I'll take either right now.' Macro unfastened his cape and let it drop onto the corner of Cato's camp bed before he eased himself down on the other end and rubbed his shoulder with a tight-lipped grimace.

'Any luck with the search party?' Cato asked. The centurion had been scouring the ruins of the colony for tools, weapons or armour that might be of use to the cohort.

'No. There's nothing left. Boudica's lot did a pretty thorough job.'

'Did you find your house?'

Macro nodded. 'Easy enough to locate. Not so easy to dig through what was left of it. I couldn't find the chest I buried under the wood bunker in the kitchen. One of those rebel bastards must have made off with it. That's ten thousand sestertii I'll never see again.'

Cato cleared his throat as he tackled the touchy subject. 'I'll cover whatever it costs to get you back on your feet. You can repay me whenever you like.'

Macro fixed his dark eyes on him for a moment and nodded. 'That's kind of you, lad. But we'll manage, Petronella and me. Somehow.'

'The offer's open,' said Cato. 'Any time.'

'Thanks. Good to know.' Macro was quiet for a moment before he indicated the scroll on the desk and changed the subject to something less personal. 'Is that what I think it is?'

Cato nodded.

'I hope you told the governor we can't do a damned thing until we get the men we were promised. We're short-handed as it is, without even taking account of the dose of Remus's Revenge that's going around the camp. A quarter of the lads are in no shape to do anything right now. And we're going to need to dig some fresh latrines just to keep our heads above the shit.'

'Charming. I've told Suetonius we need more men before we tackle the Icenians. Meanwhile, we have enough to keep up the patrols. Has Galerius got anything out of the prisoners yet?'

The mounted contingent had scoured the area around the camp for any rebels who had returned to their tribal lands. Unsurprisingly, most of the people they had encountered claimed to have had nothing to do with the rebellion, but the wounds and warrior caste tattoos of some told a different story, and these had been taken prisoner and brought back to the camp. Centurion Galerius and the cohort's interrogators had been pressuring them for any information about Boudica and the other ringleaders. Some claimed that she had fallen in the battle; others said that she had escaped and was raising a new army from within the Iceni lands. The truth, Cato suspected, was that none of the Trinovantian prisoners knew anything about her fate. Their responses were motivated by the despair of defeat or wishful thinking and he doubted that they would get any useful intelligence from them.

Macro shook his head. 'Nothing new. We might as well send 'em on down to Londinium and find a slave trader to buy them.'

'No. We'll release them when we're done.'

'Release them? What the fuck for? They'll fetch a decent price. I could use my share of that, as you know.'

'I understand. But we have to start rebuilding relations with the locals if we're going to put the rebellion behind us. If we make slaves of those prisoners, what signal do you think that sends to others in their tribe? It would only vindicate everything that Boudica told her followers about Rome. We have to offer a better vision. That begins with releasing them, unharmed.'

'Unharmed? Bit late for that now Galerius and his boys have gone to work on them.'

Cato felt his heart sink a little. 'Nothing too bad, I trust?'

'Define bad.' Macro shrugged. 'You may be right, but as far as most Romans are concerned, a barbarian is a barbarian is a barbarian. I dare say you'll find that's what the mob back in Rome thinks, and they won't give a toss about your good intentions. Or better vision, as you put it. As far as they're concerned, any tribe that backed Boudica has it coming to them.'

Cato did not doubt the truth of his friend's assessment of the public mood in the capital. They lived far from Britannia and could not hope to understand the complexity of the challenges facing those tasked with putting an end to the rebellion and taking

31

back control of the province. In Cato's considerable experience, such matters only seemed simple to the simple-minded.

'Nonetheless, the prisoners will be released. We'll see to it first thing tomorrow. I don't care what people say about it back in Rome.'

'Suit yourself.' Macro's nose was running, and he wrinkled it before sneezing. 'Jupiter's balls, this bloody climate will be the end of me. I'm telling you, when we're finished with Boudica, I'm quitting Britannia and not coming back.'

'That rather depends on whether the cohort remains stationed here.'

'Not for me it doesn't. I've signed on for the duration of the emergency. Once it's over, I'm thinking of applying for a posting to a legion somewhere warmer and less . . . barbarian. Failing that, there are plenty of gladiator schools in Italia that could use a good lanista. I know how to train men to fight.'

'Indeed you do. But is that how you really want to end your days? Pimping for the pleasure of politicians and the plebs?'

'I may not have any choice.' Macro sniffed. 'Anyway, I'll deal with all of that when the time comes. First things first. Boudica. Dead or alive. Those are the governor's orders.'

Cato regarded his friend thoughtfully. There was a time when they had considered Boudica a friend, and in Macro's case, rather more than a friend. The centurion had enjoyed a brief romance with the fiery Iceni woman before she married an Icenian noble. That was just after the legions had first come to this part of the island during the Claudian invasion. The affair might have been harmless in itself but for the fate that had befallen Boudica and her daughters when her husband had died. On receiving the news, Suetonius had given orders for the annexation of the Iceni kingdom. The procurator sent to carry out the task had taken exception to Boudica's protests and had her put in chains, flogged and made to witness the rape of her daughters.

32

Macro had commanded the procurator's escort, but had been absent when the outrage occurred. He had effected the women's escape in the hope that it would undo some of the damage. Instead, their shameful treatment had been the spark that ignited the rage of the Icenians and led to the bloodshed that followed. It was a dreadful responsibility for the centurion to shoulder, and despite Cato's attempts to convince him that he could not have known how his honourable deed would turn out, Macro would carry the burden of the unintended consequences to his grave.

There was a further aspect to the tragedy that salted the wound. The first daughter born to Boudica had been sired by Macro. Boudica had only revealed this to him after Macro had been taken prisoner by the Icenians, and his grief had been agonisingly compounded as a result.

'Dead or alive,' Cato repeated. 'When the time comes, that might not be so easy.'

Macro caught his meaning at once and drew a sharp breath before he replied. 'If she surrenders or goes down fighting, it makes no difference to me. Not any more, sir. Not after everything that has happened.'

The atrocities committed by the rebels had latterly hardened the centurion's feelings towards Boudica and her people, including his daughter. At least that was how it seemed. Cato could not help wondering at the emotional turmoil that he suspected still churned within Macro's heart. He felt a twinge of sympathy for his friend and briefly considered trying to find the words that might offer some comfort. But he knew him well enough to understand that this was not the time to do so.

'What are your orders for tomorrow, sir?' Macro continued. 'Do you still intend to lead the next patrol?'

Cato nodded. 'We'll try the settlement at Combretovium. Someone there might be willing to speak to us.'

'Fat chance of that.'

'We'll see. Give the order to Centurion Tubero to have the mounted contingent ready to ride out at first light.'

'Yes, sir.' Macro stood up and retrieved his cape, easing the sodden folds around his broad shoulders. 'Was there anything else?'

Cato waited a moment, willing the centurion to relent and open up, but the latter's face remained expressionless. He sighed. 'That's all. Get some rest. We'll need our wits about us tomorrow.'

'Yes, sir.'

They exchanged a salute, then Macro lifted the flap and disappeared into the rainy night. Cato stared after him for a moment. The weight of the duties imposed on him did not compare to the burdens heaped upon his best friend.

'You poor sod.'

CHAPTER FOUR

On the way to Combretovium

The rising sun soon cleared the dawn mist from the ground and shone brightly from a clear sky. It was as fine an early autumn day as could be wished for, Cato mused as he led the mounted column away from the ruins of Camulodunum along the track towards Combretovium. The road between Londinium and Camulodunum that had been constructed by legionary engineers ended at the colony. To go any further, travellers were obliged to use the native tracks that wound across the rolling countryside dotted with farmsteads amid the scattered forests of the region. Most of the forests had started to lose their foliage, and leaves fluttered on the light breeze. Cato was thankful for the change in season; soon the trees would be bare and less able to conceal any enemy using them to carry out an ambush. He could ill afford to lose any more men.

As to the enemy strength, he was uncertain. To be sure, most had died on the battlefield, but many thousands had fled the scene. The defeat would have shattered their brittle courage, and he hoped that as many as possible had abandoned their weapons and returned to their farms and villages. There would be a cadre of warriors who would not accept defeat, resolved to continue the fight against the Roman invaders until the bitter end. The surviving leaders of the rebellion would be sure to encourage them. Boudica and the others were marked for death and had nothing to lose. The danger was that they might find a way to keep the spirit of defiance alive and fan the flames to provoke a fresh uprising. Such a prospect chilled Cato's heart. Rome was clinging on to the province by the fingertips, and another military reverse would be sure to end in disaster for the legions. He felt the crushing burden of the task allotted to him by Governor Suetonius.

'Nice day,' Macro announced cheerfully as he eased his horse alongside Cato's mount. 'Makes a change from the shitty weather we've had to put up with recently. I'd almost forgotten how fine these lands could be in the right conditions.' He raised his head and sniffed the cool air, like a hound taking in the scents.

For all his companion's casual enjoyment of the moment, Cato knew that Macro was as keenly observant as ever, and long experience would ensure that he was alert to any danger that might present itself. Cato himself tried to clear his head of his worries and looked round at the landscape.

'We'll not reach Combretovium until this afternoon. Let's hope there's no trouble. I don't fancy riding back to the colony in the darkness.'

'I doubt there will be any,' Macro replied confidently. 'We're in Trinovantian territory. It's Boudica's lot that we need to be wary of. The Icenians are a bunch of fanatics. They hate our guts. Mind you, we've given them every reason to.'

'Same goes for the Trinovantians, though,' said Cato. 'They had to bear the brunt of the colony being sited on their lands. Our veterans helped themselves to their lands and imposed crushing taxes on them.' He shot a glance at his friend. 'That was before you arrived in Camulodunum, of course.'

'Indeed, though I doubt I'd have acted any differently,' Macro conceded. 'It's just the way it goes when Rome stamps its seal on a new province. In any case, the Trinovantians lacked the

36

balls to do anything about it on their own. If it hadn't been for Boudica stirring the pot, I dare say they wouldn't have lifted a finger against us.'

'Maybe so. But as things turned out, they were out for our blood just as much as the Icenians. They just needed a gentle push. We'll have to watch ourselves around them for a long time before we can be sure there's no further danger from their direction. I'm not happy at the prospect of Claudia, Lucius and Petronella returning to Britannia for a while yet.'

Macro nodded. 'Me neither.'

As they rode further away from Camulodunum and the land that the Roman colonists had annexed, the number of tribal settlements increased. There were still plenty of farmers tending the last of the year's crops, while others looked after small flocks of sheep or herded cattle. All paused to watch warily as the column passed by in the distance. Some ran into hiding or hurried back to their round huts to spread the word that the Romans had returned. Occasionally Cato saw bands of men, women and children fleeing to hide in the nearest area of forest. There was a peculiar atmosphere to the morning, with neither side yet understanding how the crushing defeat of Boudica's horde would play out. The local people were no strangers to the rough treatment handed out by the invaders, and doubtless dreaded retribution now that the rebellion appeared to have collapsed. Meanwhile, every Roman soldier would live in fear of ambush and Roman civilians would be looking anxiously over their shoulders at any tribesmen they passed by. The tension between the two sides would last for a long time yet, Cato mused. It would be made incalculably worse if the governor gave in to the widespread desire for bloody revenge among those Romans who had suffered during the rebellion.

Just after midday, the track crossed a low ridge and Cato

saw the settlement of Combretovium no more than two miles beyond. He reined in and halted the column before he surveyed the scene spread out below him. The Trinovantian town lay in the broad loop of a river, protected on three sides by the riverbank, while a ditch and palisade covered the side facing the track. Cato estimated there were perhaps as many as five hundred round huts beyond the palisade, as well as a large rectangular hall and several similar structures along the river, where a number of small trading vessels were moored. Thin columns of smoke trailed up from cooking fires and forges and formed a faint haze. He could make out the tiny figures of people moving between the huts and, closer to, working in the fields and pastureland outside the town.

'Looks quiet enough,' said Macro. 'The same way it was the last time I came here, before the rebellion.'

'It may look a little different close up,' Cato replied. 'We'd better be careful.'

He turned to address Tubero and his mounted men. 'Lads, we don't know what kind of reception to expect when we ride into Combretovium. We don't know how many of them sided with the rebels. We've not come here to cause trouble. We're here to gather information. I want you to use your eyes and ears, not your fists. You are not to abuse the Trinovantians. If they insult you, keep your mouths shut. If they throw filth, ignore it and don't respond. No one is to draw a weapon unless we're attacked and I say so. If anyone disobeys these orders, they'll answer to me, and I can assure you that will be far more unpleasant than any shit the locals hurl your way.'

He glanced over his men in silence for a moment as his words sank in. Then he turned his mount back towards the town and waved his arm along the track. 'Advance!'

It did not take long for the Trinovantians to respond as the column slowly picked its way down the slope towards Combretovium. Those outside reacted first, driving their animals away from the approaching Romans, while others abandoned their tools and hurried off. Shortly afterwards, men lined the inside of the palisade either side of the gates as they were closed.

'I don't think that's very hospitable of them,' Macro remarked. 'Fucking heartbreaking. If we aren't friends any more, I don't think I could bear it.'

'We should be safe,' said Cato. 'I doubt the people down there want to give Rome any excuse to treat them as enemies of the Empire.'

'All the same.' Macro patted the hilt of his sword. 'We'd best be on our guard.'

Cato halted the column a hundred paces from the ramp crossing the ditch in front of the gate and turned to Macro. 'I'm going forward to talk to them. You stay here with the column.'

'But—'

'If anything happens to me, you turn back to Camulodunum and send a report to the governor, then wait for further orders.'

'Fuck that. Anything happens to you and those bastards are going to pay for it.'

'You'll do as I order, Centurion. Is that clear?'

Macro made a face before he nodded and raised a finger to the brim of his helmet in salute. 'Yes, sir. Just be careful.'

Cato eased his mount into a walk and slowly approached the gate. Despite the warmth of the sun, he felt an icy tingle trickle down his spine and forced himself to adopt a composed expression as he sat stiffly in his saddle. Ahead he could make out the details on the faces of the Trinovantians lining the palisade. They stared back in silence, displaying neither smiles nor hatred, and that ambiguity was in itself unnerving. He saw the glint of reflected sunlight on the broad point of a spear and noticed that a handful of other men were carrying bows, though none had nocked any arrows. He reined in and cleared his throat before addressing them in the local dialect.

'I am Prefect Cato, commander of the Eighth Illyrian Cohort stationed at Camulodunum to restore order in this area. I wish to meet with your chief, or whoever speaks for the people of Combretovium.'

He spoke clearly and with as much authority as he could muster, well aware of the hollowness of his words. If the Trinovantians knew just how few men he had at his disposal, they would laugh in his face.

There was a short pause before a tall man to the right of the gate leaned forward.

'I am Vellocatus. I speak for my father, Tasciovanus, the chief.'

'Where is your father?'

'He is unwell. He is resting in his hall. Until he has recovered, I rule in his place. State your business here, Roman.'

'Very well. I wish to confer with you about restoring order to this region, following the defeat of Boudica and the collapse of her rebellion. Rome needs to work alongside our allies to repair the damage and restore authority so that we can live in peace, as we did before.'

This time there were several responses to his words from those on the palisade. Cato heard snorts of derision and angry muttering before Vellocatus raised his hands and called on his followers to still their tongues. As quiet fell, he turned back to Cato.

'Very well. You may enter. Alone. Your men stay back.'

Cato shook his head. 'My men enter with me. They will need to feed and water their horses. We come in peace. You have my word that we are not here to harm your people. I just wish to talk and buy provisions. For which I will pay in silver.' He reached under his cloak and held up his purse, hefting it so those watching could see that it was heavy with coin.

Vellocatus turned to give an order, and a moment later the gates creaked open. The Trinovantian leader emerged and approached across the ramp. Closer to, Cato saw that he was a man of roughly the same age as himself, though a little taller and broader across the shoulders. He had faded swirling tattoos on either cheek, and his dark hair fell to his shoulders, framing his beard. Pale blue eyes scrutinised Cato as the other man took stock of his Roman visitor.

There was a tense stillness before Cato decided it would be better if he dismounted to put them on the same level. He did not want to be seen as some haughty Roman officer looking down his nose at these tribesmen he must win over to restore order. Easing himself from the saddle, he dropped to the ground and held out his sword hand. Vellocatus hesitated, then grasped Cato's hand in a powerful grip.

'You and your men may enter Combretovium,' he announced. 'But you will not be permitted to stay for the night. I may speak for my father, but I cannot answer for all my people. There are a few who hold little but hatred in their heart for Rome and her soldiers.'

'More than a few, I imagine.' Cato smiled knowingly and was relieved to see a brief amused expression on the other man's face.

'Yes, more than a few. After all that has happened since your legions came to these shores, can you blame them, Prefect? You Romans have not treated us with much respect, even though the king of our tribe signed a treaty that made us allies. I wonder, does Rome habitually help itself to the lands of all its allies around the Empire? If so, I can imagine that rebellions like the recent one are a frequent event.'

'Not really,' Cato replied. 'Most provinces are handled rather better than Britannia. It takes time for both sides to get used to each other.'

'Quite a lot of time in the case of Britannia, I fear.' Vellocatus released Cato's hand and gestured towards the gate. 'You had better follow me into the town. My people will need to see that

41

you enter with my permission.'

'I understand.' Cato turned back towards his men and called out, 'Dismount! Form up on me!'

Macro's voice bellowed down the column as he relayed the order, and the auxiliaries climbed down from their saddles and led their horses down the track towards the gate. As they closed up on Cato, he introduced Macro.

'My second in command, Centurion Macro.'

A glimmer of recognition showed itself in Vellocatus's face. 'I know you. You were a magistrate at Camulodunum. I sold you and your wife some sheepskins last year.'

'I remember.' Macro nodded. 'I was the chief magistrate at the time. Now I'm back serving in the army, since there is no colony for me to be a chief magistrate of any more.'

The two men stared coldly at each other for a beat before Cato spoke. 'Lead on, Vellocatus.'

As the Trinovantian strode back towards the gate, Cato waved his men forward across the ramp and through the entrance. On the far side, a broad track stretched between the huts. The change in season, accompanied by rain, had rendered the ground muddy and churned up by hooves and wheels. Some attempt had been made to improve the footing with scattered bracken, but it had already been trodden in for much of the way. The local people lined the route, looking on in silence as the Roman soldiers and their mounts passed by. Cato was keenly aware of the suspicion and hostility in most faces. Only a handful regarded them with neutral expressions. The air was thick with the tang of cooking and the odours of dung, woodsmoke and the middens of the townsfolk.

He studied the throng on either side. The men were wearing cloaks and tunics, and some carried staffs or hunting spears, but no swords, in accordance with the terms of the treaty with Rome. The women had their hair tied back or wore it plaited, and carried their infants in slings while they kept a tight grip on the hands of their younger children, who gazed wide-eyed at the visitors to their town. Then something struck him. Most of the men were either youths or frail old-timers with grey hair and wrinkled faces and limbs. There were very few men of fighting age to be seen in the town.

The quiet around him was unnerving, and he could not help wondering if he and his men were being led into an ambush. He scrutinised the way ahead and the huts on either side as the column proceeded further into Combretovium, but there was no sign of any suspicious movement or the glint of concealed weapons. Besides, the Trinovantians would have ensured that their women and children were kept away from any ambush.

The muddy thoroughfare led down to the river, then followed the bank to a compound dominated by a large timber-framed hall. A modest fence surrounded the compound, intended to demarcate the domain of the chief rather than serve as a significant line of defence, Cato realised. His gaze shifted to the handful of craft moored to posts along the bank, and a few larger vessels anchored in the middle of the river. Two of them were the kind of merchant vessels that plied their trade between Britannia and Gaul. Their crews were at work loading their wares into small boats to ferry them ashore. A man with cropped hair and garbed in a plain tunic who was supervising the landing of the cargo greeted Cato with a relieved expression as the column approached.

'Good to see the army back on the scene!' He held out his hand. 'Titus Besodius, captain of the *Minerva*.' He indicated the larger of the two cargo ships. 'Just in from Gesoriacum.'

Cato halted his men as he replied. 'Quintus Licinius Cato, Prefect of the Eighth Illyrian Cohort. I have to say I'm surprised to see a Roman merchant here, given recent history.'

Besodius shrugged. 'To be sure, rebellion is bad for business, sir. I had a hard time finding a crew willing to come back here.'

43

'Bad for business?' Macro gave an irritated hiss. 'It's bad for pretty much everything else besides, friend. But I dare say tens of thousands of bodies and burned towns and settlements don't feature much on the balance sheets of the merchants back in Gaul.'

'This is Centurion Macro,' Cato interrupted before his friend could go on. He was keen to have the chance to talk with Besodius, who might have useful information to share. 'Will you be able to join us in the compound later on?'

The merchant nodded. 'I've just got to see the cargo safely locked away in those sheds along the bank before I take my usual consignment of wine to the chief. Keeps the old man happy.'

Vellocatus had been watching the exchange impatiently and now addressed Cato. 'There's not much time before you have to leave, Prefect. Best we get a move on.'

'I hope we can talk later,' Cato said to Besodius before Vellocatus led the column off again.

There were two guards on the compound gate, veteran warriors by the look of them; tattooed and scarred, with greying locks of hair. At Vellocatus's command they stood aside to let the Roman column pass through. Inside, the perimeter of the compound was lined with stables, pens and store sheds. There were a score or so of servants and armed men in evidence. Four of the latter were exercising with their swords against wooden posts to one side of the stable. The chief's hall rose up on the far side, dominating all the other buildings of the town. It was a rectangular structure with a shingle roof, its style revealing the hand of the Roman engineers who had built it for their ally to impress his people with.

Cato drew up and called out to Tubero. 'Centurion! See to it that the men water their horses while I arrange for some feed.'

'Yes, sir.'

'And make sure that they remain inside the compound. They are not to speak to the locals, particularly the women. I don't

44

want them getting hold of anything to drink. We can't afford any trouble. Clear?'

'Yes, sir.'

'Good.' He lowered his voice, just in case Vellocatus understood enough Latin to grasp the sense of his next words. 'Keep your eyes open and your wits about you. If you see anything suspicious, report it to me at once. Macro, come with me.'

They handed their reins over to one of the auxiliaries and walked with Vellocatus towards the entrance of the hall. The heavy timber doors were open to admit light to the dim interior. Crossing the threshold, Cato and Macro were at once assailed by the acrid odour of woodsmoke. There were trestle tables and benches on each side of the hall, and straw was strewn over the packed earth of the floor. A large table stood at the far end, in front of the folds of a heavy woollen curtain that sectioned off the space beyond. Cato could hear muttered conversation from behind the curtain.

'My father's bier is in there,' Vellocatus explained. 'He is being attended by one of our . . . healers.'

The hesitation was not lost on Cato, who understood that Vellocatus was referring to the Druids, who served a wide range of roles for the tribes of the island. Healing was only one of their skills, alongside appeasing the tribal gods and interpreting their will, adjudicating disputes within and between the tribes and, in times of conflict, rousing their followers and casting spells and curses on their foes. The Druid cults had been the bitter enemy of Rome for generations, and after Caesar had conquered Gaul, he had attempted to stamp them out. The survivors had fled to Britannia. When Emperor Claudius's legions had landed on the island, one of their principal objectives was the elimination of the Druids. Yet the latter continued to survive and to be offered food and shelter by the tribespeople, who still regarded them with veneration.

'What is the nature of his illness?' asked Cato.

'A hunting accident,' Vellocatus replied. 'He fell from his horse.'

'I could send my cohort's surgeon to tend to his wounds. He's skilled at his job. He might be able to help.'

Vellocatus stopped in the middle of the hall and turned. It was clear from his expression that he was considering the implications of accepting.

'If I send a rider for the surgeon now, he could be here tomorrow morning,' Cato continued. 'It would help if I could see your father first, then I can brief the surgeon so that he brings the right instruments and salves.'

The Trinovantian reflected in silence for a moment before he nodded. 'Very well. Wait here. Let me send the healers away first.'

He strode to the far end of the hall and ducked behind the curtain, where a heated exchange began.

'What are the odds that the old boy's hunting injury was anything but?' Macro muttered. 'I noted that Vellocatus didn't challenge you when you mentioned wounds.'

'Quite.'

'Looks like Tasciovanus was a rebel then.'

'So it seems. Him and many others in this town. If the surgeon can save his life, that might go some way towards improving relations with the locals.'

'I wouldn't place too much faith in that. As the saying goes, no good deed . . .'

The voices behind the curtain rose in anger until Vellocatus bellowed an order. There was no mistaking the threat that lay behind his words. Shortly afterwards, he drew the curtain aside and beckoned to the Roman officers. They rounded the table at the end and stepped through into the chief's private bower.

Tasciovanus lay on a frame bed covered with furs. A door at the rear opened onto a yard behind the hall, and Cato caught a glimpse of some figures in dark cloaks scurrying away. He turned his attention to the chief. Tasciovanus's head rested on a woollen bolster. A blanket covered his legs, leaving most of his torso exposed. The faded tattoos on his pale flesh were discoloured by bruises. A bloodstained poultice lay across his stomach, a foul smell emanating from it. The Trinovantian leader appeared to be in his fifties, and in good physical shape for his years. But the wound had left him weak and feverish, and he lay with his eyes closed as he muttered softly, sweat glistening on his brow.

Cato bent to lift the poultice away, fighting the urge to recoil from the stench of whatever ointments the Druids had soaked the material in. There were smears of dried blood on Tasciovanus's stomach, and off to one side of his navel a dark bulge amid which there was puckered skin around a wound the circumference of a man's thumb. Cato had seen enough of such injuries to know at once what had caused it. He made sure that Macro had a chance to examine the wound before he replaced the poultice.

'Can your surgeon help him?' Vellocatus asked.

'I think so. It looks like the kind of injury he has treated before,' Cato replied carefully. 'I'll give the order for him to be summoned. We can talk once I've done that and feed has been bought for the horses. Macro, come with me.'

As they left the bower, Vellocatus took a damp cloth from a pitcher beside the bed and began to gently dab at his father's brow.

'Hunting injury, my arse,' Macro said once they were out of earshot. 'That was caused by a slingshot, no mistake about it. And there's only one way he could have got it – by going up against some of our lads. Looks like we have ourselves a rebel. Maybe one of the ringleaders the governor sent us after. In which case, what do you plan to do about it, sir?'

'I don't know yet.'

'He's the enemy,' Macro growled. 'One of the bastards responsible for what happened to Camulodunum and Londinium.'

47

'We don't know that, Macro. He and his men might not have been involved in the attack on either. They might have been late to the party, or they might have been coerced into joining the rebellion. I need more information before I make a decision. There's more than one way to deal with rebels.'

'There's *only* one way to deal with 'em,' Macro responded, and jerked his thumb across his throat. 'That's all they deserve.'

'And where will that get us? If we start hunting down and killing anyone we suspect of being a rebel, then all we will achieve is to create more rebels. More rebels, more bloodshed and more likelihood of never restoring peace in the province. The carrot and the stick, Macro. The trick is finding which you need to use and when to use it.'

'Hmph,' Macro snorted dismissively as he patted the top of the centurion's vine cane protruding from his belt. 'The stick every time, if you ask me.'

Cato knew his friend's proclivities well enough to be aware that there was no point continuing the discussion. Macro was without doubt one of the finest soldiers in the Roman army, and his promotion to centurion had been well earned. However, that was as much of a promotion as his particular talents merited, or indeed as he desired. It was different for Cato. He had been chosen for command positions, with the very real prospect of the honour of the highest rank someone of his social caste could aspire to. One day he might be appointed prefect of the Praetorian Guard, or even the prefect with responsibility for ruling Aegyptus, the most vital of all the Empire's provinces. While Macro could fix his attention on training men and leading them into battle, Cato had to consider the wider implications of Roman policy and make decisions with far-reaching consequences.

On his shoulders rested the prospect of restoring a lasting peace in the province of Britannia, or responsibility for the failure to achieve that. The continuation of the rebellion threatened to lead to the complete collapse of Roman control of the island. The shame of such a catastrophic defeat and retreat would be associated with his name and would echo down the ages. His heart quailed at the prospect as they stopped at the entrance of the hall, where he called out to Tubero and gave the instructions to fetch the cohort's surgeon at once.

CHAPTER FIVE

In Combretovium

Vellocatus had arranged for some food and drink to be set up on one of the tables while Cato, Macro and ten of their men had left the compound to find a local merchant to buy feed for the auxiliaries' mounts. Cato had paid over the odds for the bags of oats, despite Macro's tutting.

'I know you're after winning their hearts, but anyone who lets a barbarian fleece them like that is going to be regarded as a fool rather than a friend.' Macro coughed. 'What I mean to say is . . .'

Cato looked at him with an amused expression. 'Yes? Do go on. I'm fascinated to see how you compound insubordination with some other form of transgression. You were saying I'm a fool . . .'

'I'm saying that your actions might look foolish to some, sir.'

'But not to you, eh?'

'Perish the thought.' Macro offered a shamefaced smile. 'I didn't work my way to the centurionate just to be broken back down to the ranks for underestimating the thin skin of a superior officer.'

'Glad to hear it. Anyway, I can afford to lose a little face with the locals if it means keeping the forces fed and the feed merchants of Combretovium happy.' Cato noted the surly expressions of the townsfolk who had paused to watch the small party of Romans pass by. 'Winning them over is going to be every bit as important as winning battles in the months to come.'

The Roman from the cargo ship was sitting with Vellocatus when Macro and Cato returned to the hall and took their place on the bench on the opposite side of the table.

'Just heard about the old man,' Besodius said in the local dialect as he tipped his head towards the curtain, opened wide enough for them to see an elderly woman trying to feed the chief with soup from an iron pot. She had used a second bolster to prop him up and he seemed to be struggling to swallow even the smallest spoonful. 'I don't suppose he'll be up to drinking the wine I brought him for a while.'

'The prefect has sent for his surgeon,' said Vellocatus. 'He will cure my father.'

Cato felt a prickle of anxiety. 'I said he will do his best to help him. And he will. But he doesn't perform miracles. What he can do is offer more help than those healers of yours who were there before, concocting useless potions and muttering spells.'

'I hope you are right,' Vellocatus replied as he reached for the jug and poured some wine for the two officers. 'For what it's worth, they aren't *my* healers. They were called upon by my grandmother.' He indicated the woman leaning over the stricken chief. 'She believes in the old traditions . . . the ways of the Druids.'

Macro, who had a grasp of the local customs, arched an eyebrow. 'I thought most of you Britons were believers in one or other of their cults.'

Vellocatus tore off a hunk of bread and chewed on it before he responded. 'Our world was changing even before Rome invaded. The Druid cults have been losing influence for some time. Nor were their spells, curses and appeals to the gods any help in overcoming your legions on the battlefield. Even so, they still hold sway over the older generations and those who are desperate

51

enough to believe in their claims that only through following them can Rome be defeated. After what happened to Boudica's army, there are many of us who no longer look to the Druids for guidance and leadership.'

'Are there others in the town who share your views?' asked Cato.

'Plenty. Mostly younger men like myself. But as many still heed the calls of the Druids to fight Rome to the last drop of blood. Most joined the rebellion and paid the price. The survivors have returned to Combretovium to resume the lives they led before Boudica called on them to follow her. Even now, the fire of rebellion still smoulders in their hearts.'

'I saw as much in the faces of the people we passed in the town.'

Besodius nodded. 'I've seen it too. I've been landing cargo here ever since the colony was established at Camulodunum. The people were friendly enough before the rebellion. Now, I fear some would happily stick a knife in me the moment my back was turned. Unless things change soon, I'll take my trade elsewhere.'

This was a fresh aspect of the work that had to be done to restore peace and order to the province, Cato reflected. The challenge was threefold. Firstly, those who still fomented rebellion must be hunted down and crushed. Secondly, Rome must strive to rebuild good relations with the tribes of the province. Thirdly, men such as Besodius must be persuaded that it was safe to resume trading between Britannia and the rest of the Empire. The catastrophic scale of the destruction wrought by the rebels earlier in the year had caused panic across the province, and many merchants and tradesmen had fled to Gaul or died in the conflagrations that marked the path of Boudica's horde. Such people were the lifeblood of any province. Without them there was no future for Rome in these lands.

Something else occurred to Cato, and he regarded the Trinovantian warily before he addressed him. 'Your father fought for Boudica, didn't he? That's how he came by his wound.'

52

Vellocatus hesitated. 'I told you. It was a hunting accident. He fell from his horse and pierced his side on a sharpened stake.'

'Bollocks,' Macro snorted. 'He got that wound in battle.'

'The centurion is right,' said Cato. 'We've both seen wounds like it many times before. We know exactly how he came by it.'

Vellocatus glanced fearfully towards his father, who was still being fed by the old woman. 'What will you do to him?'

'Nothing,' Cato replied. 'Provided he gives us no more trouble. The same goes for every man in Combretovium who renounces the rebels and swears to accept the authority of Rome. Including you, Vellocatus. I take it you were at your father's side when he led your warriors to join Boudica.'

Vellocatus slowly lowered his goblet, masking his reaction behind an expressionless face. 'What if I was?'

Cato sensed Macro bristling at his side and answered before his friend could speak. 'Like I said, there's a chance for a fresh beginning for us all. I suggest you take it while it's there. I will not show any pity towards those who refuse the offer and continue to throw in their lot with Boudica. What do you say, Vellocatus? Do you want peace?'

'At what cost? If things return to the way they were before the rebellion, then what is the point of your peace? One way or another we are ground down and end up little better than slaves. Better to die with honour on our feet than—'

'Yes, I know the saying,' Cato interrupted in frustration. 'But I've been a soldier long enough to know that more often than not there is no honour in death. I don't deny that Rome has treated your people badly in the past. There is no guarantee that won't happen again. However, there are many Romans who understand that things must change if there is to be a lasting peace in Britannia. We will do our utmost to make a difference so that your peoples and ours can live alongside each other without fear of oppression or treachery.'

'Fine sentiments, Prefect. But if you can't guarantee they will turn into deeds, then why should I put any faith in them?'

'Because we cannot continue as before. The province cannot endure while the tribespeople burn with hatred for Rome. And we cannot endure living with the day-to-day suspicion and fear that you will turn on us again.'

'Amen to that,' Besodius muttered with feeling.

'There is another solution to this predicament,' said Vellocatus. 'Take your legions and quit our lands. Leave Britannia and return to Gaul. That way you will have nothing to fear from us and we can have peace. Better still, we might yet become your true allies if you treat us as equals.'

Cato sighed inwardly. 'If it was up to me, I would consider that possibility very carefully.'

Macro stirred. 'Now just wait a moment—'

'Quiet, Macro. Let me finish. Much as I might sympathise with your suggestion, Vellocatus, I am only a soldier. I have no choice but to obey the orders I am given by my superiors. While you and I might agree to such an outcome, those who rank above me see things rather differently. Rome is a vast empire. Its frontier stretches from the coast of Gaul across the forests of Germania and Pannonia and far to the east and south, where trackless deserts extend to the horizon. To defend the Empire there are fewer than thirty legions and their supporting auxiliary cohorts. Frankly it is a miracle that we manage our frontiers as well as we do. The reason why the Empire is not overrun is because of its reputation for enforcing its will with complete ruthlessness. Rome does not accept defeat.'

'What about the three legions that your General Varus led to their destruction in the German forests?'

'The Germanic tribes were made to pay a terrible price for their victory in the punitive campaigns that followed. Rome dare not be seen to allow any such setback to go unavenged.'

54

'And why should you behave any differently here in Britannia?' Vellocatus demanded.

'Make no mistake, there will be repercussions for those who continue to resist, and Rome will not abandon this province while to do so would undermine the image she projects to the barbarians who live beyond the frontiers. We are here to stay. Nothing will alter that. But we do have some degree of influence over how we restore peace and find a way to live to our mutual benefit.'

'And I have to take your word for it that you will find a way to achieve that?'

Cato nodded. 'You have my word that I will do all in my power to achieve a just peace in this region.'

'But you have said that you have no power. That you must obey orders.'

'The governor has ordered me to hunt down and destroy what remains of the rebellion and to restore order in the lands of the Trinovantians and the Icenians. *How* I achieve that is up to me. If it serves my broader purpose to grant amnesty to those who give their sacred word that they will abandon the rebellion and live in peace, then I will. On my authority, in the name of the governor, the emperor and the people of Rome.'

It was a grandiose statement of intent, but Cato fervently hoped that the Trinovantian saw that he meant to hold to his promise as a matter of honour.

'If you will swear an oath of allegiance to Rome, I will let you live in peace. The same goes for your father and any of your people who do the same. A binding oath is all it takes.'

'And if we refuse?'

'Then I cannot protect you from the wrath of those back in our capital who will clamour for bloody retribution against the tribes that still challenge our rule. Our only chance of avoiding that fate is to present the emperor and his advisers with proof

55

that the rebellion is over and that the tribes have proved their renewed loyalty.'

'I see.'

'It would serve our joint interest further still if some of your people chose to march alongside my troops when I lead them against Boudica.'

Macro bristled. 'I doubt our boys will be happy having this lot on our side, sir. Given what we've seen they're capable of. Don't want to take the risk of waking up to find one of the bastards has cut your throat.'

'Should that happen, I doubt I will be troubled by waking up at all.'

Vellocatus gave a dry laugh before he responded. 'That may be a request too far, Prefect. My people might be willing to swear an oath of loyalty to Rome in exchange for peace and fair treatment, but I doubt many will be willing to fight for you. The Trinovantians have a long tradition of enmity with the Icenians, but the rebellion went a long way towards resolving that. For some, they are still our allies, while you remain our enemy.'

'Then we'll do without such people. I'll only accept those who freely volunteer.'

'And why would they do that?'

'Because the rebellion will be extinguished whether it is I who am responsible for it or another, less considerate, Roman commander. You can be part of the victory as a valued ally, or you can be an onlooker of questionable loyalty with the consequences that entails.'

'You don't give me much choice.'

'Not much, but it *is* your choice. So choose wisely.'

Vellocatus pondered his predicament for an instant before he spoke again. 'It would help to win my tribe over if your surgeon could save my father. That would place us in your debt. Such things carry much weight in the hearts of our people.'

'The surgeon will do what he can.'

'If he intervenes and fails, then I should warn you that will not be taken well. The Druids will claim that they could have cured him and that the Roman surgeon poisoned him.'

'What will you say if he should die?' Cato asked.

'I will not blame your surgeon. I was once in Londinium on my father's business and fell ill. I was treated at the hospital in your governor's headquarters. I know enough to value the quality of Roman medicine. But mine will be a lone voice in Combretovium. If he recovers, I will be sure to lead the praise for the skills of your surgeon.'

Cato nodded. 'That's as much as I could hope for. Very well.'

There was a pause as Macro reached for the jug and refilled the goblets. He shook his head. 'No pressure on the surgeon then. Wouldn't swap places with him for all the wine in Combretovium.'

'That's a fairly low bar,' said Besodius. 'Trust me, I know. There hasn't been a drop in the place since before the rebellion until I arrived with the first cargo.'

'Best enjoy it while we can then.' Macro drained his goblet and reached for the jug again before Cato intervened.

'That's enough. I need my men to have clear heads until we leave Combretovium. Speaking of which . . .' He turned to Vellocatus. 'Given the jeopardy my surgeon faces, I will not leave him in the town alone. My men and I will need to remain here until he has finished treating your father. Whatever the outcome. Understand?'

'He will not be harmed. I will make that clear to my people. As for you and your men remaining in the compound . . . I would prefer that you make camp outside. To avoid any risk of an unfortunate encounter with the less hospitable of my people.'

Macro snorted. 'I don't think so! It's bloody autumn and the nights are cold. I'm not sleeping out in the open if I can avoid it. We're offering to help save your father's life. Show some gratitude, why don't you?'

'We'll stay the night in the compound,' Cato announced, fixing Vellocatus with a firm stare. 'That's not up for negotiation.'

For an instant, the Trinovantian's nostrils flared and it appeared that he might disagree vehemently. Then he took control of his instincts and breathed deeply before he responded. 'For the sake of whatever help your surgeon can give, you have my permission to remain in the compound overnight.'

'Our horses will be stabled. The men and I will sleep in the hall.'

Vellocatus glanced towards where the old lady was dabbing the chief's brow with a damp rag. He lowered his voice and spoke in an urgent undertone. 'My father is very ill. He needs to rest without being disturbed. You can't bring your men in here.'

'I will give orders for them to respect his condition. Besides, if your people are as divided as you say, he could use some extra protection to ensure his safety.'

'*His* safety?' Vellocatus scoffed. 'It seems to me you are looking out for your own, even if that means treating the chief of my people like a hostage.'

'I can't help how it seems. I've made my decision. I suggest that you go and make arrangements for our mounts and the feeding of my men. We will, of course, pay our way.'

Vellocatus rose, tight-lipped, and strode out of the hall. Once he had disappeared from view, Macro let out a low whistle.

'For a man who was offering plenty of concessions a moment ago that I wouldn't have dreamed of, that was quite a sting in the tail, lad. You might have gone a bit too far.'

'I don't think so. It's important that our Trinovantian friend understands there is an iron fist beneath my silk glove.'

Macro chuckled. 'That is fucking poetry, that is. Or that other thing that Apollonius used to be so fond of – an ayfor . . . er . . .'

'Aphorism.'

'That's it! Just the kind of thing he would say!' Macro's grin

58

swiftly faded as he recalled the death of their former comrade, who had given his life to save Macro's own during the rebel assault on Camulodunum. He shook his head sadly. 'I never thought I'd say it, but I miss the smug bastard.'

'Me too. We could use his spying skills now more than ever. Which reminds me.' Cato turned to Besodius, who had made a start on the cold cuts of pork on a wooden platter. 'You must know the waterways and coast of this region quite well.'

'Quite well?'

Cato was only just able to make out the merchant's words as the latter spoke with a full mouth. He chewed hurriedly and swallowed before he continued.

'I know them as well as I know every street and avenue of the Aventine district in Rome where I grew up.'

'I thought I recognised the accent.' Cato smiled. 'How far up the east coast have you sailed?'

'As far as the big basin called Metaris Aest. There was a trading post at Branodunum before it was abandoned a few years ago. I used to shift wine and some fine-spun cloth to the Icenians back then, before they went cold on dealing with foreigners. Haven't been that way since.'

'But you are confident you could navigate there again?'

'Of course.' Besodius affected an offended expression as he jabbed a thumb into his chest. 'I'm one of the old hands as far as sailing these waters go. You won't find a better captain than me this side of the sea.'

'I'm glad to hear it. I've come to the right man, it seems.'

He frowned. 'What do you mean?'

'I need to understand the lie of the land. I've only ever ventured a short distance into Icenian territory and I've never seen it from the sea. I need someone who knows his way around to act as my guide. And that's you, it seems.'

Besodius shook his head. 'Can't help you, Prefect. Once I've

59

loaded up with wool bales and local trinkets, it's back to Gaul for me. I'll probably have time for one more run, two at the most, before winter comes, and that's me done until spring. I should be back this way then if you are still around.'

'That's too late for my purposes,' said Cato. 'I was thinking we could take the trip rather sooner than that. Once the surgeon has seen to the chief and the column leaves Combretovium.'

'That's not possible. Like I said, I'm heading back to Gaul.'

'Surely, as a good Roman citizen, you'll be keen to assist the army in restoring order to the province. After all, it's in your interests that we do so. The sooner we get the job done, the sooner normal trade can resume and men like you can reap your profits without worrying about any further trouble from the locals.'

It was clear that Besodius was increasingly worried at the direction the conversation was taking. 'I can't just drop my work and ferry you around, sir.'

'I'll make it worth your while.'

'It's not just the cost. It's the weather. Autumn's on us and soon the sea will be too dangerous to venture out on. *Minerva*'s a solid vessel, but even she can't take some of the storms that blow up in these waters. Then there's the sandbanks further north. Tricky buggers they are. Difficult to navigate.'

'But you did say you were the best sailor this side of the sea,' said Cato. 'And you've done it before. So it shouldn't present much difficulty.'

'I don't know about that.' Besodius scratched his beard, then helped himself to a slug of wine.

'Of course, if you're too afraid, that's understandable,' said Cato. He caught Macro's eye and nodded subtly at the captain's goblet. Macro fought to suppress a grin as he reached for the jug and topped up their cups.

Besodius nodded his thanks and took another sip. 'Don't get

me wrong, Prefect. It's not that I'm afraid. It's just that conditions can be challenging.'

'Challenging?' Cato reflected. 'Yes, I imagine so. Anyway, enough of that. Let's get stuck into this food and wine.'

Macro topped up the goblets again, and raised his own for a toast. 'Death to the rebels!'

They drank, and Cato made another toast. 'To Rome's bravest! On land and sea.'

Besodius smiled cheerfully and slurred his words as he responded. 'To bravery!'

Cato took a small sip and spoke thoughtfully. 'I've only been to sea a handful of times, and I know how terrifying it can be. It takes great heart to brave the open sea as you and your sailors do. I wouldn't want to involve you in anything that put your crew at risk. So I'll have to find someone else for the job. Can you recommend another captain with the necessary nerve?'

Besodius took the affront just as Cato had hoped. 'There is none better than me, I'll have you know,' he declared, thumping his chest. 'They're good, some of 'em at any rate. But none as good as me. And none as brave.'

'Oh?' Cato dipped the tip of his finger into some spilled wine and drew slow circles. 'Well, I'm sure that may be true. I'll just have to make do with whoever I can find. Of course, once I make it clear that they will have exclusive trading rights for all the ports serving the Trinovantian and Icenian tribes, I am sure there will be more than a few of your competitors who will consider taking the job on.'

'Now just a moment, Prefect! I was the first merchant to begin trading with Combretovium and the first one back here once Boudica was defeated. If anything shows I've got guts, then there it is. Fine, if you want to take a trip up the coast, I'll do it. I can't have you being drowned at sea because you picked the wrong captain and the wrong ship. You'll be safe with me. That I swear on my honour. Can't have your death on my conscience if you put your trust in some second-rate Junius-come-lately.'

Cato smiled warmly. 'I'm glad to hear it. I am very reassured to have you as my captain. Thank you!'

He extended his hand, and Besodius spat on his own weathered palm and shook on the deal, grinning proudly as his head wobbled slightly in his intoxicated state.

Cato took his hand back. 'We'll work out the pay and the trading agreements later on. Now's the time to drink to our partnership.'

The three men raised their goblets and toasted each other before draining them and setting them down on the table with a sharp rap.

'You'll be wanting to prepare your ship for the voyage. Enough rations for ten days at least,' said Cato. 'There's plenty of time to get your crew ready before we set sail. Might be a good idea to unload any cargo in the hold. My men can guard it for you while we're away.'

The captain's brow creased slightly as he sobered up just enough to realise what he'd committed himself to.

'It's like I said, sir. Not the best time to venture onto the high seas. Better to wait until the winter storms have p-passed.'

'There's not a moment to waste,' Cato said cheerfully. 'Damn the storms, eh? In any case, we've shaken on it. A matter of honour. The deal is done.'

'Yes,' Besodius agreed flatly. He wiped his lips on the back of his hand and rose unsteadily. 'B-better get back to the *Minerva* to supervise the last of the unloading.'

'I'll send some of my men to help.'

'Oh, no need for that.'

'Nonsense. It's the least I can do.'

The captain nodded warily and turned to walk out of the hall, swaying as he went.

Macro watched as he stumbled out of sight. 'Praise where praise is due – you played him like a cheap flute. Him and Vellocatus both. You're wasted on the army, lad. You should have had a career in politics or the law.'

'Now, now, Macro. No need for abuse.'

They shared a smile before Macro gestured after Besodius. 'Do you think we can trust him to hold good to the agreement?'

'Not once he sobers up. That's why we're going to send some men down to the river to take charge of the *Minerva* and her crew. They're to be polite and helpful, and make sure the ship stays where it is until I'm ready to embark on the reconnaissance trip.'

'Is it really necessary? Given what he said about the weather.'

'We need to know as much as we can find out. Boudica has the home advantage on land. If we can control the coast and waterways, that will help us close the net around her and what's left of her army. I'll happily take getting a little wet and cold for that.'

'What about a little drowned? I'd hate to have to break that to Claudia and your boy.'

Cato saw the genuine concern in his friend's face and responded light-heartedly. 'I'll take good care that it doesn't happen. Now you'd better get some of our boys to join Vellocatus. Five should do the job. Make sure they understand what they need to do.'

'Yes, sir.' Macro stood up and tapped his brow in salute before he left.

Cato sat alone at the table. Picking up a rib from the platter, he tore off a strip of meat and chewed as he reviewed the situation. There was no doubting the broad hostility towards Rome among the people of Combretovium. He glanced towards Tasciovanus, now resting fitfully on his bier. The chief's mother looked up at the same moment and their eyes met briefly. It was not hard for Cato to read the hatred in her expression even at a distance. Then she looked down at her stricken son and stroked his hair gently.

Cato breathed deeply. So much rested on the skill of his surgeon. If he saved Tasciovanus, he would buy Rome some gratitude and goodwill and hopefully some badly needed allies. If he failed and the chief died, Cato dreaded the consequences.

CHAPTER SIX

At Lyngomara

Syphodubnus entered the round hut and let the leather curtain drop behind him. Outside it was raining lightly but steadily. There was no sign of the sun; merely a hint of lighter gloom in the grey overcast sky. The feeling of cold dampness penetrated everywhere. The only relief came from the warm glow of the fire crackling in the centre of the hut. Most of the smoke rose through the opening at the top. There was a faint hiss each time drops of rain fell into the flames.

Boudica was sitting on a fur-covered stool to one side, leaning forward, chin resting on her folded hands, as she stared into the heart of the fire. Her thoughts had been fixed on the fate of her younger daughter lying on a makeshift bed in the next hut. Merida had seemed to be recovering well from her wound over the month since the battle, but now the girl had developed a fever, and her mother feared for her life.

'My queen?'

She looked up at Syphodubnus and fixed her adviser with a vacant look before she collected her thoughts and coughed. 'What is it?'

'The last of the chiefs you summoned have arrived. They await you in the hall of the elders.'

'Good. I'll join them shortly.'

When she made no effort to stir, Syphodubnus waited a moment and then spoke softly. 'Is there any news?'

Boudica shook her head. 'She is the same. None of the healers has been able to help her. Not even Bladocus.'

'Ah. I had hoped that he of all of them would know what to do,' Syphodubnus responded sadly.

'He has done all that he can. He has made offerings to the gods and the spirits of our forefathers. He tells me it is in their hands now. They will decide whether she lives or dies.'

'I have made my own offering and prayers, my queen.'

Boudica smiled slightly in gratitude. 'I thank you. Now go and tell them I am coming. No, wait.'

She stood up so that her height would match his. Although her people readily accepted her as their queen and war leader, she had long since discovered the additional advantage of using her stature to enhance her status.

'Tell me, cousin, how do you think they will respond?'

Syphodubnus hesitated, and she saw the doubt in his expression.

'That badly? You are my closest adviser now that all the others have been lost. Be honest with me.'

He nodded. 'Very well. I have not spoken to all of them, but I'd say that perhaps a third are willing to continue the fight. A third will not support the rebellion any further, and the others are undecided. They are the ones to convince. If you win them over, there's a chance that many of those who now wish for peace may still discover the heart to continue. But I warn you, morale is low even among those who will fight on. After a defeat such as we have suffered, there are grieving kin in every town, village and farm. The harvest has been poor enough without having so few left behind to take it in. There will be hunger this winter.

'There are many who say that the enemy cannot be defeated. They are better trained and armed, and they are ruthless and relentless. The only thing to counter that sentiment is the deep, undying hatred of Rome and the outrage at the treatment of you and your daughters. That will be passed down from generation to generation and will never diminish.' He smiled. 'You know how we Icenians like to nurse a grievance.'

'And that grievance has been earned by Rome a thousand times over,' Boudica said bitterly. 'Even if I fail to win over the tribe, I swear by Andraste that I will never know peace. As long as I can hold a sword in my hand, I will fight them to my last drop of blood and final breath. There is no other path for me.'

The cold vehemence of her words struck her adviser forcefully and he raised his hands as if to ward her off. 'You don't have to persuade me. I will follow you to the end now.'

'That pleases me,' said Boudica. 'There was a time, after my husband died, when you sought to push me aside and replace him.'

'I was wrong to do so, my queen. No one else could have rallied our tribe to fight the enemy as you have done. No one else could have shown the courage and leadership that you displayed. No one else could have persuaded the neighbouring tribes to rise up and join us. Our warriors fought with your name on their lips as they hurled themselves at the Romans. By all the gods, have you ever seen such bravery before? Time after time they charged the Roman lines, even though they were scythed down like ripe wheat. Climbing over the fallen to get at the enemy, believing until the end that one more charge would carry the day. Victory was never so close . . .'

'And now so far,' Boudica concluded. 'Lack of courage was never our weakness. But courage is not enough to defeat Rome. We must find a new way. We must change our tactics. But first we must rest what is left of our men, and recruit and train many more. When we are ready, we will take the war to them again, and next time victory will be ours.'

'I pray so, my queen. Shall we attend them in the hall now?'

'You go. I must see Merida first.'

Syphodubnus bowed his head and ducked out of the low entrance to the hut. Boudica took a moment to smooth the folds of her tunic and cloak and then reached down to the small chest under her stool to take out her gold torcs and the band that fitted round her brow. She needed to appear every bit the queen when she stood before the assembled chiefs. Inspecting her reflection in a polished bronze mirror, she nodded with satisfaction.

Outside, the rain had subsided to a clinging drizzle that beaded her cloak as she made her way to a smaller hut nearby. By the light of the fire inside, she could make out her younger daughter, covered with furs and blankets yet trembling as she moaned softly. Bardea squatted by her sister, holding her hand. She looked up as her mother entered.

'How is she?'

'Weaker than ever.' Bardea shifted to make space and Boudica looked down and saw the flutter of the pulse in Merida's thin neck.

Bardea eased the coverings back, exposing the grotesque puckered flesh and the black and purple hue of the surrounding skin. Dried blood formed patches around which pus glistened, and a nauseating odour made Boudica flinch.

'I don't know how much longer she will last, Mother. It's a miracle she has endured as long as she has.'

'Not a miracle. She has her father's strength. There was never a king of a tribe to match him. Prasutagus would have been as proud of her as he would of any son. He so wanted a boy, but in the end he knew that he had sired the best child a warrior could hope for.' Boudica glanced quickly at her older daughter. 'And he loved you no less. Be sure of that.'

Bardea nodded and replaced the coverings before reaching a palm to her sister's forehead. Boudica felt a flicker of relief, yet at the same time disgust at herself at the secret she had harboured for so many years. Bardea was not the daughter of Prasutagus. The seed had come from another man Boudica had known briefly before becoming betrothed to the Iceni prince. That would not have been such a scandal had the father been a member of the tribe, but he had been a Roman. Centurion Macro. She thought of him now with a mixture of residual affection and rage. He alone, as far as she was aware, shared the secret. Time after time she wished it had not been him, but the past could not be changed. That meant she was burdened with knowledge she dared not share with any of her people, most of all Bardea. How could she be the champion of the Icenians when she had freely given herself to a Roman?

They had been allies then, but now Macro was as much her enemy as any soldier of Rome. If the fates should ever cause them to encounter each other on a battlefield, Boudica was utterly resolved to kill him without hesitation. She thrust the thought from her mind.

'I must go. Stay with her.'

'Of course.'

She leaned down to kiss her daughter's dark curls and then left to make her way across the muddy ground to the hall of the elders. Around her, huts sprawled in all directions until they disappeared into the mist that veiled the settlement of Lyngomara. Beyond, the wetlands spread out for many miles. The fortified settlement could only be reached by a narrow track that wound its way through the marshes. There was a waterway that led to the coast, a day's journey to the north, but it was hard to trace through the tall reeds, and only a handful of locals knew it well enough to use the route. Lyngomara stood on a modest island amid this wilderness, surrounded by a stockade.

It had once served as the home of a Druid cult that had left generations before for reasons that none recalled. Only a stone altar amid a circle of tall wooden posts remained, now covered with moss and lichen. Since then it had become a sanctuary for the Icenians in time of trouble. Boudica had been there only once before, during an earlier uprising against Rome that had flared up briefly some twelve years ago. She had no fondness for the place, finding its frequent mists and lack of any far horizon confining and depressing. The onset of autumn only made the setting seem more dismal. Yet it was a safe haven that no Roman knew about. Even if they discovered its existence, there was no possibility of a surprise attack, since the enemy's cumbersome equipment would bog them down and slow any approach through the marshes to a crawl. There was some relief to be had from that knowledge, and Boudica fully intended to use the respite to rebuild her forces and take the fight back to the Roman invaders.

As she passed through the settlement, she exchanged greetings with the men and women who had followed her here. Their tone was respectful enough, but it was hard to miss the deflation in their spirits. Just over a month earlier, their hope and joy had surged on the crest of a wave that had swept the Romans before them and destroyed their towns, farms and forts, leaving smouldering ruins and charred bodies in the rebels' wake. Each victory had nurtured the growing conviction in their hearts that victory was possible, then certain. Nothing could stop the triumph the queen was leading them to. The last battle had crushed that spirit, and now the remnants of her army followed her out of dogged loyalty and undying hatred of Rome. She knew that she needed to find something more than that to put the fire back into their bellies and rekindle the belief that victory would come. She needed to find that spark now, as she faced the most important chiefs and warrior leaders of her tribe.

The hall of the elders rose up before her, and she slowed her pace as she approached to order her thoughts and calm her nerves. Two men from her bodyguard stood at the open entrance, through which she could see the glow from the hearths within.

Around them, in the ruddy glow of the flames, stood those who had come to hear her. She could hear their muted voices and could sense their anxiety and doubt even before she entered.

The conversation died away to silence as soon as she entered the hall. As she made her way past the fires to the low dais at the far end, where the oaken chair of the ruler of the Icenians stood, her nobles parted respectfully before her and bowed their heads in deference. The absence of so many familiar faces, lost in battle, weighed heavily upon her. Mounting the dais, she settled on the chair and drew herself up as she faced her audience. Syphodubnus took up his place to one side.

Boudica waited until there was absolute silence and stillness aside from the hissing of some damp logs on the fires. Then she drew a deep breath and began.

'I bid you all welcome to Lyngomara, and offer my gratitude to you for answering the call. You have been told that the reason for the gathering is to consider the path our tribe will take following the recent defeat of our forces. Many of you will doubtless think the time has come to accept that the rebellion is over and we must sue for peace and throw ourselves on the mercy of the enemy. You will say that Rome cannot be beaten and we must recognise the emperor as our overlord.

'I tell you now that while I live, while I am your queen, while a flicker of honour and pride still lingers in the hearts of our people, there will be no end to the war against Rome. Peace with Rome is little more than the acceptance of annihilation. For the Romans will be satisfied with nothing less than the destruction of our tribe. Their revenge will be a terrible thing to behold. They are a ruthless people who will stoop to every barbarity and cruelty to achieve their aims. They will not rest from seeking us out and slaughtering those they find. That is why I say there can be no peace. No attempt to negotiate a surrender. There is no hope that they might forgive and accord us the respect of an

71

ally ever again. So we must fight on, or die like dogs with no honour. These are our lands, our homes, our farms, our families, our children. If they aren't worth fighting for, then what kind of people are we? If we refuse to defend them, we are no better than slaves in chains. I will accept no such fate, and I know that you who are proud to call yourselves Icenian will understand that and share my determination to continue the fight.'

She looked out over the audience and swept their faces with her gaze, daring any to defy her. Then, moderating her tone, she continued.

'So, to the purpose of this gathering. I need more warriors to replace those we have lost. I need weapons. I need supplies. But above all, I need your loyalty, your obedience and your conviction of the justness of our cause. There will be some whose hearts quail at the enormity of the challenge facing our people. I understand that. More of us will die. Our farms and settlements will be ravaged by the enemy. But that is the nature of war, and all victories come at such a cost. I tell you the Romans can be beaten, because the hatred we feel for them is echoed in the hearts of others in every tribe in Britannia. We have already proved that we can summon a great host whose ranks are filled with warriors from every corner of the island. We can do that again. We can keep on doing it until the invader is driven from our lands. And then we shall have peace. Peace with honour. This I promise you, by my most sacred oath. But only if we keep the fire of rebellion alight. That duty has fallen to the Icenians. We are the last hope of all those tribes living under the heel of Rome. It may take us many years, many battles, lost and won, but we can – we will – be victorious. It will be a victory that will be told and retold down the ages. Our enemy will come to fear and respect us. In Rome they will shudder at the memory of defeat, and the name of our tribe will haunt them to the day their empire finally crumbles into the dust. We will be their epitaph.'

She paused to allow those before her to reflect on her message. Then she leaned back in the chair and nodded to Syphodubnus. He took a step forward and addressed the audience.

'You have heard the words of your queen. Are there any here who wish to speak?'

The crowd stirred as people looked round and some muttered to their companions. Then one of the chiefs, an older man Boudica knew only slightly, stepped forward into the glow of the nearest of the fires. He looked weary.

'My queen, there is not one person here who does not share your loathing of the Romans. They have come to our island like a plague, laying waste to our people and our traditions. They have stolen our lands, forced us to pay ruinous taxes and left many of us to starve. We are a proud people. Our warriors are the finest to be found among the tribes of Britannia and we are your loyal followers . . .'

Boudica leaned forward. 'But?'

The old man's gaze slipped away from her determined stare.

'Speak up.'

He raised his head and stiffened his back. 'But we have been defeated. Not just defeated. Crushed. The finest of our warriors are dead. Along with countless thousands of men who left their farms to take up arms and join your rebellion.'

'*Our* rebellion,' Boudica cut in.

The old man steeled himself to continue. 'They gave their lives to free us from the Roman yoke. And now their wives and children go hungry, as too few of us remain to take in the harvest and tend our crops and herds. If you try to raise a new army to continue the war, it will be comprised of old men and boys. What chance have they against the legions?'

'Remind me of your name,' Boudica ordered.

'Ganomenus, your majesty. Chief of the settlement at Branodunum.'

'Ganomenus, you are talking about Icenian old men and boys. Any one of whom is the equal of any fighter from another tribe.' It was an exaggeration, but Boudica needed to appeal to the arrogant pride of her people if there was a chance of putting that to use.

'Old men and boys all the same,' he replied. 'They are farmers, untrained in the ways of war. Even if they were willing to take up arms to keep the rebellion alive, they are not warriors and they would go to their deaths for no good purpose. Enough blood has been shed by our people already. We cannot defeat Rome. What purpose does it serve to continue a war we have no realistic hope of winning?'

'What choice do we have?' Boudica countered. 'Were you not listening to me before? Do you think the Romans will be content to let our people go back to their fields to tend their crops in peace? They mean to destroy us. The only thing we can do now is strive to frustrate that aim. As long as we live, the rebellion lives. We may never defeat them in open battle, but we can harass them, lure them into traps and ambush them. Make them bleed to death, slowly but surely. We don't have to win a great victory. We just have to outlast them. Ours is a long war. Many of us will not live to see its end, but as long as we fight, our people will be free one day. Why do you have so little faith in yourself, Ganomenus? Have we not proved what Icenian warriors can achieve?'

She turned to Syphodubnus. 'I think it is time to remind them of what Icenian courage can do.'

He nodded and moved behind the chair to retrieve a bundle of dark cloth. Pacing to the front of the stage, he let the material fall away to reveal the gilded form of an eagle, its claws clenching thunderbolts. He held it up for all to see.

'This is the sacred symbol of the Roman legions. It was taken from the hands of a centurion after he had been slain by our warriors. There is no greater shame for a Roman soldier than to let this be captured. It is proof that even their vaunted legions can be crushed by our people. Our enemy is not invincible. The defeat we inflicted on the Ninth Legion can be shared by all their legions. If we have faith in ourselves, we can do this again and again, until the eagle of every legion in Britannia is a trophy of the Icenians and the huts of our warriors are adorned with the heads of their soldiers. Their gold and silver will become our riches. We will offer their weapons and armour to our gods to honour the victories we shall win!'

The hall filled with cheers and cries of defiance as the crowd punched the air with their fists and stamped their feet on the ground. Boudica noted with satisfaction that even those who had seen the trophy many times before when it was paraded through the rebel army shouted in triumph. The captured eagle still worked its magic over her followers and charged them with renewed hope and determination.

Syphodubnus stepped down from the dais and slowly made his way down the length of the hall, the crowd pressing about him to touch the eagle so that its mystical power might flow through them also. At length he returned to his position at Boudica's side. The cheering died away, but there was a different mood in the hall now. A sense of excitement and determination had replaced the sullen despondency. Yet there were still some who looked wary, shaking their heads and muttering to one another. They would have to be dealt with later, Boudica knew. During the rebellion, a degree of dissent or a lack of alacrity could be tolerated. That was no longer the case. Now the desperate situation demanded that every member of the tribe play their part and make sacrifices to continue the war against Rome. Nothing less would do.

She rose from her seat and spoke with icy firmness to ensure that her orders were clearly understood.

'Make no mistake. We are in a fight to the death. The war

is everything and we must do whatever it takes to continue it until we have achieved victory. You will return to your people with this message and you will send me every able-bodied man to rebuild our army. They will need weapons and food, which you will also send here. Other supplies will be held in grain pits, hidden from the eyes of Rome. Those will be used to feed our people in times of hardship. While none will starve, we had all better get used to being hungry. Hunger is good. It sharpens the wits and increases the determination to survive.

'Before you leave here, each one of you is to give a full account of the number of people you are responsible for and how many of your men are of fighting age. Bladocus, chief of my Druids, will record the details. From time to time I will send men to you to fetch supplies and recruits. If they should discover any discrepancy in the details you provide to Bladocus, your lives will be forfeit and your people will be forced to supply twice the shortfall. I will not permit deceit, defeatism, dishonour or treachery. If any of you, or your people, attempt to fraternise with Romans, supply them or cooperate with them in any way, you will suffer the fate earned by all those who betray our cause. You know the stakes and you know your duty. Now you may leave the hall. Return at first light tomorrow to report to Bladocus.'

She resumed her seat as the crowd began to shuffle towards the entrance. Syphodubnus wrapped the eagle in the cloth before returning it to the small chest.

'You still have their loyalty, my queen. That was clear to see.'

'But how long will it endure? There are so few of our warrior class left. The rest are farmers, peasants. While they may be loyal for now, their courage is brittle. They live from season to season with only a dim awareness of the long term. That is why I may have to make them fear me as much as they might fear Rome. Maybe more, if we are to continue the rebellion indefinitely.'

'I think you underestimate their quality,' Syphodubnus said

76

mildly. 'They are Icenians and proud of it. They respect our traditions and the obedience they owe their queen. I think they will surprise you in the time to come.'

'I hope so. More to the point, I hope they surprise the Romans.' Boudica stared fixedly down the length of the hall. 'They will come for us very soon. We must be ready for them. From the moment they enter our lands, they must be made to live in constant fear of us. We shall wear them down one by one. Every step they take into Icenian territory will be a step closer to their graves.'

'There is one other matter to attend to,' said Syphodubnus. 'The individual we were expecting arrived just before you addressed the nobles. I arranged for him to have some food while you spoke. Shall I send for him now?'

Boudica nodded eagerly. 'Bring him to me. It's time we found out how far the Roman plans to deal with us have advanced.'

CHAPTER SEVEN

Combretovium

The surgeon of the Eighth Cohort arrived late the next morning, escorted by the auxiliary who had been sent to fetch him. Cato greeted him with relief as he entered the hall. The auxiliaries had been moved into the storage sheds next to the stables so that he would not be distracted as he went about his work. All morning Cato and Macro had been watching Vellocatus sitting alone fretting as he impatiently awaited the man's arrival.

'You made good time, Phrygenus.'

The surgeon, a dark-skinned Syrian, saluted. 'Your order said it was urgent. A matter of life and death. I rode as fast as I could.'

'Good man. It is a matter of many lives and deaths, as it happens.' Cato indicated the curtain that had been drawn across the end of the hall. 'The chief of this town has a wound to his side. He's in poor shape. If you can save him, we'll win a lot of support from his people. If he dies, many of them will become open enemies of Rome.'

Phrygenus rolled his eyes. 'No pressure then. What kind of wound?'

'Slingshot. It's still within the wound as far as I can tell.'

'No one's attempted to remove it?' the surgeon asked in surprise. 'What's been done for him?'

'Poultices and spells,' said Macro. 'Surprisingly, that hasn't worked out so well for the old boy.'

Phrygenus was about to continue, then paused as he frowned. 'Slingshot, you say?'

Cato nodded. 'That's right. One of ours. I know what you're thinking, but we can make an ally out of this enemy if you can save him.' He nodded towards Vellocatus as the latter approached. 'That's his son. Do your best to reassure him.'

'Is this him, your healer?' Vellocatus demanded. He regarded the slender Easterner and his medical chest anxiously.

Cato nodded. 'Phrygenus is one of the best surgeons in the army. If anyone can save your father, he can.'

Vellocatus gestured urgently towards the curtain. 'Tell him to get to work.'

Cato led the others to the curtain and drew it aside to reveal the old man on his bier. Tasciovanus's eyes were closed, but he was not sleeping. His lips moved and he mumbled incoherently. His mother, sitting on the far side of the bier, rose and made to protest, but a curt word of command from her grandson silenced her. She turned to leave by the doorway beyond, pausing on the threshold to scowl at the Romans before she disappeared.

Phrygenus set his chest down, leaned towards the old man and sniffed. 'That's not good.'

He lifted the blankets to expose the wound and crouched down to examine it closely for a moment before rising to speak to Cato.

'I'll have to remove the shot. Should have been done much earlier. See how the flesh has contracted around the entry wound? I'll have to open that up. He'll lose quite a bit of blood in the process and he's very weak already. The wound will have to be cleaned out and then left to drain before it is closed again. After that, it'll take him a while to recover. Provided he survives the procedure in the first place.'

79

'What are the odds that he'll live through all that?' asked Macro.

'Odds?'

'If you were a betting man,' Macro prompted patiently.

The surgeon considered this briefly before replying. 'I'd say . . . five to one against him surviving.'

'I won't be taking that bet then.'

Vellocatus had been following the exchange between the Romans with growing concern and now intervened.

'What does your healer say? Can he do it? Can he save my father?'

Cato turned to him with as reassuring an expression as he could muster. 'He says there's every chance of a full recovery if he is allowed to get to work at once and isn't interrupted while he treats the patient.'

To his credit, Macro managed to bite his tongue and nod along.

'Very well,' Vellocatus said with relief. 'Tell him he shall have everything he needs. He only has to ask and it shall be done. If he is as good as you say, then I shall be forever in his debt. But if he fails, I will hold him personally responsible and have his head.'

'What did he say?' Phrygenus asked. 'Does he understand what's involved?'

'Yes,' Cato responded evenly. 'He said he is grateful to have a fine surgeon on the job and that he and his people will do whatever they can to help. He says that whatever the outcome, he will be in your debt, and offers you the blessings of his gods.'

Phrygenus smiled warmly and patted the Trinovantian on the shoulder. 'That's very decent of him. Do thank him for me.'

'I think he understands.'

'Right, well, I'd better get started. I'll need some water and rags to clear the blood away as I work and some help with restraining the patient if he stirs. If we're lucky, he'll pass out.

Better tell our friend to wait outside. It's not going to be pretty and I don't want him jumping in if his father starts shouting.'

Cato steered Vellocatus to the door with instructions to have the surgeon's needs met. When the Trinovantian had gone, Phrygenus removed his cloak and opened his chest to take out a leather apron, a wrapped bundle of instruments, some pots of ointment and a small basket that reeked of rotten meat. He set the latter down carefully at the foot of the bier.

'What the fuck is that stink?' Macro's nose wrinkled with disgust.

Phrygenus chuckled. 'Just a little trick of the trade. You'll see.'

Cato and Macro watched with fascination as the surgeon opened out the linen roll that contained his gleaming probes, scalpels, saws and other unsavoury-looking items. As he readied those he would be using, Vellocatus returned with a bucket and a bundle of rags. He set them down on the end of the bed and paled as he saw Phrygenus's instruments.

'This man looks more like a butcher than a healer.'

'I can assure you he knows what he is doing.'

'I'll stay here and make sure that he does.'

The surgeon noted his expression and spoke quietly to Cato. 'Sir, it really would be for the best if he wasn't here to see what happens next.'

Cato turned to Vellocatus. 'You need to leave us to it. Outside. Please.'

Vellocatus hesitated, then leaned down to kiss his father's forehead before he left. Cato closed the door behind him and returned to the bier.

The surgeon moved his fingers gently over the side of the chief's midriff, feeling for the position of the shot. Tasciovanus stiffened and let out a groan before slumping back. Phrygenus waited until he was still again, then picked up a scalpel and a set of wound openers and addressed the two officers.

'I want one of you on each side. Hold him down by the shoulders and arms. There's going to be a lot of pain and I need him to be kept as still as possible while I extract the shot and any other foreign matter.'

Cato and Macro took their places and clasped the older man's limbs tightly.

'Ready?' Phrygenus asked. 'Here we go.'

Using the scalpel, he picked away the scabs and encrusted pus to reveal the entry wound. At once blood and other fluids oozed out. He wiped them away before using the other instrument to pull apart the flesh and reveal the torn muscle beneath. Tasciovanus's eyes snapped open, and he gasped and then let out a keening whine as he tried to rise. Cato and Macro pressed him back and held him as the surgeon picked up a probe and adjusted his position to go in at the right angle. He worked quickly, ignoring the grunts and cries of pain from his patient.

'Found it . . . Now if I can just . . . Damn! Keep him still . . . There.'

Cato's guts squirmed as he saw that most of one of the surgeon's hands was working around inside the wound. Tasciovanus, weak though he was, strained every sinew, the veins of his neck standing out like thick cords of rope.

'Tough old bastard,' Macro said through gritted teeth. 'For someone supposed to be close to death.'

Phrygenus frowned, then gave a satisfied nod. 'I have it. Keep him still a moment longer . . .'

His bloodied hand emerged from the cavity, a dark oval lump nearly two inches long between his fingers. He tossed it onto the foot of the bier and rinsed his hands in the bucket before shaking off the drops. Then, picking up a flask, he removed the stopper. Cato could smell the sour vinegar within. The surgeon held the wound open as he poured vinegar in until the liquid came back out almost clear. His patient writhed for a moment at this latest

82

agony before mercifully losing consciousness and slumping back limply.

Phrygenus examined the dark flesh around the edges of the wound.

'This will have to go. Time for my little friends to get to work.'

He picked up the basket and removed the lid, and Cato saw a dead fish inside covered with writhing maggots.

'That fish is well past its prime.' Macro grimaced. 'What in Hades are you going to do with it?'

'For the wound,' Phrygenus explained.

'You're kidding. And I thought the poultice was bad enough. If the stink of that fish doesn't kill him, nothing will.'

'It's not the fish I'm using. It's the maggots. They'll do a good job of eating the corrupted flesh, and then I can clean the wound again and sew it up.'

Phrygenus began to place the maggots, one at a time, until there was a squirming mass in and around the entry wound. He covered it with a light dressing and bound it in place with a strip of cloth around the chief's torso before stepping away from the bier. 'There. I've done what I can. Now we wait for the maggots to clear out the dead flesh, then stitch the wound and hope he recovers.'

Macro shook his head. 'I've seen it all now. If ever I get wounded, Cato, make sure this quack never comes near me.'

Phrygenus picked up the shot and washed off the gore in the bucket before drying it on a rag and holding it up to examine it closely.

'I can see the unit markings. This came from the forges of the Fourteenth Legion. Look there.' He offered it to Cato, who could clearly make out the 'XIV' on the side of the lump of lead. 'Doesn't take a genius to work out how the old man came by the injury.'

'What happens now?' Cato asked.

The surgeon rinsed his instruments in the bucket as he responded. 'He needs rest while he fights off the fever. He should be encouraged to take drink and food. Soup to start with.'

'How long will it take for him to recover?'

'*If* he recovers . . . a month or so. If you can spare me, I'd better stay here and keep an eye on him until he's out of danger. It'll be a few days before I know if he's going to make it.'

'Yes, you do that. I want him to have the best care – your full attention.'

'Not sure the locals are going to be so keen on having a Roman hanging around,' Macro observed. 'Do you think it's safe for Phrygenus to be left here on his own?'

'I'm not going to leave him here alone,' said Cato. 'You're going to remain here with most of the cohort to make sure nothing happens to him. I want you to make sure the men behave. We can't afford any trouble with the locals. Also, I want you to start sending out patrols along the border with Iceni territory, but don't take any risks. If you see the enemy, there is to be no chasing after them. I just want you to gauge the mood in the villages of the region. I'll be taking the rest of the men with me on a little trip.'

'Trip? You're serious about having a look along the coast with Besodius and his boat?'

'I believe that sailors prefer to call such vessels ships. And yes. Might as well do it while we wait for Tasciovanus to recover.'

'And if he doesn't?'

'Then you are to get the surgeon and the rest of the men back to Camulodunum and wait for me there.'

'What if something happens to you?'

'In that case, you take command and let the governor know. After that, I'd be obliged if you'd look after Claudia and bring Lucius up for me.'

Macro tutted. 'Don't let it come to that, eh?'

CHAPTER EIGHT

On board the Minerva

The *Minerva* was typical of the craft that plied their trade along the coast of Gaul and across the sea that separated it from Britannia. She was sturdily built, with high sides and a large hold, and her bows and stern were raised to ride the rough swells she might encounter. The mainmast was crossed by a spar from which hung the leather folds of the furled sail. A much smaller mast and spar rose behind the foredeck. Two sweeps – long oars with broad blades – were stowed on the side rails. Cato took it all in as he and four of his auxiliaries climbed aboard. He had chosen tough men who could swim well, should the need arise. He was simultaneously excited and nervous about the prospect of going to sea again. There was something exhilarating about surging across the water amid the salty tang of the air. At the same time, he suffered from seasickness whenever he was out of sight of land, or when the sea was rough. Moreover, this was going to be a journey of some days and, worse, nights. All of it along a hostile coast.

Besodius approached from the stern, where he had been talking with the man testing the bindings of the large steering oars that hung either side of the stern.

'Good morning to you, Prefect.' He smiled cheerfully.

As well he should, Cato mused, having negotiated a steep price for his services. It was silver that Cato hoped to reclaim from the provincial treasury, if ever the money could be prised from the hands of whoever was appointed as the new procurator. For now he needed to understand the landscape over which he would be fighting during the months to come. He looked up into the grey sky, from which a light drizzle was falling.

'Good? It's not the best of weather.'

'Perfect for getting down the river to the estuary. By then the clouds will have lifted.' Besodius raised his face as though taking in the odour of the air. 'Yes, I'm sure of it.'

'What about the sea conditions?'

'We'll find out, eh?' He grinned and jerked a thumb towards the rear of the vessel. 'You can stow your kit in the stern lockers. I've sorted out some spare clothes from the slop chest to make you look as much like sailors as possible.'

It had been agreed that if they encountered any Icenian fishing boats, Besodius and the others aboard would present themselves as the crew of a merchant vessel blown off course. If high seas forced them to make landfall or the ship was wrecked, the subterfuge stood little chance of saving their lives if they fell into the hands of the rebels.

They stripped off their army cloaks, tunics and boots and placed them in the lockers along with their armour and weapons. Besodius and his five crewmen looked on in amusement as the soldiers picked up the coarse, stained tunics put out for them.

'No boots?' Cato queried.

'Not having any iron studs tearing chunks out of my deck,' Besodius replied. 'And bare feet will give you better grip when things get rough.'

'Are the supplies aboard?'

'Yes, Prefect. Food and water for ten days. I've kept some of the wine cargo back in case we need it to trade with any friendly Icenians. Not that there will be many of those. We can always drink what we don't use on the way back.'

Cato glanced back across the river to where Macro and several of his men were sitting on some benches beside a market stall selling cuts of meat from a roast suckling pig. He raised his hand in farewell and the centurion and the others responded with a faint cheer.

'Let's be off, then, Captain.'

Besodius gave the order to raise the anchor and man the sweeps. As soon as the muddy anchor emerged from the surface of the river, the *Minerva* moved with the current.

'Bring her round, boys!' he called to the men at the sweeps, and the bows of the ponderous vessel slowly swung downriver. As they glided past the hall, he followed Cato's gaze. 'Do you think your surgeon will save the chief?'

'He'd better. If he wants to keep his job.'

'And his head,' Besodius added. 'I know how unforgiving the locals can be. May the gods look favourably on his ministering to an enemy of Rome.'

'May the gods be wise enough to see our enemies as potential allies to be won over,' Cato responded.

Besodius raised an eyebrow. 'Do you really believe that's going to happen? Most of the tribes in Britannia hate us. They're a proud lot and I don't ever see them willingly bending the knee to Rome.'

'Give them time, and a few decent governors, and they'll realise that Roman peace is a surer route to prosperity and contentment than the endless tribal wars and raids they endured before we arrived. Yes, I believe the day will come when they are committed allies. That's what history teaches us: whether someone is regarded as enemy or friend is just a matter of timing.'

'I admire your optimism, given the bloodshed and destruction that swept the province just a few months back. I dare say there are more than a few men of your rank and above who might not share your point of view. Suetonius for one. I've a friend who recently had a couple of the governor's staff officers on board making for Rome. They told him that Suetonius intends to make such an extreme example of the Icenians that no tribe will ever dare to rebel again. If you're the man he has chosen for the task, I don't get the impression that you and your superior see eye to eye over the fate of Boudica and her tribe.'

Cato was not prepared to get lured into any conversation that might lead him to overtly or inadvertently criticise Suetonius. Besodius was clearly the kind of man who enjoyed trading gossip and confidences with his peers. All the same, he needed a tactful response to the captain's probing of his position.

'The governor has given me my orders and I will carry them out. The matter ends there.'

He turned away and made his way forward, climbing onto the small foredeck to get a better view of the way ahead. Even though the river was easily navigable, it was nowhere near as wide as the great Tamesis, which flowed through the heart of the southern part of the province. Combretovium might one day be a minor port, but it would never equal the size or significance of Londinium.

As they left the town behind, the farmland gave way to forests that crowded the riverbank. Every so often there were signs of life. The odd clearing with a cluster of small round huts. People pausing to watch the Roman ship slowly pass by as the oars rose dripping, swept forward and dropped to thrust the vessel along. It was impossible to tell if those regarding the ship harboured mere curiosity or hostility towards her and the Romans aboard. Cato knew that they were well within bowshot from either side, and despite the serene landscape that surrounded them, he could not help maintaining the constant watchfulness of the professional soldier. He feared that it would be a long time yet before any Roman could travel through the province without fear of ambush or assassination. All he could do was his best to hasten the day when such enmity was a thing of the past. He knew that for every person who thought as he did, there were perhaps ten others, Roman and Briton, whose hatred for each other would prolong the violence. It was a tragedy, because this land, even on a hazy autumn day, had its own kind of beauty.

It was late afternoon before the ship reached the estuary, where it merged with the mouth of another river before giving out onto the open sea. They were in tidal waters, and the expanses of exposed mud stretched out around them as Besodius gave the order to anchor in the middle of the stream. Once he was sure the anchor was not dragging, he gave the order for the sweeps to be stowed and the evening meal prepared. Salted fish and bread were produced, along with a small jar of wine that was watered down from one of the small kegs of water in the hold. The crew and soldiers sat in a circle in front of the mast as they ate. In the absence of uniform and rank insignia, Cato and his men looked no different to the sailors. The difference would be far starker tomorrow, when the *Minerva* went to sea. The auxiliaries would struggle to stay on their feet as the ship rose and fell on the ocean swell. Cato was already dreading it. He forced himself to eat, knowing that he might well have no appetite for food again until he was next ashore.

As dusk closed in and the shadows thickened along the banks of the river, he posted one of his men to keep watch while the others chatted quietly with the sailors and shared the last of the wine. As a moonless night fell over the scene, Cato's wariness returned and he leaned against the mast for a while, straining his eyes and ears for any sign of danger. The chirping of daytime birds was replaced by the haunting cries of hunting owls, while nocturnal animals rustled amid the undergrowth. It took an act of will not to fall prey to an overactive imagination and project something sinister onto any sound that could not be immediately identified.

The crew and soldiers settled down to sleep, stretching out on the bare deck, covering themselves with their cloaks and using spare clothing from the slop chest to rest their heads on. Besodius stood beside Cato, his features barely discernible in the dark.

'You'd be wise to get some sleep, Prefect. There'll be precious little of that to be had in the days to come.'

'Will conditions be that bad?'

'It's hard to say at this time of year. We could have a calm day and blue skies, or a gale might blow up. Then there's the cold. There'll be rain and spray and we'll be soaked most of the time, with the wind making it impossible to stay warm. My men and I will be earning every sestertius you've paid us. Your lads should be on danger money. I'll bet they never imagined when they signed up for the army that they'd have to endure what's to come.'

Cato grunted in reply. 'What's in this for you, besides the money? If it's as dangerous as you say.'

Besodius was silent for a moment, and his normal cheery tone was absent when he replied. 'The truth is, I do need the money. I had a small fortune invested in stock in a Londinium warehouse before the rebellion. That all went up in flames. Along with my younger brother, who stayed behind to try and protect our property and left it too late to get out.'

Cato recalled the chaos of the moment the rebels entered Londinium and began to kill, loot and burn their way through the town. Thousands of its inhabitants had been caught there and perished at the hands of the enemy. Many of them were subject to inhuman torments before they died. The image of the impaled bodies of men, women and even children still haunted him. 'I'm sorry for the loss of your brother.'

'Not your fault, Prefect. There was nothing the army could have done to prevent it. Minucius should have left while he had the chance. But he felt he owed it to me to do his duty, and so he is dead. I wish I had been there to tell him to get out before Boudica and her bastards got to him. Now you know why I decided to help you. I'm no coward. You didn't have to trick me into this. I'm also no mercenary, even though I need the money. I'm doing this mainly to avenge my little brother. You have my word that I will do whatever I can to help you destroy the rebels. As Jupiter is my witness.'

The next morning dawned with a clear sky and a gentle westerly breeze. Besodius had his men up as soon as there was enough light to see their way out of the estuary. The anchor was raised, and a moment later the sail was unfurled with a soft rasp before the breeze filled out the stitched goatskin and the *Minerva* was under way. There were a few other craft in sight: small fishing boats, and a river barge moored close to shore as it waited for the tide to turn and carry it upriver. Ahead the estuary widened to give a clear view of the open sea beyond, sparkling in the morning sunlight. Far in the distance, a thin band of fluffy white clouds floated just above the horizon.

As the ship met the first swell, Besodius joined Cato at the bows. 'As fine a morning as we could wish for, Prefect! The gods must favour our enterprise. If this breeze holds, we'll have a leisurely cruise up the coast and you can start gathering whatever intelligence you need for your campaign.'

Cato forced himself to smile back. His stomach gave an uncomfortable lurch as the *Minerva* crested a larger swell and then swooped down the far side, the wake creaming along the vessel's side.

Besodius grinned and indicated two of the auxiliaries at the side rail, halfway along the main deck. One was clutching the rail as if his life depended on it while his companion was hunched over, retching. 'You'll all get your sea legs in a few days.'

'Days,' Cato muttered miserably as he fought to control his rising nausea. 'Oh, shit.'

The captain gave him a reassuring slap on the back and turned to shout an order for his crew to set the foresail. With both sails trimmed to make the most of the steady breeze, the *Minerva* surged out to sea.

Some five miles out, as far as Cato could estimate it, Besodius changed course to follow the coast at a safe distance. The low-lying landscape was the only fixed point for Cato to use to fight the increasingly uncomfortable sensation in his stomach, which began to spread up his throat. Then, with a sudden spasm, the brief breakfast of bread and hard cheese that he had consumed just before dawn spattered down the side of the vessel.

'For gods' sake, man!' Besodius shouted. 'Not to windward! Do it over the lee side! Same goes for the rest of you five-day sailors!' He grabbed the nearest of them and thrust him to the port side. He was too late to stop the man spewing across the rail.

'You can bloody well clear that up the moment things calm down. I'm not having you lot make the *Minerva* look like the gutters of Rome the day after Saturnalia.'

As the day wore on, the sun climbed above the main spar and cast a welcome shifting shadow across the deck. Gradually Cato's seasickness passed and he began to pay more attention to the coastline. Mid afternoon, they drew abreast of another river mouth and he called to Besodius.

'Can you bring the vessel any nearer to shore? I need to look in there.'

'There are some sandbanks along this stretch of coast. I can't risk running aground.'

'I need to get closer,' Cato insisted.

'It would help if I knew what you were looking for, Prefect.'

'Places we can land men and construct forts. I mean to throw a noose around the enemy and tighten it bit by bit until we have them trapped. Then we can deliver the final blow to end the rebellion once and for all.' He indicated the river mouth. 'That might be a likely spot.'

'I doubt it. That's a warren of small islands and mudbanks. It'll not serve your purpose. Besides, we're still sailing past Trinovantian territory. We won't reach the Icenian coast until tomorrow.'

'I see. I'll start the mapping then. Where will we stop tonight?'

Besodius squinted up at the sun to estimate the remaining hours of daylight and then scrutinised the coast. 'There's another, smaller river a little way along. We'll reach it in plenty of time to beach the *Minerva* overnight.'

'Is that safe, so close to Icenian territory?'

'There's no settlement nearby. We'll be fine. Gone before anyone notices us.'

Cato was not convinced by the captain's confidence. 'When was the last time you sailed up this coast?'

Besodius thought a moment. 'Six months back. First trip of the spring.'

'Much has changed since then,' Cato said drily. 'We need to be on our guard.'

The captain shrugged. 'As you wish.'

Shortly afterwards, he ordered the helmsman to close with the shore, and the *Minerva* changed course to angle in towards the coast. The swell was now coming at the stern quarter, causing even more discomfort to the ship's passengers.

'What fresh Hades is this?' Cato muttered to himself. He threw up again, then forced himself to stand with as much composure as he could manage to restore some sense of the decorum due to his rank.

Closer to the land, he could make out gently rolling hills covered with forest that gave onto scrubland and shingle at the edge of the sea. The opening of the river stretched back as far as the first curve, and he saw with relief that the waters there were much calmer.

'Take in two reefs on the mainsail!' Besodius called, and his men ran to haul on the ropes that drew up the leather folds. The *Minerva* began to lose way, and as the ship passed between the low headlands, he gave the order to take in the foresail. With the sun dipping towards the treeline to the west, the ship ghosted towards a small shingle beach beneath a low cliff. Studying the shrinking distance between his vessel and the beach, he ordered the mainsail to be taken in and the crew and passengers to move aft.

Cato had been expecting the final approach to be carried out with the sweeps. He nodded in admiration as the bows grounded softly on the shingle. The *Minerva* gave a gentle shudder before she was still, the deck reassuringly firm beneath his feet. Clearly Besodius was as accomplished a seaman as he claimed.

A rope ladder was lowered from the bows, and Besodius and Cato clambered down onto the beach.

'It's about high tide,' the captain said. 'The river level will drop during the night so we won't be able to refloat until dawn.'

'In that case, I'll post a watch on the clifftop,' Cato decided.

'Suit yourself. Me and the boys are going to forage for firewood. We've got a few spears and bows in case we spot any game.'

Cato shook his head. 'Best not light a fire. Don't want to be drawing any unwanted attention.'

'Ah, come off it, Prefect.' Besodius pointed upriver. 'The nearest settlement is six miles that way. If we wait until dark and set the fire up against the cliff, no one is going to see it. That way we can prepare a hot meal and dry our clothes. In any case, while you're on my ship, I'm the captain and I give the orders.'

Now that he was on solid ground again and the nausea had gone, Cato became aware how hungry he was. His gaze shifted to the four auxiliaries, who, like himself, had been exposed to the spray of the waves all day and were now shivering from cold as well as the exhaustion that came after seasickness. Much more of this without let-up would be bad for their morale and take the edge off their fighting ability, if it came to that. He looked over the surrounding landscape and saw that there was no possibility of the fire being spotted unless someone was close by.

'Very well. But since we're now on land, I give the orders, and I say that no fire is to be lit until I tell you.'

'Yes, Prefect,' Besodius said reluctantly, before calling up to his crew to get their hunting weapons and join him.

Cato watched the small party head along the shore towards a gully that led off the beach, then ordered his men to scour the beach for firewood. As they ambled off in the opposite direction, awkward on their sea legs, Cato took out his waxed notebook from his pack and began to draft an itinerary of the day's progress, noting landmarks and estimated distances between them. He concluded with a brief sketch of the surrounding river mouth and considered its potential as a site for one of the forts.

Dusk was closing in when one of the auxiliaries alerted him to the return of Besodius and his crew. The captain, holding a spear, was leading the way. Some of his men were clutching bundles of wood while the two at the rear carried the carcass of a boar, suspended from a trimmed branch.

'See what we found!' the captain greeted them as his party reached the ship. 'Roast pork tonight!'

As the shadows lengthened, the crew set to work butchering the boar and using axes to prepare the wood for the fire. Cato gave his watchkeeping orders to his men, who had retrieved their boots and weapons from the stern lockers. There would be two watches of two men, stationed at the top of the cliff overlooking the beach. He had discounted the idea of posting one man at a time, since two had the advantage of keeping each other awake and vigilant. Despite Besodius's assurance that they were far enough from any prying eyes, Cato's innate sense of caution along with his training and experience made him wary.

He waited until night had fallen before he gave permission for the fire to be lit. Besodius produced a tinder box and worked the flints so that the sparks caught the charred lint in the box and a tiny flame glowed. Soon the kindling was alight, and then the first of the split branches and logs were added as the fire was built up. A rosy hue lit up the surrounding shingle and the base of the cliff, and the men warmed themselves against the chilly night air. As the flames died down to wavering flickers above the glowing embers, chunks of meat were cut from the carcass to roast, and a rich aroma excited Cato's tastebuds. When the time came to eat, he found the hot pork delicious, and he closed his eyes to relish the flavour as he chewed.

'Beats cold rations, eh?' Besodius chuckled as he tore a strip off the sharpened stick he had used as a skewer.

Cato was about to agree with him when a movement behind the captain's shoulder distracted him. He froze and stared along the foot of the cliff. Then he saw it again: a figure moving stealthily towards them, with more emerging from the night. Spitting out the meat he was chewing, he set his skewer down and reached for his sword as he spoke calmly to Besodius.

'We've got company.'

CHAPTER NINE

Cato stood up and called out to the others. 'On your feet!'
The sailors and the two auxiliaries who were not on watch did as they were ordered. Besodius snatched up his spear as his men grabbed their own weapons and turned to face the figures approaching them along the narrow beach. As they came within the pool of light cast by the fire, they stopped, a scant fifteen paces away. Cato could see that there were at least a dozen of them, all armed with spears. Several had tattooed designs on their cheeks.

There was a tense silence before a voice called out in the Trinovantian dialect. 'Who are you?'

Besodius answered. 'Just honest sailors, friend, looking to trade along this stretch of coast. And who might you be?'

There was no reply, and then a man stepped forward and scrutinised those standing around the fire. 'Romans . . . Traders, you say?'

'Surely. And who do I have the honour of addressing?'

The man did not reply. His followers shuffled closer, and Cato felt his heartbeat quicken as he made ready to draw his sword. Behind him he heard some scrambling, and then footsteps on the shingle as the two men who had been posted to keep watch on the clifftop rushed to join their comrades. The odds were a little more even now, although he had no idea how good Besodius and his crew would be in a fight.

The man who seemed to be the leader of the tribesmen scrutinised the Romans before he spoke again. 'I am Garamagnus.'

Cato had been following the exchange in silence and now recognised the characteristic burr of the Icenian dialect. His fingers tightened their grip on the handle of his sword as he tensed his muscles, ready to draw the blade from the scabbard and strike.

Besodius bowed his head politely. 'Then I bid you welcome, Garamagnus. You and your men. Will you join us around the fire and share our meal?'

The Icenian sniffed at the aroma of roast meat and then nodded. He muttered something to his followers, and they edged forward and stood in an arc around the fire with their backs to the cliff. Besodius motioned for his crew to sit opposite, and Cato and his men did the same. Once both the Romans and the tribesmen were settled on the shingle, there was a slight easing of the tension.

The captain took a cleaver to the boar carcass and hacked off a haunch, which he offered to Garamagnus. 'For you and your men.'

The Icenian gave a nod of thanks before tasking two of his followers to share the haunch out among their companions. Soon both parties were roasting their meat over the low flames.

Cato looked over the tribesmen – almost all young men – before he spoke to their leader. 'What brings you to our camp tonight?'

'We're hunters. We were in the forest looking for boar when one of my men spotted your fire and your ship. It's been a while since we have seen any Romans in this area.'

'Understandably, given the recent rebellion,' Cato countered, before continuing warily, 'You are Icenian?'

'I was born an Icenian and then married into a Trinovantian clan. These others are Trinovantian also.'

'Do you come from the village further up the river?'

There was a brief hesitation. 'Why do you ask?'

'Just curious,' Cato replied innocently.

'How do you know about the village?'

'I told him about it,' Besodius intervened. 'I know the area.'

'Hmm.' Garamagnus accepted a fresh hunk of meat from one of his men and stuck it on a length of cut wood before offering it up to the fire. He turned his gaze back to Cato. 'You don't look much like a sailor. Nor do those men sitting next to you.'

Cato thought quickly. 'I am a merchant new to the island. I am paying Captain Besodius to find me people to trade with. Which is why I asked if you were from the village. I hope you don't mind.'

'I mind.'

'There is always coin to be earned in exchange for information,' he persisted in a cordial tone.

'Now you sound like a spy.'

'A spy?' He made a hurt expression. 'No, just a simple businessman.'

'What about those other men?' Garamagnus indicated the auxiliaries. 'I've seen plenty of Roman soldiers over the years. I know the type. So I am wondering why they are here. And who you really are.'

'I am a merchant, like I said. These men are my bodyguards, and yes, they were soldiers before they entered my service. That's why I hired them. The rebellion has made travel something of a risk.'

'That is true. Strangers from across the sea are rarely welcome among our peoples.'

'A pity, as there is much that could be gained by both parties through trade and friendship.'

'Maybe.'

There was another uncomfortable pause in the conversation

99

before Cato changed the subject. 'How is your hunting going? Any luck?'

'Some. We came across three boars in the forest. We speared one and wounded the others. We went after them but they got away.'

'At least you got one.'

Garamagnus gave a short, humourless laugh. 'That's what we thought. Only when we returned to the spot, it had gone. Perhaps we had not killed it after all.'

'Perhaps. They are tough creatures.'

Cato sensed Besodius stiffen beside him, and some of the sailors exchanged looks. With a mixture of apprehension and anger, Cato grasped what must have happened. He pointed to the carcass. 'We have eaten our fill. Please take the rest.'

The Icenian nodded slowly. 'Very generous of you, Roman. To give us back what is rightly ours already. Your people seem to make a habit of stealing what belongs to others. I take it that is the boar that my party killed.'

Cato turned to Besodius and spoke in Latin, forcing himself to maintain a neutral tone. 'Well? Was the boar dead when you found it?'

The captain shifted guiltily. 'There was no one there when we found it. We just considered it a stroke of good fortune and brought it back for us all to enjoy. How could I have known about this hunting party?'

'Don't be a fool. You could see the wounds on the animal. You knew how it had been killed. Why pretend that you had hunted it down? To impress me and my men? Are you trying to get us killed?'

'It was a mistake.'

'Yes. Now keep your mouth shut while I attempt to get us out of trouble.'

He shifted back to the local tongue as he spoke to the Icenian. 'It seems some of our men made a mistake.'

100

'Yes. They did. A big mistake.'

There was no mistaking the hostility in Garamagnus's tone, and around him the men of his hunting party were still, their eyes fixed on the Romans as they gripped their spears tightly.

'The captain offers his apologies, and I will pay you for the meat we have consumed,' said Cato. He unfastened the purse from his belt and shook out several denarii into the palm of his hand. The silver coins gleamed in the firelight. He offered them to the Icenian, whose eyes betrayed his delight. He took the coins and quickly put them away in the haversack hanging over his shoulder. It was a substantial sum to pay for the meagre amount of meat that had been eaten by the Romans, but Cato was desperate to avoid any violence. He and his men might have the edge, but the loss of Besodius or too many of his crew would put an end to the reconnaissance mission.

'Very well,' Garamagnus said. 'The rest of the boar is ours. We will leave you in peace. But I warn you. If you ever return here, you will not be welcome. My people don't take kindly to those who break the rules of the hunt. To steal another man's kill is the lowest form of dishonour. To claim it as a kill of your own makes it even worse. But we are used to Romans acting without honour. You made treaties with my people only to break them when it suited you. When King Prasutagus died and you laid claim to half his land, your men also abused his widow and her daughters. Small wonder that so many Icenians and Trinovantians rose up and joined her rebellion.'

'Were you one of them?'

Garamagnus looked pained. 'Yes. As were all my men here. We were not present at the great battle, though. Our warband arrived too late. When we learned of the defeat, we returned to our homes.' He glared at Cato. 'Rome may have won that battle, but the spirit of the rebellion lives on in our hearts. Like I said, you are not welcome here. I will let you leave alive this time. Be sure that you sail with the morning tide. If you remain a moment longer, we will kill you all.'

He stood up and gave curt orders to his followers, who followed suit, contemptuously tossing what was left of their meat into the fire. Then they picked up the hacked carcass and strode into the darkness. Cato heard their footsteps fade along the shingle before he released his grip on the sword handle and breathed deeply.

'Fuck,' Besodius muttered. 'That was close. Thank the gods you talked them into leaving us alone.'

'No thanks to you,' said Cato. 'You should have been straight with me about the boar so I'd have known there was a hunting party close by. We were lucky they were cautious. I'm guessing defeat has left them shaken. The Icenian wanted to see how many of us there were and what type of men he was dealing with before he made his next move. Now he knows.'

'Next move?'

'We're still in trouble. They may have the boar and the silver, but our friend knows there is even more coin to be had. That, and other loot. My guess is that they'll be back during the night, hoping to surprise and kill us while we sleep.'

'Dear gods . . .'

Cato looked at the dark bulk of the ship. 'Is there any chance of getting that off the beach without having to wait for the rising tide?'

'No. It would take far more men than we have to shift it.'

'Damn.' He considered their predicament. 'All right. Then we'll just have to be ready for them when they return. For now, I want you to let the fire die down while we prepare.'

'Maybe they won't come back,' Besodius suggested desperately. 'Maybe they'll be content with the boar and the silver and leave us alone.'

'They won't. I saw the look on his face when I gave him the coins. He wants it all. They'll be back, you can be sure of it.

102

They hope to make easy prey of us. Let's make sure we disappoint them.'

Once the fire had died down, Cato sent a man to each end of the beach to keep watch and then gave his orders to the rest. The slop chest was emptied, and together with the old cargo covers stowed in the hold and small rocks from the bottom of the cliff they made some dummy figures on the beach to give the appearance of the crew and passengers of the *Minerva* slumbering around the fire. Once that was done, Cato assembled the men below the bows to explain his plan.

'They'll make for the decoys first. Once they've been lured in, that's when we strike. You have some bows and spears on the ship. Any other weapons?'

'Just a few ship's axes and belaying pins.'

'Any slings?'

'No.'

'We can make up some of those. Fortunately there's no shortage of ammunition.' He bent down to scoop up a few pebbles from the shingle. 'These will do. We'll be on the deck. The sides are high enough to provide a decent defence. Once they're lit up by the fire, we let them have it with every missile we can let loose. If we're lucky, we'll take down enough of them to scare them off. If not, we'll have to fight them from the ship until we can escape on the rising tide. I'll give each of you your orders, and when we're ready, we build up the fire and wait.'

Besodius and his men, no doubt chastened by their responsibility for the situation, did all that Cato asked, and around midnight he piled the remaining wood onto the fire and stepped back to inspect the trap. In the wavering light cast by the flames, the decoys were convincing enough. He returned to the ship, climbed the rope ladder and turned to the anxious men spread around the bow of the *Minerva*.

'Keep down behind the rail until I give the order. When we strike, I want you all up on your feet and in action at once. And give a war cry as loud as you can make it.'

'War cry, sir?' one of the sailors asked. 'What kind of war cry?'

Cato tapped his boot on the deck. 'If this was a navy, they'd shout the ship's name. So "*Minerva*" it is. The louder you make it, the more you'll scare the living shit out of the enemy. All right, lad?'

The sailor nodded.

'To your posts, then. Stay calm, be still and don't talk.'

The figures around him eased themselves down to the deck while Cato stood with his back to the foremast and waited for the first sign of the Icenian and his band. Time passed slowly, with a wearying intensity, his strained senses alert to every sound and subtle shift in the shadows of the surrounding landscape. The flames at the foot of the cliff gradually died down to a steady wavering glow, and he started to wonder if he might have been wrong after all. It was possible that Garamagnus and his men were long gone, making for their village or camp, happy with his generous pay-off. He began to feel foolish. Supposing nothing happened and these men sat through the night in fear for no good reason? They would regard him as edgy and nervous, and he would lose any respect they might have had for him. But he'd rather be thought overcautious by those under his command than be complacent and endanger them.

Then he heard the soft crunch of footsteps on the shingle and a dark shape rushed towards the bows as one of the lookouts returned.

'They're coming, sir!'

'How far off?'

The auxiliary paused to estimate. 'Five hundred paces or so when I spotted them, but they'll be closer now, sir.'

He climbed the ladder and stood there gasping before Cato

104

ordered him to pick up one of the slings that had been prepared and stand by the small pile of pebbles further down the ship's side. 'Make sure you don't hit any of our side at the bows,' he joked.

'Do my best, sir.'

They were interrupted by the sound of someone approaching from the other direction, and Cato realised it was the other lookout. He came scrambling down the shingle a moment later. 'Sir! The enemy's here.'

'I know. Seems they're going to hit us from both sides. Climb aboard. Wait!' Cato turned to look in the direction the second man had come from. 'They're behind you?'

'Yes, sir. Plenty of them. More than we saw earlier.'

'You're sure of that?'

'Yes, sir. I waited to make sure before I reported back.'

'All right. Pull the ladder up. There's a sling for you further back. Get in position and stay down. Wait for my order.'

So Garamagnus had brought in more men to support him. Cato had hoped a brief display of force might be enough to drive the enemy off, but now it looked as if those aboard the ship would have a real fight on their hands. Turning to the crouched figures, he spoke calmly. 'We have to break the attack. When I give the order, hit them with everything to hand and don't let up until they are out of range. Chances are they'll take the damage and attack the ship. If they do, we have to keep them out. Don't let even one of those bastards get aboard. We have already proved our superiority to them on the battlefield. Now the battlefield is here. But we're still Romans, and every one of us is more than a match for a barbarian. Show them no mercy because they will surely show us none. It's kill or be killed.'

He heard the sound of footsteps coming on swiftly and crouched down. 'Wait for it, lads.'

They came out of the darkness on both sides, a mass of fleeting shadows swarming towards the fire. There were none of the familiar war cries, and Cato mentally applauded Garamagnus for the discipline he exerted over his followers. They raced into the dim loom of the flames and began to stab and hack at the decoys, their wavering shadows on the cliff behind looking like distorted giants.

Cato sprang to his feet and drew his sword. 'Now, Minervans! Let 'em have it!'

'*MINERVA*!' The cry crashed out from the deck of the ship as the sailors and auxiliaries rose and unleashed their arrows and slingshot towards the tribesmen massed in the light of the fire. For an instant the enemy was too startled to react, then the first of them was struck down and the rest turned to look around them in a blind panic. Cato picked out their leader at the same moment as the latter turned towards the ship, thrusting his spear towards the *Minerva* and bellowing at his men to follow him as he charged down the beach. He could see now that the Icenian had been joined by at least another thirty tribesmen.

'Four to one,' he calculated under his breath.

The ship's defenders continued to unleash arrows, shot and stones as the enemy rushed towards them. Cato saw several more struck by the missiles before they reached the bow of the ship and splashed along the sides to thrust their spears up at the defenders. As he had foreseen, the height of the deck provided a significant advantage, and the men with the hunting bows were able to freely loose their arrows into the tribesmen packed below them. Further back, the slings whirred and loosed their stones with equally certain effect. Then one of the attackers was hoisted up, his hands grasping the top of the side rail close to Cato. He slashed his sword down, cutting across the man's wrist at an angle, cleaving through flesh and bone. The tribesman howled with pain and tumbled back.

A quick glance round showed that most of the crew and sailors were also fighting off men trying to climb the sides of the ship.

They wielded their spears, swords, axes and clubs with wild desperation, stabbing and hacking at the dark shapes splashing in the shallow water.

'No you fucking don't!' Besodius shouted close by, and Cato saw him thrust his spear into the throat of an enemy. The man lurched back, snatching the shaft of the spear from the captain's hands, and Besodius grabbed a club and swung it at the head of the next man to try his luck. 'Get your hands off my ship, you bastards!'

There was a high-pitched cry from the other side of the ship, and one of the sailors staggered back, hands clamped over his face, before he crumpled onto the deck. But there was no time to see to him as another attacker was hoisted up, grabbing hold of the bow post and swinging a leg over the rail. Cato rushed towards him and thrust at his chest. The tribesman leaned nimbly aside and the point missed its target. Before Cato could strike again, his opponent made a wild thrust with his spear. The point caught in a fold of Cato's tunic and tore through the material to gash his side. A sharp, burning pain made him grit his teeth as he thrust his sword again, this time finding his mark and punching deep into the man's shoulder. The attacker's grip on the rail failed and he tumbled back out of view.

A barked order sounded above the cries and clatter of weapons. The tribesmen broke off and backed away before trotting up the beach and angling away from the fire to be concealed by darkness. Blood was pounding in Cato's ears and he could hear the heavy breathing of the men around him as well as the moans of the wounded sailor and the tribesmen around the bows. A handful, still able to walk, nursed their injuries as they staggered back towards their comrades. One of the seamen raised his bow and took aim, but Cato pulled his weapon down.

'He's out of the fight. Save your arrow for the others.'

'They'll be coming back for more, you reckon?' Besodius asked.

'I think so.'

A sharp crack sounded from the foremast and a pebble dropped to the deck near Cato's feet.

'Get down! Down!'

More pebbles and small rocks rapped off the mast and the sides of the ship. One of the auxiliaries was too slow to take cover and was struck on the side of the head. Staggering back, dazed, he fell and hit his head against the mainmast and was knocked out. Cato crept forward to the stem and risked a quick glance over the beach. Beyond the men hurling missiles at the *Minerva* he saw Garamagnus with several others over by the fire, stoking up the flames with more kindling. Some were tearing the clothing from the decoys and wrapping the strips around cut branches. Their intention was clear.

Cato made his way back to Besodius. 'Buckets. We need buckets.'

'Stern lockers. There's a few there.'

'And rope,' he added. 'Take one of your men with you. Get water from over the stern. Go!'

The captain and his crewman scurried to the rear while Cato turned to the rest. 'They mean to burn us out. When they start throwing the incendiaries aboard, we have to get them over the side if we don't want to be roasted.' He could not help a fleeting smile as the last word summoned up an image from earlier in the evening. 'Don't know about you, but I don't want to go the same way as that boar.'

There was a dull flare of light along the edge of the wooden rail.

'Be ready!'

An instant later, a blazing length of wood arced through the air and thudded down beside Cato. He snatched it up, gritting his teeth as the flames singed his palms, and hurled it over the side towards the deeper water. More firebrands landed on the deck,

108

and the other men followed his example or beat the flames out with their cloaks. Then one, smaller, rose higher and caught on the furled sail on the short length of the angled foremast. The flames licked at the tarred cords that bound the spar to the mast and set them alight.

'Besodius!' Cato called to the stern. 'We need that water now!'

An instant later the captain ran forward, hunched over, the rope handle of a bucket gripped in both hands. He braced himself before heaving it up. The water splashed up the mast, dousing most of the flames before drenching Cato and the others in the bow.

The tribesmen continued their attempts to fire the ship for a little longer before they ran out of combustibles.

'Watch out for boarders!' Cato warned.

Once again he risked a glance towards the beach. By the light of the remaining embers he could make out Garamagnus standing close to the cliff, rallying his men for a fresh attack. They replied to his exhortations with raucous cheers. Despite their losses, they still outnumbered the defenders. It would only be a matter of time before they got enough men aboard to swing things decisively in their favour.

There was a slim chance to stop them before the attack began. Cato looked round and saw one of the hunting bows lying on the deck, next to a quiver. Only two arrows remained. He picked up the bow and nocked the first arrow, then rose and took aim at the cluster of tribesmen around their leader. Breathing steadily, he sighted the shaft as best he could. He had used bows to hunt with and had received some training in their use during his time in the army, but he knew he was an average shot at best. He paused, breathed out slowly and released the arrow. It disappeared into the night and he could not follow its path, but an instant later he saw one of the men in line with Garamagnus shudder and drop to the ground.

'Shit,' he hissed in frustration as he snatched up the last arrow. Again he took careful aim as the enemy leader turned to look towards the men gathering around his first victim. 'Jupiter, Best and Greatest,' he prayed softly, 'guide this arrow to its target.'

He released the string, and again the arrow was swallowed up by the darkness. Then he saw Garamagnus stagger back and drop his spear, the arrow shaft protruding from his midriff. The nearest man caught the Icenian by the arms before he could collapse and held him up. The cheers died in the throats of his followers as they saw that he had been badly wounded, and there was a collective groan and some cries of rage. Cato feared they might be spurred into one final, fanatical assault, driven by the desire to avenge their leader, but then one of them called an order, and he caught the words instructing them to take up their wounded.

They approached the ship cautiously. One of the sailors rose beside Cato and readied his throwing arm.

'No!' Cato stopped him. 'They want to retrieve those still alive around the ship. Let them do it.'

It was not for mercy that he gave the order. He did not want to provoke the tribesmen into another assault. Most of the wounded were picked up and carried off into the darkness. Slowly the defenders emerged from cover to watch as the tribesmen melted away, leaving only their dead and some abandoned weapons. Cato waited as the sounds of footsteps on the shingle faded, and then a while longer to ensure that none of the attackers were returning. Then he sheathed his sword and slumped back against the foremast.

CHAPTER TEN

There was no sleep for Cato and the others for the rest of the night as they sat on the deck waiting for any sign that their attackers might return. The fire on the beach died down to a dull red glow that cast no light over the surroundings. In the darkness, every sound was magnified and the movement of animals in the trees above the cliff caused the men to start in alarm before easing back down in a cold sweat. Some two hours before dawn, a breeze picked up and the soft, sighing psithurism amid the branches fuelled the edginess of those on board. Occasionally they heard the pitiful moans from the remaining enemy wounded scattered about the bows.

Finally, the first hint of the coming dawn crept upon them as their dark surroundings slowly gave way to lighter shades and details that revealed the landscape. Cato scrutinised the beach and the top of the cliff with tired eyes, but there was no sign of the tribesmen apart from a single figure squatting perhaps two hundred paces away, keeping watch on the ship.

Besodius was using the pale light to inspect the injured aboard *Minerva*. The man who had been struck on the head was still dazed, and an ominous lump had risen on his temple. Others had minor wounds that required little attention.

'Prefect . . .' Besodius indicated the tear in Cato's tunic, which was surrounded by dried blood. 'I'll take a look at that.'

Cato had been so focused on guarding against a fresh attack that he had largely ignored the wound during the remaining hours of darkness. Now he became fully aware of the pain and stiffness in his left side.

'All right.' He made to lift the tunic over his head and winced at the sudden burning sensation. Gritting his teeth, he removed the garment and dropped it to the deck. His pale skin was crusted with dried blood about the six-inch gash, which was now bleeding afresh.

Besodius bent down for a closer inspection. 'Not too bad.'

'Easy for you to say,' Cato growled.

'I'll get it quickly sewn up.'

'Quickly?'

The captain nodded towards the river. 'The tide's coming in fast. We'll float off soon. We need to get out to sea as soon as possible.'

'Fair enough.' Cato stood with his arm raised as Besodius took out a needle and some thread from a small chest that also contained dressings and pots of ointment. 'I hope you've done this before.'

'Goes with the job. My boys get injuries all the time. Hold still.'

As Besodius set to work, Cato gritted his teeth and fixed his gaze on the tribesman keeping watch on them. Though the captain worked swiftly, by the time he was done, Cato felt almost giddy with pain.

'There. Neat job, if I say so myself.' Besodius nodded as he wiped his bloodied hands on a stained cloth. 'You've added a nice new scar to your repertoire to impress the ladies.'

Cato looked down at the puckered flesh. 'I don't think Phrygenus needs to be worried about the competition. But thanks.'

'Better not exert yourself if you don't want to tear those stitches,' said Besodius. 'And have me do the job all over again.'

112

'That rather depends on our friends.' Cato indicated the tribesman on the beach. 'Let's hope there's no repeat of last night.'

Besodius got the implied criticism. 'We'll not be spending any more nights ashore, Prefect. Not until this is over and we're back at Combretovium.'

They were interrupted as the deck shifted slightly beneath their feet. Besodius closed the medical chest and turned to his men. 'Get the sweeps out.'

As they unlashed the long oars, Cato carefully put his tunic back on and then climbed onto the foredeck to look over the scene of the previous night's skirmish. He could see the dark streaks and spatters on the shingle where the enemy wounded had been dragged away. Two bodies sprawled close to the fire. One had an arrow shaft protruding from the throat while the other appeared to have been downed by a slingshot. Around the bows of the ship were several more bodies, some on the shingle, some in the shallows. Another floated further out, carried off by the rising tide. The enemy had been bloodily repulsed. Those aboard the *Minerva* had been lucky, he reflected. None had been lost as yet, though the fate of the sailor with the head injury was uncertain. If Garamagnus had been more patient and summoned more men before attacking, Cato and the others would not have stood a chance.

His thoughts were cut short as Besodius called out the order to use the sweeps to push the ship out from the shore. The auxiliaries took their place along the oars and heaved. There was a brief stillness before the deck gave a lurch and the shingle ground under the keel, accompanied by a swirl of water. The *Minerva* was afloat. The sweeps were quickly deployed to turn her bows downriver, and she glided out into the middle of the flow and headed away from the beach. Cato made his way to the stern and stood beside the helmsman, looking back. The enemy lookout had risen to his feet. He brandished his spear and shouted something that Cato could not make out, though the defiance in his tone was clear. Then he turned away and disappeared into the trees.

It had been a salutary experience. The rebels might have been defeated in battle, but their hatred of Rome and their war-like spirit had not diminished. No Roman was safe in the land of the Icenian tribe and the Trinovantian territory that bordered it. That danger would remain until their capacity and will to fight on had been completely crushed. The task confronting Cato seemed more daunting than ever. His heart felt heavy as the ship emerged from the river mouth and headed back out to sea.

They had good fortune as they continued up the coast. The weather remained kind: mostly sunny days with patches of brilliant white cloud passing overhead, borne on a steady breeze. The swell was mild for the time of year and the *Minerva* easily rode the crests and troughs. Occasional bursts of spray carried fleeting rainbow arcs that lifted Cato's mood as he stood on deck and breathed the fresh salty air. Despite the seasickness, he was becoming more accustomed to the movement of the deck, no longer needing to clutch on to the rigging and mast to steady himself.

As they progressed, he kept notes about landmarks and the distance between them. He ordered Besodius to close up on the shore each time they encountered any more rivers or waterways that led inland. Those that had potential to serve as the sites of outposts were surveyed in detail, and Cato ventured ashore briefly while his men kept a close watch over the surrounding flat landscape for any sign of danger. There were frequent sightings of the tribespeople, and occasionally their fishing boats and smaller craft. They turned away as soon as they saw the Roman ship approaching and disappeared into the reed-lined channels along the coast. It was clear to Cato that the word had gone out to every member of the tribe to treat all Romans, civilian and military alike, as an enemy to be feared and avoided.

On the following nights, Besodius ensured that his vessel was securely anchored a good distance from the shore and that a careful watch was kept during the hours of darkness. On the third day, dusk came before they had found any river or bay in which to shelter for the night, and he gave the order to anchor at sea, in the lee of a sandbank. They spent a wakeful night on the constantly shifting deck. Not even the sailors could sleep for fear of the anchor dragging and the *Minerva* being swept ashore and wrecked. Their torment was made worse by the delirious mutterings of the man with the head injury, whose condition was getting steadily worse.

By the following morning, the wind had risen and waves were churning. The captain got the ship under way as swiftly as possible, tacking across the narrow stretch of sandbanks until they reached an inlet that opened onto a large expanse of open water surrounded by reeds. There they decided to shelter until conditions calmed, only to go aground as the tide went out, leaving the *Minerva* stranded on mud a short distance from the tidal river that passed through the area.

They were alone for a few hours before the lookout who had climbed the mast called down that a boat was approaching. Shortly afterwards, Cato saw it emerging from a channel that led through the vast reed banks. No more than twenty feet long and low-sided, it was propelled by four men with paddles, while four others sat in the middle armed with spears. It closed to within a hundred paces of the *Minerva* before it reached the mud and was forced to stop.

'Here's trouble,' one of the auxiliaries muttered as the Romans watched from the deck.

One of the tribesmen climbed over the side of the boat and instantly sank up to his knees in the clinging mud. Using his spear to prop himself up as he tested the approach to the stranded ship, his progress was glacial. He frequently slipped and struggled to stay upright, and was soon covered in filth. The apprehension of those around Cato turned to mirth, and they jeered and mocked the man as he fought his way towards them. Eventually, when he had covered no further than a quarter of the distance, one of the men in the boat cupped his hands to his mouth and called him back. The tribesman turned away from the ship and paused to loosen his belt before lowering his breeches to show his arse to the Romans by way of insult. Only to promptly stumble and fall face-first into the mud.

The Romans roared with laughter as the man pulled up his mud-caked breeches and retraced his steps to the waiting boat.

'That went well!' Besodius chuckled. 'There's no way they are getting anywhere close to us at that rate.'

'True.' Cato watched the Icenian clamber back onto the boat and sit hunched, exhausted by his efforts. The men with the paddles backed the small craft away, then headed back into the reeds. 'There's only eight of them now, but it'll be a different story if they return with reinforcements when the tide comes in.'

'They'll have no more success in getting aboard than that mob the other night. Besides, the tide has already turned. We'll be gone long before they come back, even if they bother to.'

'I hope you're right.'

The muddy basin was gradually flooded, and sure enough, the *Minerva* was soon afloat again without being troubled by hostile tribesmen. With the sweeps out once more, she made her way down the channel towards the open sea. As they approached a narrow point just before the land gave way to the ocean, the lookout, who had been climbing down the ratlines from his perch astride the yard, paused and thrust an arm out.

'There's more of them, Captain! Both sides of the channel!'

Cato rushed to the side and climbed the rope rungs to join the lookout. Sure enough, he could see men massed on the dunes, hundreds of them. He returned to the deck, hurriedly reassessing their situation.

116

'This is going to be tricky. We'll be well within bowshot when we reach that narrow stretch. The breeze is against us and we'll need men at the sweeps to get us through. What about the helmsman? Can we lash the paddles to keep the ship on course?'

Besodius nodded. 'Any alterations can be made by the sweeps. Those on the oars are going to be exposed, though.'

'Then we need to do our best to keep them under cover,' said Cato. 'We haven't got much time. Is there anything in the hold that we can use to build up the sides?'

'A spare set of sails. We can lash those outside the ratlines and run them fore and aft. They'll hide the men on the oars but won't offer much protection. That's the best we can do.'

'All right, let's get to it.'

While the sailors worked the oars, Cato and his auxiliaries lifted the folded sails stored in the forward part of the hold and hurriedly rigged them as the *Minerva* approached the narrows. Closer to, they could hear the Icenians cheering as they worked themselves up in readiness to attack the Roman ship. As the first of the enemy ran to the edge of the water to loose their arrows, Besodius urged his men on. The sailors strained to push the cumbersome craft faster while at the same time keeping in time with their companions. Arrows thudded into the loose leather folds of the spare sails, which deflected or absorbed the impact and rendered most of the missiles harmless. But every so often one pierced the stretched sections, tearing through and leaving holes that weakened the protection offered. One of the older sailors was hit and fell, gasping for breath, and Cato pointed to the nearest of his auxiliaries.

'Take his place and keep your head down!'

The loss of the sailor had already caused the bows to turn slightly, and Besodius shouted to the two men on the other oar. 'Back water!'

The *Minerva* steadied, and with the auxiliary in position, the

117

oars moved together again, with Besodius calling the time loudly enough to be heard over the jeers and curses coming from either side of the channel. Cato felt a cold sweat trickling down his back. Disaster had been avoided, just. But if the *Minerva* ran into the bank or aground, there would be no escape this time.

'By the command of Neptune, I order you to let us pass!' a voice bellowed, and Cato turned to see Sagitus, the sailor with the head injury striding towards the foredeck. Gripping the bow post, he climbed onto the rail in full view of the enemy and thrust his free hand at them as he cried out again in a deep, powerful voice, 'Put aside thy puny weapons and fall to your knees! I command it! Do as Neptune commands, you miserable savages!'

'Get down from there, you bloody fool!' Besodius shouted.

The jeers and insults of the tribesmen died away as they paused to stare at the madman berating them from the bows of the *Minerva*. The barrage of arrows ceased for a precious few heartbeats, and then one of the tribesmen shouted a response and there was a roar of laughter from the shore on both sides.

'Keep laughing, you bastards,' Cato hissed. 'Buy us time.'

But almost immediately he was aware of voices shouting angrily as the leaders of the Icenians ordered their men to resume the attack. Once more arrows rained onto the ship, slashing through the shredded side screens and splintering the timbers.

'What is the meaning of this!' Sagitus shrieked in rage. 'How dare you defy the will of great Neptune himself?'

Divine providence did indeed seem to favour the madman as arrows zipped past him and over him without any striking home. Cato saw that the channel was beginning to widen now, and he turned to Besodius. 'Help me get him down before his luck runs out!'

They crept forward, and Cato braced himself to spring up and grab the sailor's arm. Then there was a soft crack, and he looked up to see an arrow shaft sticking out of the side of the

118

man's skull. One of his eyes bulged hideously as it was pushed out from within. Startled, he half turned to look at the two men who had come to save him.

'How dare they?' he demanded in a slurred voice. 'Don't they know gods cannot be killed by arrows?'

He was about to say something else, but two more arrows hit almost at the same instant, one piercing the hand that clutched the bow post while the other tore through his throat. Blood spurted from his lips and he swung out over the water before his pinned hand jerked him to a stop. Then the flesh tore free, and he tumbled into the sea. A triumphant cry sounded from the tribesmen as Cato and Besodius scrambled back.

'Keep at it!' Cato encouraged the men on the sweeps. 'We're almost out of danger!'

The enemy began to hurry along the shore to keep pace, but the channel was widening and already there were fewer arrows reaching the ship. The deck rose and dipped through the first wave, and before too long they were safely out of range and Besodius slowed the oar rate, keeping his men at it until they were a few hundred paces out to sea.

'Get the screens down,' he ordered Cato and the auxiliaries. Looking back, Cato saw several of the tribesmen splashing into the shallows to retrieve the body of the sailor, desperate to take his head as a trophy.

Besodius told the men to cease rowing, and the blades of the sweeps splashed down as the sailors slumped over the shafts, fighting for breath, their chests heaving and sweat gleaming on their faces and limbs. He let them rest only briefly before he ordered them to ship the sweeps and set the sails. Soon the *Minerva* was sailing north along the coast, heeling on a stiff breeze as Cato and the auxiliaries prised arrows from the timbers and tossed them overboard.

Besodius left the helmsman to settle on course before he joined

Cato, a grim expression on his face. 'This ain't quite the pleasure cruise I'd hoped for.'

'Welcome to my world,' Cato replied with a wry smile.

'I'm not sure I want any part of it. In fact, I'm all for turning back right now unless we discuss a bonus.'

'The bonus is getting back in one piece after you've completed the job. Until then, find us a safe place to stop for the night. And for gods' sake, make it somewhere we can get some bloody rest . . .'

CHAPTER ELEVEN

That evening the *Minerva* entered what appeared to be a delta of some kind – a vast sprawl of channels and isolated islands large and small for as far as could be seen from the lookout perch atop the mast. Cato scanned the horizon, but the only trace of any settlement was a thin trail of smoke some miles off. All day they had seen only a handful of small huts at the water's edge. Most appeared to be abandoned, and those that weren't were lived in by timid individuals who melted into the reeds the moment they caught sight of the Roman ship.

They anchored in the middle of a large expanse of open water beyond the tidal range. Surrounded by swathes of reeds and small woods growing on the largest of the islets, they seemed to be in little danger there. The terrain did not lend itself to human habitation on any significant scale. It did not permit cultivation of grazing, and while there was fish and game to be had, these promised thin pickings.

Nonetheless, the area could serve a purpose of a different kind, Cato reflected. It would be easy to hide an army in this maze of waterways, marshes and small islands. An outsider might easily get hopelessly lost and bogged down and vulnerable to ambush. He felt his heart grow heavy at the prospect of attempting to carry out the governor's orders. This was to be no large-scale policing action to hunt down and capture a small band of desperate fugitives. It would require far more men than had been promised to Cato so far, let alone the farcically small number that had actually been provided. And he would need warships too. Again promised but not provided. He was not looking forward to confronting Suetonius with his demands. The governor already had his hands full restoring order across the rest of the province. It presented a familiar challenge to keeping order in the province – too few resources spread across too large an area. Yet, if the lingering spark of rebellion was to be extinguished before it flared up again, Boudica must be hunted down and the eagle of the Ninth Legion recovered. Only then would the rebellion be broken. Cato's task would be impossible without significant reinforcements and resources. He had to convince his superior of that.

As the sun set over the gently stirring reed beds, Cato climbed down from the mast to join the others. Their mood was subdued, having lost a member of the small, tight-knit crew, and as a consequence of the nervous and physical exhaustion of recent days. They had nearly finished repairing the damage caused by the barrage of missiles unleashed earlier that day. The arrow shafts and heads had to be worked out of the ship's timbers and the resulting splinters removed. Then the damaged area had to be pumiced in order to remove any sharp jags of wood that might cause further minor injury to the crew. The main- and foresail had been lowered to the deck, and Besodius and one of his men were sitting cross-legged going over them, removing any arrows caught in the folds and sewing up tears in the leather.

'See anything?' the captain asked.

'Nothing for miles. We're safe, I think.' Cato stood for a moment looking over his surroundings before fetching the bag containing his waxed notebook. 'I've a feeling these waterways and marshes are going to play an important part in the campaign. We'll need to establish some outposts here.'

Besodius glanced around. 'I can think of less depressing places to be posted to.'

'It won't be for long. Just until the rebels are rounded up.'

The captain paused in his stitching. 'You soldiers have always seemed to me to be a pretty confident bunch. Overconfident, I'd say. What makes you think the rebels won't be able to hide out for ever? You won't be able to keep up the search for long before someone in Rome complains about how many men are being deployed in the hunt and how little they've achieved. I wouldn't want to be in your boots when that happens.'

'*If* it happens,' Cato responded irritably. 'We'll see. How well do you know this area?'

'I've only ever come as far as this point. I didn't want to go any further since I wasn't sure I'd be able to find my way out. Besides, apart from a few hovels along the way, there's no one to trade with. Place is a backwater of a backwater. I doubt any Roman has ever gone further in than we have.'

'That's unfortunate,' Cato mused. 'I need men who know their way around every part of Icenian territory. I've never had to fight through anything as difficult as this landscape. Vast marshes, mud that can swallow you up and mists so dense you can barely see where you're putting your feet. And all of it surrounded by tribes who have every reason to hate our guts. It's going to be as tough a challenge as I've ever faced.'

'May Fortuna bring you all the luck you can get, then. If it doesn't work out, there'll always be a place for you on my ship. I could use a quick-witted business partner. I own a couple of other vessels and I have plans to expand my operation. You could do worse.'

The captain's offer was flattering. But even if Cato failed to capture Boudica and was dismissed from his command of the Eighth Illyrian Cohort, he would get by. He owned a large house in Rome and a modest estate in the countryside not far from the city, in addition to the proceeds of booty from earlier campaigns – not that that amounted to much. He had been less fortunate in that regard than most of his peers on active service. Even those on garrison duties had profited more, thanks to their connections with local businesses and lucrative side deals hiring out their men to serve as guards. Cato's time in the army, nearly twenty years now – it was hard to believe it had been so long and passed so quickly – had been taken up with special duties that had denied him the opportunity to settle into any comfortable posting. In truth, he had developed an appetite for such roles and could not see himself settling into a pampered lifestyle back in Rome.

'Thanks for the offer, Besodius. I'll keep it in mind.'

'You do that.'

'How long before the repairs are complete?'

'Almost done. Just a few more tears to fix in the foresail, and some splices to the rigging. We'll be finished while there's still light. We can go back to sea tomorrow.'

'Good. How far to Branodunum?'

The captain thought a moment. 'If the wind is favourable, less than a day's sail. You can make your notes and sketches and then we'll head back. Can't say I won't be delighted to get out of these waters and return to Gaul for the winter. Same goes for my boys. That said, I'm not looking forward to breaking the news about Sagitus to his family. Still, he's got some back pay due and that will tide them over for a bit.'

'Never an easy duty,' Cato sympathised, briefly dwelling on the many times he had been obliged to settle the affairs of the men under his command who had died in battle, or as a result of accidents or disease. 'I take it you will resume your trading with Britannia once the winter is over.'

'That rather depends on you, Prefect. If you fail to catch Boudica and the rebellion boils up again, then it may well be over for us in Britannia. In which case I'll go back to working the routes between Gaul and Hispania. If you defeat the rebels, I'll resume trading here. This is where the best profit is to be made. At least until the province is more established and the next wave of wine merchants arrive and spoil things for those of us who took the initial risk.'

As a soldier, Cato was not inclined to dwell too much on matters of commerce and trade. He knew that the fate of the Empire was as much bound up with such things as it was dependent on the army to defend its borders and maintain internal order. The invasion of Britannia marked the first expansion of the Empire during his lifetime. In the years he had served there, he had come to some awareness of the complexity of the process, involving as it did the laying down of the infrastructure, administration and commerce that followed on from military action. Things that were already well established in the other provinces he had served in. It interested him to consider for a moment the perspective of the risks taken by men like Besodius in contributing to the creation of a viable province. If it turned out that Rome failed to make a success of Britannia, the captain could take his financial hit and transfer his business elsewhere. It was different with the army. Their investment was made in terms of lives, and if the province collapsed, they would count the loss in dead comrades.

He smiled encouragingly. 'I'll do my best to ensure that you are back here in the spring and that you will continue to reap the profits you seek. You deserve them after this trip.'

The sky was clear that night, and the slim crescent of a new moon and the brilliant sparkle of the stars provided enough illumination to see any attempt to approach the ship. Those aboard slept soundly while a two-man watch kept an eye on their surroundings. A mist rose before dawn and the men woke to discover that they were covered in a light patina of dew. Standing

125

at the ship's side, Cato could barely see the dim outline of the nearest bed of reeds, and the still water had a dull metallic sheen as the sun tried to pierce the gloom.

'We're not going anywhere until this lifts,' said Besodius.

'Is the mist a regular occurrence hereabouts?'

He nodded. 'If you were ever going to imagine a place as dismal as the River Styx, then this would be it. Charon would be right at home here.'

They waited impatiently for the sun to rise and the mist to slowly dissipate. At length the captain announced that he could see well enough to get under way. As they emerged into the open water near the coast, Cato looked back with a shudder. The mythical reference was apposite, and the ethereal atmosphere of the landscape evoked all the descriptions of Britannia he had read as a child. Back then he would never have dreamed that he would one day be part of the army claiming the island for the Roman Empire.

The northern coast of the Icenian territory proved to be a mixed affair of low cliffs, pebbled beaches and marshy inlets with rolling forests beyond that stretched west until a vast bay opened up ahead of the *Minerva*. So large that the coastline that bounded it could only be seen from the masthead. Besodius pointed out thin trails of smoke rising from behind the dunes at the entrance of the bay.

'That's Branodunum. It can be reached by a small channel. When I was last here, I anchored in the deeper water and they came out in small boats to trade. That was before the rebellion. I'm not sure what kind of reception we might receive now.'

'We're posing as merchants. You have wine to sell. If I know anything about this tribe, it's that they like wine. I'd be surprised if they passed up the chance, given that you are are almost certain to be the first ship from Gaul to come this way since the rebellion broke out.'

126

'We'll see,' Besodius replied doubtfully.

He made his way aft and guided the helmsman towards the entrance to the channel that led the short distance inland to Branodunum. They dropped anchor a safe distance from the shore. As the *Minerva* slowly swung around, bows into the rising tide, the men gazed in the direction of the settlement, hidden by the dunes.

'What now?' asked one of the auxiliaries.

'We wait,' Cato replied. 'There will be someone along soon.'

Sure enough, a short time later, several figures appeared amid the tall tufts of grass on one of the dunes. There appeared to be some kind of heated exchange, with lots of arm-waving and brandishing of spears, before the men went away again.

'Doesn't look very hopeful,' Besodius observed. 'We should leave. We can anchor out in the bay for the night before we head back down the coast.'

'No. We'll wait here a while. See how they react.'

'You saw how they reacted. I may not be as familiar with the tribe as you are, but to me that did not look friendly.'

'We'll see.'

It was already late in the afternoon, and Cato knew that unless someone approached the ship soon, they'd have to move the *Minerva* out into the bay rather than risk remaining where they were. They could always return to the spot the following morning and give the locals another chance to make contact. A lot was riding on the captain's earlier dealings with the people of Branodunum.

'Boat approaching!' the lookout called down from the mast. He pointed up the channel, and a moment later Cato saw a small craft emerge from one of the waterways and head towards them. He could make out three men. Two paddling, while the third sat in the stern. As they drew closer, he could see that the Icenian passenger was grey-haired and wiry, perhaps in his fifties or older. He gave his men an order and they slowed down.

'I know him,' said Besodius. 'He's the chief of the settlement.'

'You said he was friendly enough when you came this way before.'

'That's right. Let's see how much the rebellion has changed things.'

Besodius cupped his hands to his mouth and called across the water to the boat, now no more than fifty paces away. He spoke in the Icenian dialect. 'Greetings, Ganomenus!'

The old man cocked his head to one side and stared a moment before he called back. 'Is that the *Minerva*? Captain Besodius?'

'The same. You are welcome to come aboard. I have wine for you to sample.'

The captain turned to order one of his men to bring an amphora up from the hold as the native craft approached cautiously. It stopped again some ten paces from the side of the ship, the men on the paddles keeping it level with the *Minerva* as the exchange continued.

'What are you doing here?' the old man demanded.

'We've come to trade. What else would we be doing here?' Besodius replied cheerfully.

'You have some nerve, Captain. The Icenians are at war with Rome.'

'Haven't you heard? The rebellion is over. Boudica has been defeated.'

There was a brief pause before Ganomenus gave a fresh order to his men and the boat edged closer to the side of the ship. Besodius lowered the rope ladder and beckoned. 'Come aboard. I give you my word that you are quite safe. I am not your enemy.'

The boat bumped against the ship's timbers and Ganomenus stood, balancing himself in the light craft as he grabbed at the ladder and climbed nimbly up onto the deck. One of the men held the ladder to keep the boat in position while their chief was aboard.

The old man briefly clasped forearms with Besodius before looking around at the other Romans. 'You have a larger crew than last time, Captain.'

Besodius indicated Cato. 'This is my new business partner, Cato, and his bodyguards. He's come along to familiarise himself with the coastline before he begins to trade here.'

The Icenian looked Cato up and down before he responded suspiciously, 'He looks more like a soldier than a merchant.'

'He was a soldier before,' said Besodius. 'He left the army some years ago to find a more lucrative and less dangerous life.'

'And he chose to come to Britannia, did he?' the old man asked with heavy irony.

Besodius grinned and indicated the amphora. 'Now, about that wine. Will you have some?'

Ganomenus sighed, as if making a profound concession. 'As you wish.'

'Good man!' Besodius clapped him on the shoulder in a familiar fashion and indicated the lockers at the stern. 'Let's sit and exchange our news while we drink.'

The three men took their places while a crewman poured wine for each.

Besodius raised his goblet in a toast. 'To old friends, and new. May our friendship be long and fruitful.' Cato saw that Ganomenus hesitated before he drank.

When all three goblets were drained and refilled, Besodius asked, 'And how are your people doing? Any more grandchildren? Your youngest son had just had his first boy when we last met.'

Ganomenus lowered his beaker and frowned. 'Penotagus is gone. Along with his family. They followed Boudica and never returned. Like so many others.' There was no mistaking the bitterness in his tone, and Cato decided to intervene before Besodius tried to shift the conversation back to lighter ground.

'Many families were lost during the rebellion, Roman and

129

Briton alike. It is a tragedy. And what has been achieved? Nothing but great loss of life and property. We need peace to return as swiftly as possible now that the rebellion has failed.'

'Failed?' The old man snorted. 'You speak as if it had ended.'

'Hasn't it? There was a great battle and Boudica was defeated. Most of her followers were annihilated and she fled, who knows where. It's over.'

Ganomenus shook his head and turned to Besodius. 'Your new business partner has a lot to learn about my people. Perhaps you should have chosen more wisely, Captain.'

He addressed Cato again. 'The rebellion is not over. Far from it. Even now our queen is rebuilding her forces in her stronghold deep in the marshes. You Romans will never find the place. Even if you discover the right track to take you to Lyngomara, her base is impregnable.'

'I've yet to see a tribal fortification in Britannia that is truly impregnable,' Cato replied.

The chief frowned at the comment before continuing. 'Besides, she is raising a new army and sending agents to other tribes to ask for volunteers to join her. Her spirit is unbroken and her hatred for Rome knows no limits. She will continue the struggle to the last drop of her blood and that of the last person in our tribe.'

Cato's ears pricked up as he heard the shift in tone of the last words. 'It sounds like you don't approve of her resolve to fight on.'

The old man lowered his head and was silent for a beat before he replied. 'She is my queen. I am loyal to her as I am loyal to my people. Sometimes there is a tension between the two when a leader acts in a manner that endangers those they have responsibility for. This is one of those times. The battle was lost and her army destroyed, as you say. Somehow that has only sharpened her resolve. She is now driven solely by thoughts of revenge, no matter the cost to the rest of her people.'

'Have any of her advisers tried to reason with her?' Cato asked.

'Attempted to persuade her of the pointlessness of continuing the struggle?'

'Of course they have,' Ganomenus replied sharply. 'When she summoned the leaders of the tribe, I spoke up. But my words were dismissed out of hand. She ordered us to provide food, men and weapons and threatened those who refused to comply. My other son led the rest of the contingent to join her a few days ago. There are only old men and children left to manage the land now. Winter is coming and hunger will come with it.'

Cato listened thoughtfully. 'I see. You know where to find Lyngomara.'

'Yes, of course. I know the marshes like the back of my hand.'

Cato made a mental note of the comment as he spoke again. 'Are there many in the tribe who feel as you do?'

'Some. It's hard to say how many, as we dare not risk being too open about our concerns within the tribe. I am only telling you because you are outsiders, and you have provided me with wine to loosen my tongue.' Ganomenus smiled faintly as he held up his goblet. 'It could do with some more loosening.'

The sailor poured another round.

'How do your people in Branodunum feel about continuing the rebellion?' Cato asked. 'Is there any chance that Besodius and I can begin trading again now?'

'No. It would be too dangerous. My people are divided. Many who have lost kin in the rebellion blame that on Rome and still support Boudica. If you showed your faces in Branodunum they might attack you. Even if they didn't, your presence would be reported to the queen and she would be sure to make an example of any who had dealings with Roman merchants.'

'What about you? Given what you say, you're taking a risk coming here to tell us this.'

'Of course I am. However, the men in the boat are trusted followers. They were fishing when they spotted your ship, and

131

brought the news straight to me, but it's only a matter of time before others are aware of your presence. I came here out of regard for my former friendship with the captain. I needed to warn him to stay away if he valued his life. Besides, I knew he would have wine. He always does. And wine has become a scarce pleasure these days.'

The old man drained his cup again and stood up, wiping his mouth on the back of his hand. 'I must go, before we are seen.'

The two Romans rose and Besodius indicated the amphora. 'You can take that with you, my friend.'

Ganomenus looked torn for a moment before he shook his head. 'I might struggle to explain how I came by it. Save it for happier times, when we can drink and feast in my hut once again. Goodbye, Besodius.'

He held out his hand and they clasped forearms before the Icenian faced Cato. 'Farewell, business partner of my friend.'

There was a shrewdness and humour in his expression that impressed Cato as the old man continued. 'I was not fooled for an instant, Roman. I know what you are and why you are here. I just hope that you have learned enough not to regard all Icenians as your enemy. When the time of reckoning comes for those who remain loyal to the rebellion, remember me and those like me and show us mercy. Even though some would call us traitors.'

Cato shook his head. 'I consider no man a traitor who is wise enough to prefer peace to a lost cause.'

'Really?' Ganomenus's eyes narrowed. 'I wonder if you would feel the same if our positions were reversed. From what I have learned about Roman soldiers, I doubt it.'

Cato smiled self-consciously now that his subterfuge had been exposed. 'You have me there. It is different for Roman soldiers. We are trained to be obedient, and when our leaders order us to wage war, we do it until we are ordered to stop, no matter what the cost.'

'And what do you think about that? Do you consider it wise?'

'I don't question such things aloud. What I think is a different matter. That is what passes for wisdom among soldiers.'

'I understand. I hope I have the chance to meet you again, when it is all over.'

They clasped hands, then the old man climbed back down the rope ladder into the small boat and his companions thrust it away from the ship's side and paddled back up the channel towards Branodunum. Cato watched them for a moment before his gaze moved over his surroundings, noting the easy approach to the settlement and the vantage points among the dunes and the gentle hills beyond. It would be a fine site to establish a fort on the edge of Icenian territory. From what Ganomenus had said, the sympathies of his people were divided, and that would make Cato's task easier. He felt a moment's pity for the old man. He might be forced to pick sides, with all that might cost him, sooner than he anticipated.

He reached for one of his notebooks to record his observations and then snapped it shut before he turned to Besodius. 'I've seen all I need to see. Get us out of here. We'll spend the night in the bay, then return to Combretovium.'

The captain did not hide his relief. 'Good!'

A puff of wind caused both men to turn to stare to the north. A band of cloud was edging towards them, and whitecaps could be seen far out at sea. Besodius nodded to himself.

'Not a moment too soon.'

CHAPTER TWELVE

In Trinovantian territory

'Are you sure this is the place?' Macro asked as he lay on the wet leaves just inside the treeline.

Beside him Centurion Tubero nodded as they looked down the slope towards the small village, scarcely twenty huts of various sizes in all. It was situated close to the border with the Icenian tribe. The inhabitants seemed to be going about their usual routines with no indication that they suspected they were being watched.

'My lad's directions were quite clear. There's no mistaking it. See there, beyond the village, the mere with the small island in the centre. Just as he said.'

'Hmm,' Macro responded. He was still not convinced by the opportunity that Tubero had presented to him with great excitement two days earlier. The centurion had been out with some of the men and a hunter scouring a nearby forest for game when they had encountered a farmer tending a small flock of sheep along the track from Combretovium. Macro had instructed all the patrols and hunting parties venturing close to the border with Icenian territory to question anyone they encountered about the enemy's movements. The farmer stopped by Tubero had been fearful at first, but when it was made clear that he would come to no harm, he had told the Romans of the pending visit of a small party of Icenian warriors to collect supplies to feed what was left of Boudica's army. They also intended to recruit volunteers, but the farmer was concerned that it would be more a case of coercion than volunteering. Tubero had rewarded him for his information and hurried back to report to Macro.

Now, thirty men from Tubero's mounted contingent were in a clearing a short distance behind the two officers, waiting for the order to close the trap on the Icenians when they appeared. They had moved into position the previous evening. It was already noon, as far as Macro could estimate, and there was still no sign of the enemy. Their lateness tested his patience. At the same time, he was aware that the farmer's story might be part of some scheme to turn the tables on the Romans. It was possible, he decided, but unlikely. The enemy had been annihilated and the survivors were on the run. They were the prey of the Romans sent to hunt them down and would therefore be far more likely to be in hiding rather than setting traps. Macro was confident that the numbers and superior training and morale of his men would be more than a match for any party of Icenian warriors they might encounter in the village. Assuming the enemy turned up.

'Taking their own sweet bloody time. I hope this isn't some kind of wild goose chase, Tubero. I don't take kindly to spending a drizzly autumn day lying in the damp when I could be sitting beside a fire in a nice warm hall.'

He spared a moment to reflect on the comforts of Tasciovanus's accommodation and the ready supply of wine, thanks to the recent delivery by the merchant Cato had hired to take him up the coast. All being well, the prefect would be returning soon, and Macro hoped he would have news for him of the day's small victory and a clutch of Icenian prisoners to interrogate for details about Boudica's forces. At the same time, he could not help being concerned for his superior's safety. Venturing onto the open sea was risky enough in itself. But to do so at this time of year along an enemy coast added significantly to any risk. Macro hoped Besodius was as good a seaman as he had claimed he was.

'There they are!' Tubero announced, and pointed to the end of the vale that led from Icenian territory to the north of the village. Several riders had emerged from a forest track, armed with spears and with oval shields slung on their backs. Macro bristled at the sight. Those were auxiliary shields, looted from the bodies of Roman soldiers defeated in the earlier stage of the rebellion. There were ten tribesmen, leading two large covered carts drawn by mules. Roman carts and Roman mules, Macro realised.

'Ten men and two mule drivers,' Tubero said cheerfully. 'Excellent. We'll make short work of that lot, sir.'

'Yes, I imagine so.' Macro's gaze steadily swept the rest of the vale and the village, looking for any sign of more rebel warriors or anything that might give him cause for suspicion. It was a peaceful enough scene. The villagers did not seem unduly interested in the approaching Icenians, but then of course they were expecting their arrival.

'When do we go in and get them, sir?' asked Tubero. 'Shall I tell the men to mount up?'

'Not yet. We don't want to spook any birds into flight while there's still time for that lot to turn tail and get away. Stay where you are. Let them get into the village and dismount before we make our move.'

Macro watched children run to greet the approaching Icenians and line the entrance to the village as the riders and carts passed by. Some women hurried over to keep the less cautious of their offspring from getting too close to the heavy wheels and bundled them into their huts away from any danger. A small group of men abandoned their work to gather on the large patch of open ground in the middle of the village, but it was impossible for Macro to assess whether they meant to confront their visitors or to greet them.

The riders halted, and there was a brief exchange before they

136

dismounted and their leader addressed the villagers with much stabbing of his finger.

'Our Icenian lads don't seem to be very welcome.' Tubero chuckled. 'The locals aren't too keen on being parted from their food and young men.'

The warriors now advanced on the villagers and began to push them towards their huts, bundling them inside before they began to search the storage huts for food.

'Time to make our move,' said Macro.

The two men shuffled back into the trees, then rose to rejoin the rest of the column. Before he gave the order to mount, Macro spoke to his men.

'Remember, the villagers down there are Trinovantians. We treat them as allies unless they give us any reason not to. It's the Icenian warriors we're after. Take them alive if you can, but if they don't want to cooperate, then knock them on the head. I don't want to give the game away until the last moment. So keep your war cries to yourself until I give the order to charge. After that, make as much noise as you can and let's put the fear of the gods into those bastards. Let's go. Mount up!'

Macro and Tubero led the column down the forest track that gave out onto the slope above the village a short distance from where they had spent the morning observing the locals. As the auxiliaries came out into the open, they fanned out on either side to form a line and began to trot towards the huts two hundred paces away. Macro heard a distant shout above the thrumming of hooves on the soft ground, the jingle of accoutrements and the creak of leather.

He drew his sword and raised it over his head. 'Eighth Illyrian . . . at the canter!'

He urged his mount to increase its pace, and on either side the line rippled as the men followed suit. Ahead he could see the Icenians running towards their horses. The rest of the open

137

ground was deserted now. Fifty paces from the edge of the village, Macro gave the command to charge, and the men let out wild cries as they urged their mounts towards and among the huts. He steered his horse directly towards the two carts and the Icenian warriors climbing into their saddles as they prepared to defend themselves. It would be too late for them to escape the trap. They would either have to fight or surrender now.

He was still a short distance from the carts when a war horn sounded close by, from within the village. Several more horns joined in from other huts, and at that moment rebel warriors poured from the covered wagons, with more bursting out from the entrances of the huts. The war cries died in the throats of the auxiliaries as they looked about them in horror.

'Sweet fucking Jupiter,' Macro snarled through gritted teeth. 'We've been had.'

Boudica and ten of her bodyguards had risen to their feet and readied their weapons the moment the Roman riders were spotted. Like the others, she was wearing leggings and ringed armour over her tunic. Her red hair was tied back, and woad war designs had been applied to her face and arms. Moving to the doorway, she peered out and saw the extended line of cavalry with two centurions leading from the centre. Red cloaks and crests rippled and light glinted off the blades and spear tips. An impressive sight, she thought, and then smiled coldly. The arrogance of the enemy had played into her hands. Soon most of the men charging towards the village would be dead. The message that the rebellion was not over would spread far and wide and renew the spark of resistance in other tribes.

She ducked back as the first of the Romans galloped past the hut. Turning to the man carrying the war horn, she thrust out her free hand. 'Now!'

He raised the mouthpiece, drew a deep breath and blew into

the instrument. The flat, blaring note that had been heard so often during the rebellion sounded its defiance again as Boudica burst out of the hut, followed closely by her bodyguards, roaring their battle cry as they raced towards the nearest of the auxiliaries. More of her warriors streamed from the other huts, cutting the mounted man off from his comrades. Grasping his reins, he hesitated, not knowing which way to turn. His hesitation cost him his life as one of Boudica's bodyguards, far fleeter of foot than his queen, thrust his spear into the rider's right side, the impact driving the man to his left, where the weight of his shield sealed his fate and he fell from his saddle. He landed heavily, the breath driven from his lungs in an agonised gasp, and was immediately surrounded by the rebels, who hacked and stabbed at him.

Boudica reached the scene just in time to thrust the point of her sword into the auxiliary's face, shattering his jaw as the blade plunged on into his mouth and deep into his skull. Already her men had moved on, spreading out as they rushed to find fresh targets. Boudica raised her bloodied weapon and saw that several more of the enemy had been surrounded. They were desperately trying to swerve their horses from side to side as they blocked blows with their shields and stabbed with their spears. Beyond, the bulk of the Roman column was caught between the men rushing from the direction of the carts and those charging out of the huts. They might yet escape the trap if their officers reacted swiftly enough.

The commander of her bodyguards, Varibagnus, was at her side, ready to protect his queen, but she pointed to the open slope leading to the trees. 'Don't let them get away. Find some men and cut them off. Now!'

He hesitated for a heartbeat before calling on the others in his group to follow him as he worked his way around the swirling skirmish in the heart of the village. Boudica moved on, thrusting her way towards the nearest duel, where three of the enemy were keeping a far larger number of rebels at a distance with their spears.

'What are you waiting for?' she cried out shrilly. 'Kill them! Kill them all!'

She saw the fear in the nearest man's eyes, and felt a cold rage and contempt as she pushed past him and leaped towards the nearest of the horsemen. He made to thrust his spear at her, but she dropped into a low crouch, so close to the horse that the stench of its hot breath washed over her face. With a snarl, she swung her sword, and the edge cut through the beast's knee, severing muscles and shattering bone. At once the horse collapsed and the rider pitched forward, fighting to stay in his saddle. Boudica rolled clear and came up with her sword raised as the auxiliary was grasped by hands that wrenched him down and out of view.

Beyond him, one of his companions had lost his spear and was laying about him with his long cavalry sword. She saw him strike one of her warriors on the shoulder, cutting deeply into his chest. He went down under the impact, dragging the sword with him as the rider tried fruitlessly to wrench his blade free. Another warrior stabbed the Roman in the back and yet another thrust a spear into his thigh. He swayed a moment and then jolted under the impact of other weapons before he was hauled from his saddle. The third man, quicker-witted than his comrades, urged his horse into a charge and burst through the swirl of warriors to join his companions hurriedly trying to form a circle around their unit's standard.

Boudica cupped a hand to her mouth and shouted to be heard above the din of war cries and the clash and clatter of weapons, the splintering thuds of blows landed on shields and the snorting of horses. 'Kill the standard-bearer! Kill their centurions!' She knew the Roman way of war well enough to be aware that the symbols and their officers were prized above all else. To threaten them was the surest way of shaming the men into remaining to fight.

With a fresh roar, her warriors surged towards the Romans, flowing around the knot of mounted men and surrounding them. Boudica estimated that no more than twenty of the enemy remained to fight the two hundred warriors she had deployed in the ambush. Even so, several of her men were down, and now that the initial surprise was over, the Romans were closing up and holding off their attackers for the moment. She stood back watching in frustration as her warriors struggled to close in and wield their weapons effectively. She was near enough now to make out the features of the two Roman centurions urging their men on. One was unknown to her. The sight of the other sent an icy jolt down her spine as she beheld the familiar stocky physique and then heard the inimitable bellow of his voice.

'Protect the standard! Stick it to the bastards!'

'Macro . . .' she whispered to herself. If only it could have been any Roman officer but him. There would be time to lament the iniquities of coincidence another day, she told herself forcefully. For the present she must steel her heart and do what must be done. She drew a deep breath.

'What are you waiting for? Are you men or children? Kill the Romans! Cut down their horses!'

She waved her sword above her head and blinked as drops of blood fell on her brow. Her cry galvanised her men and they surged forward again. Their long swords slashed out at the animals' legs, and those with spears piked them into the flanks and necks of the enemy mounts. Some of the stricken horses managed to stay upright, blood-flecked foam spraying through their air as they tossed their heads. Others crumpled, bringing their riders down with them. Those men who fell among the rebels were pounced on and hacked to death with swords and axes. Two were lucky enough to escape among their remaining companions.

'Eighth Illyrian!' Macro called above the din. 'On me! Don't stop for anything! Move!'

There was a sudden surge of horseflesh as he galloped through the cordon of warriors with the standard-bearer at his side. Those who had been distracted by finishing off the unhorsed auxiliaries had created a gap in the rebel circle, and now the surviving Romans charged through it, hacking to right and left as they raced through the huts and made for the open ground and the slope beyond.

'Don't let them escape!' Boudica shrieked. 'You fools!'

She ran in at an angle, targeting the other centurion, who was towards the rear of the enemy horsemen. He saw her at the same time and reined in his mount as he snarled.

'Boudica!'

He wheeled towards her and urged his horse forward. 'It ends now, you bloody witch!'

She did not hesitate, but ran to meet him, lips lifted in a feral grin. At the last instant she threw herself to the side, and as the dark shape blurred past her, she swung her sword and cut deeply into the flesh just above the rear of the beast's hock. The horse lurched, then its leg folded and its rear went down. The centurion threw his weight forward to retain his seat, but his mount rolled to the side, pinning him to the ground. His shield was thrown clear, but he managed to retain his sword as he desperately tried to free his leg from beneath the writhing horse.

One of her warriors rushed forward to strike at the centurion, but Boudica thrust him away. 'He's mine!'

She retrieved the Roman's oval shield and approached him warily as he brandished his sword and made to strike. She feinted, and the centurion's blade clattered off the shield. She taunted him with it a few more times, savouring his helplessness, before whirling her own sword and hacking at his wrist, almost severing his hand so that it flopped uselessly from a shred of skin and muscle and his weapon dropped to the ground.

Unable to defend himself, the centurion slumped onto his back and raised his remaining hand, fingers splayed. 'Spare me!'

Boudica had learned Latin as a child, and spat at him as she replied. 'You ask me for mercy? What mercy did you show my daughters? What mercy did you show my people when you continued to massacre the fugitives from the battle? What mercy did you show me when you had me scourged and stole everything from my people. No. There will be no mercy for you, Roman. Nor any other.'

Angling the bottom edge of the shield, she brought the trim down hard on his throat, just below the ties of his helmet. The centurion let out a gasp, his hand groping at his crushed windpipe. She struck him again and again, driving the edge deeper into his neck until she had pulverised his throat and his breath came as a high-pitched wheeze. He slumped back, jaw jerking. His body spasmed briefly, and then he was still. Boudica glared at him, then threw the shield aside as she bent over the corpse and hacked at the neck until the flesh and bone parted with a fresh rush of blood. She reached for the base of the crest where it fitted into the top of the helmet and hoisted her grisly trophy up for her warriors to see. There was a roar of triumph from those nearby.

Boudica looked up the slope to see that the auxiliaries had drawn ahead of their pursuers and were entering the forest track. A moment later, the last of them, Macro, paused briefly to look back. Sheathing his sword, he appeared to be staring directly at Boudica. He raised his hand in salute. Whether that was for his fallen comrades or out of respect for her for besting him, she could not tell. Then he wheeled his horse around and cantered out of sight amid the trees.

Boudica lowered the head and let it hang by her side for a moment, angry that any Romans had escaped the trap at all. But she admitted to herself that she was glad Macro had managed it. Of all Romans, his would be the death she regretted most. But die he must, along with every other Roman in Britannia, and she would not rest until that had come to pass.

Around her the warriors were cheering in triumph as they shook their weapons and held up the other heads of their foes. Now that the action was over, the villagers emerged from their huts to join the celebration, women and children just as deliriously excited as their menfolk who had defeated the enemy. Boudica felt a moment's pity for them. The village would be marked for death now. The Romans were bound to come back, in force, and exact a terrible revenge as a warning to any other Trinovantians who collaborated with the rebels. She hoped that she could persuade them to leave the place before then, but there were always those too old or stubborn to do the wise thing, and they would pay for it with their lives.

It was hard not to get caught up in the jubilation. Boudica grinned at her warriors and the village's inhabitants, all savouring the victory, however small, that had given them renewed hope. She would send word to other villages and towns about the ambush and have their trophies paraded so that all might see that Rome could be defied and defeated. More fighters would be inspired to join the new army she was raising. This time, she had resolved, they would fight more effectively. They would harass Roman supply lines, ambush patrols, burn villas and massacre their occupants, wearing the enemy down. Anything but face them in a pitched battle again. The Romans would be forever chasing their tails, marching from one end of the province to the other in a vain effort to hunt down the elusive rebels. Day by day, month by month and year by year, they would be picked off and demoralised until they were too exhausted to continue the struggle and abandoned Britannia.

Boudica was human enough to be proud that her name and that of her tribe would be at the heart of the account of the rebellion that would be passed down through every generation of every tribe in Britannia. But after a moment she thrust thoughts of that prospect aside. There was much to be done before her

144

ambitions could be realised. First, she and the core of warriors that remained must survive long enough to raise and train the new army that was to prepare the ground for victory. If what she had learned was true, the Romans were preparing to turn their might against her. And Macro would be among those coming for her. The thought chilled her blood and filled her heart with fresh resolve. No matter who they sent, they were all Romans, and Rome was the enemy of the ages. None of them must be allowed to live. Not even one she had once called friend and lover.

CHAPTER THIRTEEN

At Combretovium

Macro was waiting on the wharf at Combretovium as the *Minerva* approached under oars. The lightness in Cato's heart as he saw his best friend turned to concern as he drew close enough to see the strained expression on Macro's face and the dressing tied about his sword arm.

The return voyage had been fraught. The good weather had given way to rain and squalls blowing in from the depths of the northern ocean and the ship had been tossed about on steely grey waves as the crew and passengers were doused with freezing spray and rain. Just when Cato had been hoping that he had finally triumphed over his seasickness, it returned with a vengeance as if driven on by all three of the Furies at once. Sickness, lack of sleep, the pain from his flesh wound and cold had reduced him to an exhausted wreck by the time the ship entered the calm waters of the estuary and worked its way upriver. He and the grey-faced auxiliaries had managed a few hours' sleep before being roused by Besodius as they rounded the final bend before the town.

The helmsman steered in towards the bank, and at the last moment the captain gave the order to ship the sweeps. The crew hurriedly fed the long oars in and made ready with the mooring ropes. With a soft thud against the beam, the ship was deftly brought alongside and made safe. Cato ordered one of his men to carry his kit back to the chief's compound before he clambered ashore, the firm ground feeling oddly unsteady beneath his feet.

Macro approached and saluted formally. 'Good to see you safely back, sir. Any trouble?'

'Some, but it seems I wasn't the only one.' Cato nodded at the dressing on his friend's arm. 'What happened?'

'Oh, that? Just a scratch.' Macro sniffed dismissively. 'Anyway, the good news is that the chief is still alive and he seems to be improving. Phrygenus has played a blinder there.'

'And the bad news?'

'The bad news is that is all the good news, I'm afraid,' Macro said sombrely. 'We lost fourteen men in an ambush, including Centurion Tubero.'

'Tubero? Dead?' Cato was shocked by the loss. He had come to know the man well during the campaign to take the Druid stronghold of Mona. 'How?'

Macro briefly explained the treachery of the Trinovantian farmer who had lured the auxiliaries into the trap. 'It was well worked. We had the place under observation for some hours before we went in. I have to hand it to the villagers. They played their part well, pretending to go about their business as if nothing was planned. Most of the rebel force must have moved into position the previous night to wait for us to make our move. And they delayed the arrival of the wagons long enough for any suspicions to fade. We were lucky that they made no effort to follow us back here. They're not confident or foolish enough to push their luck just yet. But very smart all round.'

'Except for our side,' Cato responded cuttingly, weariness getting the better of tact. Macro's pained expression told him how keenly he blamed himself for what had happened.

'There was something else, sir. I saw Boudica. She was there, leading the rebels.'

'She did survive the battle then. I'll have to let the governor

147

know when I make my report.' Cato paused and turned to dismiss the four auxiliaries who had come ashore. He did not want them to overhear the next part of the exchange. Once they had gone, he turned his attention back to Macro. 'I wish it had never come to this, but Boudica is the enemy and she has to be destroyed. It's her or us, my friend.'

'You don't have to tell me that. Whatever happened in the past carries no weight with me any more. I know what has to be done and you should have no worries on that score. When the time comes, she will die. The only concession I will make is to ensure that it is a quick death. I swear this by Jupiter, Best and Greatest.'

Cato could hear the remorse in Macro's words. How much of that was down to the loss of those close to him at the hands of Boudica's rebels and how much to the part he had played in letting her escape and enabling her to raise the rebellion, he could not tell. But the turmoil within his friend's heart was evident. It would be best not to let him dwell on that.

'What other bad news have you got for me?'

'Had a message from Camulodunum. The first batch of reinforcements from the Second Legion has pitched up. Only half a cohort. Three centuries of raw recruits fresh from the training depot at Isca and led by a centurion just promoted to the rank. No sign of the cavalry cohort we were promised either, and no word about any ships from the navy.'

'For fuck's sake,' Cato said furiously. 'How can Suetonius expect us to do anything if he fails to equip us with the tools for the job? We need more men. Good soldiers, mind. Not green recruits. The only way we're going to defeat the rebels is to contain them and then crush them when they have no means of escape. Nothing else will do it.'

'Unless something was to happen to Boudica,' Macro suggested. 'If she is removed, maybe the rebellion will crumble away. We

148

could put a price on her head. Generous enough to get one of her own lot to betray her.'

'I had thought of that,' Cato responded, thinking back to the exchange with Ganomenus a few days before. 'Not everyone supports her intention to keep the rebellion going. The problem is that we don't know where she is based. We don't know the terrain. You should have seen it, Macro. A veritable maze of narrow waterways and reed beds. Without a guide, you could lose an army in those marshes. We can also assume there is blind loyalty to their queen by many in the tribe. They'll fight for her and they won't give her up for any amount of Roman silver. And she is certain to take precautions against treachery. Most of her personal bodyguard survived the battle. She'll keep them close by to protect her from traitors. Our best hope is that she will lead her forces in person, as she did at the ambush you fell for. She does that often enough, and there's a good chance she'll be killed, severely wounded or captured. Maybe, just maybe, we'll find someone willing to betray her for the right price, but I doubt it, at least as things stand. That may change once we start putting the squeeze on the rebels. Every time we destroy one of her warbands or a village, her standing in the tribe will be undermined a little more.'

'I hope you're right,' Macro said. 'But from what I saw, she's already managed to drill a disciplined force, and she leads from the front. I got the feeling they'd follow her to the gates of Hades if she gave the order. They were on us so quickly we barely had time to react. It was only because her warriors were so set on being in on the kill of our lads they'd surrounded that we managed to cut our way through. I'm lucky to be here, Cato. Have to tell you, it put the shits up me.'

Cato paused to look up and down the wharf, scrutinising the locals. Most were not paying any attention to the two Roman officers. But some passers-by looked at them with surly resentment.

'Do the locals know what happened at the village?'

149

'We came back with half the number we set off with, and carrying a few wounds, so what do you think? I doubt there's a single person here who isn't aware that we had our arses handed to us by Boudica and her mob.'

'And how have they reacted?'

'Nothing out of the ordinary so far. We're still not the most welcome of people, despite what the surgeon has done for their chief. In fact, I'd say if it wasn't for that, we'd be forced to quit the place pretty quickly.'

'I need to have a word with the chief and Vellocatus, then, and persuade them to stay on side. But there's someone else I need to deal with first.'

Cato crossed the wharf towards the *Minerva*. Besodius and his crew had stowed the sweeps and neatly coiled the sheets, and were swabbing the decks and rails with fresh water. 'Many thanks to you, Captain.'

Besodius looked up. 'I'd like to say it was a pleasure, Prefect. I really would.'

Both men grinned before Cato continued. 'You said you own some other vessels.'

'That's right. Two more cargo ships like the *Minerva*, though bigger and slower and not so easy to sail. Which is why I have other captains to command them. There's also a couple of barges I managed to get out of Londinium before the rebels came. They're ashore at Durobrivae for the winter.'

'And the ships?'

'In Gesoriacum. I'll be heading back to Gaul to join them as soon as I have re-provisioned.'

'I see. Listen, Besodius. I've got a proposition for you when you return after winter is done. I'm going to need ships to land men on the coast, and smaller boats to get them up the rivers and narrower channels. I'll make sure the provincial treasury pays you the going rate and a bonus for any risk involved.'

150

The captain hesitated. 'I'm not sure I want to be part of that, sir. And I can't speak for the other captains. We're commercial sailors. Not your navy types. We don't know the first thing about fighting.'

'You won't have to fight. At least you shouldn't have to,' Cato corrected himself, thinking it best to be as honest as he could. 'You'll just be dealing with cargoes of soldiers, rather than wine, furs and so on.'

Besodius shook his head. 'I don't know . . .'

'Listen, any chance of restoring trade to the level you knew before the rebellion, and the profits that went with it, depends upon the success of my campaign. The sooner we win, the sooner you carry on making your fortune. Alternatively, you can stick to less lucrative trade for however many years you have left in the business. Wouldn't it be better to be paid well to do your duty by Rome? After all, in the end, what's good for Rome is certainly good for you. Like I said, I'll make it worth your while.'

The captain slowly rocked his head from side to side as he considered Cato's words. 'Listen, Prefect, I can't promise anything. I'll put it to the other captains when I get back to Gesoriacum and see what they think. If they agree, I'll send you a message as soon as I can.'

'Thank you,' Cato said with relief.

Besodius raised a warning finger. 'But we won't come cheap. And we'll want compensating for any losses.'

'Your sense of patriotism is truly humbling.'

'Patriotism doesn't pay crews' wages, Prefect. Nor does it put food on the table. But if we agree to do the job, you have my word we'll do it as best we can.'

'I'm glad to hear it.' Cato reached across to clasp hands. 'I hope you have a safe voyage back to Gaul. When are you leaving?'

'First thing in the morning.'

'Then there's time for us to write a few letters for you to take with you. My family and the centurion's wife were on one of the last ships to leave Londinium before the rebels arrived. They were making for Gesoriacum. I dare say they'll be anxious about us. Will you do it?'

'Of course. And when . . .' Besodius caught himself and chuckled. 'And *if* I come back in the spring, I'll be sure to bring you their replies.'

'Many thanks.'

Cato turned away and rejoined Macro. 'Did you catch that?'

'Yes. It'll be good to get a message to them. Petronella will be tearing her hair out. She acts tough—'

Cato's eyebrows rose. 'Acts tough?'

'All right, she *is* tough, but she worries about me all the time. Dare say the same can be said of Claudia and young Lucius. They'll be relieved to know we're safe.'

'It might be best not to mention any details about either of our recent excursions.'

Macro laughed. 'Fair enough. Less said the better.'

They made their way along the wharf to the gateway in the stockade surrounding the chief's compound and headed for the hall. As they entered, they saw Vellocatus and Phrygenus sitting on stools either side of Tasciovanus's bier. The old man was propped up, and made an effort to rise as Cato and Macro approached. At once Phrygenus eased him back with an impatient tutting.

'Vellocatus, tell him he still needs plenty of rest if he is going to make a steady recovery. If he keeps trying to jump up and down, I won't be held accountable for any relapse.'

Vellocatus grinned and translated, and the old man shot a dark look at the surgeon but lay back all the same.

'There's a good little chief,' said Phrygenus before hurriedly adding, 'Don't translate that.'

Cato was relieved to see that some colour had returned to the old man's face. He was alert, and his sharp grey eyes scrutinised the Romans before he spoke. 'You must be Prefect Cato.'

Cato and Macro pulled up more stools and sat opposite the chief's son, alongside the surgeon.

'Prefect Quintus Licinius Cato, commander of the Eighth Illyrian Auxiliary Cohort, since we're getting acquainted for the first time.' Cato offered a friendly smile. 'The last time I saw you, you were in no shape for introductions.'

'I thought I was bound for the Otherworld,' Tasciovanus replied. 'But your man brought me back. It pains me to say it, Prefect, but I am in your debt now.'

'We cannot let a valuable ally die if it can be avoided.'

'Ally?' The chief was silent for a moment, his breathing shallow, then he cleared his throat. 'Neither of us are fools, Prefect. You know how I came by my wound and I know that you know. So let's be straight with one another. Two months ago, you and I were enemies. The same goes for my son and some others in Combretovium. I imagine that your governor, Suetonius, had plans to make an example of us. So tell me, how does that make us allies? Am I to be saved by your healer only to be executed by your governor?'

'Not if I can persuade him to offer amnesty to those who swear an oath of loyalty to Rome.'

'Do you think you will be able to persuade him?'

'I would have a much better chance if you and the rest of the Trinovantian tribe agreed to fight alongside my troops when I move against Boudica.'

Tasciovanus shook his head. 'Some might agree to that, in exchange for mercy. But not all those who swear the oath will be prepared to take up arms against our former allies, the Icenians.'

'You were rivals and enemies before you were ever allies. It was a grave mistake for the Trinovantians to join the rebellion. It has been a disaster for all the tribes involved. You owe the Icenians

153

nothing. Look where their actions have left you.' Cato raised his hand so that his thumb and forefinger were almost touching. 'You are this close to feeling the full wrath of a vengeful Rome. I am trying to save the Trinovantes from sharing the fate of the Icenians. I believe the emperor and the governor will be content with making an example of Boudica and her tribe. I will not be able to prevent that. But I can try to limit the punishment to her tribe alone, if I can prove your loyalty to Rome through your deeds.'

'Prefect, do I need to remind you of all the injustices you Romans heaped on my people? The veterans of your colony at Camulodunum stole our lands, abused our people and imposed crushing taxes on us. We did not choose to join the rebellion on a whim.'

'I understand that. And we Romans contributed our own mistakes to the catastrophe that befell us all. The price paid by us has been equally severe. That is why I am determined to do what I can to ensure that such mistakes are not repeated. Whether you like it or not, Rome is here to stay, and we need to find a way to live in peace together. That will not be possible while the rebellion smoulders on.'

'I'd say it was doing a little more than smouldering, given the rough handling your boys got a few days back,' Tasciovanus observed archly. 'Vellocatus told me about it.'

'It was an ambush. We lost a handful of men. It is likely that as many of her warriors fell in the resulting skirmish. While it might put some heart into her followers, it was little more than a gesture. A pinprick that Rome will barely notice. It will change nothing. Her defeat is as inevitable as the setting of the sun.'

'A pinprick, you say. But an enemy may still be bled out by a thousand such pinpricks. Vellocatus tells me that news of her ambush has already inspired some of our people to quit Combretovium to join her cause.'

154

Cato looked at the chief's son. 'Is this true?'

Vellocatus nodded. 'Nothing I said could stop them.'

'Perhaps you should have tried to be more persuasive,' Macro suggested.

Vellocatus scowled as he shot back, 'Perhaps you shouldn't have walked into the trap and given them the excuse they needed to join Boudica.'

Macro's nostrils flared and his body tensed dangerously before Cato intervened. 'What's done is done. Our lads have learned a lesson. Yours obviously haven't. I hope they are wise enough to change their minds once they understand there is no future for them if they remain with the rebels.'

'We shall see.' Tasciovanus's brow creased, and he grimaced.

Phrygenus leaned forward. 'I think it would be best if you let him rest, sir. Our friend still has a long way to go before making a full recovery.'

Cato realised there was little to be gained from further discussion in any case. He had made his case. Now he must let Tasciovanus and his people consider which path to take. He was in no position to force the issue given the meagre resources available to him.

'Very well,' he replied. 'How soon will you be able to leave the chief to recover by himself?'

Phrygenus scratched his cheek as he reflected on his patient's condition. 'He has turned out to be rather more robust than I first thought, sir. I've done all I can. It's up to him now to regain his strength.'

'So you can quit Combretovium?'

The surgeon nodded.

'Good. Then there is no need for any of us to remain here.' Cato turned to Macro. 'We'll wait until Besodius sets off to make sure no one gives him any trouble, then we'll return to Camulodunum. Have the men and horses prepare to march.'

'Yes, sir.'

'There's one other thing. I need to replace Tubero. We'll have to make a promotion. For now, I want you to take command of the mounted contingent.'

He stood and exchanged a look with the weary chief. 'You have a few months' grace, Tasciovanus. I hope you choose wisely. The same goes for the rest of the Trinovantian people. I would like us to meet as allies when next we see you.'

The chief replied in a reedy voice. 'We will make our choice, and your governor will make his. Farewell for now, Prefect Cato.'

Cato took his leave of Vellocatus as the surgeon packed up his chest, then the three Romans made for the far end of the hall. Cato indicated a table close to the entrance.

'Phrygenus, have one of the men bring me my writing case, then get yourself ready for the ride back to Camulodunum.'

Once the surgeon had gone, he turned to Macro. 'We'd better write our messages for Claudia and Petronella. It'll be the last chance to get anything to them before winter sets in. And when spring comes, there won't be time for it.'

'Aye,' Macro responded with feeling. 'If it all goes to shit, we'll be dead, or else we'll be held responsible, and you can be sure the governor and those back in Rome won't be very forgiving. If we succeed, there'll be little chance of reward given the embarrassment the rebellion has caused the emperor and Rome.'

Cato smiled. 'You have put it as succinctly as I ever could. May the gods help us.'

CHAPTER FOURTEEN

Cato and Macro rose before dawn to hand over their messages to Besodius before the *Minerva* left for Gaul. The captain reassured Cato that he would put his proposal to his comrades, then gave the order to his crew to loose the mooring cables and shove off. As the ship glided out into the middle of the river, Macro spoke.

'Do you think he'll come back to help us next year?'

'I hope so. Otherwise we're going to have a hard time of it, unless I can get the governor to part with a squadron of warships.'

'I can't see that happening, given that he's not sent us anything else he promised us.'

'I know.' Cato nodded. 'That's why I'm going to have to return to Londinium to confront him. Just as soon as I've had a chance to look over the new men at Camulodunum. If they're as green as you say, we're going to have to work on them through the winter so that they're properly trained and ready to face the enemy. That'll be your job.'

'Can't wait.' Macro smiled.

'I thought you'd like that. Suetonius may actually have done us a favour by failing to give us what he said he would at the outset.'

'How's that?'

'If we'd had enough men to risk taking the fight to Boudica straight away, they'd have been worn out from the year's earlier campaigns. We'd have had no time to reconnoitre, plan and prepare. It would have been a piecemeal effort with little chance of success. The only thing in our favour would have been the demoralised state of whatever forces Boudica still has. But they'd have been fighting for their homeland, and that, as we know from past experience, tends to boost men's determination. I don't think things would have gone well for us even if we'd been given all the men we were hoping for. At least we have time now to prepare for what's to come.'

'That's as true for the rebels as for us,' Macro pointed out. 'You can be sure that Boudica won't be sitting on her hands over winter.'

'That can't be helped.'

They watched the ship fading into the milky dawn fog that lay across the river, and then it was gone.

'I hope our letters find them,' said Macro. 'Given all the rumours that will have followed them to Gaul, they'll be worried sick about us.'

'They'll have heard about the victory. That'll be some comfort at least.' Cato pulled his cloak more tightly about his shoulders to keep out the chill. The change in the season was making itself felt. Soon the last of the leaves would have fallen and the bitter winter weather would close in. Although Cato and Macro had first experienced the Britannia climate nearly twenty years earlier, neither had grown used to it, and they found the winter months a long and depressing struggle to stay dry and warm and to stave off the boredom of being stuck in winter quarters.

'Anyway,' he continued, 'they may already have sent messages to us. I'll ask about that while I am in Londinium. Some of the replacements coming in from Gesoriacum might have brought letters with them.'

It struck him that he had hardly spared Claudia and his son a thought for many days, given the demands placed on him. Now that he had time to reflect, he realised just how much he longed for their company.

He glanced sidelong and saw Macro staring downriver, as if he could still see the ship, while his imagination stretched far further to embrace the memory of his beloved Petronella.

'Come, this moping around isn't going to do us any good. Let's go.'

They returned to the compound, where Phrygenus and the survivors of the mounted contingent were making final preparations to depart. Vellocatus came out to meet them.

'I'll be sorry to see your surgeon go. I'll never forget what he did for my father. Please tell him.' He looked past Cato and gave Phrygenus a brief wave.

'I will.'

'I don't suppose I can persuade him to stay a bit longer? Until my father is back on his feet.'

Cato shook his head. 'There's no need. You heard what he said. All Tasciovanus needs now is rest. Besides, the surgeon is needed elsewhere. Some of our men were wounded the other day and will need looking after. And then there's the units in Camulodunum. They'll be training over winter, and that always produces a few casualties.'

Vellocatus looked downcast.

'Look here,' Cato continued. 'If your father takes a turn for the worse, send a message. It's only a day's ride.'

Vellocatus smiled with relief. Then he paused a moment as he struggled to come up with the words. 'Thank you, Prefect. I never thought I'd see the day when I'd express my gratitude to a Roman.'

Macro chuckled. 'I never expected to see the day when a Briton expressed that either. Funny how things change.'

Vellocatus clasped hands with each officer in turn before making his way over to address Phrygenus, who made a show

159

of understanding the other man's words. Then the Trinovantian reached up and removed the gold torc from around his neck, placing it on the neck of the startled surgeon before bending the arms back to hold it in place.

Macro clicked his tongue. 'Now there's something you don't see every day.'

'Indeed,' Cato replied thoughtfully. 'Let's hope it's a sign of things to come.'

They left just as the sun was coming up. It warmed their backs as the small column headed along the track leading to Camulodunum. Macro had posted scouts on either flank and well ahead of the rest of the men in case the rebels were confident enough to operate far beyond the Icenian frontier. Falling into the enemy's trap had been a salutary lesson he was determined not to repeat. Cato rode alone, his mind going over all that he had observed and learned in his voyage up the coast. In truth, the task set for him by Suetonius seemed more daunting than ever. The only positive aspect of the last ten days was that there was a chance many of the Trinovantians would be won over to the Roman side. If not brothers in arms, then at least they would not renew their brief alliance with Boudica.

They made good time and reached Camulodunum just before sunset. From the rise overlooking the ruins of the colony, Cato saw that the legionary reinforcements had set up their tent lines within the confines of the temple courtyard, with the result that there was very little space for much else. Macro reined in alongside him and noticed the unsatisfactory arrangement at once.

'What in Hades are they thinking? If some bastard was to lob a few incendiaries over the wall, we could lose the lot. Not to mention the obstacle they pose to moving men around the camp in an emergency. Whoever's responsible for that, I'll be having their balls for breakfast.'

160

Macro ordered the bucina man to give the signal to recall the scouts and alert the camp to their approach. As they made their way through the scorched ruins of the colony, Cato was pleased to see that there had been considerable progress made in clearing the debris away from the walls of the temple precinct. Work had also begun on excavating a defensive ditch around the site. It was good to see that the reinforcements had been immediately put to work improving the fortifications. That went some small way towards redeeming the layout of the tents within.

The rebuilt gateway to the precinct had also been improved during his absence. A tower rose on either side, connected by a walkway above the gates.

'Someone's been very busy,' Macro commented. 'I'm almost impressed.'

As they drew closer, the gates opened and a section of legionaries trotted out. Forming up four at each side, they stood to attention. A tribune standing at the entrance saluted before he greeted Cato.

'Welcome back, sir.'

Cato recognised the man and reined in before dismounting. His back was stiff after the day's ride, and he rubbed it as he returned the salute.

'Tribune Agricola. What are you doing here? Aren't you supposed to be on the governor's staff?'

Agricola smiled and removed his helmet, tucking it under his arm. He was one of the contingent of senior tribunes from aristocratic families sent from Rome to serve with the legions on the frontier in order to gain some military experience before they returned home to take up posts in the civil administration. Those who had a taste for army life, and a modicum of ability, were permitted to continue serving for longer. Agricola was one such, and while he had impressed Cato with his enthusiasm, he still had a lot to learn.

'I put in a request to be attached to your command, sir.

161

Suetonius gave his permission and here I am. Jolly keen to be in on the final defeat of Boudica and her rabble, I can tell you.' He grinned.

'Sweet Jupiter, save us,' Macro muttered. 'We needed more men and the governor sent us this kid instead.'

Agricola turned his attention to Macro. 'Good to see you too, Centurion.'

Macro gave a slight start at the sharpness of the tribune's hearing, and tapped the brim of his helmet in acknowledgement. 'Sir.'

The column dismounted, and Cato and Macro handed their reins over to one of the auxiliaries as Agricola pointed to the corner of the precinct wall. 'I've had the men put up some temporary stalls on the other side of the camp, given the lack of space within.'

'Have you now?' Cato arched an eyebrow. He was a little irked by the changes to the camp's arrangements, not all of which met his approval. However, the tribune had been trying to demonstrate initiative, and that needed to be recognised and commended. 'Very well. Centurion, see to the mounts and then join me in my quarters.'

Macro nodded and led the column away around the outside of the half-completed ditch. Cato made his way between the honour guard Agricola had arranged for him, noting with dismay the fresh, youthful faces beneath the helmets.

'A good turnout,' he concluded. 'Very neat. I'll look forward to seeing if they can fight as well as they can keep their kit clean.'

Agricola looked wounded. 'I'm sure they will prove themselves worthy of the Second Legion, sir. The Second won a fine reputation for itself when it landed in Britannia.'

'I know that, Tribune,' Cato replied drily. 'I was serving as an optio in the legion at the time.'

Agricola's jaw dropped momentarily. 'You were an optio? How on earth . . .' he began before he could manage to stop himself.

Cato cocked his head to one side. 'How on earth did a common optio get himself promoted to the rank of prefect? Is that what you were going to ask?'

The tribune made to reply, but was not quick-witted enough to summon up a diplomatic response and mumbled something like an apology instead. Cato regarded him with a degree of sympathy. The youngster had been born into an aristocratic family and no doubt assumed that all senior officers he encountered were from the same background. His surprise would have been compounded if he'd learned that Cato had not even emerged from the plebeian class but had been born a slave. Admittedly the circumstances of his upbringing had been far more privileged than those of most Roman citizens. As the son of a respected freedman serving in the imperial palace, he had been given a fine education and raised in the comfort of his father's quarters. When his father had died, Emperor Claudius had granted Cato his freedom and enabled his entry into the Roman legions. Whether out of gratitude for his father's long service, or as some kind of joke, Cato became a soldier. A rather fine one, as it turned out.

'I earned my promotions the hard way, Tribune, rather than from some accident of birth or familial connections like nearly all the other officers of my rank. Does that answer your question?'

'Yes, sir.'

'Good. I'm tired and I need something to eat. I will speak to you later. Come to my quarters when the first hour of the night has passed.'

'Yes, sir.'

Cato left the tribune to dismiss the honour guard and strode stiffly into the camp. The crowding of the tents was even more evident close at hand; there was little space between them to provide for the free passage of men. As the senior officer present in Cato's absence, that was a black mark against Agricola. Picking his way across the interior of the temple precinct, he climbed the steps of the pediment and entered the makeshift headquarters that had been built on the remains of what had once been the temple's inner sanctum.

His manservant, Trebonius, was resting on his sleeping mat by a small brazier. He jumped up and bowed his head.

'Good to see you, sir.'

'It's good to be back in one piece,' Cato replied. He put his helmet down and extended his arms for Trebonius to unfasten the buckles and ties and remove his cuirass and greaves. Relieved of the burden, he rolled his neck and stretched as he ordered some food.

While the manservant was out of the room, Cato lit some oil lamps and arranged his notebooks on the desk fashioned from some undamaged timbers from the ruins. He began to consider how best to tackle the governor in order to obtain all the forces he needed. It was clear now that the original plan to mount a swift punitive expedition to hunt down Boudica and her followers and burn a few villages would never have worked, even if Cato had been allocated all the forces that Suetonius had originally said he would provide. The hard truth was that far more men would be needed. Cavalry in particular, given the need to respond to threats quickly and strike the enemy fast. However, the governor's army was short of mounts, due to the losses incurred during the year's campaigns. Suetonius would be reluctant to redeploy the numbers Cato required.

He sat back and sighed with frustration. If he failed to extinguish the flames of rebellion in the east of Britannia, it would surely end his army career. It was of no comfort to know that whoever replaced him would be equally unlikely to achieve success. Eventually Suetonius would grasp that and deploy overwhelming force to crush Boudica. Too late to save Cato's reputation, naturally. Would it be so bad to put active service behind him? he wondered. He could return to Italia with Claudia and Lucius and live in peace on the modest estate he owned in the hills outside Rome. There would be plenty of room for Macro and Petronella to join them if they wished. No more danger, discomfort or the burdens of command. The only concern would be keeping Claudia out of sight of those who might recognise her as the former mistress of Nero who was assumed to have died while in exile in Sardinia. The thought drew a shadow over Cato's reverie, and he forced his thoughts back to the challenges of the present.

Trebonius returned with a small iron pot of stew. 'I thought you might be hungry, sir.'

Now that the manservant mentioned it, Cato realised he was ravenous. 'Any bread?'

'I'll see what's left from the day's baking, sir.'

'Good. And wine?'

'There are two jars of Falernian left in your personal stores. You've almost exhausted the supplies brought from Londinium. If I might be so bold as to ask you to advance me some coin, I can try to replenish stock from the local farmers.'

Cato considered the possible dangers of letting Trebonius venture out alone, and decided he could be safely attached to a patrol while purchasing supplies. Then there was the certainty that he would be sure to overstate the price he had paid while pocketing the difference. That was only to be expected. 'Very well. You may take fifty sestertii from my chest.'

'Yes, sir.' Trebonius turned to go.

'One more question.' Cato halted him. 'How are things in the camp?'

It was one of the manservant's functions to keep his eyes and ears open as he made his way through the Eighth Illyrian's camp each day and relay to Cato anything that might be of concern.

Trebonius took a moment to marshal his thoughts before he responded. There was a fine balance to be maintained between keeping his superior informed while respecting the confidences of the other ranks. He had to guard against being loose-lipped either way if he was to maintain the men's respect for their prefect while at the same time keeping Cato informed about the morale of the soldiers under his command.

'To be honest, sir, the lads haven't been too happy since the reinforcements arrived. You know how it is with legionaries, they tend to look down their noses at us auxiliaries. The fact that we're veterans and the cohort has decorations on the standard makes no difference. It's even more galling that not one of the legionaries has seen any action. When they were ordered to march on Londinium during the rebellion, they didn't make it more than halfway before turning back and sitting it out in Isca Dumnoniorum.'

'That's not their fault. They were under the orders of their camp prefect at the time.'

'That's true, sir. But their attitude's a bit rich given that they were sitting on their arses when we were facing the rebels in battle.'

'Well, yes, quite.'

'The tribune's not helped matters by ordering our lads to move their tents to the rear of the camp to make space for the legionaries.'

Now that did annoy Cato. The rear of the camp was the area furthest from the main gate and closest to the latrines. It was usually reserved for the most junior unit, or one that was being punished.

'That's just not on, sir.'

'No, it isn't,' Cato concurred. 'I will deal with it. There will need to be a few changes to arrangements within the camp.'

'Yes, sir. Thank you.'

He nodded. 'Bread and wine then.'

Just after the manservant left the room, Macro appeared, eyes lighting up as he saw the pot. 'Any spare?'

166

'Help yourself.'

Macro took off his helmet and cuirass before pulling up a stool to sit. He didn't bother with the bowl and picked up the spoon to eat directly out of the pot.

'Oh, that's good!' he sighed after the first mouthful.

Once Trebonius had brought them bread, beakers and the wine jug, Cato ordered him to close the door behind him so that he could speak to Macro in private.

'I'll be riding to Londinium in the morning. I'll be leaving you in command.'

Macro lowered his spoon. 'The tribune's not going to like that.'

'That's too bad. I can't leave the men in the hands of a staff officer. Particularly one who is a divisive influence with regard to those under his command. He's already enabling tensions between our lads and the legionaries.'

'So I gather. I've heard more than a few grumbles about the tent lines since we got back.'

'Indeed. I think that the men will be too tired to cause much trouble once you start the drilling of the legionaries. Start with building a camp outside the colony. That should keep them busy and toughen them up.'

Macro smiled. 'Sounds good. I might just throw in some route marches as well. Followed by kit inspections. That'll keep 'em on their toes.'

There was a knock on the door and Cato raised a warning finger. 'That'll be Agricola. I've asked him to join us so that everyone's clear about the arrangements. Come!'

He did not offer the tribune the opportunity to sit before addressing him in a formal tone.

'I will be leaving for Londinium tomorrow. Centurion Macro will be assuming command.'

Agricola did not hide his disappointment. 'May I ask why you

167

are ignoring the usual chain of command, sir? As the ranking officer in your absence, I should be in charge.'

'Since you ask, I will make it plain to you. Macro is a seasoned veteran. You are not. There is a danger that the enemy may attack the camp, and I will not leave it in the hands of an inexperienced tribune.'

Agricola stiffened. 'Inexperienced? Did I not serve in the same campaign as you when Suetonius took the army to Mona? Was I not at the same battle as you when we defeated Boudica's army?'

'I don't deny that. But you served as a staff officer, Tribune, not a field officer. How many times have you commanded a detached force?'

'This is my first opportunity for that, sir. That's why I requested permission to serve here.'

'Which is a commendable action. You will have the chance to learn some proper soldiering from one of the finest centurions around. That can only do you some good if you are keen to pursue a career in the army, rather than serve your time as a military tribune before returning to a civilian role. Tell me, Agricola, do you have ambitions to command an auxiliary cohort, or perhaps even a legion one day?'

'Yes, sir.'

'Then you need to earn the right to do so. And that involves proper training, which Macro can give you. Something you won't get swanning around on the governor's staff. If you are prepared to accept that, I will be pleased to permit you to serve with us when we march against Boudica in the spring. If not, there is no place for you here and you can return to Londinium with me.'

The tribune lifted his chin haughtily. 'Sir, I must protest—'

'Protest noted.' Cato cut him off. 'Now, do you accept my terms?'

There was a moment of inner struggle before Agricola steeled himself to reply. 'I accept.'

'Fine. Then you will place yourself under Centurion Macro's command in all respects. You will obey his every order as if it was my own. If he says jump, you say . . .?'

Agricola spoke through clenched teeth. 'How high?'

Cato arched an eyebrow, and the tribune swallowed his indignation before he tried again.

'How high, *sir!*'

'That's it. Now that we all understand and accept the situation, you are dismissed, Tribune.'

Agricola hesitated a beat before saluting and turning to march out of the room, closing the door a trifle too loudly behind him.

Macro chuckled. 'That put him in his place all right.'

'It's what he needs. He may have the makings of a commander. He's certainly ambitious enough. See what you can do with him. I have a feeling he may well go far if he is given the right start.'

'Oh, I'll give him that all right.' Macro rubbed his hands together. 'Him and those raw recruits from the Second. Our old legion's reputation has taken a bit of a battering. That changes from now, if I have anything to do with it!'

CHAPTER FIFTEEN

Londinium

Londinium had changed considerably from the devastated condition it had been in when Cato was last there, two months previously. The main thoroughfares and most of the side streets had been cleared of rubble, and those areas that had escaped the fires which had consumed large swathes of the town were inhabited once more. Elsewhere building work was under way, and a large number of makeshift dwellings and shops had been set up by those who had returned to their homes. For all that, over half of the area occupied by the original town was a wasteland of twisted charred timbers and scorched and shattered roof tiles. Down at the river, there was a fraction of the shipping there had been before the rebellion, and a handful of sails stretched over stockades to replace the line of warehouses that had stood along the wharf. Everywhere the acrid smell of burning lingered in the air.

Unsurprisingly, the most extensive effort in rebuilding the town was centred on the complex housing the administrative headquarters and personal accommodation of the governor. Making his way along Londinium's main avenue, Cato could see the scaffolding, and men at work replacing the roof of the main hall where ceremonies, audiences and the business of running the province took place. The high wall that surrounded the complex had been rebuilt, replastered and given a fresh coat of whitewash so that it looked stark and clean against the backdrop of the rest of the town. The gatehouse too had been reconstructed and was now flanked by formidable-looking towers manned by legionaries. The duty optio saluted as he saw Cato ride up and his men stood to attention. A quick glance confirmed to Cato what he had anticipated: more men drawn from the training formation that the once proud Second Legion had become.

'Prefect Quintus Licinius Cato,' he introduced himself as he returned the salute. He indicated the gatehouse towers and their surroundings. 'I see the governor is not letting the grass grow under his feet.'

The optio grinned. 'Not half, sir. He's made it known that he wants Londinium back in the shape it was before the next year is out. At the rate things are going, I think we'll be there long before then. That'll show those rebel bastards.'

His haughty attitude irked Cato. 'Show them what? You weren't there for the battle. I suspect Londinium will be rebuilt long before the Second Legion's reputation is.'

The optio flushed but dared not respond to the superior officer's comment as Cato rode by.

The interior of the compound was like a disturbed ants' nest. Engineers, builders, gangs of slaves and soldiers were bustling about their business on all sides. Nearly all the smaller buildings – stores, stables, workshops and barracks – had been repaired or replaced and the main structure was nearly complete. Piles of rocks and stacks of wooden beams and tiles were arranged in the middle of the compound together with some temporary shelters for the slaves, mostly prisoners taken after the battle. It seemed to Cato to be pleasing rough justice that these latter were now forced to repair the damage they had caused to Londinium. It was almost certain that none of them would ever see their homes and families again. That was the price of choosing to defy Rome. The novelty of owning slaves from Britannia had not yet exhausted itself among the more fashion-conscious of the Empire's wealthiest families and there would be a ready market for the tattooed warriors. At the same time, the lanistas would be keen to add such men to their stock in the gladiator schools.

Cato made his way over to the stables, dismounted and handed the reins to one of the orderlies with instructions to feed, water and groom his horse and clean his saddle and tack. Then he heaved his saddlebags across his shoulder and made for the main building. Inside, the activity continued, with carpenters hard at work creating door frames, shelving and furnishings while other men plastered and painted the walls. Among them, struggling to concentrate amid the din, shavings and splatters of paint, clerks bent over crudely constructed tables and benches as they dealt with the administration needed to restore the authority of Rome and ensure that things returned to running smoothly as soon as possible.

Stopping a passing optio, Cato asked him where he could find the governor's chief of staff.

'Tribune Helvius? Down that corridor, up the stairs, turn right and he'll be in one of the offices on the left, sir.' He scurried off before Cato could thank him, weaving his way through the workers.

Cato followed the optio's directions and found himself on a narrow corridor with rooms ranging along each side. None of the door frames had been fitted with doors yet and neither had the windows been given shutters, which made for cold working conditions for the governor's staff. They went about their work wrapped in cloaks, while many wore fingerless mittens in an effort to prevent their hands becoming numb. After a few enquiries, Cato found the man he sought.

Helvius had managed to have his door and shutters fitted. Moreover, his room was heated to a comfortable temperature by a large iron brazier. He looked up from a desk piled with waxed slates and scrolls as Cato entered.

'Yes?' he said tersely. Then, recognising Cato, he hurriedly set down the slate he was reading and stood. 'Prefect Cato? Greetings to you, sir.'

Cato motioned to him to resume his seat before he crossed over to the brazier, set down his saddlebags and turned to warm his back as he addressed the tribune.

'I've come to see Suetonius. I need you to arrange that as soon as possible so that I can get back to Camulodunum at the earliest opportunity.'

'Camulodunum? Have you put an end to Boudica and the other fugitives already, sir?'

'No chance. We've barely started preparing for the campaign.'

'Ah.'

'Ah?' Cato prompted him.

'Well, sir, I believe the governor was anticipating that the matter would be resolved before winter set in.'

'Really? On what basis, I wonder? Given that until a few days ago I had barely two hundred and fifty men to carry out the task. I've only just received the first of the reinforcements I was assured would be with me over a month back. Even then, the men sent to me turn out to be green recruits from the Second Legion with no combat experience. I need more men, and ships. That's why I need to see Suetonius. The sooner the better.'

'I'm afraid the governor isn't here at the moment, sir. He's in Verulamium supervising the restoration of the town's civic buildings.'

'When is he expected to return?'

'Not for another two days.'

'Two days?' Cato frowned.

'You could always make your way to Verulamium to seen him, if it's an urgent matter,' the tribune suggested hopefully.

173

Cato considered this briefly before dismissing the notion. He did not want to encounter Suetonius on the road. The nature of the meeting he was intending to have with the governor called for privacy, not an audience of subordinates.

'I'll wait for him to return.'

'As you wish, sir.'

'I'll need accommodation for a few nights, of course.'

'Ah, well, that presents something of a difficulty, sir.'

'Difficulty?'

'As I am sure you can appreciate, sir, accommodation is at a bit of a premium in Londinium at the moment. Rather more people than places to stay, as it happens. Under normal circumstances I'd be happy to arrange for you to stay in the mess, but that's overcrowded as it is. Tribunes are having to sleep two to a room.'

'Then for the next few nights some of them will just have to sleep four to a room.'

The tribune looked confused, or perhaps he was so tired that his mind was working more slowly than usual. Cato sighed.

'For Jupiter's sake, man. Move two of them out and clear their room for me. I need somewhere to sleep and work until the governor returns.'

The tribune hesitated a moment before the sestertius dropped. 'Yes, sir. But they won't like it.'

Cato glared at him. 'Do I have the appearance of someone who gives a damn? Just get on and make the arrangement. Have my saddlebags taken to the room after the present incumbents have been moved on. I'm going for a walk. I expect the matter to be resolved by the time I come back. And I'll want a meal and for someone to be detailed to clean my uniform and kit before the governor returns. Clear?'

'Yes, sir.'

'Good. Get on with it.'

He left the office in a foul mood and made his way out of the building site as swiftly as possible. He had been a little sharp with the man, but the tribune's reluctance to put out his companions for Cato's sake spoke of the same inbred self-indulgence evident in Agricola. He walked along the cleared road that led down to the river. On either side, amid the ruins, he caught sight of children playing and women cooking outside crudely constructed lean-tos. Here and there were structures that more resembled the houses that had stood there before. Only a handful, of the kind owned by the better-off survivors of the disaster, had been fully repaired or rebuilt, and those were guarded at their entrances by hired heavies.

When he reached the riverbank, he turned upstream, hands clasped behind his back as he went over his assessment of the campaign's needs he intended to put before the governor. As he strolled and reflected, he was nonetheless aware of his surroundings and took in the repairs that had been effected to the bridge that crossed the Tamesis. The middle of it had been destroyed as the rebels arrived. The buildings on the far bank had been spared as a consequence and the settlement there stood in stark contrast to the shattered remains on Cato's side of the river. Rising above the flow were a handful of masts and the scorched hulls of vessels that had been abandoned or failed to escape the wrath of the rebels. To his right stood the barely recognisable remains of the warehouses that had lined the wharf, the blackened posts and beams looking like the beginnings of charcoal sketches against the distant sky. Further along, a number of cargo ships were moored, and opposite them stood the temporary replacements for the ruined warehouses. The cargo being unloaded seemed to consist mostly of building materials, and Cato could not help wondering how those returning to Londinium were managing to feed themselves. Hunger had haunted the poorer regions of the town before the rebellion, but it would be a problem for the majority of the inhabitants for many months to come.

He stopped as he came to a road that led gently up from the river towards the heart of the town and realised that this was the thoroughfare on which the Dog and Deer had once stood, the inn run and co-owned by Macro's mother, Portia. The old lady had been too frail to leave and had insisted on remaining behind to die on the premises. It was a sobering reminder of the personal losses Macro and Cato had endured. He felt drawn to the place and turned to walk up the road, slowing as he approached the remains of the inn. The sign that Macro had propped up outside the burned shell after they had returned to Londinium after the battle had gone, as had most of the serviceable timbers and furniture. Only the crumbling wattle-and-daub walls indicated the layout of the main building. Beyond these he could see that some of the storerooms in the courtyard at the rear were still intact.

A flash of movement drew his eye, and he caught sight of the back of a child disappearing into the alley that ran past the yard. He was reminded of Lucius and felt a pang for his absent son. The feeling was swiftly followed by a sense of guilt that the army had been unable to prevent the rebels destroying the home of this boy and his family. Retracing his steps, Cato turned into the alley and approached the gate that opened onto the small yard, fishing in his purse to find a coin for the boy and his family to help them buy whatever they needed to eke out a living amid the ruins. The original gates had been taken off their hinges, and now a few charred planks had been nailed across most of the gap, with a small opening covered by what looked like a strip of tent leather. He could hear voices from within, women talking in low tones. He eased the flap aside and stepped into the yard. One of the store sheds had been occupied. A short distance away, a woman was feeding firewood into the flames beneath an iron grille while another stirred the pot on top. Their backs were turned to him. On the far side sat the child, a boy, hunched over a crude fort he had built from scraps of wood.

Cato cleared his throat and held out the coin. 'Excuse me. I wonder if . . .'

The words dried in his throat and his heart missed a beat as the three faces turned towards him, their wary expressions turning to confusion and then unalloyed joy.

'Claudia?' he mumbled. 'How in Hades . . .'

The younger of the two women rose quickly. 'Cato!' Then she was in his arms, her own wrapped around his back and drawing him close. She pressed her face into the folds of his tunic for a moment before looking up and beaming. 'Oh, Cato.'

'Father!' Lucius shouted with glee and scrambled up to come tearing around the fire to join them. Cato saw that he was barefoot and grimy from playing amid the ashes and charred timbers. He eased himself away from Claudia and squatted down to scoop his son up, gazing at him with delight.

'Why, Lucius, I'd swear you have grown at least another two inches since I last saw you. You're heavier too!'

'Of course I am!' Lucius replied indignantly. 'I am eleven years old.'

'By the gods, you'll be fully grown before I know it.'

'That's because of Petronella.' Lucius rolled his eyes. 'She makes me eat everything she puts in my bowl, and she always puts in too much!'

Cato lowered him to the ground and ruffled his hair before turning back to Claudia with a more serious expression. 'I wasn't sure I'd ever see you again. Anyway, what are you doing here?'

'Ah, come on!' Petronella intervened as she bustled over and gave Cato a quick hug. 'We're not the type to give in that easily. We get that from our menfolk. Speaking of which . . .?'

'Macro's fine.' Cato thought it better not to mention the fresh scar he had added to his collection, nor how he had come by it. 'Missing you, though.' He shook his head and grinned. 'By the gods, how we've missed you! But what are you doing here? How in Hades did you come to be back in Londinium?'

Claudia embraced him again and kissed him for good measure before she stepped back and drew him in the direction of the store shed. Two charred benches had survived the fire that destroyed the inn, and these were arranged against the wall. Petronella hurried to the pot and used a rag to move it to the side so that the meal would not burn while they continued to talk.

Cato felt overwhelmed by the encounter. 'So tell me. Tell me all.'

The women exchanged a brief look before Petronella gave a slight nod and turned away to distract Lucius.

Cato felt his guts knot in foreboding. 'What happened?'

'The ship Macro put us aboard was one of the last to leave before Londinium fell. So it was crowded. We picked up more passengers the next morning from a ship that was overloaded and in danger of foundering. And then we came to the open sea. The weather was as good as could be expected for the season, and in normal circumstances we'd have been fine, I'm sure. But there were too many people aboard, and when the waves increased in size, the ship rolled from one side to another, so much that I feared we might turn over. Progress was slow, and it was dark long before we could reach the coast of Gaul.'

She paused and clenched her eyes shut for a moment as the memories flowed back. 'It was terrible that night. The ship rolled and pitched and people were crying and screaming in fright as they fought for a place as close to the mast as possible. We did our best to protect Lucius, sitting with him between us and trying to keep him warm and dry, but he still trembled all night. When morning came, I saw that some people had gone. I had not heard anyone fall in or cry for help. At the time I supposed they must have died and been put over the side. Maybe that is what happened. But I doubt it, given what came next. The ship had

178

taken on a lot of water and the captain told us we were in danger of sinking if we could not lighten the load. So he made us bid for our places. Those who had nothing were thrown overboard first. Some begged the rest of us to take their infants, but the captain threatened that anyone who did would go into the water too. So we watched as they drowned. I can still hear their screams, Cato. They fill my dreams and I wake with the sound in my ears . . .'

She steadied herself before continuing. 'Petronella used the coin from Macro's chest to pay the captain and we were allowed to stay on the deck. Less than a third of us were left by the time he decided enough had been sacrificed to make the vessel seaworthy. We continued to Gaul and reached Gesoriacum on the third day, soaked, scared and starving. We had enough money left to rent a room behind a butcher's shop, and we stayed there as we recovered our strength and waited for news of the rebellion. Each day more anxious than the previous one. Then word came of a great victory, and that Boudica's army had been annihilated. By that time, we were nearly mad with fear for you and Macro and we decided to return to Londinium and try to get word to you. But it was easier to say than do. Few captains were willing to make the journey, and those who did were laden with military supplies. It took us a month, and most of the money that was left, to get a place on a ship. When we reached Londinium and saw the scale of the destruction, it was hard to believe what lay before us. That was ten days ago. We made our way here, moved into the store shed and salvaged what we could from what was left of the inn.'

Cato looked round the yard. Despite attempts to restore order amid the devastation, it was little better than the meanest hovel. 'You can't stay here.'

'Believe me, we know that. But there's nowhere else to shelter, given the shortage of intact buildings in Londinium.'

'You should have gone to the governor's headquarters and

asked for help. You could have used my name to give some weight to your request.'

'How could I? What if someone recognised me? I'd be arrested and sent back to Rome for Nero to decide my fate. Besides, we're not married, so what status would I have even if I had tried to ask for help? I begged Petronella to take Lucius and seek assistance for the two of them as the wife of Centurion Macro, but she refused to leave me alone here.'

'And a good thing too,' Petronella added from where she had been half listening to the conversation as she played with Lucius. 'What with the gangs roaming the ruins. You can imagine what they might have done to a woman on her own. Even the two of us together are vulnerable enough. Or so they might think. But we're ready for them.' She indicated a cleaver beside the fireplace and staves with nails driven through one end propped up against the wall of the shed.

Cato felt sick with concern. 'I have to find you something better. Something safer.'

'It will not be adequate when winter sets in,' Claudia agreed. 'That's when people will start to starve. Most of the food we have managed to get hold of has come in by ship. There's never enough and the merchants have been charging crazy prices for what little there is. Winter will mean fewer ships from Gaul. People are going to die, and most of those who are left will be fighting for scraps to stay alive.' She put her arm around his waist and drew him closer. 'You are here now. That's something. You can take us back to Camulodunum with you.'

Cato shook his head. 'There's nothing left there either. The rebels destroyed the colony even more thoroughly than they did Londinium. That's where my cohort is now. We've been ordered to hunt down Boudica and her followers.'

'But then you will have a camp. And your soldiers,' Claudia responded, a trace of desperation in her tone. 'We'll be safer there.'

'You won't,' Cato responded. 'I don't have enough men there to guarantee even our own safety. That's why I have come back to Londinium, to ask the governor for more men. Our camp is close enough to Icenian territory to make it a target and we don't know if the Trinovantians will remain loyal to Boudica or not. It's too dangerous for you to be there. Macro would agree with me.'

'I'm sure he would,' said Petronella. 'We can't go there, love. Cato's right. It would be dangerous, and it would give him and Macro more to worry about when they need to concentrate on defeating the enemy.'

Claudia released Cato and stretched her arms. 'Well, we can't stay here much longer! We'll either starve or be murdered in our sleep.'

Lucius looked up, and Cato saw the heartbreaking fear in his son's eyes. That decided him. 'I will not let you stay here. You must come with me to headquarters and I'll make arrangements for you to be sheltered and looked after there. I know there's a risk that you will be recognised, so we'll have to do what we can to change your appearance and identity. Few people give slaves a second glance. We'll say that you belong to Petronella. There will be somewhere safe for you to stay until Macro and I have completed our work and can come back for you.'

'What then?' asked Petronella. 'You said there's nothing left of the colony. Everything Macro and I owned has been lost. What will become of us?'

'I don't know,' Cato admitted. 'But we'll think of something when the time comes. What matters now is making sure the three of you are safe. Pack whatever you can carry.'

He glanced round at the ruins of the inn and the ramshackle shelter that they had been using. 'Let's get out of this place.'

CHAPTER SIXTEEN

Governor Suetonius returned to his headquarters four days later. He had been delayed by having to deal with a band of brigands that had been using a nearby forest as a base from which to launch night raids on Verulamium, now vulnerable thanks to the destruction of the town's defences. Cato was sitting with Lucius and the others under the covered porch of the barracks block that had been set aside to accommodate the families of soldiers and officials who had lost their homes during the rebellion. He had found time for the boy's education while waiting for the governor's return. The reading matter chosen from the limited selection in the officers' mess was Herodotus, the kind of narrative that inspired boys and young men to read, he calculated.

It was mid afternoon when the governor rode into the compound with his staff and escort. Cato set the scroll down and stood up. Lucius's eyes gleamed with excitement at the sight of Suetonius and his retinue in their crested helmets and gleaming cuirasses. Petronella was indifferent and barely looked up from her sewing. Beside her, Claudia reached up to pull her woollen skullcap down to her eyebrows. Her blonde hair had been cut short and was tucked under the fringe of the cap. Her face was deliberately smudged with traces of soot to give her the appearance of a characterless drudge who would be easily overlooked. Cato had drilled it into his son that he must say nothing about her true identity, nor her relationship with Cato, and he had solemnly sworn an oath on his honour that he would do as instructed.

'Stay here,' said Cato as he emerged from the porch and approached the governor as the latter halted in front of the headquarters entrance and dismounted. The other riders followed suit, and the officers handed their reins to their orderlies and stretched their limbs, stiff from the day's ride. Suetonius did not hide his surprise as he caught sight of Cato.

'Prefect! What brings you to Londinium? It's too soon to have achieved a victory. How goes the hunt for our enemy?'

'That's what I need to talk to you about, sir.'

'It can wait until after I've had a rest and a meal. Better still, join me and my officers for dinner and we can talk then.'

'I'd rather we spoke now, sir. In private.'

The governor looked none too pleased at the request. 'How urgent can it be, Prefect? You have me worried now.'

'Sir, I have already been away from my command for six days. The sooner I can return to continue my preparations for the campaign, the better.'

'Preparations?' Suetonius frowned and then breathed deeply. 'All right. I will see you in my office shortly.'

He turned and made his way to the entrance of the main building, followed by his officers, some of whom cast curious glances at Cato as they passed by.

Cato hurried back to the barrack block, where Lucius regarded him eagerly.

'What did the governor say to you?'

'Nothing of importance yet. We're going to talk more in a moment.'

'Can I come and listen?'

'I don't think so. Besides, it would be very boring. Now, I need to fetch some things.'

He entered the small suite of rooms that made up the centurions'

183

quarters and fetched the saddlebags containing the plans he had made for the campaign. On his way out, he paused to speak to Claudia. 'I'll be a while. Save me something to eat. I dare say I won't be invited to dine with Suetonius.'

She made to reach for his hand to give it an encouraging squeeze, but he shook his head.

'Be careful,' she whispered.

The door to Suetonius's office opened and one of the junior tribunes stepped out to address Cato. He had been kept waiting longer than anticipated and the light was already failing outside. Further down the corridor, orderlies were already using tapers to light the lamps hanging from brackets on each side.

'The governor will see you now, sir.' He stepped to one side and ushered Cato through the doorway.

Like the rest of the headquarters, the room had recently been replastered and painted, but the faint tang of burning still lingered. Suetonius was sitting on a cushioned chair beside a brazier. A small table next to him held a silver platter of meat and some bread along with a small silver jug and goblet. Still chewing, he pointed a chicken leg to indicate a spot opposite his chair, and Cato followed his direction and set his saddlebags down beside his feet. He had memorised all that he needed to say, along with counter-arguments to oppose the responses he anticipated from his superior. He stiffened his spine and returned Suetonius's gaze.

The governor reached for his goblet to wash down the last fragments of food, then regarded Cato coolly.

'You were ordered to hunt down Queen Boudica, destroy what is left of her rabble and capture her or produce her body. What efforts have you made to effect this?'

Cato outlined his reconnaissance trip to Combretovium and the observations he had made during the voyage up the coast, together with his misgivings about the nature of the terrain.

'She could go to ground there, sir, and it would take an army to track her down.'

'An army is precisely what I cannot give you, Prefect Cato. I fear you are exaggerating the difficulties that present themselves to you.'

Cato felt a surge of anger and forced himself not to react. He took a moment before he replied in an even tone.

'I am not asking for an army, sir. I am asking for the forces you said you would give me to achieve the task you set. I was promised the pick of the army and a squadron of warships. You said that to me in this very building just over two months ago. Instead, I have had to make do with what is left of my auxiliary cohort and three centuries of men fresh from basic training who only turned up at Camulodunum less than ten days ago. There has been no sign of any warships, let alone a squadron. I have no cavalry, apart from the survivors of my cohort's mounted contingent. Five hundred men in all. Five hundred men to subdue two of the most powerful tribes in Britannia spread across the entire east of the province. How can you expect anyone to deliver the result you demand if you refuse to give them the tools to do the job?'

Suetonius slammed his palm down on the table at his side, making the platter, jug and goblet rattle. 'You forget yourself, Prefect Cato! How dare you presume to address me in such a manner? I am well aware that you have a clutch of admirers in high places back in Rome, but you have nothing like the political influence that I wield, so I would strongly advise you not to behave like some jumped-up son of a senator. You are a subordinate officer and you will respect my rank, if not my person. Do you understand me?'

'Yes, sir.'

There was a tense silence as the governor continued to glare at Cato, and then his expression softened a little. 'I well recall what

I said to you that day. We had only crushed Boudica a few days before and there was every reason to believe that it would be a simple mopping-up exercise. I had assumed that the scale of our victory would have a salutary effect on all those who sympathised with her cause, or at least saw the rebellion as an opportunity to exploit the disruption in the province. I had hopes that the tribes would fall back into line after they received the news. I did not anticipate that I would be firefighting across the province in an effort to restore order. The garrison of Britannia has been at full stretch. I simply have not had the time, nor the men, to provide you with the forces I had hoped to.

'That said, I am pleased to say that we are finally reimposing the authority of Rome, and we will soon have the peace and security we enjoyed before this bloody business began. I still intend for the Icenians to receive the harshest of treatment in order to send a message to every barbarian on this wretched island who might be foolish enough to ever consider raising a hand against us in future. Accordingly, you will get the men I promised you as soon as they become available. The same goes for the squadron of warships, should you need them.'

Suetonius sat back in his chair and smiled benignly. 'Come now, Prefect. There's no need for us to be at odds over this. You can return to Camulodunum confident that you will have what you need to carry out your orders.'

Cato sensed that he was expected to make some conciliatory response, as if he should be grateful to his superior. He steeled himself to move to the next step he had planned for this encounter.

'That is a most welcome prospect, sir. However . . .'

'What else?' Suetonius sighed impatiently. 'Go on, man! Out with it.'

Cato saw the chance to use the governor's own argument to strengthen his case. 'As you said, sir, at the time, we were certain that the morale of the enemy had been shattered. If I had been able to move swiftly, we could have caught up with Boudica and stamped out the last flicker of rebellion. However,' he continued with emphasis, 'since I have been delayed waiting for reinforcements, the initiative has passed to the enemy. Boudica has used the time to rally her followers. She intends to rebuild the rebel army, recruiting from outside of her tribe, and continue to wage war against Rome. She is using the eagle captured from the Ninth Legion to persuade potential allies that our legions can be defeated. That's powerful propaganda, sir.'

'How do you know this?' Suetonius demanded.

'I heard it from the son of a chief of the Trinovantes, as well as one of Boudica's own chiefs.' Cato related the intelligence he had gained at Combretovium and Branodunum.

Suetonius listened attentively, and reflected a moment before he spoke. 'So we have a chance to win the Trinovantes over, or at least some of them, while the others remain neutral?'

'Yes, sir.'

'I had settled on the fate of the Icenians as soon as I heard about the razing of Camulodunum and the massacre of the Ninth Legion. But I have not yet decided if the Trinovantes should share the same punishment. If what you say is accurate, it would be more profitable to win them over than grind them under my heel along with Boudica and her dogs.'

'Precisely, sir. Carrot and stick. The destruction of the Icenians and leniency towards those who choose to be our allies will be effective examples to set before the other tribes of Britannia.'

'Yes, indeed.' Suetonius nodded.

Cato felt a surge of satisfaction that he had won that round for Tasciovanus and his people. Now came the trickier part.

'There's something else I learned that will be of use to us, sir. When I spoke to the chief of the settlement at Branodunum, it was clear that he had grave reservations about Boudica continuing the struggle.'

'So?'

'If there are others like him, we can find ways to drive a wedge between Boudica and elements within her tribe. That will weaken her position. It might even bring her down and lead to her being ousted in favour of a leader who is keen to make peace with Rome.'

'I see. I'm not sure I like the sound of that.'

'Sir?'

'Think about it. If we were to make peace with a new Icenian leader, where's the stick? If Rome is to be feared enough to ensure that she is not challenged, we can't be seen to be handing out carrots to all and sundry. Someone has to be beaten severely enough to terrify others to stay in line. That someone has to be the Icenian people. All of them. I will certainly not be offering leniency to anyone who replaces Boudica. As far as I am concerned, the Icenians are vermin, right down to the last woman and child. If it serves our purpose to sow dissent in their ranks, then by all means do so. Strike whatever deals you like with Boudica's rivals. If they think that will save them, they are sadly mistaken.'

Cato was not altogether surprised by the double-dealing proposed by his superior, though the vehemence of his desire to utterly destroy the Icenian tribe was disturbing. But at least he had planted in the governor's mind the notion that not everyone in the tribe supported the rebellion. With luck and diligence he could cultivate that understanding and ease Suetonius into a more merciful mood. He needed to persuade his superior that too much stick was every bit as dangerous as too much carrot, if not more so. After all, that was what had caused the rebellion in the first place.

Cato nodded, then indicated his saddlebags. 'Speaking of defeating the enemy, I wonder if I might seek your advice on the plans for the campaign.'

188

'By all means.'

He moved the bags over to the desk and took out a map of the east of the province that he had borrowed from the headquarters staff to help him refine his thoughts while awaiting Suetonius's return. The governor rose from his chair and joined Cato as the latter opened out the map and positioned two oil lamps to illuminate it. The geographical details of Icenian territory had been sparse when Cato had first looked at the map, but he had carefully added new information and corrected some of the errors. Now it provided a reasonably accurate representation of the region, although much of the interior of Boudica's domain, especially the wide swathe within the northern coastline, was blank.

Leaning over the map, he traced a line with his finger. 'This is roughly the border between Icenian and Trinovantian territory, sir. You can see that Camulodunum and Combretovium are well within the latter. Too far back. I'll need to shift my base of operations across the frontier, I think.'

Suetonius inspected the map and nodded. 'That would be best. Where did you have in mind?'

'Here, sir. Venta Icenorum.' Cato tapped the map.

'The Icenian capital?' Suetonius smiled. 'You don't believe in doing things by half. Why there?'

'I know the area, and so does Centurion Macro. The Iceni town is in a shallow vale with a river that is navigable all the way to the coast. There's an open stretch of sloping land not far upriver that would be ideal ground to construct a fort. It can be supplied by road or river. It's my intention to burn the town and drive its people away to the north. They'll be extra mouths to feed for the settlements still loyal to Boudica, besides being a means of spreading the word that we have staked our claim in the heart of her realm. That won't do much for their morale.'

'Indeed. What then?'

Cato indicated other positions to the west. 'I'll establish a line of forts here, within half a day's march of each other, with signal stations set up every mile. With the line being patrolled regularly, it will seal off the tribe and prevent any significant reinforcement of Boudica's force from outside. For the same reason, it will be necessary to build forts to cover access to rivers from the sea.' Cato pointed out the sites he had observed from Besodius's ship. 'Once Boudica and her followers are cut off from the rest of Britannia and we start destroying their food supplies, the rebellion will wither away. I believe that is likely to force her hand and she will come out fighting rather than be starved into submission. When that happens, she and her followers will be defeated and she will be captured or killed.'

'And how long do you think this will take?'

'If the forts are in place by spring, our patrols can make sure that no crops are planted and any livestock is either carried off or killed. They'll start to starve long before this time next year, sir.'

'A year is a rather longer time than I'd anticipated the job to take, Prefect.'

Cato was reluctant to remind his superior of his failure to act when there was a chance to finish Boudica off. Any satisfaction that might be gained from making the point was vastly outweighed by the outrage he might provoke from Suetonius. Instead, he decided to play on the man's vanity.

'I appreciate that, sir, which is why I am submitting the plan to you for refinement. I've gone as far as I can. I can see that it needs improvement.'

Suetonius stroked his top lip for a moment as he pondered. Cato watched him closely for any indication that his scheme was about to be shot down, or that the governor was wise to his deeper game.

The governor sighed. 'Your plan, while being somewhat crudely conceived, is certainly robust, like taking a hammer to

190

crack a nut. What you have failed to account for is the number of men necessary to put it into effect. All these forts, for example, will have to be garrisoned, and men will be needed for patrolling the line, as well as striking into enemy territory. If you think you can achieve all that even with the men I promised you at the outset, then you are mistaken, Prefect Cato.'

When Cato offered no response, Suetonius counted off the number of forts that would be required. 'I make it at least twenty forts. Assuming a minimum of a century stationed in each, plus the men in the signal posts, we're talking about . . . three thousand men. Then there's patrols and strike columns. They'll have to be mounted so they can react quickly. Boats will be needed to control the waterways and warships to block access from and to the sea.'

'Yes, sir. I can see that now.' Cato did his best to look contrite and grateful in response to his superior's comments. 'How do you think I should proceed?'

Suetonius returned to the table to pour himself more wine, then bent over the map again. 'You've done the groundwork, Prefect. You've made a good job of it as far as it goes. But your assessment of the number of men needed is woefully out. Leave this with me for now and I'll consult with my staff officers in the morning regarding the forces that will be required.'

Cato felt his spirits soar but kept his expression subdued and thoughtful.

'Yes . . .' Suetonius muttered to himself as he examined the map and then took a sip of his wine, 'I am confident that I can make this work.' He looked up at Cato. 'I'll send for you once I've refined the details. Dismissed.'

'Yes, sir.' Cato saluted, closed the flap over his saddlebags and turned away from the governor to stride towards the door.

Outside in the corridor, he let out a deep sigh and smiled broadly as he whispered, 'Hook, line and sinker.'

CHAPTER SEVENTEEN

Lyngomara

It was a fine autumn morning with clear skies, the lightest of breezes rustling the last of the leaves in the trees that surrounded the sacred grove. Overhead, crows swirled like scraps of dark cloth around the high boughs where they had built their nests, giving vent to their raucous cries. The air was cold and those in the funeral procession exhaled thin grey wisps as they trod slowly towards the burial mounds of the Icenian rulers. The Druid, Bladocus, led the way, muttering invocations to the tribe's gods to accept the dead girl into the Otherworld. She lay on a wicker bier, carried by six of Boudica's bodyguards. The bier was garlanded with mistletoe and holly, whose bright red berries contrasted with the black shroud that covered her body. The red tresses of her hair had been combed out, braided and arranged around the chalk-white skin of her face.

Boudica walked ahead of the bier, with Bardea at her side, both wearing green tunics and cloaks. Merida had died two days ago, despite the best efforts of Bladocus and the tribe's healers. It had been a long, painful death and Boudica felt exhausted and drained of emotion after witnessing the suffering of her younger daughter. Behind the bier paced Syphodubnus at the head of the long column of nobles, relatives and warriors. The handful of common folk of the hidden settlement had earlier formed an avenue from the royal enclosure to the edge of the sacred grove. Many had sobbed and wailed as the procession passed by. Boudica was thankful to leave that behind as they entered the grove where the ordinary people were not permitted on such occasions.

Ahead, in the open space between the trees, lay the slab of the altar, roughly fashioned from a rock that had been brought here from the far side of Britannia many hundreds of years earlier. Its surface had been smoothed by weathering and stained with the blood of sacrifices – fowl, goats, pigs and, more rarely, horses and even humans when the occasion demanded a sacrifice of the highest order. One of Bladocus's Druids of the First Ring, the most junior level of the cult, stood beside the altar with a kid goat, its hide gleaming white. It bleated as the procession approached.

Bladocus stepped round behind the slab as the bier was set down to one side. He waited until the mourners had filed up to form an arc before the altar. When they were standing still and silent, he raised his arms to the sky and intoned in his deep voice, 'Spirits of the ancestors of the great Iceni people, hear my words! We bring you a daughter of royal blood to join the shades of her ancestors in the Otherworld. Merida, second-born of King Prasutagus and Queen Boudica. Beloved daughter and sister. Flower of our tribe. Dutiful and brave, though her life was short, she honoured us with the courage with which she fought at the queen's side against our Roman enemies. We grieve for her as we grieve for all those who sacrificed their lives so that our people might be free. Andraste, goddess of the Iceni, we humbly beg that you favour Merida with all the gifts of a warrior when she is welcomed into the Otherworld. We make this sacrifice that you might bestow such a reward on one who has earned it through the shedding of her blood in your honour!'

He nodded to the other Druid, who bent to lift the kid up onto the altar. At once it began to struggle in protest, its little feet kicking out. The Druid managed to pin it down on its side before

Bladocus drew a narrow curved blade from within his cloak. With his spare hand he grasped the kid's muzzle and clamped it shut, then eased the head back to expose the throat. It was over in an instant. The blade cut so swiftly that the beast was still trying to bleat before it realised it had come to any harm. As the bright gore pulsed from the severed blood vessels and pooled rapidly across the top of the altar, the kid struggled briefly, spasmed and then went limp as its eyes glazed over in death.

Bladocus wiped the blade on the hem of his cloak and sheathed it. Then he daubed his forefinger in blood and stepped over to the bier, where he painted a crescent to represent the moon on the pale skin of Merida's forehead.

He turned to Boudica and spoke gently. 'It is time, my queen.'

Boudica nodded, and her bodyguards raised the bier onto their shoulders again as Bladocus turned to lead the procession through the trees at the end of the clearing towards the burial mounds. There were more than twenty of them of various sizes, according to the status of the ruler and the size of their family. The older mounds were overgrown with bushes and trees, the names of those interred long forgotten. The funeral procession wound its way through to the most recent mound, covered only in grass. The path leading to the timber-framed entrance was free of debris and had been cleared of the nettles that had sprung up since King Prasutagus died. Bladocus had to duck to enter, and was followed by Boudica, Bardea and the two strongest of the bodyguards, who carried the bier between them. The short passage gave onto the burial chamber, supported by props and beams. There were niches on either side. Only one was occupied, the remains of the corpse covered in a dark shroud, damp and mouldy after a year underground.

As the bodyguards eased Merida's body into the adjacent niche, Boudica paused to touch the covered head of her dead husband, filled with sorrow that neither he nor his daughter had been granted a longer life. If Prasutagus had lived, it was possible that the rebellion would never have occurred. As for Merida, she had not known love, marriage or motherhood, her only experience of men the Roman soldiers who had raped her. Boudica felt a tide of sadness welling up and had to struggle to keep it at bay.

'Father . . .' Bardea said softly, and began to reach out to touch his body.

'Don't.' Boudica brushed her daughter's hand aside.

Bardea drew back with a surprised expression that gave way to anguish, and Boudica's heart twisted. But she could not in all conscience let her surviving daughter dip further into the deceit concerning the truth about who her father really was. She forced herself to speak in an emollient tone.

'Let him rest in peace. We are here to bury your sister.'

The bodyguards left the chamber, and the light from outside illuminated Bladocus as he offered the final prayers and supplications and then drew the shroud up to cover Merida completely. Boudica felt an overwhelming sense of loss, knowing that she would never see her younger daughter's face again. At once a wave of memories washed over her – the glistening screwed-up features of the tiny infant at birth, then the softened expression of the toddler, eyes bright with curiosity and simple delight, followed by the mischievous glint of childhood. Even the first rages of her later years now became the cause of agonising regret where they had once occasioned the patient disappointment of her parents. She fought back her tears as her throat tightened painfully.

Indicating that the others should leave first, she waited a moment longer before she spoke.

'Farewell, beloved daughter. Go to your father. Tell him I will come as soon as I have done what I must for our people.'

Then she turned slowly and paced up the slope into the sunlit world above.

The bodyguards resealed the chamber with the slab of stone that had been heaved to one side at first light when the preparations for the funeral had been made. Then the mourners made their way through the mounds and the grove beyond as the disturbed crows looked down and filled the air with their discordant din.

Later that day, Boudica met with Bladocus and Syphodubnus in the round hut she used as her private quarters. They sat on stools as they discussed preparations to renew the rebellion.

'We now have over a thousand warriors in the camp,' said Syphodubnus. 'And more are promised from the villages who have responded to your call to arms.'

'Warriors?' Bladocus scoffed. 'How many of them are trained fighters? Half? A third at best. The rest are a mix of volunteers and those we have coerced into joining the rebellion.'

'That may be true,' Syphodubnus conceded. 'However, you've seen how their spirits have been raised by the success of the trap we set for the Romans. Even the most reluctant of our recruits now knows that Rome can be outwitted, and they are keen to repeat the exercise. Sure, there are some who are unfamiliar with the ways of the sword, but they have the desire to fight and are keen to learn. Our warriors will train them hard over the winter, and when spring comes, they will be a force to be reckoned with.'

'I hope so,' Bladocus responded. 'But we'll need more men, men with experience. And we can only get them from other tribes.'

'Which is why I have sent envoys to the Parisi, Corieltauvi, Catuvellauni and Brigantes to ask for volunteers to fill out our ranks.'

'Good luck with the Brigantes,' Bladocus sneered. 'Their queen, Cartimandua, sold her people out to Rome long ago when she betrayed Caratacus and handed him over to them.'

Boudica knew that was a particularly sensitive issue for the Druid. He had groomed the Catuvellauni prince to become warlord of his tribe and to lead the coalition that had resisted the legions when they invaded nearly twenty years before.

'Cartimandua's control over her people is not as firm as some might think,' Syphodubnus replied. 'There is a faction that is opposed to her treaty with Rome. If we could make common cause with them, we might raise a fresh rebellion in the north. The Brigantes are a powerful tribe. Second only to the Iceni. If they were to ally with us, it would surely inspire other tribes to join the struggle against the invader.'

'First you would have to depose Cartimandua,' Bladocus pointed out. 'And the Romans were quick to jump to her aid last time that was attempted.'

'They were not preoccupied by restoring control to the rest of the province at the time. Now they are thinly stretched. If Cartimandua is to be replaced, the circumstances are propitious.'

Bladocus shook his head dismissively.

'What about the Trinovantes?' Boudica intervened. 'Will they stand with us? I know the people of the village we used for the ambush were willing enough, but what of the rest of the tribe? Surely if we could tap their reserves of manpower, that would make a considerable addition to our strength?'

'Indeed, majesty,' Syphodubnus nodded. 'Their senior surviving chief, Tasciovanus, led the Trinovantian contingent of the rebel army. But he was wounded. The last I heard, he is not likely to recover. In which case, power will pass to his son, Vellocatus.'

'A pity. Tasciovanus is loyal to the cause. I am not aware of his son's sympathies. Perhaps we should pay Combretovium a visit and test the waters. Show the captured eagle to their people, along with the heads we took at the ambush. After all, the Trinovantes have almost as much reason to hate Rome as we do. However, if they are wavering then we need to make sure that they understand that there are no neutrals in this conflict.'

'I agree, majesty.'

'What about the Romans at Camulodunum?' Bladocus asked. 'Our spy reports that the auxiliary cohort there has been joined by three centuries of legionaries. It could be risky going to Combretovium with them in the area.'

'I doubt it,' said Syphodubnus. 'The spy says they have not ventured far from the colony since the ambush. There is a lot of activity – patrols close by, the construction of a fort outside the ruins. But my guess is that they do not intend to move against us until after the winter. They'll use the time to get their men ready and draw in reinforcements. Those they have there at present are not nearly enough to pose any threat to us.'

'Not yet,' said Bladocus.

Boudica leaned forward and clasped her hands together. 'Then the sooner we try and win over the Trinovantes, the better. Let's get to them before the Romans gather sufficient forces at Camulodunum to frighten them off. Have my bodyguard made ready to march, Syphodubnus. I'll take my chariot and a hundred mounted men. That should be enough to impress Tasciovanus – or, if he has died, his son.'

'When do you propose to leave?' he asked.

'As soon as we can today.'

'So soon? Your majesty has only just buried a daughter. The people are grieving. It is the custom to mourn for five days at least.'

'Let them mourn,' Boudica replied. 'I will do my mourning on the road, as I will every day of what is left of my life. But I will not let it get in the way of continuing the rebellion. The best way to honour my daughter's memory is to work towards the defeat of Rome, the destruction of her legions and towns and the slaughter of her people.'

The bitterness in her voice and the fanatical glint in her eye took Syphodubnus by surprise, and he cleared his throat as he stood up. 'Very well. I shall give the orders.'

After he'd left the hut, there was a pause before Bladocus

spoke. 'It's good to see that your martial spirit is undimmed, my queen. Very good. Whatever our friend Syphodubnus may think about securing allies and more warriors from the other tribes, everyone still looks to you as the leader of our struggle. They want to see that strength of purpose. That fire in your eyes. They draw strength from it. You inspire them. I know something about the Romans' ways. What they fear above all else is a powerful woman. That is why they vilified Queen Cleopatra of Aegyptus, to the far south of the Empire. You will give them cause to fear you just as much, if not more. She was merely a Greek, soft and cultured, while you are a flame-haired barbarian warrior.' He smiled. 'I can imagine how their histories of this time will strike fear into the heart of every Roman.'

'Fine words, Druid,' Boudica responded. 'But I too know something of Rome and its history. I don't intend to meet the same fate as Cleopatra. I will not be humbled as she was. I will have my victory. But if I am to be defeated, I will go down fighting, a sword in my hand and blood in my mouth. I will not clasp a serpent to my breast to ease my passing,' she said fervently. 'Never.'

Three days later, at dawn, Boudica stood tall in her chariot as she led her men through the mist into Combretovium. Those who were already abroad in the town turned as they heard the rumble of wheels and hooves. As she passed by, they muttered to each other in fear and awe, but none, she noted, offered a cheer. It was possible that they were surprised to see her unscathed at the head of a powerful column of warriors. They had heard of the rebels' defeat and the rumours surrounding the fate of their leader. Some claimed that she had died in battle, succumbed to wounds or taken poison. Others that she had been captured by the Romans and was already en route to Rome to be dragged through the streets before being presented to the emperor. Yet here she was, proud, defiant and very much alive. She wondered how they might react once they had recovered from their shock. Would they renew their support for her? Would they be afraid and reserved? Or would they be angry? She felt reassured by the men at her back. They would guarantee her safety and add weight to her words when she spoke to Tasciovanus and his son.

The Icenians continued down the main thoroughfare and reached the open gates of the chief's compound. One of his men made to step into the queen's path to challenge her, but the chariot continued without slowing and he only just managed to leap out of the way in time. As her mounted men entered behind her, they filtered out to each side but remained in their saddles. Boudica ordered her charioteer to draw up in front of the entrance of the hall, then she drew a deep breath and called out in a clear voice.

'I am Boudica, Queen of the Iceni! I demand to speak to Chief Tasciovanus!'

A handful of curious women and children had emerged from the huts within the enclosure and looked on expectantly, but there was no reply to her words so she repeated them.

There was movement within the dim interior of the hall, and a frail-looking figure in a cloak emerged onto the threshold, his hand resting on the shoulder of a burly retainer. He began to speak, pausing to cough before he continued. 'Queen Boudica, you are welcome to my hearth. Will you take food and wine with me?'

'Later. I would speak to you, your advisers and your warriors. Send for them now.'

Tasciovanus did nothing to hide his distaste at being addressed in such a peremptory manner, but a glance at the horsemen holding their spears caused him to respond cordially. 'As you wish. Please honour me by being a guest of my hall.' He gestured towards the interior, and Boudica gave a grave nod and descended from the rear of the chariot. Syphodubnus quickly ordered four of his men to accompany her in case there was any attempt at treachery.

She walked at Tasciovanus's side as he shuffled to the middle of the hall, where there stood a chair covered with furs that had been set up close to the fire. He eased himself onto it and commanded the man who had supported him to fetch another chair for Boudica and set it opposite him. As she waited, she regarded him with pity. She had known him since her childhood, when he had been a powerful warrior. Even as recently as the rebellion he had been a man to be reckoned with. But now he looked thin and drawn and had aged significantly since the last time she had seen him, after the sacking of Londinium.

'I was told that you had been wounded.'

He nodded. 'A Roman slingshot.'

She raised her eyebrows slightly. 'Such a wound is often mortal even if it does not kill its victim outright.'

'Then I have been fortunate to survive.'

'Indeed. Where is your son?'

'Vellocatus? He's not here. He's out in the forests with a hunting party. He will not be returning for some days.'

'A pity. My words are for him too, as your heir.'

Tasciovanus smiled weakly. 'You don't seem to have much faith in my recuperative powers. I hope to live for a while yet.'

She nodded thoughtfully before continuing. 'The question that faces us at present is how one chooses to live. On our knees, bowing our heads to Roman overlords, or on our feet, proudly standing up to them and fighting for our freedom?'

'The second proposition, while appealing, comes with certain risks attached to it.'

'That is always the price of freedom.'

'True, in which case the question becomes how much of a price one is prepared to pay. And how much is one prepared to demand others pay as well.'

Boudica's expression hardened. 'You do not sound like the man who stood at my side when we marched on Londinium only months ago. Have you already given in to Rome, Tasciovanus? Have you already chosen slavery over freedom? Have you no sense of duty to your people?'

Now it was the old man's turn to become hard-faced. 'Tell me, Boudica, what has the rebellion achieved? How many of our people have died? Are we any more free of Roman oppression than we were before? I stood at your side in good faith and so did my tribe. I was severely wounded in your cause and many of my warriors were killed fighting for you. I will not take lectures from you concerning duty to my people. We have paid a heavy price already. If we choose to continue the struggle against Rome or we choose peace, that is a decision for us to make. Not for you to browbeat us into. I hope that is clear.'

Setting out his position, as reasonably as he could manage, had strained Tasciovanus, and now he slumped back in his chair and closed his eyes briefly.

Boudica regarded him with a mixture of sadness and contempt. He had been a figure to look up to, but now he was a tired, beaten old man. No longer prepared to stand up for his people against the arrogance and cruelty of Rome. A coward, she told herself. And a fool. Did he really believe that peace with the Empire was better than slavery? He was a lost cause and she had to hope there were others in the tribe who still had fire in their bellies and a yearning to cast off the Roman yoke to stand tall and breathe the sweet air of freedom.

The old man opened his eyes again and stared at her. When he spoke, it was as if he had been reading her thoughts.

'You talk a lot about freedom. It's a fine word, to be sure. A fine sentiment. But what do you think it means? Does it mean the same thing for you as queen of your tribe as it does to the lowliest Icenian farmer scratching a living off the land? You are fighting to retain your hold over your people. For power and riches and the right to control the lives of many others. If you win, that is your prize. If you lose, Rome will rule the Icenian people in your place. Do you really think either of those results makes much of a difference to the common people? I can't speak for you on that point. As far as I am concerned, I no longer believe I have the moral authority to ask my people to die for a word as slippery and insubstantial as the morning mist. If they are to fight and die, let it be for their very survival and for no lesser reason. That is my position, Boudica. You may make your case to my people. If some choose to follow you, I will not stop them. But if they choose not to, you have no right to force them to fight.'

She was silent for a moment. 'I see.'

The warrior moved away from his chief's side to build up the fire, then Boudica resumed in a neutral tone.

'You were lucky to survive your wound.'

Tasciovanus nodded. 'Very lucky, according to the surgeon.'

She frowned. 'Surgeon? What surgeon?'

'From the garrison at Camulodunum,' he stated in a challenging tone. 'He saved my life and I am in his debt.'

She felt her heart grow cold with fury. 'How can you stomach the thought of being in debt to a Roman?'

He shrugged. 'Easily, if the alternative is death. I wonder how you stomach having the deaths of so many of your people and mine on your conscience?'

The blood drained from her face as she stood up abruptly. 'I will not waste any more breath on a man who would betray his tribe to Rome. Let's see what the real men of Combretovium have to say when I speak to them.'

As Boudica strode towards the entrance, Tasciovanus sighed sadly. Despite their different views, he still admired the Iceni queen and shared her disgust and anger at the way Rome had treated her and her daughters. He had willingly gone to war to avenge such outrages and shared her anguish at the catastrophic defeat of the rebels at the hands of the legions. But he feared there was no chance of ever overcoming the Romans' superiority. Even though the rebels had destroyed the Ninth Legion, there would always be other legions to replace it. They would surely always win in the end. Perhaps, deep inside her mind, Boudica herself feared that to be true but was so consumed with hate that she would not admit it to herself or anyone else. As a result, she was prepared to continue the war until she ran out of warriors, her own and those of other tribes. Too many of his people had died already, he reflected. Even if she persuaded some to join her, he had already decided to forbid them to leave, despite what he had said to her shortly before. They had sworn an oath to obey him, and he would hold them to it.

He felt himself shivering and eased forward in his chair to better warm himself by the fire while he waited for his men to gather in the compound to hear Boudica's appeal.

Boudica's lips were pressed together in a grim line as she strode over to Syphodubnus, looking up at him with a wildness in her expression that frightened him. When she spoke, her voice was low and emotionless.

'I want you to pick four men you can absolutely trust to do your bidding and take them into the hall. Cut off Tasciovanus's head, wrap it in his cloak and bring it to my chariot. One of his men is with him. He will try to defend his chief and must be killed too.'

Syphodubnus glanced round and saw that the nearest men seemed not to have heard her words. He quickly dismounted and moved closer to her.

'My queen,' he whispered urgently, 'what are you thinking? You can't do this. How do you think his people will react to such an outrage?'

'He has been collaborating with the enemy. The Romans were here and he allowed himself to be treated by their surgeon.

204

He speaks as if they are his allies. He has betrayed his people, he has betrayed the rebellion and he has betrayed me. Have you forgotten what the Romans did to me, Syphodubnus?'

'Of course not. But—'

'Don't you dare question my orders. I have told you what to do. Now see to it. At once.' She turned away before he could protest further and returned to her chariot.

The first of the Trinovantians were arriving at the compound, and Syphodubnus ordered half his warriors to form a cordon to keep them as far back from the hall as possible. Then he picked his four men and set off to carry out the orders of his queen.

When the last of the settlement's men of fighting age had entered the compound, Boudica ordered the gates to be closed and guarded by her warriors. The Trinovantes regarded the mounted Icenians warily. Scanning their faces, she could see that many were distrustful and afraid as they muttered among themselves. Slowly she raised her hands, and the crowd, at least five hundred strong, fell silent. She made no effort to address them, instead allowing the tension and expectation to build. At last she lowered her arms, drew a breath and began. She spoke just loudly enough for her audience to hear, her voice calm and clear.

'You all know who I am. Many of you have seen me before when you proudly marched at my side. You were there when we won our victories at Camulodunum, Londinium and Verulamium. Some of you were in at the kill when we caught and destroyed a Roman legion. We are comrades, you and I, and I have come here as your ally, as your friend, as your leader, to ask that you take up arms once again and rejoin our struggle against Rome. It is a matter of honour. *Your* honour.'

She gazed over the sea of faces and swept her arm round in an arc, her finger pointing at them. 'Honour demands that you wage war against the enemies of your people, and what greater enemy has any tribe in Britain confronted than the Romans? They are like a plague sweeping across our lands, destroying all in their path and feeding off those who are left like the bloodsucking leeches they are. What kind of a person permits themselves to be abused by Rome – robbed, raped and humiliated? What kind of person is so lacking in pride and honour that they would bow their head to accept the yoke that Rome wishes to burden them with?

'I am not such a person. The blood of my ancestors flows in my veins. Just as it flows in the veins of the Iceni warriors. Just as it flows in the veins of the proud people of the Trinovantes. I know your worth. I have seen the courage of your men at first hand and pay homage to such heroes.'

She plucked a spear from the holder on the chariot and brandished it as she called out across the compound, 'Honour to the brave Trinovantes!'

Her bodyguards picked up the cheer and thrust their own spears into the sky. The men in the crowd looked around at the horsemen, and a handful joined in. Boudica kept the chant going as the volume swelled until she could see only a few faces that regarded her with indifference or disapproval. A movement to the side caught her eye and she glanced round to see Syphodubnus and his men emerging from the hall. Her adviser was holding a bundle, which he placed on the bed of the chariot. She lowered her spear and let the sound die away before she continued.

'I speak for all the Iceni when I say that we open our hearts to those of your tribe who fought with us, bled with us and died alongside our fallen. They were our brothers. We mourned their deaths as we mourned those of our own kin after the great battle in which we suffered defeat. Our first defeat. But when you go to war, you accept that there will be defeats as well as victories along the road to the final triumph. *Our* triumph! Who among you is with me?'

Once again the crowd cheered, many of them now in a wild fervour, she noted.

'Death to Rome!' she cried out.

'Death to Rome!' the men of both tribes thundered back, over and over again until she signalled for quiet.

'Before we march against Rome, we must root out those who would betray us. Those who would stab us in the back for Roman silver. Those cowards who hold their honour so cheap that they would sell their souls and shame their people. Those who turn away from the sacred rites of our Druids and embrace the dark practices of the enemy. They are traitors! Traitors!' She paused. 'And what do we do with traitors?'

'Kill them!' the crowd roared. 'Death to traitors!'

Boudica reached down and flipped back the folds of the bundle by her feet. Grasping the locks of grey hair, she raised Tasciovanus's head and held it out to the crowd. Their cries faded in their throats as they looked on in shock.

'Here is your traitor,' she said. 'The dog who turned on his people for the sake of a few scraps from his Roman masters' table. So perish all those who betray their people. Let this be a warning to those who harbour the same treachery in their hearts. You are either for the rebellion or you are our enemy. There is no other way. Tasciovanus chose to be our enemy. *Your* enemy.'

She lowered the head and let it drop onto the folds of the cloak. 'You can choose to march with us now when we leave Combretovium, or you can join us later if you need longer to say your farewells and settle your affairs here.' She eased her toe under Tasciovanus's head and swept it off the chariot to thud onto the ground. She made no attempt to hide her contempt and disgust. 'I will leave this as a reminder of the fate of any who stand in the way of the rebellion. Along with the heads of any others who betray the cause.'

CHAPTER EIGHTEEN

At Camulodunum

As Cato reached the crest of the last hill before Camulodunum, he reined in to inspect the progress Macro had made in his absence. The tent lines in the interior of the temple precinct had been restored to the neat, well-spaced arrangement of before. Meanwhile, the new fort was nearing completion a short distance outside the ruins of the colony. It was well situated on slightly elevated ground yet close enough to a bend in the river to give easy access to a water supply. A substantial ditch and rampart extended most of the way around the perimeter, and legionaries toiled away in the bright sunshine as they laboured to complete the defences. Timber-framed towers rose at each corner, with gatehouses in between. Within the rampart the legionaries' tent lines occupied one corner, leaving plenty of space for other units when they arrived. Cato could make out the stakes that had been set up to mark out the locations for the construction of the headquarters, granaries, barrack blocks and stables. Further out across the landscape he could make out the foraging parties sent out to procure timber cut from the nearest forests, and mounted pickets keeping watch for any sign of the enemy.

'Good job,' he muttered to himself, then flicked the reins and urged his mount down the road towards the colony.

Macro was easy to pick out, standing on top of the bare earth rampart looking down on the legionaries. He held his vine cane horizontally behind his back and his crested helmet turned as he watched the men like a hawk. As he saw Cato approaching, he summoned one of the legionary centurions to take over before making for the nearest of the gateways to cross the ditch and greet his superior.

'You've done wonders since I set off for Londinium.' Cato grinned. 'I should stay away more often.'

'Well, of course, it's a lot easier to get things done without some jobsworth looking over your shoulder all the time.'

They shared a laugh before Cato indicated the fort. 'Seriously, though – you've done a fine job, brother.'

'This isn't all I've had the legionaries working at. There's been plenty of marching, weapons drill and inspections. They're tired as fuck and really pissed off with me, but they're coming on nicely.' Macro's smile faded. 'For the most part.'

'There's been trouble?'

'I'm afraid so, sir. I've had to have one of the officers arrested for refusing to obey my orders. He's been held in the cage for the last three days.'

'What happened?'

'He felt that drilling and digging with the rest of his lads was . . . demeaning. Yes, that was the word he used.'

'Which of the centurions was it?'

Macro sucked in a breath. 'Ah, well, here's the thing. It wasn't a centurion. It's Tribune Agricola.'

'Damn, that's awkward.' Agricola came from an aristocratic family with powerful political connections. They were not going to be best pleased when they discovered that he had been accorded such disciplinary action. A man of lesser rank would have faced far worse punishment, of course, but people of their class considered themselves as living apart from hoi polloi. 'I'd better have a word with him before he decides he wants to kick up a fuss.'

'Probably a good idea.'

'I made it clear to him that I was leaving you in command. Any disciplinary action you have taken was in my name. You did the right thing and I'll stand by that.'

'I know, lad. I wouldn't expect any less. Anyway,' Macro changed the subject, 'how did it go with the governor?'

Cato briefly related the details of the encounter, to Macro's growing delight.

'Sounds like you played him perfectly.'

'I hope so. Before I left, he sent out the orders for the reinforcements to be attached to my command. That should bring us up to a full cohort of legionaries, four infantry cohorts of auxiliaries and two mounted cohorts, in addition to replacements for the Eighth Illyrian. There will be warships from the Britannia squadron. Four biremes and six liburnians, as well as some smaller boats. Along with the sailors and marines, that gives us over four thousand men. I just hope nothing happens to cause him to change his mind.'

'It's more than you were hoping for, but perhaps less than you need, sir. Given that the lion's share of that will be used for garrisoning the forts and outposts that form the cordon around the Icenian heartland.'

'I know. I hope we've managed to persuade Tasciovanus to provide us with some levies from the Trinovantes. We'll see. On a brighter note, I have some good news for you.'

'Oh? I could do with some.'

'Petronella is in Londinium.'

Macro's eyes widened. 'What?'

'She's with Claudia and Lucius. I found them while I was there. They returned from Gaul after they heard about the rebels being beaten.'

'Thank the gods they are all safe.' Macro's surprise and relief quickly gave way to concern. 'What in Hades does she think she is doing? I told her not to return until she heard from us that it was safe to do so. She never listens! Mind of her bloody own, that one.'

'Which is one of the reasons you married her, my friend.'

'Tell me more,' he demanded. 'Is she well?'

Cato gave a full account as they walked back to the temple precinct together. After hearing about their experiences at sea and afterwards, Macro was greatly relieved that they were now safely accommodated at the governor's headquarters in Londinium.

'There will be time over winter for you to take some leave and go and see them,' said Cato.

Macro nodded his thanks. 'I hope we can bring an end to this business and stamp out the rebellion. I don't think I could cope with having to get them out of harm's way again.'

Both men were silent as they recollected the scenes of chaos, terror and bloodshed as the rebels entered Londinium while Macro found places for their families on one of the last ships to escape the doomed town.

They passed through the gate of the precinct and entered the Eighth Cohort's temporary camp. Cato handed his reins to one of the duty soldiers and retrieved his saddlebags.

'I'll see to Agricola. You can return to training duties.'

'Yes, sir.'

They exchanged a salute and went their separate ways, Cato heading up the temple steps to enter the inner sanctum. He handed his bags and cloak to Trebonius.

'Some food, sir?' the servant asked.

'Yes. Bring me whatever you can find. I'll have it after I've attended to another matter. I understand that Tribune Agricola is under arrest.'

'Yes, sir.' Trebonius rolled his eyes. 'You should have heard

211

the fuss he made about it. Quite ungentlemanly language and behaviour, if I may say so.'

'Where is he?'

'At the back of the pediment, sir. The centurion had some shelters put up there to serve as cells in case he had to discipline any of the legionary recruits.'

'Shelters?' Cato's imagination was already conjuring an image of the prisoner's surroundings that was only going to make matters worse in terms of resolving the problem. 'Right. Get my cloak cleaned, the saddlebags unpacked and then bring me some food and wine.'

'There's no wine left, sir. Just water.'

'Fine. Water then.'

Cato left the sanctum and paced round the pediment with its half-completed columns, still stained by smoke. In the space at the back, four cages had been constructed, each six feet in each dimension, with tent leather on top and the sides to keep out the rain. The front of each cage was comprised of sturdy timber posts with locking bars secured by wedges. Two auxiliaries on guard duty stood to attention as Cato rounded the corner. Two of the doors were open. A legionary in his red tunic sat in the rear of the nearest, and Cato paused to snap at him.

'On your damn feet when an officer is present!'

The legionary scrambled up and stood to attention, his head bowed because of the low roof.

'What's your name?' Cato demanded.

'Gaius Bullo, sir.'

'What are you in here for?'

'Drunk while on duty, sir. Five days in stir and ten on latrines, sir.'

'Drunk, eh? Lucky you. You must be good at foraging. I thought the last of the wine had been recovered from the ruins of the colony. You may have a useful skill there, Bullo. I need

212

resourceful men. But I don't need drunkards. I don't want to see you in the cells again. Understand?'

'Yes, sir.'

Cato nodded and moved to the next cell, where Agricola was leaning against the wooden bars, his legs slightly bent so that he didn't have to tilt his head. He made no attempt to greet Cato or salute. His jaw was lined with bristles and he sniffed slightly as he glared at his superior.

'I have to say I expected better from you.' Cato shook his head

'I was thinking the same about your friend Centurion Macro.'

He ignored the jibe. 'He says you refused to obey an order. True?'

'He told me to take a pick and get into the ditch.'

'So?'

'I am a senior tribune, not some bloody squaddie. I will not be treated like one.'

'Did he call you sir when he gave the order?'

'What?' Agricola frowned. 'What if he did?'

'Then he treated you with the respect accorded your rank and you have no cause for complaint.'

'There is a chain of command, sir,' the tribune protested.

'Yes, there damn well is!' Cato snapped back. 'I am your superior officer and your commanding officer and I give the orders. My orders were that Macro was in charge and he was to drill the reinforcements who had joined the Eighth Cohort. That includes you. Is that understood?'

'Yes . . . sir.'

Cato folded his arms. 'I take it that part of the reason you requested a transfer to my command was because you wanted to get away from the governor's staff and do some real soldiering. Am I right?'

Agricola nodded.

'Then you've come to the right place. I don't think you realise how fortunate you are. As Jupiter is my witness, I have never met a better soldier than Macro, nor one who can train men as well as he can. Learn all you can from him and it will set you on the path to a successful military career, if that is what you want. The best senior officers are those who paid attention to the veterans they served with in the early days of their army life. I am no exception to that. I wouldn't be standing here as a prefect lecturing you on the subject if I hadn't been willing to listen to Macro from the outset.'

He let his words settle in the young man's mind before he continued in a milder tone. 'For what it's worth, I think you show promise. More so than most tribunes, who just want to get through their service period as fast as possible without getting too dirty or exposing themselves to danger. The fact that you applied to serve here proves that you have a bit more about you, and I respect your willingness to get stuck in. But you need to know what it means to be a soldier before you can be trusted to command any. Being an officer isn't just about giving orders in a loud voice.' He offered a smile. 'That's what optios and junior centurions are for. You have to be able to think like a soldier and understand their ways if you are to get the best out of them. And that's how Macro and I are going to treat you for now. If and when we think you are ready to command troops in the field, you will get the chance to put what you have learned into effect.' He paused before he offered his conclusion. 'That's the deal. If you are happy to play your part, then say so. If not, you can pack your kit and fuck off back to headquarters. Which is it to be?'

Agricola scratched his chin before he replied. 'I'll stay here, if I may, sir.'

'Good, that's settled. Now, how long were you sent to the cage for?'

'Five days, sir. Can I be released?'

'How many days have you been inside?'

'This is the third, sir.'

'Then you only have two left. Hopefully you'll have learned your lesson and that will be the end of it. Make yourself comfortable, Tribune.'

Cato turned away and returned to his quarters. Trebonius had set up a tray on his campaign desk. There was a bowl of greasy-looking stew, a hunk of bread and a jug of water.

'Is this all you could find?' Cato complained as he sniffed the stew.

'At short notice, sir. Which is what you gave me. If you had wanted a small banquet, it would have been best to let me know in advance.'

'Less of the backchat, if you don't mind.' Cato looked up sharply. 'Seems like discipline has completely gone to shit while I was in Londinium.'

'I'm not sure whether mind-reading was one of the requirements when I was appointed as your servant, sir.'

'Let's put it to the test,' said Cato, and he gave Trebonius a hard stare. 'Can you guess what I am thinking now?'

'I have a fairly good idea, sir.' Trebonius nodded towards the door.

'Well done. You get to keep the job. Wait a moment.' He frowned. 'There was one jar of wine left before I went to Londinium. Where is it?' It was not unknown for some servants, and slaves for that matter, to take a fairly liberal approach to their masters' personal stores of petty luxuries.

'Stolen, sir.'

'Really?'

Trebonius affected a mortally offended expression before he continued. 'Why, yes, sir! I caught the thief in the act. Managed to give him a whack on the head with one of my pans as he made off. He dropped like a stone. Unfortunately, so did the jar. Wine went all over the place. Quite a mess. I had the toerag clear it up before he was taken away.'

Cato was angry. He had been looking forward to sharing the last of his wine with Macro to toast the safe return of their families. 'The thief, what was his name?'

'Bullo, sir. Legionary Gaius Bullo.'

The dying days of autumn saw a marked change in the weather. The temperature dropped, the skies became cloudy and rain arrived, carried on biting easterly winds. None of which made the slightest difference to the training regime at Camulodunum. Having completed the fort, Macro set the legionaries to making marching camps 'in the face of the enemy', as the army termed it. These were the fortifications put up by units when on campaign in enemy territory, and were far more substantial than basic marching camps, which were more of a discouragement than a real set of defences. Ditches were dug, ramparts built and palisades erected on top. Gatehouses set up and tents pitched. All within the space of a few hours. When they'd finished, Macro had them strike the tents, dismantle the palisades and shovel the soil and turf from the ramparts back into the ditches before leading them on a route march through the countryside around the colony. Then it was back to Camulodunum to repeat the process.

The legionaries hated him for it to start with, then swiftly began to take pride in the speed with which they could set up a field camp and tear it down again. The same went for the route marches. The harder Macro pushed them, the more resilient they became, and determined to keep up with their colleagues. To encourage them to greater efforts still, he devised competitions between the three centuries and the men formed ever closer ties with their comrades as they sought to outdo their rivals in digging a defensive ditch or completing a formation change on the patch of open ground outside the colony that was used for marching

216

and weapons drills. Tribune Agricola was attached to the First Century as acting optio, in which role he was worked as hard as the rankers but allowed to develop some authority and carry out limited command tasks.

As the men became fitter and more proficient, Macro introduced mock attacks by day and then later under cover of darkness, and was quick to pounce on any failings that might cause avoidable casualties in actual combat. 'Always remember,' he bellowed at morning parade, 'Roman soldiers are the best because our drills are like bloodless battles and our battles like bloody drills! It may seem like hard work now, but in the long run sweat saves lives.'

Cato observed the training with approval, noting the steady improvement in the performance of the legionaries. Meanwhile, the auxiliaries spent their time on the buildings inside the completed fort. Rows of long, low barrack blocks were constructed out of timber and turf with bark shingled roofs. More extensive timber buildings were built to serve as granaries. They were raised up on stone foundations to limit the ingress of any vermin that might feed on the sacks of grain brought up to the colony by supply columns sent from the warehouses in Londinium. The largest and most complicated of the structures was the headquarters block, with its lofty and spacious main hall, administration offices, armourer's stores and strongroom where the most important records, wills and savings and pay chests, along with each unit's standards, were kept under constant guard.

As soon as the buildings were completed, Cato moved the Eighth Cohort into the fort, where his men occupied the barracks in the prime location, closest to headquarters. A month after his return from Londinium, the first of the promised auxiliary cavalry units arrived, commanded by Prefect Quadrillus, a veteran who had fought in the great victory over the rebels that summer. They were assigned their barracks and horse lines before the men set to work building the stables that would shelter their mounts through the winter months. Strong columns were sent out to patrol the border of the Icenian lands, with strict orders not to engage the enemy for fear of a repeat of the trap that Macro had been lured into the previous month. The remaining units were expected to reach the colony any day.

Before then, Cato took two squadrons of cavalry and rode north to the great bay he had seen from Besodius's ship, marking on his map the sites where he planned to build the forts and outposts that would screen the Icenian border. It was clear that the work would require a considerable number of men, and he would have to approach Suetonius to ask for the survivors of the Ninth Legion based at Lindum to help. Content with his plans, he led the column back to Camulodunum some eight days after setting out. Macro was waiting for him at the main gate, his expression grave.

'What's happened?' Cato demanded as he dismounted.

'Vellocatus is here. He arrived a few days after you left. Came with a small warband to offer his services.'

Cato smiled. 'Excellent! But why the long face?'

'It's Tasciovanus. He's dead.'

'His wounds?'

Macro shook his head. 'Boudica. She took a column to Combretovium while Vellocatus and his companions were out hunting. She murdered Tasciovanus, convinced most of his men to turn against us and killed those who refused to side with her. You'd better come and speak to him.'

CHAPTER NINETEEN

Vellocatus was sitting alone in the corner of the hall of the headquarters building. He was carving a design into the shaft of a spear by the light of the window above him. So engaged was his attention that he did not notice Macro and Cato until they were standing at his side. He raised his eyes and nodded a greeting before he lowered his knife and blew away the small scattering of shavings on the table.

'Macro told me about your father,' Cato began gently. 'I'm sorry. He was a good man. I regret that I didn't get the chance to know him better.'

The Trinovantian nodded.

Cato indicated the bench on the other side of the table. 'May we?'

'It's your hall, Prefect Cato. Do as you wish.'

There was a dull carelessness in Vellocatus's voice that alerted Cato to the scale of the turmoil in the young man's head.

'From what Macro tells me, you were fortunate not to be there when Boudica arrived.'

'Fortunate?' Vellocatus repeated in a dry, mocking voice. 'I'm not sure how you would qualify that word. My father is dead. They cut his head off,' he said through gritted teeth. 'They did the same to some others, and left the heads of fathers, brothers and sons on stakes in the compound.'

He clasped his hands together, working his right thumb over the flesh on the back of the other as he continued. 'We heard the cries of their families as we returned to Combretovium that evening. Boudica and her men had left earlier in the afternoon, along with over three hundred of those who volunteered to join her rebellion. May all the gods of our tribe damn them to eternal suffering when they enter the Otherworld. I heard what happened from one of the serving women at my father's hall who saw the whole thing. Boudica had her men kill any who dared to speak up against her. They were unarmed and cut down without mercy by the cowards who call themselves Icenian warriors. Many of our men saved their own lives by keeping their mouths shut. They bought their lives with still tongues while their comrades were butchered all around them. The dogs. They are little better than those who betrayed my father and our tribe by joining Boudica's band of murderers.'

'You should not be too hard on those men who said nothing,' Cato said. 'What could they have done that would have made any difference? They would have died for nothing. This way they are alive and can seek revenge for their murdered comrades when the time comes.'

Vellocatus sneered. 'If they do anything of the kind it will only be out of shame.'

'I'll settle for that,' said Macro. 'Frankly I don't give a shit why your men might fight, as long as they fight well.'

Cato looked at his friend sharply, and Macro shrugged but fell silent.

'Do you think those men would back you if you returned to Combretovium and asked them to?'

'I'll be damned if I ask those cowards to fight at my side! If you want them, you ask them.'

Cato realised this was not the best time to make such plans. 'It doesn't matter now. I'm just honoured to have you and those men you have brought with you as our allies. Together we will defeat

Boudica and avenge your father and those who were murdered with him.'

Vellocatus picked up his knife to continue scoring the pattern on his spear shaft. 'When the time comes, I will take Boudica's head and mount it on a stake in front of my father's hall for the crows to pick to pieces.'

Cato was deeply saddened by his words. This was where events had led them all – Britons and Romans alike. The injustices of Roman rule begat further injustice, oppression and ultimately rebellion, from which violence begat violence in a vicious cycle of depravity and hatred that piled atrocity upon atrocity until all were victims. If left long enough, such things could perpetuate down the generations long after anyone recalled the circumstances out of which the horrors originated. The sole hope that this might be prevented lay in the swift destruction of Boudica. Even as he knew this, he could not help being aware of the terrible waste it entailed. She had once been an ally and a friend, and would have been a powerful advocate for Rome had she been treated with respect. The thought gnawed at his conscience, and not for the first time he felt a certain equivocation about the cause he had given his life to. Often Rome stood for all that was best in the world. But sometimes she made grave errors, and was the very source of evil, forcing the best among her people to make great sacrifices in terms of blood and reputation to draw her back onto the right path, all the while being castigated by loud villains posturing as patriots.

He breathed deeply and stood up, indicating to Macro to follow him. They left Vellocatus to continue working on his design, a torrent of dark thoughts swirling through his mind.

'How many men did he bring with him?' asked Cato when they reached his office on the far side of the hall.

'Thirty-two in all. Just those who were out hunting with him when Boudica paid her visit to Combretovium.'

Cato was disappointed by the number. 'Barely a squadron, then.'

221

'On a brighter note, one of them is Pernocatus.'

Cato searched his memory, then made the connection. Before the rebellion, they had hired Pernocatus as a guide when they went hunting in the forests around the colony. 'Good. Perhaps we can go out to look for boar again. It would be a relief to put some fresh meat on the table.'

'Aye.' Macro smiled briefly at the thought before turning back to the matter at hand. 'You want to put the Trinovantians on the strength of the Eighth Illyrian, or enlist them in Quadrillus's cohort?'

Cato knew that the other prefect was unimaginative and inflexible. If Vellocatus's band was added to his unit it was likely he would resent them as barbarians and treat them badly. Badly enough to sabotage the alliance Cato was painstakingly trying to build with the Trinovantes. For a moment Cato was tempted to fill out the ranks of his own depleted cohort, but then he hit upon a better idea.

'No. We'll treat them as a unit in their own right, with a standard of their own design, their own code of discipline and their familiar ways of fighting.'

'Why do that?' Macro frowned. 'Why not just add them into our lot? We need the men.'

'I don't think they will be happy to be subjected to our ways, Macro. They'd be difficult to train and would resent the kinds of punishment our men are used to.'

'My heart bleeds for them. Soldiers need training, sir. Their sort most of all.'

'I fear it would be more trouble than it is worth. Besides, thirty-two men added to the cohort is going to be of far less value to me than the example they will set if they are allowed to serve as a separate unit.'

'What example is that lot going to set anyone? Can't see our lads or the legionaries looking up to them.'

'It's not them I am thinking about. We'll win more Trinovantian recruits to our side if they can serve under one of their own and fight according to their ways. There's also considerable value in allowing other tribes to see that those who were once Boudica's most loyal allies are now standing against her. My strategy is to isolate her militarily from the rest of the province and force her to retreat into a smaller and smaller space until we can pin her down and finish the job. It would help our cause if she was also seen to be isolated politically among the tribes. Better still if, as I have reason to believe, there are elements among her own people who oppose her. They might be willing to join Vellocatus's unit if they can't stomach fighting under a Roman standard.'

Macro considered the arguments for a moment and pursed his lips. 'Sometimes I wonder if you are becoming more politician than soldier, the things you come up with.'

'Goes with the job, I'm afraid. The higher you rise, the further you see and the more complicated your options.'

'Then I'm glad I am stuck with being a centurion,' Macro decided. 'I'm happy doing what I'm good at and I'll leave the slippery stuff to those with an appetite for it. Not that I'm saying you are slippery, lad. You know that, right?'

Cato laughed. 'Perhaps there is a place for your kind of straight talking in the Senate. It would be a welcome change.'

'I doubt it,' Macro grumbled. 'I'd be more likely to stick a blade in their guts than a witty barb.'

'I can think of a few who might deserve it.' Cato opened the saddlebags that Trebonius had placed on his desk to take out his waxed notebook. 'Where are Vellocatus and his men being accommodated at the moment?'

'I let them have the temple precinct since we're no longer using it. There's more than enough room for them in the sanctum, and stabling for their horses. I've provided rations and feed from our stocks, but they've been sending out parties to find game. I'd say they are eating rather better than we are.'

'I want them moved to the fort. Make sure they get good barracks.'

'Can we trust them inside our defences?'

'I don't think our young friend was faking his hatred of Boudica and desire for revenge. But you are right to be cautious: my enemy's enemy is not always my friend. Have them watched for now – nothing obvious, mind – and if they give the slightest cause for concern, report it to me at once.'

'Yes, sir.' Macro's tone alerted Cato to something else on his friend's mind.

'You have any other reservations about moving them into the fort?'

'There's often tensions between men of different units, particularly legionaries and auxiliaries. Adding Trinovantian warriors to the mix ain't going to be helpful.'

'Then use that. I've seen how you provoke the men's competitive spirit. I dare say our lads will want to prove they are better than the Trinovantians, and Vellocatus and his men will want to show they are more than a match for any Romans. It'll be a good way for them to let off steam. Who knows? It might even bring them closer together. We'll also need a translator. Find one of our lot who can speak the dialect and assign him to Vellocatus to help him get used to our camp routine and to understand his orders and trumpet signals.' Cato paused. 'I think that covers it. Ah, one last thing. How is Agricola coming along? Showing any promise?'

'Surprisingly, he's turned out to be a pretty good optio. I don't know what you said to him, but it certainly shook the lead out of his boots. He has been throwing himself forward in all the drills and exercises and doing his best to lead the way for those in his unit. He's even managed to win their respect and get on with the lads without having to sound like them too much, if you get my meaning. Have to say, I'm impressed so far.'

'Excellent. Let me know when you think he's ready to lead in the field and we'll put him to the test.'

224

They exchanged a nod and Macro left. Cato smiled slightly to himself as he spoke aloud. 'Tribune Agricola, the army may make a man of you yet.'

Over the next month, the rest of the reinforcements arrived and were accommodated within an enlarged fortress that now covered more ground than the ruins of the neighbouring colony. All the legionary cohorts had been drawn from the Second Legion, and Macro was looking forward to subjecting them to the same rigorous training programme that he had begun with the first arrivals.

After Cato had welcomed them from the reviewing platform to the side of the parade ground outside the fort on a cold autumn afternoon, he handed over to the centurion, who walked slowly along the front rank tapping the tip of his vine cane against his greave as he addressed them in his best drill instructor voice, which carried clearly to the men in the rearmost ranks.

'You may think you are real soldiers. You may think that wearing the armour of a real soldier makes you look the part. You may think that being able to march fifteen miles without tripping over your feet and falling flat on your face means you have mastered field drill. You may think that being able to lob a javelin further than you can spit or walloping a training post with a wooden sword is all it takes to be a real warrior. If you think any of that, then, ladies, you are in for a bit of a fucking disappointment. We live in sad times. The Second Legion, the Augusta, used to be the finest bloody legion in the army. I know, I served in it and was promoted to centurion before any of you green wankers were even born. Back then it was a fighting unit. Tough as nails and rightly feared by any hairy-arsed barbarian foolish enough to tangle with us.'

He had reached the end of the front line and his tone altered as he turned about. 'Times have changed, ladies. Now the Second is little more than a training depot where recruits go to get their heads shaved, be issued nice new kit and have two square meals a day before they are taught to march in a straight line and flash a few weapons about. Normally that would lead to better things, but thanks to our rebel friends, training has been cut short and the governor's headquarters have sent you out to do the work of real men.' He laughed, then turned towards the front rank. 'When I look at your bright, eager faces, all I see is one great big fucking mistake made by some staff officer who is as clueless as you lot of beauties.'

Cato saw Tribune Agricola, standing in front of the colour party, trying hard to suppress a grin but not succeeding. Cato himself was enjoying the show just as much while keeping his expression severe as he looked down on the ranks of the recruits. He had seen his friend do this many times before, but it never ceased to be entertaining, even if it scared the life out of most of the men on the receiving end.

Macro approached a tall recruit and looked up into his face. 'You, lad, you look like you have the makings of a bloody centurion! Don't you fucking look at me!' he screamed as the hapless young man's gaze flickered towards his superior. 'Look straight ahead! You are on parade and you look straight ahead like your life depends on it! You're not ogling tarts back in the Forum now, sunshine! Do you understand me?'

The legionary nodded, and his poorly fastened chin strap caused the brim of his helmet to tip forward over his eyes.

'Holy fucking Jupiter!' Macro reached up to grab the top of the helmet and jam it even further forward so that only the tip of the recruit's nose was visible. 'Is that better, lad? Does your fucking helmet offer better protection for your pretty face now? Even though you can't see a fucking thing and if you were in battle, looking as stupid as you do, some great big barbarian would carve your balls off before you knew he was there. Well?'

The legionary dared not move, despite looking ridiculous. He began to mumble a reply, but Macro shouted over the top of him.

'What's that? I can't bloody hear you! I asked you a question. Does your helmet offer you better protection now?'

'No, sir!' the legionary shouted back.

'Quite fucking right it doesn't, soldier! So don't let me ever catch you on parade with your helmet perched on your pointy head as loosely as a drunken tart on top of a lad on his first visit to a brothel. Got it?'

'Yes, sir!'

Macro turned about smartly and resumed his progress along the front rank. 'Laughing boy back there proves my point. Right now you lot are a shower of shit on my beloved parade ground. That does not make me happy. And when I am not happy, you can be bloody sure that *you* will not be happy. It is my job to make everyone happy, no matter how exhausted it makes you, no matter how much shit you have to crawl through during training, no matter how many blisters you get on your feet from route marches or on your hands from weapons drill. I will train you to be real soldiers. Maybe even good soldiers. And if that time comes and you prove yourselves worthy of the Second Legion, then and only then will you deserve to call yourselves proper legionaries. But that is only the beginning of the hard work. You see, ladies, the reputation of my beloved Second Legion has taken a bit of a battering since you and your camp prefect decided not to turn up for the match against Boudica and her lads. You missed a good one there. Very tight it was. But those of us who were there stood our ground and won the battle, while you lot fucked off back to Isca Dumnoniorum and hid under your blankets. That sort of thing ends now. You will restore pride to the Second Legion. You will make barbarians quake when they hear the name of the legion. You will win a fine reputation for the Augusta. Do I make myself clear?'

'Yes, sir!' came the ragged reply.

Macro snapped round and thrust the head of his vine cane at

the men. 'Bollocks! I can't hear you! Say it again. Loud enough for Boudica to hear it!'

'YES, SIR!' the recruits roared as one.

He smiled. 'That's better! You see, that makes me happy. Brings out my naturally sunny character. So let's be having more of that in the days to come!'

Striding over to the edge of the review platform, he saluted Cato. 'Second Legion detachment is standing ready, sir! Do you wish to address them?'

Cato took a deep breath before he called out, 'Do what Centurion Macro tells you. Do it well, and do it for the Second Legion Augusta and the Senate and people of Rome, in that order. You may dismiss the men, Centurion.'

Macro turned about. 'Second Legion! Dismissed!'

The legionaries stood to attention for the count of three and then relaxed and began to make their way off the parade ground, Agricola among them. The two officers watched the men passing by for a moment before Cato spoke.

'The introduction was delivered with your usual gusto, brother. What do you make of them?'

'There's not much difference between them and any of those that have gone before. To be sure, I have less work to do since they've been through basic training at the depot. There will be the usual mix of good men, troublemakers, skivers and whiners, but I'll have them in good shape before we lead them against the Icenians. There'll be a lot of hard work first, of course. To be honest, I'm getting a bit long in the tooth for this sort of thing.'

Cato smiled. 'I doubt it. You live for this. It's when you're at your happiest – turning boys into men and men into soldiers.'

Macro's reply was delivered with earnest cheerfulness. 'Absolutely, lad. I fucking love this life!'

CHAPTER TWENTY

Winter came with grey skies, cold rain and blustery winds that swirled the fallen leaves around and swayed the bare branches of the seasonal trees. Early frosts laced the ground and the buildings of the fort in gleaming white crystals and added a sharpness to the dawn air, whose first breath cut into the lungs. The world seemed to shrink back into itself and the sun struggled to break through the morning mist. There was a clarity to the landscape that appealed to Cato, and he rose as soon as it was light to walk round the fort, wrapped in his cloak, as he went over the business of the coming day and reflected on the preparations for the campaign.

The last of the reinforcements and replacements had arrived in the final days of autumn, by which time over four thousand men and a thousand horses were living within the walls of the fortress. The first of the mounted cohorts to arrive was tasked with guarding the supply wagons moving up and down the road from Londinium. In addition to the daily needs of the men and beasts under his command, Cato was building up stocks in the fortress's granaries, ready to feed his force when they marched into Icenian territory. Smoke rose daily from the blacksmith's forge as javelin heads, slingshot, sword and dagger blades and arrowheads were turned out in large quantities to replenish the stores that had been used up during the rebellion.

Macro's training regime continued, made still more testing by the cold and damp that was alien to most of the legionaries recruited from Italia. The replacements for the auxiliary cohorts were generally drawn from the regions to the north of the Empire, whose inhabitants were used to similar conditions, or worse. All quickly grew used to the discomforts of the climate and the clinging mud that persisted until the winter frost hardened the ground. Ice appeared in the horses' troughs and the cisterns built to contain the men's drinking water. It had to be broken with fists to start with, then, as the winter deepened, with picks.

Macro was challenged by the need to teach Vellocatus and his men how to respond to the notes of bucinas and cornus, and their position in the line of march. They were also issued with tents and had been shown how to erect them in lines. In addition there was the thorny issue of pay. Cato had to cover the cost out of his increasingly meagre resources before the governor, at length, gave his approval for the new unit, naming it the First Trinovantian Cohort of Scouts, even though it had grown to barely a hundred men as volunteers trickled in from Combretovium and the other tribal settlements. Vellocatus chose the image of a boar to serve as the emblem for the unit's standard, as the beast had been his father's favourite animal to hunt. Within a month, the Trinovantians had picked up enough Latin to respond to commands and thereafter to start fraternising with the Roman soldiers.

In order to reassure his tribal volunteers, Cato sent one of the auxiliary infantry units to garrison in Combretovium over the winter to ensure that the inhabitants would not be subject to another visit from the rebels. At the end of November, he took two centuries of legionaries and one of the mounted cohorts north to start construction of the line of outposts intended to contain the rebels. At the same time, two of the surviving cohorts of the Ninth Legion began work on the fortifications, starting from the sea and working south towards Cato's column. The governor supplied the necessary garrisons for the completed outposts from the units that became available as order was restored to the rest of the province. By the year's end, the Romans controlled the tracks into and out of Icenian territory. Once winter had passed and the seas off the east coast became less prone to storms and gales, the warships and marines would add to the strength of Cato's force and be available to launch attacks along the coast and up the rivers and waterways into the heart of Icenian territory.

When brief opportunities presented themselves for Cato and Macro to relax, they went hunting, with Pernocatus serving as their guide. Their prey was easier to see in winter conditions, and they returned from most trips with boar and deer to supplement the usual rations. Cato was even able to give Macro a short period of leave to celebrate Saturnalia with Petronella and the others in Londinium. He took with him letters written for Lucius and Claudia, along with small gifts of Trinovantian jewellery that Cato had bought in Combretovium. When he returned, full of cheer at being reunited with his wife, Cato listened to his account of his time in Londinium with a sharp pang of regret that his responsibilities made it impossible for him to share the occasion. His sense of regret was even more pronounced as he read and reread the letters Macro had returned with, in the privacy of his quarters. He had spent so little of his time with his son as Lucius had grown up, and the sense of a loss he could never recoup lay heavily on his heart.

The need for him to remain at Camulodunum was underscored by the reports of enemy activity from the cavalry patrols he regularly sent along the edge of Icenian territory. The enemy were making their own preparations in readiness for the next campaign season. Raiding parties frequently crossed into Trinovantian lands to seize grain hordes and livestock as well as weapons. There were frequent brushes with Roman patrols and casualties on both sides.

As the new year began, the first snow fell, a light dusting

overnight that covered the fort and the surrounding landscape in a virginal veneer. It contrasted starkly with all that lay exposed, as if there was only white and darkness in the world. The men emerged from their barracks for morning assembly rubbing their hands and stamping their feet on the hard-packed snow. Their exhaled breath coiled about their helmets and pinched faces as they were called to attention, presences and absences accounted for before they were dismissed to ready themselves for training or other duties. Small groups indulged in snowball fights between the barrack blocks until bawled at by their officers. Cato smiled at the delight that snow evoked, before he recalled the horrors of a winter retreat he had once endured in the mountains to the west of the province. That was an experience he fervently hoped never to repeat.

The winter was unusually bitter, with the temperature dropping below freezing, even during daylight, for almost the entire first month. With the bone-numbing cold came more snow. Sometimes it fell like small feathers, swirling lazily in the still air under looming clouds, muffling voices and all other sounds. Then there were the blizzards, carried on winds that hurled ice crystals into men's faces so forcefully that it felt like tiny pins pricking their exposed skin. Snow piled up against the buildings and walls of the fort and filled the ditch outside. Almost all definition of the topography was obliterated, so that it was hard to tell the distance between features. The prolonged cold soon dispelled the soldiers' delight in the snow. Foraging for wood had become much harder as they had to wade thigh-deep through drifts to get to the nearest trees and cut them down, then haul them back to the fort to cut up for firewood. Even with sledges and ponies it was exhausting work, and the wood had to be rationed to eke it out. The men in barracks were confined for much of the day in small rooms, eight in each, with bunks lining the timber and turf walls. Dressed in spare clothing and clutching their cloaks

232

about them, they were only permitted to light fires outside, due to the risks of cooking indoors.

The severe weather hampered lines of communication, so that the supply convoys struggled to get through to Camulodunum and Cato was forced to put the troops on reduced rations rather than work through the stores he had accumulated for the campaign. The men grumbled, and with regular exercise denied them, tensions between individuals, and between units, led to fights. Fights led to punishments and punishments bred resentment. Things came to a head one morning as Cato was doing the morning rounds of the rampart with Macro.

He paused mid stride on the walkway and cocked his head. 'What in Hades?'

Macro stopped beside him and listened a moment before he caught the angry shouts in the distance. The noise swelled and Cato scrambled down off the ramp at a trot.

'Come on!'

They ran through the barrack blocks towards the source of the din, and turned a corner to see the alley between two buildings filled with brawling soldiers.

'What the fuck is this?' Cato bellowed, but only those nearest to him broke off and edged aside with guilty expressions. He cupped both hands and called out again. 'Break it up!'

More men stopped, but the fighting continued at the far end. Macro raised his vine cane and charged through the crowd, knocking aside those too slow to get out of his path. When he reached the men still punching each other, he laid about him with his club.

'You fucking heard the prefect! Break it up! Now, you dozy bastards!'

The soldiers drew back among their comrades, and now Cato could see that they were from the legionary barracks and the auxiliary barracks on either side of the alley. They had all fallen

233

silent and were shuffling in the cold morning air until Macro bellowed at them to come to attention.

'Where are your officers?' Cato demanded.

Two men stepped forward from each century, bruised and bleeding from the exchange of blows.

Cato pointed to the ground in front of him. 'Here. On the double!'

They trotted over and stood in one rank before him. He assumed a furious expression.

'Since when has beating seven shades of shit out of comrades in the run-up to a vital campaign been a smart idea, gentlemen? If any of the enemy are spying on this fort, they'll be laughing themselves sick. You four are supposed to enforce discipline, not let your bloody men degenerate into a mob knocking chunks off each other. What have you got to say for yourselves? How did this nonsense start?'

'Just a minor disagreement, sir,' the auxiliary centurion said. 'Difference of opinion about the allocation of firewood.'

'A difference of opinion? If this is how you settle a difference of opinion, I can't wait to see what you do to the enemy when you really have to fight.'

Cato glared at them in turn and then turned to Macro. 'Centurion Macro, what punishment would you recommend for these fools?'

'Centurions demoted to optios, sir, and optios demoted to the ranks. We can't have officers allowing this sort of bollocks to occur.'

'No, we can't.' Cato saw the anxious looks on the faces of the four officers and the bitterness in their men either side of the alley. Such a punishment would only lead to recrimination, tensions and further blows being exchanged. 'However, I have a better idea. Have the general assembly sounded.'

Macro looked at him questioningly. 'Sir?'

'You heard me. I want all the men on the parade ground. Boots, tunics and cloaks only.'

The mid-morning sun was struggling to break through the clouds as the last of the units formed up on the parade ground. The legionary cohort, being the senior formation at the fort, occupied the place of honour on the right flank. The auxiliary cohorts were arrayed to the left, with the men from the auxiliary unit involved in the brawl immediately adjacent to them. Only the duty century remained in the fort, and a squadron of auxiliary cavalry formed a picket line a mile out, their dark shapes set against the snowy landscape.

Cato climbed onto the review platform to face his command.

'This morning,' he began, 'I encountered a disgraceful display of ill-discipline in the fort. Men fighting like dogs rather than soldiers. This cannot and will not be tolerated. Therefore, in order to set an example to the others in their unit, the men of each cohort will share in the disciplinary measures to be taken against those responsible for the fracas. I have decided that only a trial by combat will suffice, given the scale of the disgusting breach of discipline I witnessed. All other cohorts will retire to the boundaries of the parade ground!'

The centurions and optios relayed the order, and men trotted away to form a cordon two ranks deep along the edges of the open area so that only the legionaries and the men of the Tenth Cohort of Gallic Auxiliaries remained. A tense atmosphere settled across the snowy scene before Cato continued.

'Each cohort is to form up, fifty paces apart, facing each other!'

Before they even had a chance to hesitate, Macro bellowed, 'You heard the prefect. Move your arses! Move! Move!'

Once they were in position, Cato regarded them with a steely expression. 'This is a trial by combat. There will be no exchange of physical blows. Any man who does so will be on latrine duties until spring arrives. Victory goes to the side that causes their opponent to drop their standard. You may arm yourselves with snowballs only. Commence punishment!'

There was some nervous laughter from the units around the edge of the parade ground and confusion on the faces of the men facing each other.

'What the fuck are you waiting for?' Macro shouted, bending down to scoop up some snow, pat it into a sphere and hurl it at Tribune Agricola, who was the nearest of the legionaries. The snowball burst on his shoulder. He instantly recovered from his surprise and returned the shot, missing Macro by a good six feet.

'Tribune Agricola, sir,' Macro spoke in a dry tone, 'that was pathetic. What are the rest of you waiting for? Get stuck in!'

The men of both units were laughing now as they surged forward, and the air filled with snowballs flying in all directions as the two cohorts were cheered on by those around the edge of the parade ground. Macro turned to stride towards the reviewing platform to join Cato, and was instantly struck by half a dozen snowballs hurled by men from both sides. He let out a savage roar and turned to throw one back before scurrying out of range. He scraped the snow from his shoulders as he took station beside his superior.

'Well, that seems to have done the trick,' Cato observed as he watched the men bombarding each other. 'Taken the sting out of tensions in the fort nicely.'

'Indeed.' Macro nodded. 'A novel approach to discipline, but effective nonetheless.'

Every time a group of men from either side made a dash towards the opposing cohort's standard, they were quickly surrounded, pelted with snow and ice and driven back. The spectators were soon shouting themselves hoarse. Then the inevitable happened, as Cato had anticipated, and the first of the non-combatants joined in. Within a short time, the entire parade ground was an inchoate melee of men engaged in the novel form of trial by combat. There was no respect for rank, with the officers taking

236

the brunt of it and trying to cluster together to defend themselves in a desperately unequal struggle.

'How long shall we indulge this for?' asked Macro, grinning at the spectacle.

'If they don't wear themselves out first, give it half an hour and then form them up to return to the fort. With luck they'll have had too much fun and be too tired to start any more fights.'

'Let's hope.'

Cato's attention was distracted by one of the pickets riding down from the ridge to the west of the fort, sprays of white kicked up by his mount as his cloak flapped behind him. Then Macro saw him as well.

'Could be trouble, sir. Shall I put an end to it?'

Cato looked round at the other pickets, who were still in position. 'I don't think it's anything to do with the enemy. Let 'em go at it for now.'

He left the platform, giving the snowball fight a wide berth as he made towards the horseman. As the latter reached him, he reined in and caught his breath. 'Beg to report, sir. There's a mounted column coming up the road from Londinium.'

'Ours?'

'Yes, sir. Officers and escort.'

'How far off?'

'Couple of miles when I saw them. The decurion sent me to report. They'll be a lot closer now.'

'Very good. You can return to your post.'

The auxiliary saluted and turned to canter back up to the ridge. There was only one likely explanation for the approaching riders. Governor Suetonius had decided to pay the fort a visit.

Cato and Macro were waiting beside the track as Suetonius and his entourage approached. The governor returned Cato's salute, then he and his staff surveyed the mayhem of the snowball fight.

Some of the men had briefly turned to regard the approaching riders before returning to the fray, and the governor was largely ignored by those enjoying themselves.

'What's the meaning of this, Prefect?' Suetonius asked curiously. 'Can't say I am familiar with this form of assembly or weapons drill.'

'It's a matter of dealing with a minor disciplinary infraction, sir. I also saw it as an opportunity to get the men into the fresh air to enjoy some exercise.'

'They certainly seem to be enjoying it.'

'May I offer you the hospitality of my headquarters, sir?'

'Certainly,' Suetonius replied as he swung his leg over the saddle and dismounted. One of the staff officers edged his own horse forward to take the reins. The governor stretched his shoulders and rubbed his posterior. 'It's been a long, cold ride and I could do with something to eat and a fire to thaw out my arse.'

As they made their way towards the gate, he cast a professional eye over the defences. 'You've done a good job here, Prefect. Of course, such field defences are not going to serve much purpose when the campaign begins. I imagine you and your column will be moving so quickly you'll barely have time to throw up a decent marching camp each night.'

'I'm not sure Centurion Macro would tolerate anything slipshod, sir,' Cato responded in a light tone, and Macro muttered a crude affirmation under his breath.

Just then there was a burst of snow on the side of Suetonius's helmet. The little group stopped abruptly. Macro turned and filled his lungs to roar in the direction of the miscreant, but Suetonius cut in first. 'A moment, Centurion.'

He took a few steps towards the parade ground, his face fixed in a hard, uncompromising expression. The nearest of Cato's men shuffled back in anticipation of his wrath. Then Suetonius bent over, scooped some snow together, eased himself upright and threw it in a high arc. It disappeared into the throng, and he gave a nod of satisfaction before turning to rejoin his staff and escort. Cato raised a warning finger at the nearest men not to reciprocate.

Suetonius rolled his neck. 'Haven't done that in years.'

Cato breathed a sigh of relief, and was glad when they had passed through the gates of the fort and were well away from any further errant missiles.

The escort dismounted and took charge of the officers' horses while Cato ordered Trebonius to arrange for feed and stabling before preparing food for the visitors. The governor had brought six of his tribunes with him as well as a secretary, and the prefect's office was uncomfortably crowded as the men arranged themselves around the brazier to warm up. Suetonius made some general enquiries about the condition of the men and their readiness for the campaign. Then he announced that the warships assigned to support the operation would sail from their base on the south coast to Combretovium as soon as weather conditions permitted. In any case, they had orders to relocate to the town by the end of February at the latest. That last piece of information sparked off a rapid chain of thoughts in Cato's head as he tried to divine the real reason for the governor's presence.

Trebonius entered with a jug of heated wine and a tray with some plain samianware beakers and set them down on the desk. As the officers crowded round to help themselves to refreshments, the manservant glanced down at the snow and mud they had trodden across the floor and rolled his eyes disapprovingly before addressing Cato.

'I have a man preparing some stew, sir. Do you wish me to include the last of the venison?' His voice held the hint of a plea for Cato to deny the request.

'Yes, that will do very well.'

The sigh was audible. 'As you wish, sir.'

Once the door was closed, Cato asked, 'Will you and your men require accommodation for the night, sir?'

'No. We won't be staying long. Just long enough to assess your readiness and to issue your orders.'

'Orders?'

'There's been a change to our plans. Two days ago, a ship arrived from Gaul carrying our new procurator, Julius Classicianus, and Polyclitus, one of Nero's freedmen. Polyclitus has been sent by the emperor to report on conditions in the province and to determine if it is salvageable. That was the word he used,' Suetonius added bitterly. 'I reassured him that I was making good progress in restoring order across those areas where opportunists had used the rebellion as an excuse for lawlessness. Of course, the matter that he is most interested in is the final defeat and capture of Boudica. He has orders to bring her to Rome in chains as soon as possible. Emperor Nero is impatient to confront the barbarian woman who has caused him so much embarrassment and heartache. Polyclitus was adamant that Boudica be taken alive. Which means you taking every step to ensure that she is not harmed in the course of defeating what is left of her army.'

'Easier said than done,' Macro observed.

'Thank you for your considered opinion, Centurion,' Suetonius responded cuttingly. 'I am aware of the difficulties involved even if our friend from Rome is not. The fact remains, those are the emperor's orders. You can always take the matter up with him directly if you wish. No? Then I'll continue. Nero demands that we move against Boudica at once.'

'In the middle of winter?' Cato responded. 'In the middle of *this* winter? Surely Polyclitus understands that it is almost impossible to campaign in such conditions.'

'I am sure he understands, but his master in Rome does not. Nero's grasp of the realities of life outside the confines of his palaces and pleasure boats is rather limited.'

That Suetonius was willing to express such criticism in front of the gathering of officers was a measure of his frustration and disapproval, Cato realised. Any one of his tribunes might let his words slip when they wrote to their families or after they returned to Rome. If it should ever reach Nero's ears that one of his most senior officials had spoken so critically, the governor would be a marked man.

'How soon can you have your men ready to march against Boudica?' Suetonius asked.

Cato's mind raced to grapple with the details. He had made plans for the campaign, but they were based on the operation being conducted in spring, when the snow would have long since melted and the tracks and forests of Icenian territory would be negotiable. They also included the deployment of warships and their marines to control the coast and waterways. To take the fight to the enemy in the depths of winter represented orders of complication and difficulty that were hard to contemplate.

'Well?' Suetonius pushed him.

'Sir, we lack the supplies to support such an advance.'

'Then you will have to live off the land.'

Cato's mouth fell open at the crassness of the comment. But he understood the predicament his superior was in. Suetonius knew as well as Cato did the challenges of fighting in winter across hostile terrain. But he had been given his instructions and had to pass them on, no matter how sound the objections that could be raised against them. Anyone who directly defied the emperor's order, or even challenged its realism, might as well offer up his throat to the Praetorian death squad sent to deal with him.

'I can have the men ready to march within two days, sir.'

'Good. Let me know the moment you have taken Venta Icenorum and captured Boudica.'

'Captured, or killed, sir?'

'Captured, Prefect.' Suetonius fixed his eyes on Cato uncompromisingly. 'I advise you to do everything in your power to take her alive. Your life, and mine, might depend on that.'

241

CHAPTER TWENTY-ONE

On the march to Icenian territory

Two days after the governor had given them their orders, the men under Cato's command marched out of the fort at Camulodunum and followed the barely traceable track north to the lands of the Icenians. The other half of the cohort that had been sent to Combretovium was left behind to defend the fortress and the supply line to Londinium. It was immediately obvious that heavy supply carts were not going to manage the snowy conditions, and Cato ordered the engineers to remove the wheels and axles and fix runners beneath the wagon beds so that they could be drawn as sleds by their mule teams. As they departed, the snow was still thick on the ground and the temperature only rose above freezing for a few daylight hours, if at all. The Eighth Cohort took the lead under Macro, making slow progress through the knee-deep snow and barely crawling through the drifts they encountered before stopping to clear them away for the units that followed.

The limited progress was exhausting and by midday they had advanced no more than four miles. Cato relieved the Eighth Cohort and ordered Prefect Thrasyllus and his cohort to take over the role. Behind them the other units moved forward in fits and starts, forced to stamp their feet to keep them from going numb when the column was halted, then shuffling forward until the next order to halt was given.

As the afternoon grew dim, Cato ended the day's march on the edge of a large pine forest. A squadron of cavalry moved out to form a picket line to watch for the enemy. Meanwhile the infantry downed packs and started to clear the snow from a large rectangle marked out by the legionary engineers, then set to work breaking up the frozen ground to prepare the ditch and rampart. The work was not completed until two hours after sunset, and then the men had to erect their tents. Few had the energy to light fires and cook a hot meal. Most huddled in their cloaks and chewed on bread and strips of cured meat.

In his command tent, Cato was fortunate to have the light and warmth of a small blaze in the portable iron brazier that Trebonius had packed. Although the edges of the tent were securely pegged down and the flaps fastened, gusts of icy air still penetrated within, and Cato sat on his folding chair with an extra cloak around him, trying not to shiver.

'More wood,' he ordered. 'Build the fire up.'

Trebonius did as he was told from the small stock he had foraged from the forest while the marching camp was under construction. There was a cough from outside the flaps before Macro spoke.

'Permission to enter?'

'Come,' Cato replied.

The centurion fumbled with the pegs until he had opened a gap big enough to squeeze through and then hurriedly refastened them. He turned round, ruddy-faced, and smiled as he held his hands out towards the fire. 'Ah, now that's a welcome sight! It's cold enough out there to freeze the nuts off a statue.'

Cato cocked an eyebrow. 'Now there's one I haven't heard before.'

'I know. Just made it up.'

There was a brief pause in conversation as Trebonius added some split logs to the brazier.

'Six miles we've come, in my reckoning,' said Cato.

'Bloody pitiful.'

'At this rate it's going to take us ten days at least to reach Venta Icenorum. That's assuming there are no blizzards and the enemy don't try to hold us up. Which they almost certainly will.'

'Why is it so important to Suetonius that we take the place?'

Cato recalled the governor's final comments before he had set off for Londinium. 'It will look good when it is reported back to the emperor that we have captured the enemy capital.'

'Some capital!' Macro snorted. 'Just a large collection of huts clustered about a hall most senators wouldn't even keep their horses in.'

'Oh, you can be sure that by the time the message reaches Nero's ears, the Icenian capital will have turned into a city. You know how it is. Rome needs some good news, and those up the chain of command need to put a gloss on our achievements to win favour with their superiors. Every skirmish we report will be a battle won. Every enemy casualty will become a warband and every ten of ours will become one lightly wounded. Any retreat forced on us will become a regrouping before the next advance to victory.'

'Such cynicism, brother. In another life you could have been a historian.'

'Some historians might take exception over your view of their profession.'

'Not the ones who make money.'

Cato chuckled. 'Anyway, besides the propaganda value for the emperor, there are sound reasons for capturing Venta Icenorum. It will be a kick in the teeth for the enemy. If a Roman column can range that far into their territory and occupy their capital, that will surely damage Boudica's standing with her people and undermine any effort she makes to persuade other tribes to join her cause. It may even draw her into battle, and we can conclude matters there and then.'

'I doubt she'll play into our hands so easily,' Macro demurred. 'Not after the hiding the rebels got last time they risked a set-piece battle.'

'I agree. But I don't think she can afford to give the place up without some kind of fight. In any case, we'll take the town. It'll serve us well as a forward base for the rest of the campaign. I just hope we won't be extending our line of communications too far. I dare say there will be thin pickings in the area as far as living off the land goes. Especially at this time of year.'

Macro nodded. The enemy would be sure to adopt a scorched-earth policy in order to weaken the invaders. The column would rely on supply convoys which would be vulnerable to harassment as they passed through Icenian territory. The only counter-measure that would protect Roman supply lines would be to build a line of forts along the route and provide powerful escorts for the wagons and carts. All of which would leave far fewer men available to locate and attack Boudica's force.

'You could ask Suetonius for more reinforcements.'

'I think I've got as many as I was ever going to get,' Cato responded. 'And the governor will not accept any excuses if I fail.'

'So don't fail, lad. You haven't so far. No reason to start now.'

As ever, Cato was reassured, and a little unnerved, by his friend's faith in his abilities. Luck had played as much of a role in his past successes as sound judgement, he told himself. Any fool could be favoured by good fortune and credited with intelligent foresight when things turned out well. It seemed to Cato that when he succeeded, it was more than likely that most officers would have done the same in his place given the information and resources available. It just made sense to him to act as he had. There was no particular magic to it. At the same time, he was aware that he had acquired something of a reputation as a gifted officer and was respected by those above and below him. A respect he did not feel worthy of.

He offered his friend a reassuring smile. 'I'll do my best.'

Macro grinned back. 'I'd expect no less.'

For the next two days, the column struggled on. It snowed again the following night. Fortunately there was only the lightest of breezes to cause any further drifting, for that occasioned the longest delays. On the evening of the third day, the sky cleared and the moon shone with such intensity that it was possible to see clearly for miles across the surrounding landscape. The night air was sharp to the breath and the temperature lower than anything they had yet experienced. When dawn came and the sun rose into a cloudless sky, its faint warmth grew in strength through the day so that by noon the snow had begun to melt on the boughs of the pine trees and the bare limbs of seasonal species.

Four days after setting out from Camulodunum, the column had increased its pace and crossed into Icenian territory. Soon afterwards, they spotted the first sign of the enemy: mounted warbands on either flank, keeping pace with the marching Romans as they toiled across the snow-bound countryside.

Prefect Quadrillus came galloping up the side of the column, angrily ordering aside any stragglers who had fallen out. His face was bright with excitement as he reined in beside Cato, just behind the leading cohort.

'Sir! Have you seen?' He pointed out the nearer of the two enemy bands, a mile or so to their right, riding along a low ridge that ran parallel to the Roman column. 'I could take my cohort and chase down those villains. We could use a few prisoners to interrogate.'

'No. Leave them be.'

'But sir—'

'Look at the ground between us and them,' Cato cut in. 'There's deep snow there. Who knows what lies underneath? If you tried to cross it at any speed, you'd injure some of your horses and maybe throw some of the men. In any case, the enemy would be long gone before you got anywhere near them, unless they were luring you into a trap.'

Quadrillus looked over the ground and then across the column to the other enemy band, desperate for any excuse to go after them.

'Your time will come, Quadrillus.'

'Will it, though? I'll be quitting the army next year. This will probably be my last chance to distinguish myself.'

'You did your duty during the Mona campaign and you played your part in the defeat of the rebels. Surely there's no need to go glory-hunting after that? Why, man, you'll be dining out on stories of that battle alone for years to come.'

'Yes, sir.' Quadrillus looked chastened.

'Go back to your men and see that they keep their eyes open. They'll need their wits about them when they form the picket line when we make camp. We're in Icenian territory now. I don't want any nasty surprises.'

They exchanged a salute and Quadrillus wheeled round to ride back to his cohort.

'Bit eager, that one,' Macro observed.

'He is now,' Cato replied. 'He wasn't quite so keen to get to grips with the enemy during the battle. He might think he has something to make up for.'

'Ah, I see. Still, better late than never.'

Cato nodded. As he continued riding, he kept watch on the two enemy bands tracking them. Neither made any effort to draw closer nor to drop back to the sledges of the baggage train in the hope of pouncing on any gap that opened up or on any sledge team that fell behind. His standing orders for the advance were that the baggage train must be protected at all costs and that the progress of the rest of the men depended on the pace set by the sledges as much as by any obstacles in the path of the column. As it was, the enemy seemed simply to be observing them. Even if Boudica was not with either group, she would certainly be aware of the approaching Roman column very soon. What she did next would tell Cato a lot about her resolve and the scale and quality of the forces she had built up over the winter.

As the sun edged down towards the horizon, he saw a large area of open ground ahead of them, on a slight rise. He gave the order for the engineers to advance and mark out the campsite, accompanied by four squadrons of cavalry from the Eighth Cohort under the command of Tubero's replacement. Acting Centurion Pillatus had proved to be a diligent commander of his squadron, who embraced the cavalry officer's dictum of ensuring that the horses were looked after before the men and the men before himself. If he survived the campaign, Cato was determined to ensure that his permanent promotion was approved by Suetonius. The engineers' posts with their coloured strips of cloth fluttering from the top were in position as the weary infantry trudged onto the site, downed packs and set to work.

From his vantage point on top of a nearby hillock, Cato could see the enemy riders moving back the moment the Roman pickets rode forward. He had expected them to put up a fight against the Roman scouts and had Quadrillus ready with half his cohort in case they needed to rush to the aid of any of their mounted comrades. Just as the sun set and the blue hue of dusk settled over the landscape, he saw movement beyond the enemy band to his right. It was hard to be certain in the fading light, and he strained his eyes, to no avail. Yet he was sure there was a dark sprawl emerging from a forest no more than four miles away.

He rode down the slope to the senior centurion commanding the legionary contingent. Centurion Torcino was overseeing the raising of his tent by a section under the command of Agricola, who was berating one of the men.

'Not like that, you dopey bastard! If you keep pulling on that rope while the other men are hammering in the pegs, how do you expect the pole to stay straight?'

The two officers turned to salute as they saw Cato, while the men continued with their work. Cato dismounted and gently stroked his horse's neck as he spoke. 'Torcino, your cohort is on duty tonight.'

'Yes, sir.'

'I think we might be getting a visit from our Icenian friends once it's dark. From that direction.' He indicated the right flank. 'They will probably launch a diversionary attack on the opposite side of the camp before their main effort. I want your cohort stood to until midnight. If there's no attack by then, I'll have Thrasyllus's lads take over until dawn.'

Torcino gestured towards the perimeter of the fort, where the men were struggling to prepare the ditch and rampart. 'They're going to be all in after a day's march as it is. Several more hours on duty through the night ain't going to be fun.'

'I'm not asking them to enjoy it. Although if trouble does kick off, they might just enjoy turning the tables on the enemy. Isn't that so, Tribune Agricola?'

'Yes, sir.'

'I want four centuries ready for the main attack, if it happens,' Cato instructed. 'One on hand for the diversionary attack and one in reserve. Make sure you change the sentries hourly. We can't allow tired eyes and ears to miss anything.'

'Yes, sir.'

'If there's any sign of movement from the enemy, send word to my command tent at once.'

Cato woke in his tent as Trebonius gave his shoulder a gentle shake. It took a moment for his head to clear and for the happy dream of riding through a forest on a sunny day with Lucius

249

propped up on the saddle in front of him giggling hysterically to fade.

'What is it?'

'Message from Centurion Torcino, sir. A sentry reports movement to the east of the camp.'

'Right.' Cato sat up and swung his feet over the side of his travel cot. As he laced up his boots, Trebonius fetched his cloak and sword belt. A moment later, Cato emerged from his tent into the chilly air. Only a handful of clouds laced the sky, edged with silver by the three-quarter moon. Tribune Agricola saluted him.

'Movement?' Cato queried at once. 'What exactly?'

'The man said he heard voices and other sounds, sir.'

'Did he see anything?'

'No, sir.'

Cato looked round. The clear sky and the snow would make it very difficult to approach the camp unobserved. It was possible that the sentry's weariness had caused him to imagine what he had claimed to hear.

'Did anyone else hear or see anything?'

'No, sir,' Agricola replied, and Cato felt a surge of irritation that his badly needed sleep had been interrupted for a false alarm. However, he was not going to take any chances. 'All right, I'll come.'

'Do you want me to rouse Centurion Macro, sir?'

Cato hesitated. 'No. He'll be on his feet soon enough if anything happens.'

They made their way through the tent lines with their sounds of snoring and the occasional muttered exchanges of those unable to sleep. As they approached the side of the fort facing the east, Cato saw the dark lines of the legionaries who had been roused and now stood in silence, formed up with their shields and javelins grounded as they waited. Torcino was easy to spot thanks to the plume of his transverse crest. A legionary was standing beside him, and Cato returned their salutes as he strode up to them.

'Is this the sentry?'

'Yes, sir.'

He appeared to be a smooth-faced youth, and Cato hoped that Macro's training had toughened him up enough not to let his imagination run wild. 'What's your name, lad?'

'Marcus Saterllius, sir!' He had responded clearly, just as he was used to doing.

'Shh!' Cato hissed. 'Sweet Jupiter, man, your voice will carry a long way on a still night like this. Keep it down.'

'Yes, sir, sorry.'

'All right. Quietly tell me what you heard.'

'Voices, sir.' The legionary turned to point at an angle towards the nearest trees of a small forest not far from the foot of the rise. 'That way. And weapons. Well, metal on metal at any rate.'

Cato looked at him closely. He seemed alert enough. 'All right. Well done. Return to your post.'

As the legionary climbed back onto the low rampart, which was as high as could be managed in the frozen conditions, Cato turned to Torcino. 'If there is an attack, I expect the rebels will start with a diversion. Make sure you wait here until the real attack develops from the direction of that wood. Once they're within fifty paces of the ditch, get your men up on the rampart and give the bastards a volley of javelins. Even in this light they'll make an easy target.'

'It'll be quite the surprise.' Torcino grinned cheerfully.

'Indeed. Let's get up there and have a look.'

The three officers climbed the wooden steps of the rampart and joined the sentry. Cato scanned the forest but could not pick out any details. He was about to ask Saterllius to pinpoint the direction when the flat note of a horn sounded from the forest. At once there was a roar as the enemy warriors shouted their war cries, and an instant later dark shapes streamed out of the trees and began to surge up the snow-covered slope towards the ditch. As the last of them emerged, Cato saw that they could not amount to more than two hundred men at most. Too few to present any danger to those in the fort, and foolish to make such a racket and lose the opportunity to surprise the defenders. Yet he could not help admire their reckless courage. As they drew closer, Torcino bellowed the order for his men to man the rampart, and they surged up and took their places.

'Ready javelins!'

The legionaries braced their feet and drew back their right arms, angling the tips of the weapons up.

Torcino judged the best moment to unleash the volley, then shouted, 'Release!'

Men grunted with effort along the rampart, and Cato just managed to pick out some of the dark shapes of the javelins against the starry sky. It was impossible to hear impacts or the cries of any wounded due to the din being raised by the attackers. However, he saw several men go down, sprawling dark against the snow.

Torcino cupped his hands to his mouth and shouted along the length of the rampart. 'Let 'em hear it, boys! Up the Augusta!'

The legionaries echoed the cry, almost drowning out the shouts of their enemy. Some firmed up their nerves by clattering the flats of their blades against the trim of their shields as they waited for the Icenians to cross the ditch and charge up to the palisade. Several war horns were sounding from the rear of the enemy, adding to the cacophony, so that it was hard for Cato to make out what Tribune Agricola, a short distance along the rampart, was trying to say to him at first. The tribune was pointing back across the interior of the fort and shouting something.

Cato shook his head.

The first of the Icenians had reached the ditch and stopped there, hurling stones and small rocks up at the defenders. The puny missiles were easy enough to block with the heavy legionary shields, and only two men were injured before they took cover. The rattle of stones striking the shields made it even harder to make out the words as Agricola continued to point in the opposite direction to the attack. He pushed past Torcino and cupped a hand to Cato's ear, shouting into it.

'Sir! Listen! The other side of the fort.'

Cato strained his ears but it was impossible to make anything out. He descended the rampart and tried again. This time he heard it, the sound of cries of alarm from the far side of the fort, where the real attack was developing. The enemy had fooled him. They had timed their moment to perfection in revealing the men emerging from the forest whom Cato had spotted earlier. Only instead of reinforcing the warband he had expected to make the attack, they had quietly worked their way round to reinforce the band opposite and had launched their attack under cover of the din made by the diversionary force. It was neatly done, he conceded. Round one to the Icenians. The thoughts surged through his head in an instant. And then one further realisation. The sounds emanating from the far side of the fort were close to the baggage train park.

'Tell Torcino to take two of his centuries off the east wall at once and get over to the other side at the double. Go!'

Cato ran to the century that had been held back in reserve and ordered the centurion to follow him, then turned towards the supply sledges. All around him the men of the other units were emerging from their tents as their officers called them to rally on the standards.

'Out of the way! Out of the way!' Cato called as he ran through the tent lines at the head of the legionaries. Some were too slow to react and were thrust aside, tumbling into the snow or against the leather of their tents, and curses and insults followed Cato as he desperately struggled towards the far side of the camp. The din from the diversionary attack continued to sound louder than the noise from the main assault. He realised that the enemy to the west were deliberately restraining the Celts' usual habit of making as much noise as possible when they fought. Boudica had instilled some discipline in her men, he realised. At the same moment he saw that the units answering the call to arms were moving in the wrong direction, so that they were becoming more and more of an obstacle to legionaries thrusting their way across the camp.

'To the west rampart!' he yelled as he pushed forward. 'The enemy is to the west!'

The men, roused from sleep, were confused, and Cato's order competed with the counter-orders of the officers still responding to the diversionary attack. Stopping as he found an auxiliary centurion buckling on his helmet, Cato grabbed the man's arm.

'I am Prefect Cato,' he said, to ensure there was no mistaking his identity in the gloom. 'I want you to find as many other officers as you can and tell them to make for the western rampart. They are to ignore the noise to the east. Clear?'

'Yes, sir.'

'Then go, man! Run!'

He pushed on until at last he reached the open ground on the far side of the tent lines, close to the quarter where the sledges were packed tightly together, the mules tethered nearby. Along the rampart he could see the dark forms of his men fighting to defend the palisade. To his left, close to the baggage train, there was a dull glow from outside the camp, and then the first of the fire arrows and small bundles of blazing kindling arced overhead and dropped among the sledges with some overshots landing amongst the tents beyond. Cato turned to the centurion of the legionaries who had followed him across the camp.

'Get your men over to the baggage train and douse those incendiaries.'

'But we have no water, sir,' the centurion gasped.

'Then use snow. Beat the flames out with your cloaks. Piss

on them if you have to. Just don't let the baggage train go up in flames.'

He gave the man a shove and then stood aside to let the legionaries hurry past as the first flames licked up from one of the sledges. Making for the nearest section of the rampart, he saw one of the legionaries lying in the snow, moaning softly as he bled out from an arrow wound to his throat. Snatching up the man's shield, Cato scrambled up into a gap between the two nearest men. Now he saw the full scale of the attack. The rebels were all along the wall, hundreds of them. To his left, illuminated by their incendiaries, was a large group unleashing a constant barrage of arrows and small fiery faggots ignited by torches that in turn had been lit from the blaze that was now consuming the rear of a chariot. Before them, a mass of warriors was pressing up against the palisade, and Cato feared they must surely overwhelm the defenders there. Even though their attackers lacked the numbers to overwhelm those in the camp, if they managed to destroy the baggage train, the Roman column would be forced to retrace its steps in humiliation. Boudica would have won a significant victory.

As he slithered down the rampart, he saw a group of auxiliaries approaching, an officer at their head.

'Come on, lads!' a voice bellowed. 'Towards the flames!'

'Macro!' Cato called out in relief. 'On me!' He indicated the threatened stretch of the rampart. 'We have to hold that. Keep them out, or the baggage train is lost. How many men with you?'

'Perhaps fifty or so.'

'That'll have to do. Let's go.'

The two officers led the auxiliaries along the narrow gap between the rear of the rampart and the sledges. Legionaries were scooping snow onto the burning sledge and beating out the smaller flames on the fringes. There was a cry of alarm from the rampart.

'They're coming over!'

Cato saw a compact group of men locked in combat a short distance ahead, and in the moonlight he could make out the spiked hair and kite shields of the enemy warriors as they thrust aside the defenders and cleared space for more of their comrades to climb over the palisade. He drew his sword and pointed. 'There! Cut 'em down!'

He reached the spot at the same time as the first of the warriors slithered down the rampart, and the two men collided, shield to shield. At once Cato took a half-step back and then slammed his shield forward, throwing his full weight behind it. He heard the man grunt, and drove forward again, this time forcing his opponent back so that he stumbled and fell. The warrior tried to raise his shield to cover his upper body. Aiming the point of his sword at the man's face, Cato stabbed again and again until his foe lay prone, choking on blood and whimpering in agony.

Macro and several of his men pushed past and then turned to face the rebels coming over the rampart. Others had reinforced the defences and were forcing back the flanks of the small knot of Icenians fighting desperately to retain their foothold on the rampart. Cato joined Macro's group, bracing his legs and raising his shield as he held his sword level. A dark shape faintly rimmed with silver loomed above him and leaped forward. Cato thrust his sword up, feeling it tear into the warrior's guts an instant before his full weight slammed into Cato's shield, driving him to his knees. He heaved the shield to tip the man aside at the same time as he tore the sword free. The warrior, though wounded, hacked at the shield with his axe in a vicious flurry of blows that splintered wood and cut through the metal trim. Cato bore the brunt of the attack for a few heartbeats and then slashed his sword at his opponent's knee, cutting through the flesh to shatter the bone. The man fell to one side and Cato brought the edge of the heavy legionary shield down on the side of his head, knocking him cold. He stabbed him in the throat for good measure before recovering his position and facing the rampart once again.

To his left, Macro and the others had dispatched those attackers who had made it to the foot of the rampart and were now climbing up to finish off the handful still within the palisade. The struggle was over very swiftly, the last of them cut down as he tried to scramble back over to safety. Cato caught a bright blur above him and just had time to angle his shield up to deflect a fiery bundle of sticks. It landed beside him, away from the nearest wagon, and he turned his attention to the other incendiaries still arcing over the defences. There were fewer of them, he noted, and he hoped the enemy were using up their supplies. Behind him, the legionaries were fighting several fires among the nearest sledges. Most were being easily controlled and doused with snow. Only one presented any danger to other vehicles nearby, but Torcino and his men had surrounded it and were doing their best to smother the flames with snow.

'They're falling back!' Macro called out.

Cato went up to join him and saw the dark figures streaming back from the ditch outside the camp. The burning chariot used to carry the fire to light the incendiaries illuminated the surrounding snow for a considerable distance around. By its glow, Cato saw a group of warriors on horseback fifty paces further back, their faces ruddy in the firelight. One was a woman. He could see the patterns painted on her face, and the long tresses of red hair. She stared towards the flames within the fort for a moment, then turned her horse and led her followers away.

CHAPTER TWENTY-TWO

By the light of dawn, the scale of the damage done during the attack was assessed and Macro made his report to Cato as the men took down their tents and prepared to demolish the defences and make ready to march.

'Three sledges and their contents burned out. Ten more damaged but are being repaired. Most of the supplies loaded on them were saved. Eight dead, twenty-four injured, eight of whom are walking wounded. So far we have counted over fifty enemy bodies. I have to say, I'm getting more than a little worried by the way our Icenian friends have upped their game. First that trap in the village, and now this. The attack was well timed and the diversion cleverly executed. We were bloody lucky that they didn't get more men over the western rampart before we fought them off. I imagine their plan was to use the incendiaries by hand. It's only because we had that century of legionaries on the spot that they were forced to throw them into the camp. Just as well you had Torcino's men stand to.'

'Yes, but most of the men were on the wrong side of the camp and the rest were heading in the wrong direction once the attack went in.'

'It was close, I agree, but I'd say we got off relatively lightly, considering how things could have gone.'

'That's down to Agricola. If his ears hadn't been sharp enough to pick up on the main attack, we'd have lost far more of the baggage train. And many more men.'

'Good for him. Maybe it's time we gave him a little more responsibility. He's earned it. One of the casualties was Centurion Torcino.'

'Torcino? Last time I saw him was after the enemy had been driven off. What happened?'

'Slipped and went head-first into the flames. Got himself burned quite badly before his men pulled him out.'

Cato winced. He himself had suffered bad burns many years before, when he was an optio, and could imagine the agony Torcino was enduring. He turned his thoughts back to what Macro was suggesting.

'You think he's ready to take over Torcino's century, and the legionary cohort?'

Macro nodded. 'He's smart, he's got guts and he understands the men. They'll follow him willingly. To be honest, he's more than a cut above the senior tribunes I've dealt with in the past. Reminds me a bit of you when you got your promotion to the centurionate. He might have the makings of a good general if he chooses to make a career in the army rather than the Senate.'

Cato considered his friend's suggestion. Agricola would be much younger than most of those who won promotion to the centurionate, but youth should never be a disqualifying factor when all the other qualities required for the rank were present. 'Very well. You've been training him, so I'll let you tell him. Make sure he understands what's expected of him from now on. It's a big responsibility and I'll be watching him closely.'

'Yes, sir. It'll be my pleasure.'

As the sun rose, the temperature was appreciably less cold and Cato saw that the branches of the trees were starting to drop their snowy burdens, the boughs giving a little shiver as the white clumps dropped to the ground. The clouds cleared early in the morning, and for the first time in many days, the men felt the warmth of the sun as they trudged on. By mid afternoon, the churned snow was turning to sludge as the column passed over it, and the mule teams began to slow as the sledges became harder to pull. Cato decided that it would be time to replace the runners with wheels when they made camp that night. They were now well within Icenian territory, and by his reckoning they should reach Venta Icenorum by the following evening.

The enemy had resumed their stalking of the convoy, only now there were many more of them, perhaps three or four hundred mounted men on either flank. Cato ordered the column to close up, with his two cavalry cohorts on either side while the mounted contingent of the Eighth Cohort formed the vanguard. The rear was covered by Vellocatus and his men. The arrangement slowed the column down, as their pace was governed by the slowest element, but it afforded the best protection to the vital supplies carried by the baggage train. All day the Romans watched the enemy warily, waiting for any sign that they were preparing to attack.

When the column halted for the night and prepared its defences, Cato doubled the number of men on duty and threw out a screen of cavalry with orders to ride back and raise the alarm at the first sign of danger. Satisfied that he had made the camp as secure as possible, he retired to his tent, determined to get some sleep to help him recover from the nervous exhaustion of the last few days. He found Agricola waiting for him outside. He had a centurion's helmet and a fine cane tucked under his arm as he stood to attention and saluted.

'At ease.' Cato nodded at the helmet. 'Where did you get hold of that?'

'It belongs to Torcino, sir. He had one of the men bring it to me when he heard that I had taken over the cohort. Only on loan, though. Same goes for the vine cane. Until he recovers and resumes command.'

'A nice gesture,' Cato noted. 'You should feel honoured.'

'Yes, sir. I do.' Agricola regarded the helmet with a reverent expression. 'Now I have some idea what it takes to earn this.'

Cato regarded him sympathetically. 'You seem reluctant to put it on, Tribune.'

Agricola gave an awkward smile. 'Well, yes. I'm not sure I have earned the right.'

'Centurion Macro thinks you have. His judgement is good enough for me. How is Torcino doing?'

Agricola's smile faded. 'He . . . he doesn't look good, sir. The surgeon says he's lost the sight in one eye. His face and arms were badly burned. Phrygenus did not seem very confident about him recovering enough to return to duty for a while . . . if at all.'

'That's too bad. He was a good centurion of the old school. We need officers like him. And now you're going to step up and take his place.'

'Yes . . .'

'Was there anything else?' Cato asked as he opened the tent flap, indicating that he was keen to dismiss Agricola.

'I just wanted to say thank you, sir.'

Cato smiled. 'You may not feel grateful for long. Commanding a unit is a more thankless task than those who seek it realise. Make sure you listen to the advice of the other centurions and your optios. Some of them are veterans. They know what they're about.'

'Yes, sir. I will.'

'Goodnight then.'

Agricola saluted and turned to stride away. Cato regarded him with a touch of nostalgia as he disappeared among the tents, recalling the moment when he himself had first been awarded his transverse crest and vine cane. It seemed so long ago. Almost another lifetime. He wondered if in twenty years' time Agricola

261

would be standing watching another junior officer take the first steps towards high command. For the first time, Cato felt old. He was a generation apart from the new recruits and the young men who led them. He had long since been comfortable with the idea that he was a veteran, but this was new. The burden of years and the harsh regime of the army had hardened him, but now he had an understanding of how Macro had been feeling in recent years. The sense that time in uniform was limited and there was less of it ahead than behind. Perhaps when the campaign was over he would have time to rest and reflect on whether he should hang up his sword. For a while at least.

He entered the tent and let the flaps fall into place. Trebonius had made up his campaign bed and laid some spare cloaks over it, and the gentle flames licking up from the brazier had taken the edge off the cold night air. The manservant appeared from the much smaller section of the tent that he occupied. He helped Cato take off his armour and handed him one of the cloaks.

'Will you be requiring anything before you sleep, sir?'

'Just another ten years of youth.'

Trebonius looked puzzled for an instant, then nodded. 'If I could find that for you, I'd be the richest man in Rome, sir. But . . .'

'I know. Then I shall just have to make the most of the time that is given to me by the gods. Go. Get some sleep.'

'Yes, sir.'

With the improvement in the weather and the thawing snow, the column made much better progress until a new problem emerged in the form of mud. It did not unduly hinder the experienced infantry and cavalry, but began to suck at the newly replaced wheels of the heavy supply wagons. At noon, Cato summoned Macro, Quadrillus and Vellocatus. To the third he posed a question.

'I make it around ten miles to Venta Icenorum. What's your estimate?'

Vellocatus took a moment to convert his people's measure of distance into the Roman equivalent. 'No more than six or seven, Prefect.'

Macro considered this. 'We could make it before the day is out. Even if we have to fight for the place, it would spare us having to put up a camp.'

Cato mulled over the options. 'All right. I'll take Quadrillus and Vellocatus's cohorts on ahead to see what preparations the enemy have made. Macro, take command of the column. Keep the pace up as best you can. The sooner you reach Venta Icenorum the better. Especially if we have to fight for the town. If it looks like there's no chance of taking it today, I'll send word for you to make camp.'

'Yes, sir.' Macro nodded. 'Would it be better to take both auxiliary cavalry units with you?'

'No. There'll be enough of us to fight our way out of any trouble. Besides, you'll need mounted men to discourage any raids the enemy might attempt.'

'As you wish.'

Cato looked round at the other officers. 'All being well, our lads will be sleeping in cosy Icenian huts tonight and feasting on their food!'

The mounted column set off at a steady trot, with Vellocatus's scouts leading the way a few hundred paces ahead of Cato and Quadrillus's cohort. They quickly drew ahead of the main column, which was lost to sight after the track rounded a gentle hill.

Cato was intrigued to see how the enemy would respond to the division of the Roman forces, and soon had his answer. One of the parties of rebel cavalry appeared on their right flank, with no sign of any riders to their left. At the same time, he saw a small group detach themselves and gallop off to the north.

'I don't think we'll be catching them by surprise,' Quadrillus observed drily.

'There was never any chance of that,' Cato replied. 'But we might at least catch them less prepared when the mounted column arrives in front of the town.'

'You intend to attack before Macro arrives?'

'We'll see.' Cato glanced at him. 'I thought you cavalry types were all about dash?'

'There's dash and there's rash, sir. The trick of it is telling them apart.'

'Fair enough.'

Two hours after leaving the main column, one of Vellocatus's scouts came galloping back to them.

'The town is in sight, sir. Vellocatus has halted about a mile away, just beyond those trees.'

'Very good. Any sign of an enemy force?'

'Yes, sir.'

'How many?'

The Trinovantian shrugged. 'Many. More than many.'

Cato sighed inwardly and made a mental note to have Vellocatus train his scouts to estimate numbers in a way that extended beyond their ability to compare them to their largest flock of sheep.

'Let's take your men forward, Quadrillus.'

He led the way as the auxiliaries rippled forward into a canter, quickly closing the distance to the gap in the trees where the track crossed the crest of the hill. On the far side the ground opened out onto snow-blanketed farmland on either side. About a mile further on lay Venta Icenorum, a sprawl of hundreds of round huts of various sizes surrounded by a sturdy-looking oval stockade perhaps quarter of a mile across. In the centre of the settlement was an inner compound dominated by the hall of the Icenian rulers. Between the Roman force and the town the enemy had formed a battle line, made up of some five hundred infantry, with a hundred cavalry on either flank.

'Not enough to threaten us, but just enough to deter us,' Cato mused.

'Until the main column comes up,' said Quadrillus.

'Quite. So I wonder what they are planning to do. Surely they can't mean to make a stand with just those men?'

'There's more of them in the town, sir.'

Cato saw bands of men, some armed with spears, moving between the huts and wondered if this was yet another trap. Did the structures conceal many thousands of Boudica's rebels, waiting to spill out and surround the Romans? Then he noticed something else. A dark column some distance to the north-west of the town. His pulse quickened as he estimated their number to be in the thousands. Then he saw that they were moving away from Venta Icenorum. His gaze snapped back to the figures within the palisade, and it was then that he noticed there were no women, children or livestock to be seen. Moreover, there were only a handful of traces of smoke from hearth fires within the town.

'They're abandoning the place. Look there. That's the civilian population fleeing.'

Quadrillus squinted and then gave a grin. 'You're right. Excellent. I dare say our men will be rubbing their hands at the prospect of having a decent shelter to sleep in tonight.'

'I imagine so,' Cato replied. 'But they might have to fight for it first.'

There were warriors emerging from the town gate to join those formed up outside. They extended the line as parties of mounted men and even some chariots came in from the surrounding countryside and formed up on the flanks. Soon there were as many as a thousand men facing Cato and his mounted column.

Quadrillus was uneasy. 'Sir, perhaps it's time for us to rejoin the main column.'

'I don't think so. They're not making any move towards us. All the same . . .' Cato turned to Vellocatus. 'Send some of your men to patrol the treeline on either flank. If they spot anyone in the forest, they're to report back at once.'

'Yes, sir.' Vellocatus nodded and rode over to his scouts to issue the orders.

When there was still no sign of movement from the enemy, Cato gave the order for his men to dismount and stand by their horses.

'Why don't they attack?' Quadrillus demanded. 'They must know that the main column is still some miles back.'

'What would be the point? They know we'll just turn about and ride off if they make a move towards us. It would be a wasted effort. All the same, it's interesting to see that Boudica has instilled sufficient discipline in them to prevent any hotheads trying to get at us. They are definitely getting better at this. Thanks be to Jupiter that they didn't learn such lessons before the rebellion kicked off. The situation might be very different if they had.'

The winter sun had begun to sink towards the horizon and Cato estimated there was no more than two hours of daylight left. Another small group of chariots had joined the enemy massing in front of them, and as it proceeded along the line, the warriors cheered and brandished their weapons. Boudica was standing on the leading chariot, spear raised as she returned their greeting.

'What I would give for a battery of bolt-throwers right now,' said Quadrillus. 'It's long-range, but a couple of volleys would pick her off.'

Cato did not dignify such wishful thinking with a reply, but he watched Boudica closely as she paraded before her warriors. They fell silent as she addressed them with much waving of her spear. She was too far away for her words to be heard, but the periodic cheers and jeers of her men in response were proof that they were in good spirits and ready to put up a fight. Although

266

the odds would be in his favour when the rest of his men reached the scene, Cato was not keen on starting an engagement as the daylight failed. Vellocatus's scouts had not reported the presence of any rebels on either flank that might indicate another ruse by the enemy, but night actions were fraught with danger, and Cato willed Macro to arrive as swiftly as possible.

A moment later, one of the optios rode up from the rear with the welcome news that the main column was approaching. Shortly afterwards, Cato greeted Macro briefly before the latter ordered the deployment of the Eighth Cohort a short distance down the slope. One by one the other units came up and positioned themselves on either flank, with the cavalry forming up last of all. Thrasyllus's cohort remained to the rear, to act as the reserve and also to guard the baggage train. By now, the sun was just above the horizon and long shadows stretched out across the snow as the temperature dropped. Cato moved down the slope to join Macro, who was standing beside the colour party, shield to hand.

'Just give the order, sir.'

Cato was ready to do so, but a nagging doubt suggested that this was all too easy. Why would Boudica risk a set-piece battle when she was at such a disadvantage in terms of numbers, and given her previous experience of the danger of fighting on Rome's terms?

His speculation was interrupted by the sound of a war horn. Three short blasts, but no more, unlike the constant blaring that traditionally accompanied an attack by a Celtic army. Behind Boudica, her infantry turned away and began to file off around the settlement. The cavalry closed up behind the chariots.

'What in Hades is she playing at?' Macro growled.

Beyond the diminished enemy line Cato could just make out men moving amid the huts, and the twinkle of torches. They rapidly proliferated as the Icenians lit scores of them. One by one the structures were set on fire, and soon the Iceni capital was a sea

267

of flames and billowing smoke and the bloody red hue contested the gathering icy blue gloom of the coming night. Boudica's chariots rumbled away, escorted by her cavalry, following the retreating infantry and the distant civilians. The Romans were left to look on in awe as the fire spread and consumed the round huts. In the very heart of the blaze, the royal hall was consumed by an inferno before the roof collapsed in an explosion of sparks and brilliant flashes of lurid yellow and orange.

'Quite the spectacle,' Macro said in a hushed tone.

The last glimmer of the setting sun died on the horizon and every man in the Roman ranks felt his heart sink at the thought of another night in the open and the frustration of the campaign dragging as the enemy refused to stand and fight. Cato's gaze remained fixed on Boudica and her escorts until they were swallowed up by the twilight. He nodded in salute to her ruthlessness. She had waited until all his men were gathered to watch the immolation of Venta Icenorum and any hope of the shelter it afforded to them. He could sense the heavy blow she had struck against the morale of the soldiers around him.

Boudica had wanted to teach both the Romans and her own people a lesson by waiting until the last moment before having her capital fired. The message was clear. The Icenians would leave nothing behind. This was now a war of complete destruction. Whichever side claimed victory would raise its standard over a wasteland of smoking ruins and the bodies of the fallen.

CHAPTER TWENTY-THREE

The thaw continued over the days that followed, and patches of grass and soil began to appear across the landscape. It became easier to break up the ground, and Cato ordered the construction of a fort outside the burned-out sprawl of round huts that was all that remained of the Iceni capital. The dismal scene was all too redolent of that at Camulodunum and he was reminded of a saying from some religious text he had once encountered in Judaea – 'an eye for an eye'. How well that fitted the cycle of death and destruction that the rebellion had inflicted on the province of Britannia.

Once the fort was completed, the men were rested for a day while they cleaned their kit and repaired boots and other items that had suffered during the harsh conditions of the advance. It was also an opportunity to wash and dry clothes around fires fed with timber, easily foraged from the remains of Venta Icenorum. The cavalry units were sent out to scout the surrounding area and search for food and prisoners to question, but even when they found inhabited farms and villages, there were lean pickings. No attempt was made to attack the mounted units, and the only sign of the enemy was the distant parties of horsemen keeping the Romans under observation.

Cato was keenly aware of the governor's demand for the campaign to be concluded as soon as possible, but there was no question of blundering about trying to pin down an elusive enemy while operating at the end of a precarious line of communications stretching back to Londinium via the fort at Camulodunum. Suetonius's instruction to live off the land was not going to be possible to follow. As soon as conditions had improved, Cato sent the empty wagons back, escorted by Quadrillus and his men. It would take at least ten days for them to return with fresh supplies. If it rained, that time could easily double and the column would have to go on reduced rations until the next convoy arrived. He wondered if the rebels were suffering from similar privations, or whether they were able to be fed off whatever they could glean from the farms and settlements still under their control.

The river at Venta Icenorum was navigable as far as the sea, and Cato sent a message to the garrison at Combretovium to watch for the arrival of the warships and Besodius's cargo ships. If the merchant put his vessels at the service of the army, Cato's column could more easily be resupplied from the sea. Just one cargo ship could carry the equivalent of fifteen wagonloads and deliver the supplies in half the time it took overland, and without the added burden of having to carry feed for the draught animals.

At the same time, Cato was drawing up the plans for the next phase of the campaign now that Boudica appeared to be avoiding battle on open ground. One fine morning, two days after the construction of the fort, he called a conference of senior officers in his command tent. He had drafted a map of the region, including the coastal layout based on the notes from his reconnaissance voyage the previous autumn. The map now hung to one side of the tent from a frame Trebonius had crafted. Cato used a vine cane to illustrate the main features as he addressed the officers.

'As you can see, Venta Icenorum is situated in the heart of enemy territory. From here we can strike in any direction. We also control the western frontier of Iceni territory, and once the weather moderates, the navy will control the coast and the rivers.

That's all very well, but the direction the enemy retreated in leads me to think that they are falling back on a base in this area here.' He paused to indicate a large blank area on the map. 'I have learned that it has the name Lyngomara and that it is surrounded by marshes, with one narrow track that leads to the island upon which the settlement is built. Other than that, I have no details.'

'If there's only one approach, and it is as difficult as you say, then it's going to be a tough one to crack, sir,' said Prefect Thrasyllus. 'A small force could hold off an army many times the size of our column. Even if we had a decent artillery train, it would be difficult to get in position, and we couldn't bring enough weapons to bear to make much of an impact in any case.'

'That is all true, but you are only looking at this from one side. A single route into their base means it is as much a trap for them to get out of as it is a challenge for us to enter. Besides, from what I saw of the area, there are plenty of channels through the marshes that a boat, and possibly a craft as big as a liburnian, can negotiate. If that's the case, we can use such vessels as artillery platforms and to land marines and our men. Once the navy arrives, we'll have a chance to penetrate the waterways of the marsh.'

One of the other prefects, a narrow-faced officer with an aloof manner, leaned forward. 'What does our Trinovantian friend know about this place? Let's not forget that his tribe was allied to Boudica less than a year ago.'

Cato had never warmed to the man and did not like his tone now. 'Why don't you ask him, Prefect Fulminus? He's sitting just there.'

Fulminus glanced at Vellocatus, who sat stiffly, arms folded. 'Well, Vellocatus? What do you know of Lyngomara? Do tell us.'

The Trinovantian shot him a withering look before he gave his answer to Cato in his own tongue. 'I know little more than you, sir. Lyngomara is not just a settlement. It is where the Druid cult of the Iceni tribe has its sacred grove. Such places are kept secret from outsiders for a reason, particularly after the Romans came to our shores. I would be surprised if its location was known to more than a fraction of Boudica's people. I have certainly never been there. Nor has any Trinovantian that I know of. I give you my word of honour that is the truth.'

'I believe you,' Cato reassured him before translating his words to the other Roman officers. Fulminus still looked sceptical as he responded.

'Well, if this man will not help us, we will need to find a member of Boudica's tribe who does know the location of the place. If we can capture some of the locals and hand them over to our interrogators, they'll give up the information soon enough.'

'Did you not listen, Fulminus? Boudica's stronghold is in a location unknown to most of her people. If we start torturing Icenian peasants, we'll be none the wiser and more hated than ever.'

'Does it matter what these barbarians think of us? The Icenians lost any right to be treated fairly when they rose up against us, burned our towns and butchered our people. It's no secret that the governor would happily condone the extermination of the entire tribe.'

'That is not official policy,' Cato responded sharply. 'When this is over, we'll need to rebuild the east of the province. If we wipe out the Icenians, how much more difficult will that task be? More to the point, the Iceni people are fine farmers and horse breeders. As such they represent a rich source of taxes for the provincial treasury. I'm sure an educated man such as yourself knows enough about finance to grasp that it is not sound economics to start slaughtering the Empire's taxpayers. If you disagree, feel free to make your case to the emperor when you are next in Rome.' Cato glared at the other officer, challenging him to respond.

Fulminus stirred uncomfortably. 'Sir, that is hardly fair. I do not mean to question imperial policy.'

'That is wise of you. I will not go about torturing peasants to death for information they cannot provide me with. If we capture some warriors, that's different. However, as you may have noticed, they have been keeping their distance since the attack on our camp. But we do need to locate Lyngomara, I agree.'

'And what happens if we do, sir?' Thrasyllus asked. 'What if we locate it and there are no navigable approaches? Just the track you mentioned. Do we try and starve them into submission?'

'That might be an option, if the governor allows us the time to see it through. But he wants Boudica defeated as soon as possible. Besides, it's likely that she has not been idle over the winter. The scarcity of food discovered by our foraging parties suggests she has been amassing stockpiles of supplies to feed her warriors. It might take months to starve the enemy into surrender. Maybe even years. Added to which we'd need to set up siege lines to ensure that they remained bottled up. That's tough enough in decent terrain. I've no experience of attempting it in the middle of an expanse of marshland, and I don't know of any commander who has. Chances are that the enemy will know the ground well enough to get supplies through our blockade.' Cato scratched his head. 'It's likely that we will have to launch a direct attack on their defences when the time comes.'

'It won't be the first time we've gone in head-first,' said Macro. 'Remember those hill forts we took in the early years of the conquest? They were pretty formidable-looking, but they didn't keep us out for long.'

'I remember them well. But we were able to make good use of our artillery to soften them up. We won't be able to do that over the ground we'll be advancing along here. This is a much tougher proposition.' Cato paused. 'But I'm getting ahead of myself. We have to find Lyngomara first. I have an idea how we might go about it. The key to defeating Boudica depends as much on undermining the rebels from within as it does on bringing

273

our strength to bear on them in battle. I believe that her decision to burn Venta Icenorum was intended to deny its inhabitants the opportunity to surrender to us. If they'd done so and weren't treated badly by us, that would set an unfortunate example, as far as she is concerned, to other settlements. The Icenians might well ask themselves why they should remain loyal to a queen determined to continue a war she cannot win. If the choice is between the hardships of a forlorn cause or accepting peace on our terms, I dare say many will go for the latter. And where one settlement goes, others will follow. That will bleed Boudica of recruits and supplies. At some point there will be dissent among those who are loyal to her now. When that happens, we shall find the man who will lead us to her secret lair.'

'That may be if rather than when, sir,' said Fulminus. 'In any case, when the governor briefed me before I joined your command, he was clear that we were to show no mercy to the rebels. He made no mention of showing them the kind of leniency you are suggesting.'

'We know that, but the enemy doesn't. Boudica is aware that I prefer negotiation over bloodshed. So let her think that she needs to terrorise her people in order to discourage them from dealing with us. It will only make matters worse for her. At the same time, hunger will be a useful weapon for us. Assuming she has stripped the villages and farms of food for her warriors, and our men are taking what is left, the Icenians will want to know why their families are hungry. Why she is starving them. I can think of nothing more likely to sway someone's mind than fear for the lives of their children. As for what the governor may have said to you, I am acting in accordance with his orders. I will show no mercy to Icenian rebels, but that leaves a certain amount of latitude concerning those Icenians who choose not to be rebels.'

'I think you are deliberately misinterpreting his order, sir,' said Fulminus.

'The chain of command runs through me, Prefect Fulminus. I am obliged to act on my understanding of the orders given to me by the governor. Just as you are obliged to obey my orders. It is not for either of us to imagine what is in the mind of the governor. Do you understand?'

'Oh, I understand you, sir. Whether the governor will is a different matter.'

'If we defeat Boudica, I think you will find that your concerns over interpretation of orders will become irrelevant.'

'And if we don't defeat her?'

'Then I imagine someone like you will replace me.'

There was an awkward silence before Cato continued. 'For the moment, we keep foraging for food and we destroy what we cannot carry away, but we don't inflict any violence on the Icenian peasants unless they resist. Every effort will be made to capture enemy warriors and bring them back to the camp to interrogate them for information that will lead us to Boudica's hideout. For your peace of mind I will ensure that your orders are given to you in writing and leave as little room as possible for misinterpretation. Does that satisfy you, Prefect Fulminus? If we are successful, the orders will be available for that day when you have some scribe write your memoirs. If I fail, I am sure you will be delighted to have kept the receipts.'

Fulminus nodded. 'Precisely.'

Cato sat down behind his desk. 'That concludes matters for this morning, gentlemen. Dismissed.'

The officers saluted and shuffled out of the tent. Macro remained behind and made a face at Cato. 'You're going to have to watch that one.'

'Prefect Fulminus?'

'I don't trust him. He wants to be the governor's blue-eyed boy.'

'He's just ambitious. Something that all officers should be.'

'I have no problem with that, as long as he achieves his ambitions without pissing all over yours. I'd be careful if I were you, lad. I know his kind. He's a thruster. He'll do whatever it takes to win the approval of his superiors and get promoted. He's dangerous.'

'Only if I make a mistake. And I don't intend to do that.' Cato yawned and rolled his neck, then winced when it gave a soft crunch. 'And if I do make a mistake – nothing fatal, mind you – what's the worst that can happen? I get stripped of my command and retire to my modest estate outside Rome to live out my life in peace. I could use the rest.'

Macro smiled. 'I know you. You'd be bored out of your fucking mind within a month. Before the first year was over you'd be begging the emperor for a new command. Somewhere on a far-flung frontier as close to danger, and as far from politicians, as possible.' He gestured at the tent around them. 'You live for this. Just as I do. There'll come a time when we're too old for it. When we can no longer keep up with younger men. When our bodies start to weaken and our enemy finally gets the better of us and knocks us on the head. Or our weakness becomes a source of humiliation. That's when we accept that our time has come, and only then do we retire from the army.'

Cato considered his friend's words. 'You know me well, brother. But that time is closer for you than for me. If it wasn't for the rebellion, you'd be living out your days with Petronella in Camulodunum, hunting, drinking and swapping tall tales with other veterans.'

'I thought I was ready for that,' Macro reflected. 'But in all honesty – and as much as I love my Petronella – I'd rather be here with you and the rest of the lads doing what we do best. Some of us are born to this life. What's the sense in pretending otherwise?' He raised his sword arm and flexed his bulky bicep. 'As long as I'm up to the job, I'll keep at it. I know that I may not have many years left before I'm forced to quit, so I'll make the most of that time.' His mood changed. 'You know, of all the enemies we've faced – Germanians, Parthians, Numidians, Judaeans and all the wild-eyed Druids and barbarians of Britannia – I've feared none of them as much as I fear time. That is the greatest enemy of all.'

Cato nodded. Although it was a commonplace sentiment that Macro had expressed, it was no less true for all that. It struck Cato then that he was at a turning point in his own life. Up until now he had lived it looking forward, with thoughts of all the things he could do when time permitted. He had been too complacent about the span of his life, despite the quotidian perils of being a soldier. Now, when he had pause to reflect, it seemed that every day counted and was not to be rushed through in order to get to the next. He was in his late thirties. Even allowing for good health and being spared the dangers of the battlefield, he was halfway through his life. There were likely more days behind him than lay ahead, and he felt as if he had squandered so much time already. That sense was most acute when he considered how little of his life he had spent with his son and, more recently, Claudia. He was suddenly overwhelmed by the need to be with them, free of the duties that weighed upon him. To have that moment of calmness when time ceased to be your enemy and you became grateful to have time at all.

Both men had been occupied by their thoughts. Now they were aware of each other again and felt slightly guilty about such self-indulgence when there was work to be done. Macro broke the silence.

'I'd better be getting on, sir. I'm leading one of the patrols today. I need to make sure my lads are ready.'

'Yes. Keep your eyes open. Send Trebonius to me.'

They exchanged a nod and Macro ducked out of the tent, leaving Cato alone. He folded his hands behind his head, closed his eyes and stretched his back.

'Sir?'

He stirred to see Trebonius standing on the threshold.

'You sent for me?'

'I need you to take down my orders. Get a waxed tablet.'

As Trebonius prepared, Cato cleared his mind and concentrated on framing his words so that they would be as unambiguous as possible and thereby spare Fulminus the effort of twisting them to suit his own purposes.

CHAPTER TWENTY-FOUR

On the road to Camulodunum

A month had passed since the burning of Venta Icenorum, and winter was drawing to an end. The last of the snow had melted days before and the bitter cold had given way to a bracing chill in the mornings. Above, the sky was a deep blue, with scattered clouds easing their way from one horizon to another on a soft breeze. None of this was of any comfort to Boudica as she waited, sitting on the stump of a tree a little aside from a large party of her warriors and their mounts. They were in a clearing, some half a mile in length, close to the edge of a vast forest through which ran the track that linked Camulodunum to the Roman fort outside the scorched ruins of the Icenian capital. The enemy's engineers had made a good start to the job of improving the route along which their supply convoys supported the small army that was ravaging the Icenian settlements. Where the track passed through muddy stretches, they had laid corduroys of logs, and the trees and scrub had been cut back for thirty paces on either side in order to remove cover for ambushers or those who might harass the convoys and their escort with arrows or other missiles. The clearing marked the extent of their progress through the forest before they had been moved much further up the track to improve its condition closer to Venta Icenorum.

The damp brown stumps of trees looked like rotten teeth,

thought Boudica as she surveyed the despoiled ground stretching out around her. That was the Roman way for you. If they needed to lay down a road, they did so in a straight line with no regard for the landscape. There was a harsh efficiency to everything they did. It was evident in the style and decoration of the villas she had seen – all lines and sharp angles, so different from the graceful, intertwined curves and swirls that Celts preferred and the circles of their huts and communities. The Romans scarred the landscape and imposed unnatural forms upon it, whereas her people lived more in harmony with their surroundings.

Dismissing such speculations, she concentrated on the matter at hand. Her spies had reported on a supply convoy setting out from Camulodunum some two days earlier, and she had decided to make an example of it to demonstrate that the rebels could still strike far from their base at Lyngomara. This far outside Icenian territory the Romans would feel safe enough to be a little complacent, she calculated, and her scouts had proved her correct. Being very careful to remain out of sight, they had tracked the convoy the previous afternoon, noting how the escorts had posted only a handful of pickets to watch for danger during the night. This morning they had set off without sending forward a patrol to screen their advance. Instead, the hundred or so mounted men escorting the thirty wagons that made up the convoy rode at the front and rear of the column. They were still some miles away, but soon it would be time for her warriors to move into a position from which to launch their attack.

Syphodubnus approached her. 'It would be best to get our men in cover now, in case they send any scouts out ahead when they reach the edge of the forest.'

'In a moment.' She looked up at the sky and fixed her gaze on a kestrel hovering above, wings shifting from side to side before it soared a short distance and resumed its search for prey. 'How long do you think it will be before the enemy discover the location of Lyngomara?'

'There's no sign that they have any idea so far, majesty. If they did, they would surely have advanced towards the marshes by now.'

'True,' she conceded. 'But it's only a matter of time before we are betrayed.'

'Betrayed?' Syphodubnus frowned. 'Who would do such a thing? Those of our people who know where it is would never reveal anything to the Romans. They are loyal to you and our cause.'

'They are afraid of me,' she countered in a bitter tone. 'I have seen to that.'

Only five days earlier, she had ordered the execution of the chief of a village who had sold cattle to the Romans. Cattle he had hidden from her own warriors when they had come to requisition supplies to support the rebellion. There had been others who had shared the same fate since the Romans had entered Icenian territory. Against her expectations the invaders had failed to act with their usual brutality, and that she ascribed to the man who was leading their column. If only they had sent other men against her. Not Cato, nor Macro. Men she could hate without reservation. Men who lacked any understanding of her people and whose arrogance would have been sure to lead them into danger. Cato was too shrewd for that, she knew, and so far he had frustrated her by refusing to pursue any of the raiding parties she had directed against his forage columns. Was he playing a long game? Waiting until she lost patience and chanced her arm in battle? If so, he would be disappointed. All the same, she needed to give her followers small victories to keep their spirits up and prove to others that the rebellion was still alive and worthy of their continued support. Like the example she was just about to provide.

'Sometimes it is necessary to rule with an iron fist,' Syphodubnus sympathised. 'A good ruler understands that even as they regret its necessity.'

'It may well seem like necessity to you and me at this moment,' she replied. 'I wonder if those who write the history of these times will agree. We will be judged, Syphodubnus. Me most of all. Will history remember me as a hero or a villain, and will those who judge do so fairly?'

'I dare say the Romans will vilify you. But our people will remember and honour your name through the ages.'

'Even if it cost their ancestors so much blood and suffering? What a great healer to reputations time can be.'

She stood up and sighed. 'Get the men in position. Remind them there is to be no movement, no sound until the signal is given.'

'They know. We trained them well over the winter. I've never known fighters like these. Ferocious, ruthless and disciplined. If only we had had more like them twenty years ago. The Romans would not have got more than a few miles inland before we thrashed their legions and sent them tumbling back into their ships to leave Britannia and never return.'

'If only,' she agreed before gesturing to him to go.

Syphodubnus strode back to the waiting men. Five hundred of them. The survivors of her bodyguard had done a fine job of selecting and training the warriors to replace those who had fallen. Her adviser was right: these men were the finest body of fighters ever raised in Britannia. More than a match for the Roman army, as the latter was about to find out.

The men led their mounts out of the clearing and into the shadows beneath the pine trees on either side, disappearing from view. Two smaller parties with felling axes were already in position, hidden at each end of the clearing. Boudica waited a moment, watching and listening for any sign of her men, but they were well concealed and quite still. With a nod of satisfaction she crossed the open ground to join those on the right of the track. Syphodubnus was in command of the party on the other side. Picking her way through the shadows, she found her warriors standing by their mounts in a long line. Indicating to the three with war horns to follow her, she moved close enough to the edge of the forest that she had a clear view of the track and then lay down to wait. The group with the war horns crouched a few paces further back. They made a faint rustling sound among the pine needles and then there was silence.

Time seemed to slow down as she lay in concealment keeping watch for the enemy's approach from the left of where she was positioned. The birds that had fled when the warband had entered the clearing were slowly returning, chirping as they searched for food. A stag appeared from the end that led to Camulodunum. It bounded forward a short distance then stopped abruptly, antlered head raised and dark muzzle twitching as it sniffed the air suspiciously. Behind it a small group of does and spindly-legged fauns waited for their cue. A moment later the stag burst into motion and tore across the open ground into the forest a short distance beyond Syphodubnus's men. The other deer followed, disappearing from sight, and Boudica heard the faint crackle of twigs before the sounds faded and quiet returned. But only briefly. The first faint rumble of wheels and hooves grew steadily in volume, then she could make out individual voices, cries and the occasional crack of whips. She felt her heart quicken as she lowered her head and pulled a fallen branch in front of her to conceal herself better.

A few beats later, eight men armed with spears, the first of the enemy's mounted escort, appeared. They clopped along the track, casting cursory glances from side to side before appearing satisfied that they were safe and continuing their conversation. As they drew parallel with Boudica's hiding place, she could make out their conversation and was gratified that there was no indication they'd been alerted to any danger. Indeed, they seemed to have no concerns at all and were good-humoured as they enjoyed the fine weather and peaceful surroundings. The rest of the mounted column emerged from the forest track, and then came the mule teams drawing the first of the wagons. A drover led them while a driver sat on the bench holding the traces in one hand and wielding a whip in the other to crack over the heads of the beasts if their pace slowed. The wagons were piled with sacks of grain and other rations for Cato's men, and oats for their horses. The Roman advance party had already disappeared from sight amid the trees, and the head of the vanguard was approaching the end of the clearing, but the rearmost wagon had not yet appeared, such was the spacing between the vehicles. Boudica cursed under her breath. She had hoped that the entire supply column and escort would be within the clearing when the trap was sprung. There was no hope of that now.

Turning her head, she caught the eye of the nearest of the men with war horns and mouthed, 'Now . . .'

They rose to their feet and blew almost at the same time. The overlapping notes blasted out and there was a flurry as birds burst into flight. Behind her, Boudica could hear movement all along the line as her men climbed into their saddles and steered their horses through the trees towards the open ground. The wagons were still rumbling forwards, the mules unaware of danger even as the drovers and drivers looked around them in fear. The mounted escort had drawn up as the soldiers also turned towards the sound. Boudica rose and stepped out into the open, a single figure who drew every eye as she snatched a breath and cried out as loudly as she could in the tongue of her enemies, 'Death to Rome! Death to Rome!'

For an instant she was alone, shouting her war cry as she drew her sword and paced towards the road, her blade pointing at the wagons. She could see the looks of incredulity on the faces of the men on the nearest wagons before one of them laughed and shouted back, 'You and whose army, you daft barbarian witch!'

Then his expression froze as the warriors emerged from the gloom. One led Boudica's mount to her, and she swung up into the saddle and took the reins before hastening after her men as they made for the line of wagons at an easy trot. Away to her right, at the edge of the clearing, she heard shouts of alarm as the first of several trees crashed down across the road. They had been prepared earlier and required only the last few blows from an axe to cause them to fall. The sight of the Icenian riders broke the spell, and the commander of the Roman escort began to shout orders before he was drowned out by the war cries of Boudica's men and a fresh chorus of blaring notes from the war horns. The first drover abandoned his wagon and sprinted for the trees on the far side of the clearing. The driver jumped down to follow him, and others started to follow suit. One, more courageous than his comrades, drew a sword and made to defend his wagon. Three warriors closed in on him, feinting with their spears, forcing him to parry away one attack at a time before he was run through. He lurched and clutched his spare hand to his stomach, then collapsed as his attackers thrust their spears into his torso again and again.

Boudica hung back from the fight, watching as her warriors cut down any of the enemy who remained with the wagons. To her right she saw that the vanguard of the Roman escort had wheeled round and were riding to meet the warriors on the right of the Icenian line. Beyond them, the advance party of eight auxiliaries had ridden back and were now surrounded by the axemen and being picked off. To the left, the first of the enemy rearguard had entered the clearing and were galloping forward on either side of the wagons. The warriors on the left of the line turned to meet them, and she heard the sharp cracks of blows landing on shields and the distant metallic clink of blades clashing. It was almost time for the next stage of the ambush. She looked from side to side to be sure that the convoy's escort was fully engaged, then twisted in her saddle to look back at the three men blowing the horns and made a cutting action across her throat.

They lowered their instruments, red-faced and gasping, and the last echo off the surrounding trees died abruptly.

At first there was no sign of movement on the other side of the clearing, then the Romans who had run into the trees to escape came tumbling out of the shadows wearing terrified expressions. Hard behind them came Syphodubnus and his men. They ran down the fleeing drovers and stabbed them with their spears before moving on to pile into the flank of the auxiliaries riding down the left of the wagons. A group at each end of the line broke off to cut across the road and charge into the rear of the auxiliaries already engaged by Boudica's warriors. Outnumbered and trapped, the Romans were doomed, but still put up a desperate resistance as they were ground down by the Icenians.

Boudica felt a fierce flush of triumph as she turned her horse towards the nearest melee. She rode between two of her men and made for the side of an auxiliary as he slashed open the arm of the warrior to his right. He looked round just in time to see her raise her sword to strike. It flashed down and cut into the top of his shield as he thrust it up and ducked at the same time. With a savage cry, Boudica worked the blade free as the auxiliary backed his horse off a short distance and made ready to thrust his own sword at her. She saw there was no way past his shield and angled her blade to cut into the neck of the Roman's mount instead. It sliced through mane, hide and muscle, and the beast let out a snort and lashed out with its rear hooves before rearing up, blood spraying from the wound. The Roman swayed violently in the saddle, arms flailing as he fought for control. Boudica raised her sword again, pausing to time her strike as the panicked Roman horse pivoted round, exposing the rider's right side. Then she slashed down, cutting into his forearm just above the wrist. The soldier's sword dropped as his fingers spasmed.

Boudica edged her horse closer and met the defiant gaze of the auxiliary as he gritted his teeth and snarled.

'Die!' she snarled back, stabbing him in the face, driving the point of her sword into his skull and twisting it from side to side.

Retrieving her weapon, she glanced about her at the warriors and Romans locked in combat. Then she caught sight of the standard of the Roman unit, and close by, the crested helmet of the commanding officer.

Turning to two of her men, she ordered them to follow her as she steered her mount towards the standard. The two warriors pushed forward on either side and the wedge worked its way through the fighting horsemen, blocking blows with their kite shields. Syphodubnus appeared directly ahead of her with a small group of his men. His cheek had been opened by a Roman sword and was bleeding profusely.

'Majesty, go back!' he cried.

She shook the red locks of her hair and made to surge past him, but he sheathed his sword and grabbed at her reins. Boudica pulled sharply, and her horse swerved aside before she urged it on.

'Stay with her!' Syphodubnus shouted to his men, and the group pressed round their queen as she continued towards the ring of auxiliaries trying to defend their officer and the standard. Crouching low, she urged her mount into a final spurt and burst through a gap between two of the auxiliaries. The Roman officer's eyes widened as he saw her, and he kicked his heels in as he raised his sword to attack. His thrust was rushed, though, and Boudica easily parried the blade aside before striking him on the side of his helmet with her hilt as he passed by. Both riders pulled hard on their reins to turn their horses for a fresh exchange of blows.

'Protect the queen!' Syphodubnus shouted desperately from outside the ring.

Boudica kept her head down and her sword out as she aimed the point at the Roman officer's throat. His lips lifted in a ferocious smile as he made to block the blow and return the compliment by smashing the hilt of his weapon into her face. But at the last moment, Boudica undercut his sword and angled her blade up so that the tip tore along the unprotected flesh beneath his arm from wrist to elbow. It caught in the sleeve of his tunic, and the sword was ripped from her hand as they passed each other again. She hissed an angry curse as she drew her dagger and wheeled her horse round. The Roman was close, facing her, blood coursing from his injured arm as he raised his sword.

'This time you die!'

He made to strike, but was thrust aside by one of the Icenian warriors, who had unwittingly backed between them as he hacked at one of the men protecting the standard. The Roman officer roared with frustration and struck out at the interloper instead, slicing through the back of his neck. The Icenian's body went limp and folded forwards before he dropped from the saddle and lay motionless, save for his jaw working furiously and soundlessly.

Boudica knew there was one chance left to her. She had to get close in order to use her dagger. As her horse moved in, she kept low and reached out to deliver a series of frenzied stabs to the Roman's thigh.

He howled with pain and rage, but before he could react, he was struck in the side by a spear. Boudica saw Syphodubnus tear the weapon back to deliver another strike, and the breath was driven from the Roman officer's lungs. At once she switched her gaze to the standard-bearer, but he had already been engaged by two of her adviser's men, and the rest had broken the ring and were dealing with the surviving auxiliaries. More warriors surrounded the standard-bearer and he was stabbed from all sides. He clung to the standard for as long as he could before it was torn from his grasp, and he let out a helpless groan before his head was struck off by a sword-wielding Icenian.

Boudica picked up her sword and remounted to see that the fight was almost over. A handful of the enemy remained in the saddle, and one, bent low, had managed to reach the treeline and swiftly disappeared, pursued by three of her men desperate not to let a single Roman escape.

Gradually the sounds of fighting ceased. The fatally wounded Roman officer was kneeling on the ground, hands clasped over a bloody rent in his scale armour. Elsewhere her warriors were rounding up prisoners and finishing off those too badly wounded to move. Others were attending to wounded Icenians and collecting the bodies of their dead comrades.

Syphodubnus was standing still as one of his men wound a dressing over the crown of his head and under his chin. When he addressed Boudica, his voice was muffled, and she could not help a brief smile of amusement amid the surrounding carnage. But her adviser was not amused, and his forehead wrinkled in a frown as he upbraided her.

'What were you doing? You could have been killed.'

She lifted her chin proudly. 'When my warriors fight, I fight with them.'

'And if you die, who will lead us?'

'If I die, there will always be others as long as the spirit of our rebellion lives.'

'Boudica . . .' He shook his head helplessly.

She strode past him to confront the Roman officer. His chest was heaving as he fought for breath, and he looked up at her from under the brim of his helmet, eyes full of uncompromising hatred. She regarded him with contempt and addressed him in Latin.

'What fools you Romans are. So blinded by your arrogance that you blunder into one trap after another.'

'Fuck you, bitch.'

She sniffed, then took out her dagger and stepped round behind him. Grabbing the metal crest holder, she yanked his head back to expose his throat and leaned close to his ear. 'This is for Merida.' Then she cut his throat and stepped back. The officer gurgled, both hands clawing at the gushing wound, and Boudica kicked him in the back so that he collapsed onto his face. 'Die, you Roman pig.'

She wiped the blade of her dagger on the hem of her tunic and sheathed it before looking round the clearing.

'Burn the wagons,' she ordered Syphodubnus. 'Kill all the mules.'

Syphodubnus gave a disapproving frown. 'Majesty? Why not just cut them loose?'

Even though Boudica shared her people's affection for horses and their lesser kin, her heart had hardened out of the need to hamper the enemy, however that could be achieved. 'The Romans need these mules to haul supplies. We spare them now and they'll be rounded up and bringing more supplies to our enemy in Venta Icenorum. Kill them.'

'As you order. What about the prisoners?'

'Kill them all, except one, and leave their heads in the rearmost wagon. Have that moved far enough away from the others to ensure it is spared from the flames. The last one we'll crucify. He may last long enough to tell those who come looking for the convoy who was responsible for this.'

'I think the Romans might work that out for themselves.'

Boudica rounded on her adviser. 'Nevertheless, I don't want them to be in any doubt. Do it.'

CHAPTER TWENTY-FIVE

Near Branodunum

Cato and Macro stood on top of a dune overlooking the channel where four warships, a bireme and three smaller liburnians were beached on the mud close to a grassy bank. The winter storms had given way to calmer seas that could be readily negotiated by the warships and cargo vessels under Cato's command. Gangways stretched from the ships to the shore and marine skirmishers could be seen moving towards the settlement at Branodunum. Further out, where the channel opened onto the sea, two large cargo ships and two barges were slowly approaching under sail. They had come up from Londinium, where they had been sent to pick up engineers and materials to construct a fort at Branodunum, from where Cato intended to strike into the marshes to hunt down the rebels. He had been aboard the bireme for some days, waiting for Besodius and his ships to arrive, before sailing up the channel and landing close to the Icenian settlement. The cargo ships were carried on the light spring breeze that caused the clumps of grass that grew across the dunes to sway gently.

The fort would command the channel which led from the sea and penetrated some distance into the marshes before it gave way to shallow runs of water that snaked through the reeds and small islands stretching out across the northern expanse of Iceni territory. Cato indicated the hump of rising ground where the channel divided half a mile further inland. The larger branch led towards the Icenian settlement, while the narrower one meandered off into the marsh. 'That's the site for the fort. It should offer a good view of the surrounding area as well as commanding the channel.'

Macro nodded. 'Easy to defend as well, with water, reeds and mudbanks on three sides. The only practicable approach will be up the slope to the main gate. A hundred men and, say, four catapults would control any access to the sea. Although I can't see that the navarch is going to be too happy about parting with any of his artillery.'

The navy's squadron commander had been passed over for promotion for many years, and was prickly as a consequence and inclined to protest against any challenge to his authority.

'Turpillius has his orders,' Cato replied. 'If I tell him to surrender his bolt-throwers and catapults to the army, he will do as I say or answer to the governor.'

'You sometimes have to wonder if we're all on the same side,' Macro grumbled.

Cato slapped his thigh lightly. 'Deal with one problem at a time. That's all we can do.'

They waited as the *Minerva* glided towards them. Cato could make out Besodius standing at the bow, and returned his wave before the captain turned to order his men to lower the sail and prepare to anchor in the middle of the channel. One by one the other cargo vessels anchored behind him. A moment later, a skiff was lowered over the side of the *Minerva* and Besodius climbed down to row ashore. Cato and Macro descended from the dune to meet him.

'I'd lay good money on it that you didn't expect to see me again!' The merchant grinned as they clasped forearms.

'Nonsense.' Cato smiled. 'I knew you for the true patriot you are. Able and willing to serve Rome.'

'Of course,' Macro added, 'it has nothing to do with the small fortune you are being paid for your services.'

'Isn't it wonderful when commerce and patriotism coincide?' Besodius responded before dipping a hand into his sidebag and taking out a capped leather tube. 'I was given this to bring to you while my ships were being loaded at Londinium.'

Cato took the message container and removed the small scroll within. He read the contents with a grim expression before replacing the scroll and tucking the tube into his belt.

'Bad news?' Macro queried.

'Boudica's destroyed the supply convoy we were expecting. She struck while it was still deep inside Trinovantian territory. Burned all the wagons and massacred the escort.'

'Shit. They're getting bolder if they're prepared to strike that far outside their turf.'

'Or desperate enough to take such a risk in order to give that impression. Either way, that's a hard blow for us.' Cato paused for a beat. 'Anyway, it's good to see you again, Besodius.'

The captain nodded towards his ship. 'I brought a few jars of wine with me from Gaul. Whenever you're ready.'

Cato shook his head and indicated the column of marines formed up and ready to advance along the narrow track to Branodunum, just over two miles away. 'We'll have to deal with the pleasantries later. Come!'

The column of marines was drawn from the four warships, under the command of the centurion from the bireme. He saluted as Cato and the others approached.

'Men are ready to move off at your order, sir.'

'Very good.' Cato returned the salute before he addressed the marines. 'Although Boudica and the rebels are the enemy, there are many among the Iceni who do not support her cause. Therefore you will not harm any inhabitant of Branodunum, or take or damage any of their property, unless I order you to. Any

293

marine who disobeys that order will answer for it.' He glared at them to ensure that none doubted the consequences of defying him. Then he turned towards the bireme, where Turpillius was leaning on the side rail watching proceedings. 'Make sure your men keep their eyes open. If we have to retreat from Branodunum, be ready to move your ships offshore in a hurry.'

'We'll be ready, Prefect. I'll move my ships at dusk in any case.'

'Not without the shore party aboard first. Is that clear?'

'As you command.'

There was an insolence to the man's tone that set Cato's teeth on edge, but any confrontation in front of the marines would be an unhelpful distraction at the moment. He resolved to deal with the man in private later on.

'Let's be off,' he ordered the centurion.

With Macro and Besodius at his side, Cato led the way along the raised path twisting through the maze of muddy channels to the nearby settlement. The line of skirmishers kept pace a quarter of a mile ahead, watching for any sign of the enemy as they picked their way forward. Cato could see only a few isolated figures looking on from a safe distance. A shepherd, no more than a boy, came into view a hundred or so paces ahead of the skirmishers. He stopped to stare for a beat, then turned and drove his flock back towards the settlement as fast as he could.

'I wonder what kind of reception Ganomenus will give us this time,' said Besodius. 'Has the winter hardened his doubts about Boudica, or has he fallen into line behind her cause?'

'We'll find out soon enough, if the old boy is still alive and still the chief.'

The skirmishers had been ordered to halt as soon as they were within sight of Branodunum, and Cato and the others caught up with them as they climbed a gentle slope and looked down on the settlement. A few hundred round huts clustered together next to a stretch of open water that led to the sea in one direction and off into the marshes in the other. A number of boats were beached on the sandbank at the water's edge: sturdy seagoing fishing vessels and smaller craft with lower sides and shallow draughts designed to navigate the marshland beyond the settlement. Fishing nets hung from frames in the open ground between the huts and the boats. Cato could make out some baskets of fish by gutting benches. That work had been abandoned now as people ran among the huts to spread the warning that Roman soldiers had been sighted. Already some were hurrying from the far side of the village along paths that led into the reeds, shrubs and clusters of trees that stretched for many miles beyond.

'It looks like our visit is not appreciated,' said Macro.

'There's Ganomenus.' Besodius pointed out a small group of men who had emerged from the huts and were warily approaching the Romans. Sure enough, Cato could pick out the familiar features of the chief at the head of the group and was relieved to see that he still appeared to be in charge of his people.

'Let's go and say hello,' the captain continued.

'Wait,' Cato commanded.

Once the skirmishers had fallen in with the rest of the column, he gave the order to continue down the path towards the settlement. He halted the marines when they were no more than fifty paces from Ganomenus and his party and proceeded with Macro and Besodius. He could see the nervousness in the Icenians' expressions. Ganomenus, however, seemed glad to see them, and advanced holding out his hand.

'Greetings, our Roman friends.'

Cato felt some of the tension in his body ease at the word 'friends'. If the old man spoke in those terms openly before these others, it indicated that their loyalty had shifted away from Boudica over the winter months. He saw that the men looked gaunt and hungry and that none of them seemed to be under the age of fifty – the residue from Boudica's recruitment of the locals, Cato presumed. He took the chief's hand and pressed it firmly.

'It's good to see you again, friend,' he replied in the Iceni dialect. 'I hope you and your people have fared well since we last spoke.'

Despite the cordiality of his comment, it was as much a provocation as a question, and the old man's response played into his hands.

'We have never known such hunger.' Ganomenus shook his head sadly. 'We lack enough men to catch fish to feed our people and there is not much left of our herds and stores of grain.'

Cato arched an eyebrow. 'Boudica?'

The chief nodded. 'Her men have come every month since we last met. Each time they have taken more of the food we had set aside for winter. And she has sent a message to surrender the last of our young men to her. We cannot survive much longer if the rebellion continues.'

Cato nodded sympathetically. At the same time, he was concerned by this latest report regarding her continued search for recruits. The losses she had endured so far against Roman patrols and skirmishes with forage parties could not possibly have exceeded the number of those who had volunteered or been pressed into taking up arms. Somewhere in the marshes she was amassing a formidable force to lead against her Roman opponents. It had come at the price of undermining the loyalty of chiefs like Ganomenus and the Icenian peasants, but Cato suspected that such concerns had long ceased to worry Boudica. All that mattered to her now was ensuring the rebellion survived from month to month to keep killing Romans.

Cato refocused his thoughts. 'I would speak with you about our purpose here and our need for guides to navigate the marshes. You and the other leaders of Branodunum.'

'By all means. May I offer you the hospitality of my round hut?'

He dipped his head in gratitude. 'We would be honoured.'

Ganomenus hesitated before he continued. 'I would ask that your men remain outside our settlement while we talk.'

'Now wait a moment,' Macro cut in. 'If you think that three Roman officers are going to walk into the heart of an Icenian village by themselves . . .'

'Who is left to do you any harm?' Ganomenus replied. 'All that remains are a few old men, children and women.'

'Given that the cause of all this bloodshed is one of your women, you'll pardon me if I don't dismiss the danger so readily.'

'Are the men of Rome so terrified of an Icenian woman?'

Macro's eyes narrowed. 'I know her. Probably better than you do, my friend. Boudica is more dangerous than almost any Roman soldier I know.'

Cato interrupted. 'Yes, well, while it's rather interesting to dwell on the martial capabilities of the Icenian queen, let's not inflate her prowess. Ganomenus, the marines will not enter your settlement. Besodius, you remain with them.'

'Me? Why?' the captain demanded.

'If there is any trouble, two dead Romans is better than three.' Cato turned back to the chief to address him in the Icenian dialect. 'Lead us to your hut, Ganomenus.'

The tribal party began to move off and Cato approached the marine centurion to give him his orders. 'We're having a discussion with the village elders. They're prepared to talk to us only on condition that you and your men stay out of their settlement.'

'Do you think that's wise, sir?'

'Probably not, but that's what is about to happen. Keep your lads formed up and watchful. If there's any sign of trouble, you come for us at once. We'll be in the largest of the round huts.'

'Yes, sir. Your funeral.'

'Let's hope not. Don't forget what I said earlier. No one is to be harmed, unless they offer violence. If some of the kids here make faces, or lob mud or turds at you, I don't want them to come to any harm.'

'Not even a clip round the head, sir?'

'Not even that. Clear?'

'Yes, sir.'

As they paced quickly to catch up with the Icenians, Cato glanced at Macro. 'I'd rather you didn't talk up Boudica with our friend there. We don't want Ganomenus thinking Rome is running scared of her.'

'Well, aren't we? Given all the men and resources being thrown against her.'

'That may be true, but let's try not to give him any reason to change his position. We've got him on the cusp of serving our interests and I don't want to jeopardise that.'

'If you say so, sir.'

'Listen, I know what Boudica once meant to you, despite everything that has happened since. We have both fought alongside her and know how formidable she is. We've also both owed her our lives at one time or another. But you've repaid that debt, and more. She is our enemy now. We need to believe that we will defeat her and Ganomenus needs to believe that too.'

'I understand.'

Ganomenus's round hut was the largest in the settlement. The interior was fifty feet across, and the roof was supported by four large beams that rose from the middle of the structure, leaving a large square space in the centre for a rock-lined fireplace whose smoke escaped the interior through the reed-thatched vent high above. A sturdy wooden seat with ornately carved decorations in the swirling designs favoured by the Celts stood opposite the entrance. Lesser chairs were arranged on both sides. The floor was cobbled with flint from nearby beaches and covered over with reeds. Ganomenus sat in the most prominent of the chairs, then the other elders took their places. Some women brought stools for the Romans to sit on opposite the chief, and set down jars of mead and clay cups for the men before departing.

Cato took a mouthful of the sweet drink and made himself smile appreciatively before he explained their presence.

'The last time we spoke, you said that the channels and waterways about Branodunum reached as far into the marshes as Boudica's stronghold.'

'Yes,' Ganomenus agreed cautiously.

'In which case we will build a fort, to cover access to the sea and to use as a base to penetrate the marshes while we search for Boudica's lair at Lyngomara.'

'A fort? Here?'

'Not right here in Branodunum. A couple of miles closer to the sea.' Cato indicated the direction. 'Where the channel divides.'

'I know the place.'

'It will be large enough to deter Boudica from sending any more of her warriors to take your food and abduct your men. And it will be large enough for you to take shelter there if the rebels approach your village.'

Ganomenus's eyebrows rose. 'You would protect us from the rebels?'

'If necessary, yes. We would do what we could to ensure your safety, but the longer this struggle continues, the more likely it is that Boudica and her followers will make you suffer. Your best hope of avoiding starvation and the pointless sacrifice of your men is for her to be defeated as soon as possible.'

Cato looked at each of the elders in turn and saw that his words were having an effect.

'She will be defeated, have no doubt about that. It is only a matter of time before we discover her lair and destroy it. That will take longer if we have to locate it ourselves, but if we were to be led to the place, the suffering of your people would come to an end very swiftly.'

Ganomenus glanced at his companions before he responded. 'You speak the truth, but what you ask for is the betrayal of our queen.'

'Has she not betrayed her people?' Cato replied in a harsher tone. 'Did she not betray you when she incited the Iceni into a rebellion she knew she could not win? Did she not betray you when she led your brave warriors to a shattering defeat in battle against the legions? Is she not now betraying you by stealing the food from your mouths, starving your children and forcing your men to fight for her doomed cause? How much more can you endure, Ganomenus?'

There was a shocked silence, then the youngest of the elders, a bald individual with a scarred face, leaned forward with an angry expression. 'How dare you speak of our queen in such terms? Begone, Roman! Before we take your head and send it to Boudica as a gift.'

Macro grasped the handle of his sword and began to rise before Cato reached out and eased him down. Ganomenus and most of the other elders had turned on their outspoken comrade and were berating him, talking so fast it was impossible for Cato to keep up. He stood up slowly to draw their attention.

'If you will help us end this, Rome will be grateful and will prove its gratitude by giving you the food you need and the promise that those warriors from Branodunum who are now fighting for Boudica will be returned to you as free men when the rebellion is crushed. If, on the other hand, you choose to oppose Rome, you need to be aware of the consequences of that choice.'

He took the leather tube from his belt and extracted the scroll from Suetonius, holding it up for the elders to see. 'This is a dispatch from the governor that I received earlier today. He informs me that one of our supply columns was wiped out by the rebels.' He unravelled the scroll and his eyes scanned the contents before he continued. 'Suetonius writes, "Roman losses were two hundred and sixty-seven men. There were no survivors. In accordance with my policy regarding the collective punishment of the rebel tribe, you are to execute ten Icenians for every Roman life lost, without regard for the combatant or non-combatant status of those selected for execution. The sentence is to be carried out as soon as possible."' He replaced the scroll in the holder and took a half-step towards the elders.

'I have my orders. If I am to stick to the terms set out by the governor, then by rights I should begin here, today, with you and your people. In truth, I am the only thing standing between you and the certain death ordered by the governor. So you can either accept my protection and have your people fed, or you can choose loyalty to a doomed cause led by a queen who has long since forfeited the right to any loyalty you ever owed her.' He pointed the leather tube at Ganomenus. 'Which is it to be? My centurion and I will return to my soldiers now to await your decision. I suggest you choose wisely and quickly, for my patience is wearing thin. Come, Macro.'

They left the round hut and strode back towards the marines, who were now formed up in a line two deep, fifty paces from the edge of the settlement. Besodius puffed his cheeks in relief when he saw them.

'You take some chances, Prefect. You really do. Even though I've known the old boy for years, I'd never have gone in there on my own. Not since the rebellion.'

'I wasn't alone. I had Centurion Macro at my side. Besides, they knew what would happen to them if there was any attempt to harm us.'

'Fair enough. Did they agree to provide the guides?'

'They weren't happy about the idea,' said Macro. 'But the lad made them an offer it would be fucking unwise to refuse.'

301

'I can imagine what that means.'

'I expect their reply any moment,' said Cato with a cold smile of satisfaction. 'You'll see.'

There was only a brief wait before Ganomenus and the others emerged from the settlement and approached Cato. There was a look of resignation in the old man's eyes as he drew himself to his full height. 'We accept your terms, Prefect. On the understanding that you give your sacred word concerning the safe return of our men serving with the rebels.'

'If they surrender or are taken alive, they will be returned. I swear this by Jupiter, Best and Greatest, on my sacred honour, as Centurion Macro and these other men are my witnesses. For your part, I require that you undertake to reveal the location of Lyngomara and swear loyalty to Rome henceforth.'

Ganomenus raised his right hand and placed it over his heart. 'I swear it, by all that is sacred to my people.'

'And this oath is sworn on behalf of all those who live in the settlement?'

Ganomenus glanced at his companions for reassurance, and they nodded. 'It is.'

It was then that Cato noticed the absence of the man who had protested so vehemently back in the round hut. 'Where is he? The man who refused to forsake Boudica?'

'He was unwilling to put the lives of our people before his loyalty to the queen and so we were obliged to end his.'

Cato was surprised at the old man's decisiveness. Ganomenus had burned his bridges as far as Boudica was concerned and now depended on Roman victory to save his neck.

'Very well. Be ready at dawn tomorrow to guide me to the location of Boudica's base. And understand this – if I am betrayed, or fail to return, the governor's order with respect to the executions will be carried out at once.'

'I understand, Prefect.'

'Tomorrow then. At dawn.'

Ganomenus nodded and led the elders away. Macro watched them for a moment before he spoke. 'That's all very well, but how are you going to explain to Suetonius that you refused to carry out his order to execute that mob?'

'If we destroy Boudica and end the rebellion, I dare say the governor will be pleased enough with the result to overlook such matters. In any case, he never gave such an order.'

Macro frowned. 'But you read the scroll . . .' Then the sestertius dropped and he grinned. 'You made it up.'

'Every word. But it did the job, didn't it?'

'Fuck me, lad. You've got a mind as sharp as a scalpel, and balls of steel.'

'Good. Because I'm going to need them when Ganomenus takes us deep into the marshes to lead us to Boudica's lair.'

'Us?'

'I don't imagine for an instant that you'd want to miss out on it.'

'True. If only because I know I'd get a hiding from Petronella if I didn't go along and anything was to happen to you.'

CHAPTER TWENTY-SIX

Leaving the navarch with instructions to oversee the construction of the fort and ensure that there was no friction with the local people, Cato and Macro set off with Ganomenus. They left their armour behind and only carried their short swords and daggers. It took two days for the old man and his grandson, Hardrin, a burly lad of fourteen, to navigate the narrow channels through the marsh, with Cato and Macro taking turns at the paddles. Their boat was wooden-framed and covered with hide, no more than ten feet long with a beam of three feet. Despite the careful stitching and a recent coat of fat, the craft leaked steadily, and Cato and Macro were obliged to sit in cold water until Ganomenus landed them on solid ground just long enough to drain the boat before they resumed. The first night they camped on a small island surrounded by rushes. Cato would not agree to lighting a fire, so they sat huddled together, eating the cold fishcakes Ganomenus's wife had packed for them and washing them down with the watered-down wine from the jar that Besodius had given them. There was no room for a tent on the boat, so they slept in the open, wrapped in their cloaks.

The sounds of the marsh at night were unfamiliar and unnerving: the dry rustling of reeds stirred by the lightest of breezes, the booming call of bitterns and the splash of waterfowl and other animals. They conspired to suggest the presence of an enemy close at hand and moving stealthily towards them. Cato and Macro took turns at keeping watch but neither could sleep when the other took over. There was a thick mist at first light that rendered the rising sun merely a faint orb of light amid the gloom and fine drizzle. Moving stiffly and shivering from the cold and damp, the Romans helped to ease the boat out between the reeds before climbing aboard. Ganomenus and Hardrin took the first spell at the paddles, gently propelling the boat along while making as little sound as possible. Cato did his best to make notes of distances, direction and landmarks as they wound their way through the channels. All four strained their ears for any sign of other men on the water or the islands they passed.

They had encountered a man in a coracle on the first afternoon who had been arranging a net as they approached. As soon as he saw them, he abandoned the net and made off into the reeds as fast as possible. There was no further encounter until noon on the second day. Cato and Macro were working the paddles when Hardrin, who was in the front of the boat, turned suddenly and raised a finger to his lips. All four froze, and Cato tilted his head. At first nothing seemed out of order, then he heard voices, low and indistinct. Ganomenus stabbed a finger towards the bed of reeds to their right, and the two Romans steered the boat into concealment as swiftly and quietly as possible.

When they were far enough in among the reeds, Ganomenus hissed, 'Everyone stay down and be silent!'

They did as he said, and for a moment nothing moved but the ripples they had stirred. They could hear the voices growing louder, and then the plop and swish of paddles. Cato saw the top of the reeds stir as displaced water reached the sides of the channel, and then a boat twice as large as Ganomenus's surged by. Six men were on the paddles while six more sat on benches. Another stood in the bows, holding a spear, scanning the way ahead. He glanced round sharply, his eyes passing directly over the boat in the reeds before he spoke harshly to his companions. 'Keep it down! Do you want every Roman patrol between here and Londinium to hear you?'

'Oh, give it a rest!' one of the others responded. 'What Roman patrols? They're too scared to enter the marshes. Scared of us and scared of losing themselves in here for ever. Just stop shitting yourself, boy, and do something useful like keeping an eye open for some game.'

The boat passed and the voices faded away. Ganomenus rose and listened a moment longer before he nodded to the Romans. 'Let's get moving again. We're close. They must be patrolling the waterways around Lyngomara. We'll have to be very careful from now on.'

Cato and Macro took up the paddles and eased the boat out into the channel. The mist had almost cleared. The danger now was being spotted by a rebel warrior or camp follower, or even a marsh dweller, who might raise the alarm and bring down another patrol upon them.

After about a mile, they came to a fork and Ganomenus told them to stop. Cato and Macro rested on the paddles while the old man frowned and chewed his lip.

'What is it?' Macro asked.

'I'm not sure which . . . It's been a few years since I last came this way. I think it's to the right.'

'Think?' Macro responded harshly. 'Don't think. Be certain, damn you.'

'Yes . . . yes, the right.'

The boat eased its way forward, and soon the reed beds closed in on either side so that the craft was brushing through them. The water here was brackish, with a foul odour of rotting vegetation. Another mile further on, Cato was almost certain the old man had lost his way. He was on the verge of turning the boat around when he saw a thin trail of smoke up ahead. Then another. The boat grounded softly on mud just before a low bank that marked the end of the channel. He could hear more distant voices, a steady hubbub from many more than would comprise any patrol. Ganomenus grinned with relief as he pointed. 'Just over there, Prefect. Go and see.'

Macro eased himself over the side and promptly sank up to his thighs in the ooze. He steadied the boat as Cato joined him, and the two of them waded effortlessly towards the bank and into the tall grass that grew amid tangles of bare brambles. Macro reached down and scraped as much of the filth from his legs and boots as he could before rinsing his hands in the water. Cato followed suit, and then the pair cautiously lowered themselves to the ground and crawled up the bank. Beyond were more reeds, and then open water that stretched out on both sides. A few hundred paces away lay a large island covered with round huts. To their right, at the end of the island, was a hall built on a mound with a sturdy stockade surrounding it and what appeared to be a ditch separating it from the rest of the island. To the left, the huts gave way to another large island, half of which was covered by oaks and other trees.

The two officers examined the scene for a while before Macro spoke. 'Quite a set-up. There must be at least a hundred round huts over there. Assuming they're mostly billets, we could be talking a thousand rebels.'

'At least.' Cato nodded. 'We need to work our way right round and see how it looks from the other side.'

Macro surveyed the rebel base again. 'That's going to take us some time.' He glanced back at the two Icenians in the boat. 'Do you think we can trust them to still be here when we return?'

Cato thought a moment. 'Better to err on the safe side.'

He slid down the bank and ordered the others to get out and drag the boat up onto the grass. When that was done, he spoke to Ganomenus. 'We're going to scout out the area around Lyngomara. I need you to come with us.'

The old man gave him an angry look. 'Why? I've given my word that I'll help you.'

'And the best way you can help me now is to come with us. Your grandson stays with the boat.'

Hardrin was alarmed. 'You're going to leave me alone?'

'I have to,' said Cato, not unkindly. 'I need a man I can trust to keep guard while we're away. Can you do that?'

The boy glanced at his grandfather, who gave a nod.

'You'll be fine, Hardrin,' Cato continued. 'Keep quiet and keep your head down. If we're not back by nightfall, take the boat back to Branodunum. We'll find a way to rejoin you there.'

Ganomenus shot him a quick look of understanding before he spoke to the boy in a reassuring tone. 'We might get lost, or we might be delayed. If we don't return, you must let the Romans know how to find this place. Can you do that?'

Hardrin nodded.

'Good boy!' Ganomenus patted his cheek, then hugged him briefly before drawing back to crouch beside Cato. 'We'd better get moving, Prefect. There's only a few hours of daylight left.'

They worked their way carefully along the bank, keeping it between themselves and Lyngomara, pausing to creep up and survey the settlement from a different perspective. It soon became clear that there were a large number of men on the island. Through the gaps in the huts they saw that there was open ground in the middle of the settlement where rebels were being trained to strike at straw dummies with their swords and spears. Others were testing themselves in duels, and the faint clatter of weapons carried across the water to the three men. The stockade at the end of the island did indeed turn out to be separated by a channel, over which stretched a narrow trestle bridge joining it to the rest of the settlement.

'That strongpoint looks like a pretty formidable spot for a

308

last-ditch defence,' said Macro. 'Assuming we can take the rest of the place first. This won't be anything like as straightforward as those hill forts we knocked over in the early days of the invasion.'

'Let's keep moving and hope we find a weak spot in the defences.'

Further on, the bank gave way to more reeds and they had to move very carefully through them in order not to cause the tops to sway in a manner that might betray their presence to a sharp-eyed lookout on the wall of the stronghold. They emerged onto more dry ground only to discover there was no continuous bank to conceal them, just an uneven series of humps and yet more reed beds. They were forced to crawl between those places where there was cover, and it was well over an hour before they had rounded the stockade and began to make their way down the far side of the marsh. It was hard going, and Ganomenus started to struggle and slow them down. At the same time, Cato had come to a much fuller appreciation of the challenge presented by Boudica's base.

They were opposite the trees on the island adjacent to the settlement when Macro, taking the lead, paused and crouched down.

'What is it?' Cato whispered.

'Look over there.' Macro raised a hand and pointed out the stakes running along the edge of the trees. Most had objects impaled on them, and suddenly Cato saw what had caused Macro to pause: a helmet with the transverse crest of a centurion on it.

'Trophies,' Macro spat bitterly.

'We'll deal with those once Lyngomara is taken,' Cato reassured his friend.

'And maybe set up a few trophies of our own,' Macro replied.

Cato looked round and saw that the sun was sinking towards the marshes behind them. 'Come on, brother. We need to keep moving.'

A little further on, they saw that the island was connected to the next solid stretch of ground by a causeway resting on stout posts driven into the bed of the small broad that surrounded the settlement and the wooded area that Cato assumed to be the sacred grove he had been told about. There was a fortified gatehouse at each end from where sentries watched over the approaches. As they crept closer, Ganomenus tugged on Cato's arm. 'Wait.'

He drew them both further into cover before he explained. 'We're close to the track that leads through the marsh. It's on the other side of the second gatehouse. We'll have to get across it before we can get round the far side and back to the boat.'

'So?' Macro queried.

'The track is bound to be patrolled. We'll have to be careful to cross it without being seen. It's not far from here, so we go on in silence. I'll lead the way.'

Macro was about to protest when he was stopped by a look from Cato. 'You know what you're doing, Ganomenus. We'll follow you.'

The Icenian set off and Macro followed him. Cato glanced around to be sure they were not being watched and then tailed the others. As the mixture of reeds, brambles and stunted bushes began to thin out, the old man crouched and waved the two Romans down. Cato crawled alongside him and saw the track not thirty feet away. It was rutted and worn, and barely wide enough to move a cart along. He glanced up at the sky and saw that the sun had dipped below the tops of the reeds and glinted between them as the breeze eddied across the marsh. There would be no more than an hour of daylight left to find their way back to Hardrin.

He crept forward to the edge of the track and looked in both directions. To his left there was a slight dip as it ran down to the gatehouse; the other way it bent to the right, out of sight of

310

the lookouts. Turning, he gestured to the others, taking the lead as they moved parallel to the track, making for the bend. They followed it round until they were safely beyond the line of sight of the gatehouse. The track continued for another hundred paces before making another right turn into the marshes.

'We'll cross here,' Cato decided, and was about to step forward when he caught sight of movement further along the track. He could see the head of a man above the reeds, and he desperately signed to the others to get back. They ducked into cover just as a chariot rumbled into sight at the head of a column of rebel warriors.

Pressed against the ground behind a tall clump of grass, they kept still as the column approached. Cato was tempted to raise his head as the chariot passed by, accompanied by a crack of the reins as the driver called out to his team. He had to force himself to stay down and pray to the gods that they were not seen. The warriors following the chariot trudged by raggedly, accoutrements tapping against their shields. There was muted conversation, and Cato guessed they were returning from a route march, exhausted and only thinking of a meal and sleep. They kept coming, more and more of them; then at length the rear of the column passed by and the sound of their footsteps faded as the last men rounded the corner and descended the slight slope to the gatehouse.

'Thought there was no end of 'em for a moment there,' said Macro. 'Must have been hundreds of the bastards.'

'We move fast now,' said Ganomenus. 'We have to get back to the boat.'

He rose and jogged towards the track, and was almost across it when someone called out. Cato and Macro just had time to drop back into cover. Ganomenus froze, then turned slowly towards the voice and gave a shrug as he shook his head and pointed to his ear.

'I can't hear so good!'

The two Romans drew their swords and braced themselves.

For an instant Cato considered retreating further and waiting to see if Ganomenus managed to bluff his way out of the encounter. But it was more than likely that whoever had spotted him would take him in for questioning. Even if he managed to talk his way out of trouble, it would waste valuable time.

'The old fart is deaf,' a second voice commented.

'Deaf or not, he has no business being here.'

'Oh, leave him be. He's harmless. I'm starving and I don't want to spend any time dragging this poor bastard in front of Syphodubnus. He'll probably have him killed and chucked into the water in any case.'

Ganomenus flinched.

'He heard that all right,' the second voice continued suspiciously. 'Something ain't right here.'

Cato saw the two men move stiffly into view, shields slung across their backs and using their spears to prop themselves up as they approached Ganomenus.

'What's your game, old man?'

Cato rose to his feet, followed at once by Macro, and the two stole silently towards the warriors. At the last moment, Ganomenus could not help glancing towards them, and one of the warriors turned, his jaw dropping.

'Romans . . .'

His mouth was still gaping as Cato thrust the point of his sword into his side, driving the breath from his lungs and carrying him off his feet. The other warrior had faster reactions and swung, lowering his spear tip towards Macro. The centurion scrambled to a halt to prevent himself being skewered and parried aside the point. The warrior feinted and lunged again, driving him back. Macro's heel caught in a rut and he fell, dropping his sword. With a cry of triumph, the warrior raised his spear to make the kill. Then Ganomenus threw himself at the man, knocking him aside so the spear point bit into the mud of the track instead. As

312

both Icenians went down, Cato sprang forward, pausing to make sure his strike did not injure Ganomenus before he stabbed the warrior in the chest as he covered the man's mouth with his spare hand. As the old man rolled clear and stood up, the two rebels bled out, gasping as they writhed feebly before becoming still.

'Get 'em off the road,' Macro grunted, still slightly winded from his fall.

They wiped their blades and sheathed them before dragging the bodies a good distance into the reeds, along with their spears. Cato indicated the blood on the track and the smears on the grass and stalks that marked the trail of the corpses.

'That's going to give the game away if anyone comes back this way before dark.' He glanced up at the grey sky. 'Unless it rains first.'

'Those two beauties are going to be missed. Let's hope they leave it too late to search for them today.'

There was no time to disguise the scene further, and the three men plunged into the reeds on the far side of the track, hurrying across the difficult terrain, keeping low when the settlement was in sight, wading through water and mud and breaking into a trot across patches of drier ground. Ganomenus found it harder and harder to keep up with the two Romans, and they had to sling his arms over their shoulders as they carried on. The gloom of dusk gathered over the marsh, and Cato feared they might lose their way. At the same time, he was straining his ears for any sign of alarm that would indicate that the bodies had been discovered. But Fortuna seemed to have blessed them as those in the settlement occupied themselves with lighting fires to cook their evening meal or resting after the day's training.

As they reached the low embankment, he muttered, 'We're close. Not far now.'

They continued for a short distance before he paused and looked across the water. 'I think we've passed the place.'

313

'Can't have,' Macro answered. 'We'd have seen the boat.'

They retraced their steps, scanning the water's edge. It was Ganomenus who spotted the deep groove in the mud where the bottom of the boat had been dragged out of the water, barely visible in the failing light. 'There . . . that's where it was.'

Cato felt his heart sink. He slumped to the ground and rested his hands on his knees. Macro squatted beside him as the old man stared out into the channel with an anguished expression. 'He left us . . .'

'We're in trouble,' said Macro. 'Once they find the bodies, they'll send every man they can spare to find us.'

'I know.' Cato forced his tired mind to think through their options, but only one offered any real chance of survival. 'We can't go back to Branodunum. We have to take the track out of the marshes. There's no other way.'

'Hardrin's still here, still close by,' Ganomenus insisted. 'He wouldn't abandon us.'

'I'm not so sure,' said Macro. 'He's only a kid. He got scared and took off. Hardly surprising.'

'No.' Ganomenus shook his head. 'You're wrong. You'll see.'

He had recovered his breath now and folded his hands carefully before blowing into the narrow gap between his thumbs to emit a low hooting sound. He waited a moment and repeated it, then there was a rustling sound among the reeds a short distance away and the dark shape of their boat emerged.

'Thank the gods,' Cato muttered.

Hardrin brought the boat to the water's edge. 'I heard the rebel boat returning. I thought it best to be better hidden until you returned. Even then, I had to make sure it was you.'

'It's all right, lad,' Macro said as he climbed aboard and ruffled the boy's hair as the first drops of rain began to fall. 'You did the right thing. Never doubted you.'

CHAPTER TWENTY-SEVEN

There was a steady downpour as Boudica reined in a short distance from the small group of warriors standing with Syphodubnus. Her adviser stepped forward as she dismounted. No words were exchanged as he led her a short distance from the track over the flattened undergrowth to where a group of her warriors stood. They parted to reveal the two bodies that had been discovered by a hunter from the settlement. The faces and exposed skin were bone white with marble mottling after several days in the open. Their spears and shields lay amid the reeds where they had been hidden along with the corpses, although the stalks had been trampled by the men who had discovered them and dragged the bodies up to the track.

The two men had been missed the night they had failed to return with the column that had been taken out for a route march. They had been reported as stragglers, but when they had failed to return to Lyngomara the following morning, a search party was sent out to find them. When there was no sign of them along the track, Boudica assumed that the two men had deserted. That was a grave concern, given that they might fall into the hands of the Romans and be tortured into revealing the location of the rebel stronghold. However, when their closest comrades were questioned, they were adamant that the two missing men had given no indication that they were considering deserting.

But they would say that, she mused. If they had suspected their comrades had been about to abscond and said nothing about it to their superiors, they knew they would be severely punished. The stern discipline that she had insisted on in order to harden her men for the war against Rome had its drawbacks.

Syphodubnus squatted down beside one of the corpses and indicated the wound to the chest. 'A sword did that. The same with the other one. He was caught in the side and the point pierced his heart.'

Boudica bent to inspect the wounds and nodded. Then she asked the question that so much depended upon. 'Our swords, or theirs?'

Syphodubnus shrugged. 'Hard to say. But they were killed with the point. These wounds weren't caused by cuts, which most of our men are trained to deliver with long swords. If I had to make a decision, I'd say these were caused by short swords. But then we have equipped a number of our warriors with captured armour and weapons.'

'So it's possible they were murdered by some of our people. Perhaps some drunken argument that got out of hand? Or a clan feud? You know how such things can go back generations.'

'It's possible,' Syphodubnus conceded, 'but I don't think so. These men were stragglers. They never made it back even as far as the outer gatehouse. They must have been killed here on the track. I can't see any of our people coming out to lie in wait for them. Besides, the men on the gate that night reported no one leaving the settlement. There's also the manner in which they were hidden. The killers barely took the time to move them out of sight. They were in a hurry. If this was a murder carried out by someone here, I think they'd have done a better job of concealing the corpses.'

Boudica straightened up. Syphodubnus rose, and she gestured to him to follow her a short distance away from the other warriors.

'If this wasn't the work of one or more of our men, then the most likely explanation is that they were killed by the enemy. Almost certainly scouts. In which case we have to assume that they have finally discovered where we are.'

Syphodubnus nodded. 'It was only a matter of time.'

'I know.' She sighed. 'I just wish we had had more time to prepare. They'll be coming soon, and they will anticipate that we'll find the bodies and know that they're coming. All the same, we can prepare a few surprises for them. If we whittle down their numbers, we might yet turn this around and destroy the column Suetonius sent to deal with us.'

'Then he'll send another, and another . . .'

She looked at her adviser sharply. 'If that's what the enemy chooses to do, then it's to our advantage. We can defeat them in detail and each column they send against us will be more afraid than the one before.'

He smiled. 'You never lose heart, do you, my queen?'

'I lost that a long time ago. I'm a dead woman, Syphodubnus. If you accept you are dead, there is no reason to fear the enemy. You've already embraced the worst that can happen and there is nothing they can do to distract you from the need to keep killing them by whatever means necessary for as long as the gods permit. That is all that matters. If, by some miracle, we prevail, and we break their will and they withdraw from Britannia, then and only then will I rediscover my heart and think about the future again. I have a daughter left. I would see her find a fine match, have many children and live to old age in peace. But I will not allow myself to think on that. There, it is gone.' Her face was like stone once again. Cold, hard and unyielding.

'Have all the members of the high council arrived?' she went on.

'Yes. They were waiting to be summoned when the bodies were discovered. I thought you would want to deal with that first.'

'Quite right. I'll speak with them now. They'll need to be told that the Romans know where we are. The fight has come to us and we must be ready.'

'Yes, majesty.'

Boudica paused to look down the track, as if she could already hear the enemy approaching. Then she indicated the bodies. 'Have them buried beside the track.'

'No ceremony in the sacred grove?'

'There isn't time. Besides, they don't deserve the honour. They failed to keep up with the others and allowed themselves to be killed by the enemy. I don't want the other men to be disheartened by the sight of their bodies. Bury them here.'

'As you command.'

The hall was cool and clammy and the heat from the hearths could not rid the place of the odour of damp and the sour scent of decay. The small group of nobles who commanded the warbands of the tribe had been gathered to discuss the progress of the rebellion. Or lack of it, Boudica mused as she entered the hall and strode between the lines of men before taking her seat at the far end. They were not going to like the latest messages received from the envoys she had sent to the other tribes to try and agree an alliance against Rome. She was wearing her usual garb of a plain tunic, leggings and cloak and had made no effort to appear before them in any of the trappings of royalty. She settled for a moment and composed her mind before addressing them.

'I asked you here for another reason, but first I must reveal that the crisis we all hoped to put off for some time yet is upon us. It is almost certain that the enemy have discovered the location of Lyngomara and may already be marching on us.' She briefly described the discovery of the bodies and what that meant for the rebels.

She was pleased to scc that most of her nobles responded with fatalistic expressions. Only a few looked anxious and afraid. She mentally recorded the faces of the latter with a view to ensuring that they were replaced by more reliable men after the meeting.

'There are two paths of action open to us. Firstly, we take our men and advance to meet the enemy in battle. I have no doubt that the hard training that they have gone through over the winter means they will give as good an account of themselves as any warriors who ever lived in Britannia. Be that as it may, we shall still be outnumbered four to one. Even allowing for the superiority of our warriors, it is likely that we would be defeated. Again. Such a defeat would be impossible to recover from and the rebellion would be over, the Icenian tribe would be crushed and the survivors would become the slaves of Rome. The second path is the one I have anticipated from the outset. We remain here and defend Lyngomara. The settlement has all the advantages of a natural fortress. It can only be attacked on a narrow front, and the Roman forces will break upon our defences as waves break on a rock. We have the advantage here, and even though they outnumber us, that will count for nothing when they come at us along the narrow track.'

'What if they don't come from that direction?' asked one of the nobles.

'What choice do they have?' Boudica retorted. 'They can't get their men through the marshes, and even if they did, we are surrounded by water.'

'Then how did the scouts find the place?'

It was a good question, Boudica realised. How had the Romans managed to get close enough to Lyngomara to leave the bodies where they were found? It was unlikely that they had come down the track, as that was regularly patrolled and they would surely have been spotted at some point. In that case, they must have found a way through the mass of channels that snaked through the marsh. Though the nearest waterways were used by Boudica's men to move to jump-off points from which to attack the Romans, the enemy scouts would have found it easier to evade the rebels there than if they had tried the track. And if they had been able to do that, then others would be able to as well.

'A fair point,' she conceded. 'I will give orders for watch to be kept over the marshes, but any concerted attack from that quarter would be impossible.' She tried to imagine the heavily burdened legionaries and auxiliaries struggling through the mire and reeds, frequently forced to drag their boats over shallows or dried-out strips of land. And where would they get sufficient boats from in the first place? All the same, it could be done.

'Not impossible, maybe,' she corrected herself. 'But impractical, to say the least. But no matter which direction they choose to attack us from, we shall be ready, and we will make sure they pay dearly for every assault they attempt. We will wear them down and they will be forced to retreat, and then we shall go after them, like hounds snapping at the heels of their prey. We will bring them down and tear out their throats.' She had found the comparison so compelling, she was unaware of her fanatical expression and the gleam in her eyes. Now, as her mind cleared and she recovered her austere mask, she spoke in a calmer tone. 'We will defend Lyngomara. We will defeat every attempt by the enemy to set foot on the island. We will drive them back in confusion. We will rout and destroy them, and none will be spared. Does any man here doubt my word on this?' She glared at the rebels in the hall and was relieved that none dared challenge her.

'Good. Then we will make our stand against the Romans here.'

The noble who had spoken earlier raised his hand, and she turned to him. 'You wish to speak, Anesca?'

He nodded. 'Majesty, the enemy outnumber us. What has

become of the aid we asked for from the other tribes? If they could send us but a fraction of their warrior strength, we could face the Romans on equal terms.'

The question had brought them back to the reason for the gathering in the first place. Boudica drew herself up in her chair, grasping the carved arms as she gathered herself to answer.

'There will be no help from any other tribes. The envoys I sent have either been rebuffed or they have been met with betrayal. Some were handed over to the Romans, while others were murdered to appease the enemy. It is possible that those captured have been forced to reveal our location. Only a handful of the warriors of those tribes brave enough to defy their leaders have been able to join us here. Most were unable to get past the Roman forts and patrols along our western border. They were killed or captured or managed to escape and return to their tribes. We are alone. No one is coming to our aid.'

There was silence in the hall, apart from the crackle of the flames in the hearths.

'The other tribes will earn the scorn of history. If we have to face Rome alone, then very well, alone it shall be. And so much greater will be the glory we earn for the name of the Icenian people when we are victorious. I would not have unwilling, timid allies fight at my side. Timorous cowards eager to kiss the feet of their Roman masters rather than stand and fight with honour for the freedom of all our tribes. When the Romans are finally driven from our shores, the victory will belong first and foremost to the Iceni, and above all else to those who are here today. We are a band of warriors unlike any other, and this is the greatest test of our people. The greatest test of any tribe in Britannia. We are the few, the lucky few, to whom this great honour has been entrusted, and we must summon up the courage, determination and skill to defeat the great evil that is embodied by Rome and everything it stands for. And may all those who live after us on

321

this island recall and relive our deeds. We are on the eve of a battle between the forces of darkness and light.'

She rose from her chair and opened her arms, raising them as she continued, her voice trembling with passion. 'We must prevail and be the spark that becomes the flame that becomes the inferno that engulfs and consumes Rome so that the forces of oppression perish amid the flames!'

Her eyes were wide and her nostrils flared as she gazed at her nobles, but it was not clear whether their expressions evinced awed inspiration at her words or abject terror.

Over the following days of fine spring weather, there was frenzied activity in and around Lyngomara. The morning mists dispersed soon after dawn and the sun shone amid fluffy white clouds and bathed the marsh in its warmth. Teams of Boudica's warriors, stripped to the waist, laboured to improve the defences of the settlement. They built up the height and strength of the sequence of gatehouses and protected their flanks with sharpened stakes sunk into the bed of the marsh with their tips hidden beneath the brackish water. The reeds and undergrowth were cleared away for some distance around the expanse of water that surrounded the settlement. Concealed ditches with more sharpened stakes were prepared along the track. Parties of warriors were sent out to forage for food to supplement the reserves already gathered in. Blacksmiths worked over forges to prepare arrowheads, javelin tips and caltrops. The last were a weapon that Boudica had seen in action when she had fought alongside the Romans years before: small iron objects with four prongs an inch long that could be scattered in grass to injure horses and unwary foot soldiers. Such injuries were often crippling, and enemies of Rome had rightly come to fear the devices. Now the Romans would be paid back in kind.

Scouts were sent out of the marsh to gather intelligence on enemy preparations, but they were intercepted and driven off by their more numerous Roman counterparts, and Boudica reluctantly recalled them to carry out more productive tasks. Meanwhile an ongoing series of skirmishes were fought by warriors and auxiliaries at the edge of the marsh where the track leading to the settlement began. The enemy now knew about the hidden entrance, and the camouflage that had been used to hide the end of the track was now superfluous and had been abandoned.

Within the settlement, further lines of defence were constructed or improved and the ditch between the settlement and the stronghold upon which Boudica's hall stood was widened and deepened, the bridge replaced with a narrow suspended structure that could be swiftly cut away if the rebels were driven back to this final redoubt. If it came to that, Boudica knew the rebellion would be defeated. At that point all that would remain would be to kill as many of the Roman attackers as possible before she and the last of her followers were overwhelmed. That at least would demonstrate the courage of those who dared to defy the greatest empire in the known world.

One night, after she had dismissed her advisers, Boudica sat with her elder daughter beside the hearth, supping on stew. Both were exhausted from the efforts of recent days. Their minds were preoccupied with the preparations and the prospects of victory or defeat in the coming battle. Neither uttered a word as they ate, gazing absently into the flames. At length, Bardea set her bowl aside and spoke quietly. 'Can we win? Can we defeat the Romans when they come for us?'

'Of course we can,' Boudica replied at once. 'We are the Iceni. The best warriors—'

'Mother, you are talking to me, not addressing the men. For once, be my mother, and be honest with me. I have a right to know the truth. I have suffered as you have suffered at the Romans' hands. I was by your side when we marched on their

323

towns and faced them in battle. I was there when we fled the battlefield, and I have been with you as we continued the fight from here. I have done all you have asked of me and never expected anything in return. All I want now is to be told the truth. Mother to daughter. Is that too much to ask?'

Boudica, so used to having her mind filled with the demands of building her army, orchestrating attacks on the enemy and preparing for battle, was suddenly speechless. As she stared back at her daughter, she saw the fear in the girl's eyes and the desperate need for reassurance and understanding. Recent years melted away and she saw the child who had been so cheerful, alert and full of delight, humour and mischief. Unspoiled by the outrage she had endured at the hands of the Romans. That and the violence that had followed had aged her prematurely, and the girl she had once been was lost for ever. An overwhelming wave of sadness and guilt chewed through Boudica's stomach, and her heart filled with the dark tragedy of it all.

'I am so sorry, my dearest daughter. I have failed you. I have failed you as a mother. I have become something else. Something I never wanted to be.' She felt the great burden upon her increase as she realised the full cost of the cause that she had permitted to define her existence for the previous year. She felt tears welling up inside her and longed once more for the strong arms of her dead husband to hold her, to comfort her. To let her be the person she was before the horror had engulfed them all.

'You are still my mother,' said Bardea. 'I love you and I am proud of you. I will stay with you to the end. I just need to know what that end will be.'

Boudica clenched her eyes shut and balled her hands into fists as she fought to control the conflicting emotions raging inside her. Every muscle in her body ached with the strain of it. At last she regained her grip on herself and breathed deeply before she opened her eyes and cuffed away the tears that were forming there.

'The truth,' she began. 'Yes, I shall tell you the truth. I don't know if we can defeat the Romans. For all the training we have done over the winter and all the preparations we may make, the truth is that they wage war better than we do. Particularly the men leading the army we shall face. I saw Macro when we ambushed the enemy in the Trinovantian village. Of all the Romans I have ever known, he is the greatest of their warriors. You saw how he defeated our champion in single combat last year when he was our prisoner. Who else is capable of such a feat? And where Macro is, you can be sure his friend Cato is nearby. I fear him even more. He has the sharpest wits of any man. If there is a way to defeat us, he will know of it. He is also the darling of fate. His intelligence is matched by his good fortune. That is why I fear what is to come.'

'Then you think they will win?'

Boudica hesitated, and her daughter leaned closer and took her hand and squeezed it tightly. 'The truth, remember.'

'The truth is that nothing is certain.'

'But it is likely?' Bardea pressed her.

'Yes.' Boudica nodded, and felt such relief and release at the uttering of a single word that she repeated it in a firmer voice. 'Yes.'

'Thank you,' Bardea replied. 'Then I will try my best to be ready for the end when it comes. I will not be taken alive. They will not rape me again.'

A fresh wound opened in Boudica's heart, and it took all her courage to speak an even harder truth.

'I don't want you to die. I want you to survive, to live and have the life I had hoped for you.'

'I am not going to leave you,' Bardea said sharply. 'I have learned how to wield a sword. I am not helpless and I will not abandon my mother or my people at their time of greatest need.'

Boudica raised her free hand to try and reassure her daughter.

'I could order you to leave. I could have some of my warriors take you from here to a place of safety. But I know you well enough to realise that you will find a way to escape from them and come back here. No. I will not do that. But there is something I need to tell you now. Something I should have said long ago but lacked the courage to do because of the pain it would cause to you, your . . . father and many others. If I tell you now, it may be a way of saving your life, and nothing means more to me than that.'

'Save me? How? What do you mean?'

'You said you wanted the truth. The whole truth.'

'Yes. No secrets.'

Boudica shook her head wearily. 'That is what the young always say they want. One day you may understand that you should be careful what you wish for. All right then. No secrets. Prasutagus was not your father.'

Bardea became very still, hardly breathing as she stared at her mother to try and gauge if this was the truth or some attempt to manipulate her through deception.

'He is, was, the father of Merida. I am sure he wanted to believe that you were his. He never asked me directly, but I know he had doubts. He loved you as his own and you must always be grateful for that.'

'If not him, then who?' Bardea demanded.

Boudica opened her mouth to answer, but the words would not come, and she winced.

'Tell me.'

She tightened her grip on her daughter's hand. 'Macro . . . Macro is your father.'

She felt her daughter flinch. 'No . . . NO!'

Bardea tried to snatch her hand back, but Boudica resisted her and caught hold of the folds of her tunic, gripping the material tightly. 'Yes. That is the truth. You should have been told before. That is my fault. No apology will ever make up for it.'

326

'No!' Bardea shook her head, tears of rage in her eyes.

'It's true. And he knows too. I told him last year. He never suspected either.'

'How?'

'How?' Boudica smiled slightly. 'How do you think? We met after the Romans took Camulodunum in the first year of the invasion. At that time the Iceni were allies of Rome. There was something instant between us.' She felt a moment's warmth as she recalled it. 'But neither of us expected anything more, and I was betrothed to Prasutagus soon afterwards. Soon enough for everyone to believe that you were his daughter when you were born. But I could see your real father in you. Have you never wondered at the differences between you and Merida?'

Bardea's cheeks were lined with tears as she looked numbly into the hearth.

'You have the blood of Rome as well as the Iceni flowing through you,' Boudica continued urgently. 'That may save you yet. When the time comes, you must tell the Romans who you are. You must demand to speak to Macro. If I am any judge of character, he will offer you protection and raise you as a father should. He is a good man, even if he is our enemy now.'

'He is a Roman.'

'When we were being held by the Roman procurator, Decianus, and abused by his men, it was Macro who set us free and helped us to escape. That cost his people dear. The consequences of that decision will weigh on him for the rest of his life. He made it possible for me to rouse the tribe into the rebellion that has been the cause of so much bloodshed and suffering. Do not judge him too harshly, daughter. He has his own demons to bear. But he will protect you if you let him. And you must. So much has been taken from all of us already and we must do what we can to see that some good comes out of this. If I have to die, then let it be knowing that you will

327

live. I beg you. And I beg your forgiveness for not telling you the truth before.'

'You beg me?' Bardea said fiercely. 'So you should. You traitor!'

She slapped her mother across the face. It was a hard blow, delivered in rage, and her knuckles split Boudica's lip.

Boudica tasted blood in her mouth as she held out her arms, her eyes pleading. 'My dearest daughter . . .'

'No! Don't you dare!' Bardea turned and ran down the hall. As she neared the far end, Syphodubnus entered, followed by another man. They stepped out of her way and eyed her curiously as she charged by, crying freely.

Wiping the blood from her lip, Boudica composed herself. 'What is it?'

As her adviser came closer, she could make out the face of the man behind him and felt herself jolted back into her role as the leader of the rebellion.

'Majesty,' Syphodubnus began, 'the Romans are coming. Pernocatus rode here to warn us the moment his unit was told to prepare to march against Lyngomara. He knows their strength, the weapons they will bring to bear against us. And there is more, but I thought you should be told right away that they are coming for us.'

Boudica nodded slowly. 'The time has come. Spread the word and raise my standard above the first gatehouse where the enemy will see it when they reach us. Tell our warriors that the gods have at last given us the chance to face the Romans in battle and show them what vengeance means.'

CHAPTER TWENTY-EIGHT

'That's nasty.' Macro made a face as he looked down at the three auxiliaries at the bottom of the ditch. They had been impaled on stakes. Two of them had died in place, unable to free themselves; the third had managed, by some superhuman effort, to do so, but had bled out before he could climb the side of the ditch.

'Indeed.' The trap had been concealed just beyond a corner of the track. Covered with a light trellis of pine branches and a thin layer of mud, it must have been almost invisible to the auxiliaries who had been chasing the Icenian rearguard. 'Have the bodies removed and the ditch filled in. We don't need any further damage to the men's morale.'

He nodded towards the auxiliaries filing past the ditch on either side, looking down anxiously at the three corpses.

'What the fuck are you lot gawking at?' Macro bellowed at them. 'You've seen dead bodies before and you'll see plenty more of 'em before this lot's over! Keep moving! You, Optio, come here!'

He ordered the man to take two sections and do as Cato instructed before turning back to his friend. 'That's the third one today. Eight dead, including this lot, and twelve wounded.'

'Third?'

'There's another a hundred paces further along. Cunning

bastards set one up on the track and made it easy enough to spot, only there were others to the side. Got four more men from Thrasyllus's cohort. I've told them to take their time and check the ground ahead of them as they go. Shame we don't have any prisoners we could drive in front of us to spring these traps.'

'Even if we did, it would mean a delay bringing them up from Venta Icenorum. We'd lose two days at least. It's a pity. The vanguard will just have to watch their step.' Cato removed his helmet and skullcap and mopped his brow. This was the second day the column had been advancing along the track through the marsh, and the enemy had contested almost every stretch of the route. They had thrown up fieldworks blocking the way, forcing the column to halt while men were sent forward into a hail of missiles to assault the ditches and earthworks and drive the rebels off. The enemy gave ground rather than mount any do-or-die effort, and fell back to the next line of defence, leaving the Romans to dismantle the obstacles and continue the advance. It was a slow and tiring process. The Icenians had also launched harassing attacks from the marsh on either side of the track, releasing volleys of arrows and light javelins before melting away, steering clear of the caltrops they had sown in the grass beside the track. After suffering several casualties the Romans were wary of chasing the enemy into the marshes and paused to clear away the small, but very effective weapons. It was apparent that the rebels had been ordered to avoid any direct contact with Cato's men, for the present at least. It was a shrewd decision. Nothing infuriated and frustrated soldiers more than suffering a steady rate of casualties without being able to hit back. Jeering and shouting accusations of cowardice at the fleeing rebels was no compensation. Particularly when every follow-up unit passed the dead and wounded being carried to the rear. If it had been up to Cato they would have simply besieged the enemy and starved them into surrender, no matter how long it took. But time was

330

against them. Rome needed a swift victory to crush the spirit of rebellion simmering across the province before a fresh uprising could occur elsewhere.

Boudica had prepared well for this, Cato conceded. The rebels were fighting in a new manner that suited the ground and revealed a far more disciplined approach. Only a handful had been wounded so far, and they had been carried away by their comrades before they could fall into Roman hands, emphasising the one-sided casualty rate endured so far.

'We can't have advanced more than ten miles into the marsh in total,' Macro estimated. 'At this rate it'll take nearly two more days to reach Lyngomara, if Ganomenus's estimate is accurate.'

Following their return from the reconnaissance trip, Cato had taken the old man back to Venta Icenorum to lead them to the edge of the marsh, where he revealed the concealed end of the secret track. They had encountered the first of Boudica's warriors almost immediately and had had to beat a hasty retreat as the enemy drove them off with arrows.

The Roman losses of the first day's advance had been reduced by interspersing groups of men armed with slings and bows between each of the infantry centuries. That had proved to be an effective response to the harassing attacks from the flanks, as well as a means of clearing the enemy away from the fieldworks set up across the track, and the column had made better progress. Until it had encountered the new danger in the form of the traps, such as the one Cato and Macro were standing in front of.

'We'll just have to be patient, brother. We have the rebels where we want them. They can't escape along the track. Ganomenus has returned to the coast to guide the naval squadron in from the north and the cavalry cohorts and Vellocatus's scouts are covering the edge of the marsh to the south and west. We must push on while doing our best to avoid any more traps they have set for us. The real contest will happen when we come up against the approaches to Lyngomara. The enemy are bound to have made significant improvements to the defences we saw before. Be that as it may, they are in for a shock when our warships get in on the act.'

Macro shook his head. 'Fat chance of that. You saw how narrow and twisting the channels through the marsh were. And that's without taking into account the shallow stretches. We'd be lucky to get even Besodius's barges within a mile of the place.'

'I have some ideas about that,' Cato replied. 'We'll see when we link up with the squadron closer to the settlement. If we can bring sufficient artillery to bear on their defences it may tip things in our favour.'

'Artillery or no, we'll still have to make a frontal attack,' said Macro. 'It's going to be a costly and hard-fought business. Nothing like the action we've seen so far. They're not going to just lob a few arrows and spears and run off. They'll fight like bloody lions when their backs are against the wall. You know how dangerous a Celt is when he's cornered. And with the training Boudica has given them, they'll be an even harder bunch of lads to deal with. Then there's us with a handful of veteran auxiliary cohorts, topped up by fresh recruits and the lads from the Second Legion. I've done the best I can with them over the winter, but this will be their first battle. Who knows how they're going to cope?'

'If you trained them, they'll cope as well as any men facing their first taste of battle.' Cato paused and cocked an ear forward along the track. He could just make out the shouting of orders followed by muffled thuds. He replaced his cap and helmet and fastened the straps. 'Come on. We need to get up there.'

The advance to the rebel stronghold took three days. The enemy fought one delaying action after another, inflicting a steady toll on the auxiliaries leading the way. After the warriors had been driven back, there would be a further delay as the obstacles were demolished and traps searched for and marked by the engineers before follow-up troops filled them in. The presence of missile troops in the Roman ranks discouraged any further harassment from the flanks, and that provided considerable relief to the men. It was one thing to see your foe across a battlefield, quite another to live moment to moment waiting to be struck by an arrow, javelin or slingshot from an invisible enemy.

It was late afternoon on the third day when the first of the rebel gatehouses came into view, the recently raised tower looming above the top of the reeds. It was the Eighth Cohort's turn to lead the advance that day, and Macro ordered the men to halt while he and Cato went on a short distance to examine the enemy's defences, taking care to remain safely beyond the range of any arrows.

'Watch your step, lad!' Macro said suddenly, pulling Cato back.

In front of them was the slightest depression in the muddy track. There was open ground on either side where reeds had been trampled, and Cato had a sense of having been there before. Then he realised they were on the very spot where he and Macro had killed the stragglers. A glance to the side revealed the mound just beyond the place where the bodies had been left.

Macro was cautiously testing the ground with his right foot, leaning back as he did so. Sure enough, the surface gave a little, and then a little more as he applied additional pressure. A small patch of earth shuddered and fell away, leaving a hole several inches across. Looking round, he spotted the rotten stump of a tree. Carefully making his way to it, he wrenched off a lump of the sodden moss-covered timber and retraced his steps to the track. With a grunt, he heaved it onto the centre of the depressed area, and the trap caved in with a rustle of branches and a thud as the lump hit the bottom of the ditch. A large opening exposed the lethal tips of the stakes and the caltrops scattered below.

He clicked his tongue. 'Lucky escape. Another step and we'd have been skewered.'

It was warm even for spring, and Cato felt a trickle of sweat between his shoulder blades. The strains of recent months had taken their toll. He felt tired almost all the time. He had lost concentration for a moment and would have blundered into the trap had Macro not stopped him. He took a moment to force himself to sharpen his attention before he replied.

'Hopefully that'll be one of the last of them.'

'I doubt it. They're bound to have other things up their sleeves. Have to hand it to them, the rebels have played a good game so far. But their luck's run out. From now on it's going to be head-to-head fighting.'

Cato nodded. There was always something reassuring in the way Macro discussed the prospect of bloody battle with such casual detachment. When they had first met, he had assumed it was the veteran's way of dealing with nerves, but he had soon come to realise that it was simply the mindset of a professional totally at home in such a dangerous environment. In the many years that Cato himself had served in the army, he had never managed to develop the same degree of stolid assurance and had had to perform as if he had. He envied his friend.

They worked their way around the trap and advanced until they had a clear view of the outermost gatehouse. It stood across the track, fifty paces on from the edge of the sacred grove. They could see a further fortification rising up behind the gatehouse. A stockade had also been erected, curving round to cover each flank. The heads and shoulders of enemy warriors lined the top of the tower. Most were wearing helmets, some of which were of Roman pattern, the spoils of war. As the two Roman officers came into view, the defenders shouted war cries and brandished their weapons in a showy challenge. Macro gave them a cheery wave before he stood, hands on hips, stocky legs astride, and surveyed the defences.

'They've been busy. That tower wasn't there when we scouted the place.'

'And there'll be plenty of other improvements put in place. We're going to have our work cut out.'

'Made no easier by the governor insisting we take Lyngomara in short order. They're not going to pose any danger to the rest of the province while they're cooped up. And even if they have stored up provisions for a siege, their supplies won't last for ever.' Macro glanced round at the marsh. 'Not that I'd be keen on spending too much time camped out here waiting for them to surrender. But it would be the sensible option.'

Cato had made the same argument in a dispatch to the governor the moment the route through the marshes had been discovered. However, Suetonius's response had made it clear that no delay would be tolerated. The rebel stronghold was to be attacked at once, the rebellion crushed and Boudica's body brought to him, alive or dead.

'We're going to need a camp. There was that island we passed over a mile or so back. Agricola's engineers can clear and level the ground for the men to put up tents. When it's dark, we'll send some units from the Eighth forward to scout the approaches to the gatehouse and mark out any remaining traps. Then tomorrow we'll send in the first attack and put their defences to the test.'

'Who gets first crack at them?' Macro asked.

Cato had already considered this. In the normal course of events, such a task would be handled by the heavy infantry of the legions. But there was a danger that Agricola's inexperienced men would baulk at the challenge facing them and be thrown back. That would be a serious blow to their morale. In Cato's experience, it was necessary to entrust green troops with a fight they would win to embolden them for future battles. It would be better for a veteran unit to soften up the enemy before giving the legionaries their first taste of battle.

'I think the Eighth would be the most suitable for the job. Are your men ready for it, Centurion Macro?'

'Does the emperor shit in the palace?' Macro grinned. 'The lads will do us proud.'

That evening, the men of Cato's column completed the construction of the marching camp on the island. The limited space was just large enough for the infantry and their baggage train. The irregular shape of the island meant that there was no possibility of establishing the usual rectangular layout, and the engineers were obliged to erect the defences accordingly. The headquarters tents were set up on the highest point, some ten feet above the rest of the camp, from where the enemy gatehouse and the trees of the sacred grove could easily be seen. As darkness swallowed up the last of the daylight, Cato could make out the glow of fires in the enemy stronghold, and in the still air he caught snatches of their revelry as they too prepared for battle. Around him he heard the sounds of his own men as they finished putting up their tents and began to build up cooking fires using the combustible material the legionaries had cut back to make space for the camp. Although there was plenty of cheerful banter throughout most of the tent lines, he could guess at the more subdued atmosphere among those of the Eighth Cohort as the men prepared themselves for the coming attack. A frontal assault on fortifications was one of the most challenging tasks that could be demanded of soldiers, and was likely to be costly even if successful. Cato felt a moment's anger directed towards Suetonius, who had issued orders for men to put their lives at risk for the sake of a politically expedient quick result.

Just after Trebonius had set his evening meal on the campaign table, a marine was escorted into Cato's presence by one of the sentries. He was smeared with mud and looked exhausted as he stood to attention and saluted.

'At ease,' said Cato.

'Beg to report, sir, I have been sent by the navarch.'

'He has succeeded in getting his vessels through the marsh, then?'

The marine shook his head. 'The bireme couldn't make it more than a few miles up the channel from Branodunum before it became too shallow to proceed any further. The liburnians fared better and reached a point no more than five miles short of the enemy's stronghold, sir. Only the smaller craft can get any closer. The problem is not the width of the channels but the depth of the water.'

'I see.' Cato considered the situation for a moment. He needed artillery to batter the enemy's defences, and the only available artillery was on the warships. He had considered requisitioning it to support the assault along the track, but it would make little impact in the restricted space. He needed a floating battery that was capable of delivering a more powerful blow.

'How did you get through to the camp?' he asked the marine.

'Used one of the hide-covered craft supplied by Ganomenus, sir. That and a bit of wading. Was easy enough once the morning mist had risen.'

'Are you confident you can find your way back to the squadron? Where is the navarch?'

'On one of the liburnians, sir. I know the way.' The marine nodded towards the darkness outside the tent flaps. 'In daylight, that is.'

'Good, then I'll need you to take me to him tomorrow. Now find yourself something to eat and get some rest. Dismissed.'

'Yes, sir.'

'Trebonius!'

The steward appeared at the entrance to the tent.

'See that the marine is fed.'

'More cooking,' the steward muttered as he stalked off. 'Join

337

the army, they said . . . see the Empire. All I'm seeing is bloomin'
pots and pans.'

Cato ignored the man's grumbling and focused his mind on
the implications of the marine's report. It was vital to find a way
of getting at least some of the warships to bring their firepower
to bear on the enemy's defences.

Macro used the morning mist as cover while the Eighth Cohort
infantry moved into position. A section was sent ahead to drive off
the rebels who had been keeping watch in front of the gatehouse.
Galerius and the First Century were to make the initial assault,
and stood ready with their ladders. Ahead of them, and on either
side of the track as far as the marsh allowed, men from another
century stood by with their slings, waiting for the order to pelt
the defences as their comrades moved forward to attack. Four
more centuries were ready to follow up if the gatehouse was
taken. The remainder formed the reserve, sitting down either
side of the track to the rear.

Cato, in full armour and carrying an oval cavalry shield, stood
beside Macro and Galerius at the head of the leading unit. He
looked over the auxiliaries nearest to him. Many of the faces
were familiar to him from the previous year's campaign in the
mountains. The others he did not yet recognise – replacements
sent to restore the cohort to full strength. The men stood silently,
but there were noticeable tics that revealed their anxiety: tapping
toes, drumming fingers on the hilts of their swords, and the many
other ways that nerves betrayed them. As they waited for the mist
to disperse the tension, they could hear orders being called out
from the direction of the gatehouse and smell the faint odour of
woodsmoke from the enemy's fires.

One of the younger auxiliaries in the second rank, shorter
and thinner than his comrades, suddenly leaned to the side and
vomited. Those around him chuckled until Galerius hissed at

them to keep silent. Macro turned to the youth and gave him a smile.

'Never mind, lad. Better out than in. Just don't piss or shit yourself, eh? None of your mates should have to walk through that.'

The young auxiliary nodded his head solemnly, then pressed his lips together and stared ahead with a determined expression.

The sun had risen clear of the mist and the Romans began to feel its warmth. Features that had been no more than vague shades of grey resolved into shrubs, trees and clumps of grass, and they could see further and further down the track. Then Cato could make out the gatehouse, less than a hundred paces away, with more detail appearing at every moment. The enemy began to jeer. Macro adjusted the grip on his shield and rolled his shoulders in preparation.

'Slingers! Make ready!'

On either side the auxiliaries fitted lead shot into the pouches hanging from the thongs and tested their swing as they awaited the next order.

Macro waited a little longer so that the target could be easily seen. The enemy were already lining the top of the tower and the palisade on either side, their faces clearly visible.

'Slingers! Release at will!'

There was a whirring sound as the auxiliaries spun their weapons up to the side then overhead before releasing as their throwing arms snapped forward. It was just possible to follow the trajectory as the lethal lead missiles, the size of plums, sped towards the gatehouse. Due to the din from their war cries, the enemy could not hear the telltale sound of the slings getting up speed to launch, and they were only aware of the danger when the first volley crashed home, splintering the timbers of the palisade and gatehouse. At once they dropped out of sight and their shouted challenges died in their throats. Cato couldn't tell if any casualties had been inflicted, but the barrage had certainly shut them up and shaken them.

'All right, Galerius,' said Macro. 'In you go.'

The centurion spat to clear his mouth and called out, 'First Century! Advance!'

The auxiliary cohort moved off, shields raised, boots squelching on the soft earth and mud. They went forward four abreast, weaving past the sticks with small strips of cloth that marked the last few traps before the gatehouse. Ahead of them, some of the enemy rose warily from behind the shelter of the defences. One of them raised a cheer that was immediately silenced, and they looked on soundlessly as the slender Roman formation approached. Cato couldn't help but admire the improvement in their discipline, and felt sad that such men could not have been put to better use, rather than dying for a doomed cause.

He saw the first of their arrows arc up from behind the palisade and fly through the clear morning air, hanging for an instant before plunging down to land just in front of the head of Galerius's century. The men would be in effective range within a few paces.

'Slingers! Make ready,' Macro ordered.

There would be time for just one more volley before there was a danger of inflicting friendly casualties with poorly executed shots.

'Release!'

This time the rebels were ready, and ducked down the moment the slingers released their missiles. The shot struck the defences without hitting any of the defenders. They were speedily back on their feet, and now it was their turn to unleash a barrage.

'First century! Halt!' Galerius ordered. 'Form testudo!'

His men raised their shields over their heads and closed up so that the shields overlapped. Once they were in position, Galerius, on the right of the front rank, gave the order to resume the advance. A constant rain of arrows and javelins arced from the gatehouse and palisade and clattered down onto the shields. Some managed to pierce the surface enough to encumber the shields and make them awkward to handle, but the formation held its nerve and kept to the steady pace called out by the centurion. Cato saw one of the men pull out of position and crouch beside the track, covering his body with his shield while he struggled to snap off the shaft of the arrow that was embedded at an acute angle in the top of his thigh.

As the head of the testudo reached the narrow causeway across the water-filled ditch in front of the gatehouse, the enemy added small logs to the missiles crashing onto their attackers. These were much more effective in breaking up the Roman formation, and Cato and Macro looked on with concern as Galerius stood with his back to the gate and his shield overhead, ordering his men to spread out on either side. The ladder carriers managed to erect two to the right and one to the left, while the one in the centre proved too short to reach the top of the tower and was hastily repositioned. While two of his comrades steadied the risers, the first of the auxiliaries began to climb up to the palisade, doing his best to protect himself with his shield as he ascended to the left of the gates. He only made it halfway before he was struck by two arrows and tumbled off the ladder to splash into the ditch and be impaled on the point of a submerged stake.

One by one the men of the First Century climbed the ladders. At least half of them were struck down before they could reach the top and draw their swords to engage the defenders. Even those who made it faced an unequal struggle, and not one was able to climb over and gain a foothold within the palisade. The frenzied efforts of the rebels made that impossible.

Cato had seen enough. 'Pull 'em back.'

Macro nodded and trotted halfway down the track to ensure that the order was clearly received above the clamour of battle.

'First Century! Withdraw!'

Galerius repeated the command, and the testudo re-formed

and slowly backed away, with the centurion steadily calling the time. Only when they were safely out of range of the renewed barrage of rebel missiles did he halt his men, form into a marching column and trudge back to Cato. Macro lingered a moment longer, studying the defences over the top of his shield while deflecting a few arrows that were on target. Then he moved to the nearest of the injured men, still kneeling beside the track, and helped him to his feet before both pulled back to where Cato was standing.

As medical orderlies helped the wounded move to the rear, the two officers stared towards the gatehouse for a moment without speaking. The bodies of the auxiliaries, some still and some moving, scattered along the final stretch of track and in front of the gatehouse, along the bottom of the palisade and in the water of the ditches, made for a sombre sight. At least twenty men had been lost, Cato estimated. While he watched, the rebels leaned over the palisade to pull up the ladders and throw them down inside the defences.

'That didn't go too well,' Macro announced. 'Buggers are putting up a spirited resistance. We're not going to have much luck with those defences.'

'No,' Cato replied sourly. 'We're not.'

He had done as ordered and attacked at once, and the attack had failed. He would be sure that was clearly stated in his next dispatch to the governor. Now a more measured approach was required. 'Time for a ram, I think.'

Macro nodded. 'A ram. Definitely.'

'And a mantle to protect it. Tell Agricola to get his engineers on to it straight away.'

'Yes, sir.'

'Have the Second Century remain here to keep an eye on the rebels. The rest of the cohort can return to camp. We'll rest the column until the ram comes up. Meanwhile, it's time I had a word with our navy friends.'

CHAPTER TWENTY-NINE

'It's no good, Prefect Cato. We've tried every channel Ganomenus can find.' Navarch Turpillius shrugged his broad shoulders. 'There's no way we can get anything larger than one of Besodius's barges any further than here.'

'Have you tried?' Cato responded impatiently.

'Certainly.' Turpillius thumped the side rail of the liburnian. 'That's why we're aground now. I was forced to leave the bireme near the edge of the marsh and continue aboard this. I'm waiting for another of my liburnians to tow us off. Then I'm pulling my squadron back to join the other biremes anchored off Branodunum before we get into any more difficulties.'

'Your ships are going nowhere until I give the order. I need your artillery and I need every ship we can get on the water around the rebel stronghold.'

'And how do you propose we do that, exactly?' The navarch smiled slightly as he folded his arms. 'Do enlighten me, Prefect. I'm all ears. I'm telling you, we can't get anything across that last stretch that's large enough to bear the weight of even one of my catapults or bolt-throwers. With all these reed banks and mud flats there's no way of dragging them over, and no way of dredging a channel. Face it, we've done what we can and my squadron can't be of any further use to you.'

Cato turned away to look in the direction of Lyngomara,

tantalisingly close yet too far. Ganomenus and Besodius stood a short distance off, keeping clear of the confrontation. As he viewed the channel before him, it did not seem possible that there was no way to resolve the problem. The artillery carried by one liburnian would tip the scales in his favour, and there was surely some way to get the liburnians through, even if doing the same for the larger biremes was impossible. He scratched his jaw irritably before he addressed Ganomenus.

'This channel, how close does it get us to Lyngomara?'

The old man thought for a moment. 'Within half a mile or so. Not far short of the place we encountered the enemy patrol boat. After that, there are the reeds, that grass bank and the open water beyond. But your navarch is right, the channel is too shallow for his warships.'

Cato studied the deck of the liburnian. Besides the catapult in the bow turret and the bolt-throwers aft of the mast, there were the marines, the sailors, baskets of artillery ammunition and other supplies. All of which amounted to a considerable weight burden.

'What if we stripped the ship of everything portable? Its draught would be considerably less.'

'Of course,' the navarch agreed. 'I went through all of that with your Icenian friend there. But even if we lightened the ship, it still wouldn't get through the shallows between here and Lyngomara.'

It was maddening. Cato looked at the channel ahead of the liburnian once again before he spoke to Besodius. 'Could we get your barges close to the rebel stronghold, even with a full load?'

The captain spoke briefly with Ganomenus. 'We think it can be done, yes.'

'Good.' Cato nodded with relief. 'Then here is what we're going to do.'

Once Cato had explained his intentions, Besodius set off in a small skiff to bring two of his barges forward. Turpillius went in another boat with orders to break down the artillery aboard the bireme and carry the components into the marsh aboard other liburnians. Meanwhile Ganomenus was sent towards Lyngomara to measure the depth of the channel and mark the deepest route that could be charted towards the enemy settlement. Cato himself remained aboard the grounded liburnian to oversee the dismantling of the artillery and the landing of the components on a grassy mound that rose above the reeds nearby. After the catapults and the bolt-throwers had been removed, he ordered that everything loose be taken off as well. Stores, ammunition, sails and the main spar all went ashore until there was a gentle lurch as the buoyancy of the vessel was enough to break the keel out of the mud in which it had become embedded. The trierarch in command of the liburnian thumped the side rail with delight.

'We're afloat!'

'Now for the ballast,' said Cato. 'Get that off the ship as well. We'll have another use for it later.'

The trierarch raised an eyebrow but got his men to carry out the order. It was an unpleasant job, as the heavy rocks used to give the ship stability were down in the bilges, where some of the water coming over the deck ended up, along with other unsavoury fluids. The crew formed a chain to bring the rocks up on deck and from there load them into light craft to take to the shore. Inch by inch the liburnian floated higher. When Ganomenus returned from his mission to measure the depth and mark the channel, he was impressed.

'But it's still not enough, Prefect.' The old man slapped the bow post of the warship. 'She's made of heavy timber in order to weather the open sea. She won't make it over the shallows.'

'We'll see.'

Just after dawn the next morning, Cato set off with Ganomenus to examine the route the latter had established. He had marked it with a line of withies, making it easy to follow. When they reached the expanse of reeds that spread out before the grass bank where they had hidden the boat during the scouting mission, Cato shipped his paddle and surveyed his surroundings.

'We'll need to cut a gap in the bank wide enough to get the warships through. And we're going to have to do it without alerting the rebels. We know the water level is the same on either side of the bank, so there'll be no problem when we open the channel.'

Ganomenus listened to him with a sympathetic expression. 'What is the point of going to such effort if there is no means of getting your warships this far?'

Cato gave him an enigmatic smile in return. 'Just humour me, my Icenian friend, while I make some estimates and calculations.'

He took a waxed tablet from his sidebag and made some notes, then read back over them and nodded before snapping the tablet shut and putting it away.

'Back to the ship.'

An hour or so before noon the following day, the lookout spotted the small convoy of liburnians and river barges approaching. Turpillius halted his warships in the deeper water while the barges continued under oars until they reached the lightened ship on which Cato stood. As Besodius climbed onto the deck, he glanced round.

'You've stripped it back to the bare bones, and then some. What's the plan, Prefect?'

'I need you to get your barges on either side of the liburnian. Once they're in position, you can start loading the ballast from that island over there.' Cato indicated to where the crew and most of the marines stood watching the arrival of the other warships.

'And then?'

'Then we lash the barges securely to the sides of the liburnian before we unload the ballast.'

346

'What's the point of—' Besodius began, before he stopped and laughed as he grasped the purpose of the exercise. 'Oh, that's clever!'

'Thank you.' Cato could not help a surge of pride before his natural cautious instinct reasserted itself. 'I just hope it's enough. Only one way to find out. Let's get the men to work.'

All afternoon the sailors and marines toiled to load the ballast rocks into the barges, taking care to distribute them evenly. As the hours passed, the vessels sank lower into the water, until eventually there was scarcely six inches of freeboard left on each heavily laden craft. Then they were eased against the hull of the warship and lashed securely in place using all the spare ropes. Once Cato was satisfied with the preparations, he gave the order for the barges to be unloaded. The men, most of whom had not yet divined his purpose, grumbled at what looked a further pointless exercise. But slowly the lightened barges began to lift the empty warship higher out of the water, the ropes creaking under the extra load, wringing the water out of their coils.

Turpillius had himself rowed up from the moored liburnians and nodded approvingly as he stepped aboard.

'I have to admit, you've solved the problem neatly, sir. Admirable! I can't wait to see the expression on the rebels' faces when our warships penetrate to the heart of their marsh.'

'Indeed. But there's still plenty of work to be done. It's vital that we don't reveal our intention until the last moment. Which means we'll have to bring each of the liburnians into position under cover of night. Along with the artillery and ammunition. The masts will have to come down and they'll need to be camouflaged and the men kept quiet and out of sight during the day. The danger will come once we get the first ship into position. It'll take some hours for each of the others to be raised up by Besodius and his barges. I dare say there will be some attempt made to deal with the threat posed by the warships. Your

347

marines will need to drive off any attacks the rebels are likely to attempt.'

'We can handle them, sir.'

'Good. Now that you've seen how the system works for getting the warships to ride high enough, you take command here until I get back with some engineers and men from the main column to prepare the channel. They'll have to work at night as well. The critical thing is that we keep the noise down, and stay out of sight during daylight.'

'Ain't going to be easy, sir.'

'No. So make sure that every man under your command understands that it is imperative he plays his part. One shout, one loud splash and we lose the element of surprise.'

'I understand, sir. You can rely on the navy.'

As night fell over the marshes, Cato returned to the main column with a convoy of small boats. As he explained his plan to Macro, his friend grinned with delight at the prospect of the rebels waking up to find themselves under bombardment from Roman warships.

'I dare say hardly any of them have ever seen a liburnian off the coast, and even those who have won't believe we have managed to get them right up to Lyngomara. Why, I can hardly believe it myself. If that's how I feel, I imagine our bloody rebel friends are in for an infinitely greater shock!' Macro rubbed his hands together in delight.

'How are the ram and mantle coming on?'

'The ram is finished. It'll be with us in a couple of days. The mantle will take a couple of days longer. It would be too cumbersome to bring down the track, so I told the engineers to transport the components here for final assembly. I'll have the track between the camp and the gatehouse prepared while we're waiting. If all goes well, we should be ready to deploy the ram

348

in . . . say, six days' time. How does that square with the navy's effort?'

'Six days should be sufficient. The attack begins at dawn on the seventh day, then.'

Macro's expression became serious. 'Do we give them a chance to surrender before the ram touches?'

Cato considered the protocol for besieging a fortress or walled town. It was the custom to offer the defenders an opportunity to negotiate a surrender before the ram struck its first blow. If they refused to give in, and the ram was deployed, it was understood by both sides that there would be no obligation by the attacker to spare lives or property when the besiegers broke through the defences. Much as he might wish to avoid bloodshed, Cato did not believe that Boudica and her followers would surrender. Their dedication to their cause had reached a fanatical pitch and there was no point in offering them the chance. Besides, if they saw the ram and pretended to negotiate, they might just buy themselves enough time to put in place some effective counter-measures. The best chance of success lay in surprising the rebels.

'No. It's too late for that. I doubt Boudica is contemplating surrender. Neither is Suetonius for that matter. Neither of them is willing to give ground and so they don't leave us any choice. It's a fight to the death. Let's just hope it's theirs, not ours.'

Macro nodded solemnly. 'It's a fucking shame. Given everything we've been through. You, me and Boudica. If only things had been different.'

'I wish it were so.'

'The gods will play their games. I just wish the bastards would play them with someone else for a change.' Macro looked steadily at Cato. 'Let me give them a chance before the ram is ready. For the sake of what has passed between the three of us.'

'Even after everything that has happened as a result of the

rebellion? After the deaths of Parvus, Apollonius and your mother? After the deaths of so many of our comrades?'

'Yes. After all that. Haven't we seen enough bloodshed already?'

'Yes, we have. All right, you have my permission to put it to them, but I don't expect them to accept any terms we might offer. Parley with them, but swear to me that you will take no risks. I don't trust them to honour any truce. Keep your distance.'

'I will.'

'Swear it. On your honour.'

'I swear.'

The next day Cato returned to the liburnian with fifty legionaries, including several of the engineer specialists, together with all the picks, baskets and tools needed to prepare the channel and camouflage the works. They spent the day helping to strip down the other liburnians and tow them as far forward as the depth of the channel permitted before anchoring them fore and aft. Then, as dusk came, Cato gave the order to their boats to follow him as he led the way with Ganomenus, following the trail of withies. As night fell, they were less than a mile from their destination. Cato could pick out the faint glow of campfires at Lyngomara and the Roman camp away to the west. They continued cautiously. It was highly unlikely that the rebels would venture out beyond their stronghold to deter anyone from exploring the marsh. All the same, he did not want to risk running into a patrol. If that happened, they could not be allowed to escape and report back to Boudica.

As the convoy approached the low, dark mass of the bank, Cato called a halt. He turned to the optio in charge of the engineer party and spoke softly.

'Keep close to the boat ahead. No noise. Pass it back.'

He waited long enough for the order to be transmitted down the line and then readied his paddle and whispered to Ganomenus, 'Slowly now.'

They entered the narrow run of open water between the reeds. Every so often the sides of the boat rasped against the stalks loudly enough to set Cato's teeth on edge. Then they were through, and the bank lay directly ahead. The two men held their paddles in the water to slow the craft, and it grounded with a barely perceptible lurch. Climbing out, they hauled it out of the water and dragged it along the bank for a short distance to clear the way for those that followed. One by one the boats emerged from the reeds and disgorged their passengers and tools. When the last of the party was ashore, they gathered around the optio as he issued his orders. Meanwhile Cato crept to the top of the bank to scrutinise the scene beyond. There were fires and torches burning in Lyngomara and their reflections gleamed off the surface of the water, only slightly distorted by the shimmering caused by the lightest of breezes and the ripples left by fish, waterfowl and other creatures abroad at night.

The optio joined Cato and examined the bank stretching out on both sides. Cato had described it to him in as much detail as possible, but now he could see the terrain for himself, the engineer appreciated the full scale of the challenge he had to overcome in a matter of days.

'We have to dig out at least sixty feet of this, sir. That's on top of widening and deepening the channel. From what I've tested of the ground, that muck is going to be difficult to shift. I'll need more men.'

'How many?'

He made a quick calculation. 'At least another hundred if we're to meet the timetable you gave me for the job. Even then—'

'I'll get you the men,' Cato interrupted. 'Anything else I need to know, Corbulus?'

'We're going to have to cut away a lot of the reed bank, sir. The rebels will become aware of that pretty soon.'

'Then we'll need to find some way of concealing our work.'

'I've thought of that, sir. We can float a screen of reeds on rafts

351

across the channel. If we put them in place at the end of each night's work, we should be able to fool them, from a distance anyway.'

'That's good,' Cato approved.

'The main problem is going to be the last phase of the operation. Once we've prepared the channel and cut away the embankment on our side, we still have to deal with the side visible to the enemy and any shallows beyond. That's going to take a night's work in itself, at least, and we're bound to alert them to what we're doing.'

'That may be.' Cato put himself in the enemy's place for a moment. 'If they hear any noise, then most likely they'll double their guard, or have their men stand to during the night and wait to see what we're up to at first light. By then, we need to be ready to get the first liburnian through the channel.' He shifted onto his side to face the optio. 'Can it all be done in time?'

He saw the faint gleam of Corbulus's teeth as the latter smiled. 'Give me a long enough lever and I can move the world, sir.'

'You can have the longest I can provide. Just get it done.'

Cato remained with them that night to monitor progress and ensure that the work was carried out as quietly as possible. Two men were assigned to serve as lookouts on each flank while a third kept watch from the top of the bank. The stretch of the embankment to be cut away was clearly marked, as was the width of the channel. It was the latter that caused Cato the most concern, since the men working on the task would be moving through water and inevitably creating noise as it sloshed about them. It was exhausting work, as the reeds had to be pulled from the bed of the swamp and taken a sufficient distance along the bank to be dumped. The men dredging the channel had an even more onerous task, dislodging slimy clods of mud and decayed vegetable matter and heaving them into baskets before carrying them away.

At the first sign of daylight, Cato gave the order for the work to cease, and the men climbed out of the channel and found themselves a place to lie down along the bank. They were soaked through and covered with filth, and most fell asleep as soon as they had made themselves as comfortable as they could. It was impressive to see how much of the reeds had been cleared away, and the narrow channel had already been widened to ten feet. Along the bank, work had begun to cut away the stretch of bare earth upon which most of Corbulus's men were resting.

'I'll be back with more men and supplies,' Cato informed the optio as Ganomenus eased one of the boats into the water. 'Just make sure you keep the men out of sight. I don't want any of them giving in to curiosity and popping their heads up to have a look over the bank.'

'Don't worry, sir. I'll make sure they understand what'll happen to anyone who gives us away to the enemy.'

Cato and the Icenian made their way back down the channel to where the liburnians and the barges were anchored. The last of the warships was being stripped of its loose gear and two of them had already had their masts removed. As Cato approached, it occurred to him that the small towers at each end of the vessels would be difficult to conceal when they were moved up to Corbulus's position.

'They'll have to be taken down as well,' he informed Turpillius after the officers had exchanged salutes and greetings on the deck of the vessel that had been bound to the barges.

The navarch looked horrified. 'Sir, these are imperial navy warships. You take those towers down and they'll look no better than Tiber barges.'

'Right now, I need such barges rather more than I need to worry about the appearance of your ships, Turpillius. Have your carpenters remove them. In any case, that'll help to lighten the load and make the going easier further up the channel.'

The navarch was about to protest again when he saw the uncompromising expression on Cato's face.

'Yes, sir.'

'While that's being done, Corbulus needs a hundred more men. Have that many marines sent to him this afternoon. They can take supplies with them. Enough for five days.' Cato paused to look at the towers again. 'How soon can you take these down?'

Turpillius puffed his cheeks. 'Five, maybe six hours, I'd say.'

'Good, then you can move this one up tonight. Get it into position behind the reeds, and have the barges sent back here before dawn tomorrow to prepare the next ship. We'll shift one each night and then reassemble the artillery once the liburnians are in place and ready to go through the channel into the broad. Make sure everything is done under cover of darkness. Nothing is to move while there's light.'

'Yes, sir. I understand.'

'Good. I'm heading back to the camp. I want you to send me a report on the progress of the engineers and the ships every morning. If you need anything else from the camp, or there's any trouble, let me know at once.'

The navarch nodded. Cato could see that the man was daunted by the task ahead of him and needed a few words of encouragement. 'If all goes to plan, we'll crush their defences, defeat the enemy and put an end to the rebellion before the month is out. The governor will be delighted, and you can be sure that he will award your squadron a battle honour if my after-action report has anything to do with it. And then you can put your towers and masts back up and get your warships back to sea where they belong. How does that sound?'

'It sounds just fine, sir.' Turpillius smiled. 'Just as long as everything goes to plan.'

'Of course. It will, as long as everyone plays their part,' Cato replied. That included the enemy, he reminded himself, mindful of the ways in which Boudica might wittingly or unwittingly interfere with his carefully constructed plans and bring them all to ruin.

CHAPTER THIRTY

Five days later, at dawn, Boudica rose to make her daily round of the defences. From the top of the outer gatehouse she could see the enemy camp with its neat tent lines and the insect-like activity of the Roman soldiers as they drilled on the levelled parade ground, as they did every morning. Closer to, she could easily make out the details of the armour and weapons of the auxiliary century standing to behind the ditch and palisade that had been constructed across the track, safely beyond the range of the rebels' slings and bows. The bodies of the Roman dead from their first attack had begun to stink, and so the rebels had piled them further up the track the previous night. The Romans had already removed them for burial at first light.

'There's been no sign of any preparations for an attack?' she asked the warrior commanding the morning watch.

'None. Same as the last two days, majesty. The only signs of activity are the forage patrols they are sending out into the marshes on foot and boats.'

'Boats won't do them much good,' Boudica observed with satisfaction. She had anticipated that the enemy would either bring boats with them or construct them on site in order to give them the option of assaulting Lyngomara over the water. Stakes had been prepared along the edge of the broad, both above

355

and beneath the surface, beyond which a palisade was being constructed. It would be complete within a matter of days.

'What kind of boats?' she asked, just to lay any doubts to rest.

'Small. Just large enough to carry four or five men at a time. And only a handful of them at that.'

'I see. Keep an eye out for any more.'

Boudica stared at the Romans looking back at her from down the track, then shifted her gaze to sweep across the marshes that surrounded Lyngomara. Away to the north, across the mere, ran a broken embankment with reeds growing on either side. Beyond, the marsh was wreathed with the dawn mist. There was no sign of movement in that direction. No sign of life at all. She wondered at that for a moment. Where had the waterfowl gone? Then her eyes were drawn to a flight of geese to the west, above the trees of the sacred grove, and she turned to watch them for a moment, smiling – a moment of innocent pleasure.

She nodded to the warrior. 'Report any developments to me at once.'

'Yes, majesty.' The man bowed his head.

Boudica climbed down from the tower and walked the palisade, exchanging greetings with the men on duty and offering words of encouragement or humour as she passed by. Their morale was excellent, she thought. It was a pity the same could not be said for some of their chiefs. The men who had failed to show sufficient spirit at the last meeting of her advisers had been demoted and relegated to menial duties within the stockaded strongpoint at the far end of the island, where their defeatism would not infect the other men. She had been tempted to execute some of them to set an example, but Syphodubnus had advised against it. The men were in good heart; why present them with a grim spectacle? Better to punish the men concerned by humiliating them in the worst possible manner according to their warrior code. Strip them of their arms and make them work as peasants. Very soon they would be prepared to do almost anything to win back her favour, and their weapons.

Leaving the outer works, Boudica made her way back along a narrow neck of ground to the second gatehouse, which guarded access to the sacred grove. Here too the warriors carried out their watchkeeping duties with diligence and had nothing to report. She passed through the gate and entered the ring of oak trees that surrounded the altars and wooden henge. Apart from the stakes and the stockade being erected around this part of the island, there were no other defences being prepared here. She regretted this, as a sturdy redoubt in the centre of the grove would have exacted a heavy toll on any Romans who managed to breach the outer defences. But to construct one there would have offended the superstitious nature of many of her followers, who would have feared some kind of divine retribution from the gods and ancestor spirits to whom the grove was dedicated.

She made a quick inspection of the warriors working on the nearly finished palisade. The men were stripped to the waist as they laboured to manoeuvre the posts into their holes and then bind them to the previous one in line. Syphodubnus was there with Bladocus, supervising the work, and the two men bowed their heads at her approach.

'How soon before the palisade is complete?' she asked.

'By the end of tomorrow,' Syphodubnus replied.

'Sooner would be better.'

Bladocus fixed her with his piercing gaze. 'Expecting trouble?'

Boudica gave a wry smile. 'There are thousands of Romans camped a mile away. Yes, I'm expecting trouble. There's no sign of immediate danger . . .'

'But?'

'I think they're up to something. Maybe anyone under siege experiences this. I wouldn't know, as it's my first time. It's just that I find it hard to believe that the Roman army sits still and waits. That's not their style. It's certainly not the style of Prefect Cato.'

Bladocus pursed his lips. 'I heard a story from a Roman some years ago. I don't know how true it was, but I could believe it. Seems there was this Greek city that a Roman general intended to capture. It was built on a steep hill with high walls and was deemed impregnable. Anyway, the Roman general calls for a parley and the city's leader agrees to speak to him. He tells the Roman that he has no chance of taking the city by assault. The Roman replies, that's fine, we'll just starve you out. The Greek laughs and says that his people have enough food in their granaries and water in their cisterns to last them ten years. The Roman general shrugs and says, fair enough, then we'll take the city in ten years and one day's time. The next day the city surrenders.'

Syphodubnus blinked. 'What? Why?'

'Why do you think? The Greeks knew that once the Romans set their mind to something, they will achieve it, no matter how long it takes.'

'Is that what you think is happening here?' asked Boudica.

'It might be. We can't get out of here. It's true we prepared for this. We have enough food stored in our grain pits to last us for several months, and as we have demonstrated to the Romans, our defences are sound. Any attempt to attack our stronghold is going to fail, and cost them dearly in the process. They may choose to sit, as you put it, and starve us into submission. If that is their plan, we need to consider what we will do in response.'

'If they choose not to fight us, we will break out of here and take the fight to them. I will not wait to starve to death, and I will not surrender.'

'What about escape?' Syphodubnus suggested quietly. 'There are enough boats to carry us and a few hundred of our followers. We could easily lose them in the marshes.'

'What would be the point of that?' asked Boudica. 'There is

358

nowhere for us to go where Rome would not be able to find us. The fight is here. This is where we face them. We will not be hunted down like dogs. We will stand our ground and fight, and die if need be, like warriors.'

'Brave words,' Bladocus said approvingly. 'Spoken like a queen of the Iceni.'

Boudica was not in the mood for flattery, and gestured in the direction of the settlement. 'I want the ditch between the sacred grove and Lyngomara widened.'

'Is that necessary?' asked Bladocus. 'It's adequate as it is, surely.'

'I won't be satisfied with adequate,' she replied. 'Besides, if we are going to be under siege for any length of time, we're going to need a schedule of works to keep the men occupied. Idleness leads to discontent. That I will not have. Make your plans to widen the ditch.'

'Yes, majesty.'

She was about to add an instruction to do the same with the ditch between the settlement and the strongpoint around the hall when they were interrupted by a warrior racing out of the sacred grove. He scrambled to a halt in front of Boudica and bowed his head.

'Majesty, you are needed at the outer gatehouse.'

Boudica's pulse quickened as she glanced in the direction the man had come from. There was no sound of any horns raising the alarm. No sound from distant Roman instruments. No shouting or sound of fighting.

'What's happening?'

'It's the Romans, majesty. They have sent some men forward who wish to speak with you. Two officers.'

Boudica exchanged a quick glance with Bladocus and Syphodubnus. 'Go back and tell them I'm coming directly.'

The warrior nodded and turned to run back the way he had come.

359

'Well, Bladocus, it seems we're about to find out whether our Roman visitors are cut from the same cloth as the general in your story.'

Returning to the top of the tower on the outer gatehouse, Boudica saw two Roman officers in red cloaks standing ten paces in front of their advance field defence. A few paces behind them was a soldier carrying a bucina, the polished bronze of the instrument burnished by the morning sun. All three men carried oval auxiliary shields. One of the officers was tall, with a plumed crest atop his helmet. The other was shorter, stockier and had the transverse crest of a centurion. She recognised him immediately, even at a distance.

'Is that her?' Tribune Agricola asked, shading his eyes.

'I doubt it would be anyone else,' Macro replied, taking in the red hair of the woman regarding them from the top of the gatehouse. 'Let's get this done.'

He turned to the bucina man. 'Three blasts every ten paces, until I tell you to stop.'

'Yes, sir.' The auxiliary raised the mouthpiece, took a breath and blew. The note would carry some distance in such a flat landscape and alert the enemy to their approach, as was the custom in seeking a parley. Macro drew his sword and made a show of setting it down on the road so that the defenders would see he was not armed. He did the same with his dagger and nodded at Agricola. 'You too.'

'Is that wise?'

'Do you think it would make any difference if we went there armed?'

Agricola considered this briefly before he responded. 'I suppose not.'

As soon as the tribune had disarmed himself, Macro advanced towards the gatehouse at a slow, steady pace, accompanied by the repeated notes of the bucina. Agricola fell into step alongside him.

360

'This feels rather dangerous,' the tribune muttered.

Macro gave him a sidelong glance. 'You asked to come along.'

'I might not get another chance to see Boudica up close. It'll be quite a story to tell the family when I go back to Rome.'

'*If* you go back to Rome,' said Macro, half teasing the young aristocrat. 'There may well be a bit of violence involved if I fail to persuade them to surrender. Don't count your chickens, and all that. Remember, I am doing the talking. You keep quiet unless you are spoken to. You are here to bear witness to what is said. And to look suitably decorative in your nice shiny armour and finely decorated helmet and plume. Keep your chin up, shoulders back and concentrate on looking proud and dignified rather than arrogant and entitled. I know that may not come naturally to you, but give it a try. If that doesn't impress a lady, I don't know what will.'

Macro's words were intended to calm the younger man's nerves. In truth, he knew that Boudica would be rather more impressed by the array of medals Macro wore on his harness, and the scars from his wounds. At least that was what she had told him when they first met nearly twenty years before.

They were no more than thirty paces from the gatehouse when Boudica called on them to halt. Macro drew up and indicated to the bucina man to lower his instrument.

'What is it you want, Centurion Macro?'

'I have come to discuss terms, Queen Boudica,' Macro replied formally.

'What terms?'

'You know well enough. Surrender terms.'

'You've had one taste of battle and you're already willing to give in?' Boudica said in an incredulous tone.

The man standing next to her translated the remark into the Icenian dialect, and her warriors roared with laughter and jeered and gesticulated at the three Romans below them on the track.

361

As the laughter died away, Macro grinned and touched his helmet in casual salute before he continued.

'Your surrender, Queen Boudica. I have been authorised by my commanding officer, Prefect Cato, to give you the opportunity to discuss terms before we attack and take Lyngomara.'

'Roman arrogance!' she snapped back at him. 'What makes you think you could ever breach our defences and defeat my fearless warriors?' She stretched her arms out and her comment was translated again, to even greater acclaim this time.

As the noise died down, she turned away and disappeared among her followers.

Agricola was startled. 'Well, that was short and sweet. A woman of few words.'

He made to back away, but Macro growled at him. 'Stand still. Wait until I say.'

They stood their ground for a beat, and then there was a rumble as the locking bar was removed and one of the gates slowly swung in. Boudica emerged accompanied by a nobleman and another individual in a dark tunic and cloak, his face a mass of swirling tattoos that Macro recognised as Druid symbols. Four warriors armed with spears escorted them. The party strode across the causeway and stopped a short distance from Macro and Agricola. The latter's hand twitched anxiously before he tucked the thumb in his belt and stared back defiantly.

'You want to discuss terms,' Boudica began in a haughty tone. 'Very well, my demands are as follows. Firstly, you lift the siege and leave the marsh. Secondly, you demolish the fort at Venta Icenorum and retreat from our land, never to return. Thirdly, your governor returns every sestertius the Iceni have been forced to pay in taxes since Rome blighted our island. Fourthly, and finally, your emperor gives orders for your legions, your auxiliary cohorts, your citizens to quit Britannia by the end of the year, never to return. In exchange for meeting those terms, we agree to spare you and any of your comrades who have dared to besmirch our soil. If you do not accept, I cannot guarantee your safety.' She folded her arms.

'The arrogance of the bitch,' Agricola whispered.

'Silence,' Macro commanded.

Then he replied loudly, in the Iceni dialect. 'My terms are as follows. Queen Boudica and all her followers are to lay down their arms, open the gate to Lyngomara and surrender. All will be treated as spoils of war to be sold into slavery, subject to the will of the governor and through him the emperor.'

'Meaning that you cannot guarantee that our lives will be spared even if we surrender,' said Boudica. 'Your governor is not a merciful man, I hear.'

'He may exercise mercy provided that you submit to him. Certainly I and my superior, Prefect Cato, will do all in our power to ensure that you and your followers are spared.'

'That's very considerate of you,' Boudica responded with heavy irony. 'So you demand that we surrender in the hope that we are spared. I fail to see how that is supposed to convince us to concede.'

'If you don't, you will surely die,' Macro replied.

'We all die in the end. The only thing that matters is the choice over the manner of our death. You can either die here in this marsh, Roman, or you can die in comfort surrounded by your family back in Rome.'

Even as he admired her brave words, Macro's heart was heavy with sadness that she was as intransigent as Cato had said she would be. He stepped closer to her and spoke quietly in Latin so that her followers would neither overhear nor understand.

'Boudica, you are trapped. You cannot escape. When Cato gives the order to attack, you will be defeated. Be in no doubt about that. You and your followers will all be put to the sword if you make us take Lyngomara by force.'

'Try it, and see what happens.'

'You know what will happen,' he responded earnestly. 'Many will die on both sides. You can prevent that, if you surrender.'

'Only if Suetonius honours your word that we will be spared.'

'Cato and I will do our best to makes sure he does.'

The mask of aloof disdain on Boudica's face slipped momentarily. 'I know you would. But I also know that Rome does not tolerate rebellion. Our lives are forfeit.'

Macro lowered his voice further still. 'Then get out of here. Take your daughters and escape. There must be a way through the marshes. For pity's sake, flee while you can.'

'I cannot – will not – abandon my people. I am their queen. If I was to turn my back on them now, I would carry the shame of that to my grave. You understand?'

Macro nodded reluctantly.

'If our positions were reversed, Macro, would you flee?'

'No . . . no, I wouldn't,' he admitted. He looked at her with aching sadness, knowing it would be for the last time while she still lived. 'Then there is nothing more to be said.'

'There is one thing. My younger daughter is dead. Bardea still lives. She is your daughter too, Macro. Your flesh and blood. Swear to me that you will do what you can to spare her. To protect her if Lyngomara falls,' she added in a barely audible voice. 'Do that for me, for the sake of the love we once shared. For the sake of the friendship we once had. For the sake of the dangers we shared in battle. Swear it!'

Macro swallowed and nodded. 'I swear it.'

There was a glimmer of relief in her eyes, and for an instant her features softened into those of the young woman he had first met so many years before as she spoke with affection. 'May your gods protect you, Macro.'

He began to raise his hand to offer it to her. The cold mask slipped back into place and she stepped back with a sneer and spat on the ground at his feet as she spoke loudly in her own tongue. 'The parley is over. Begone, Roman, and prepare to die!'

Her warriors cheered as she turned and led her party back towards the gate. Macro watched her disappear from view, then the gates closed with a sombre thud.

He paced over to Agricola. 'It's time we left. Turn around slowly and keep at the pace I set. I don't want those barbarians thinking we fear them.'

As they made their way back along the track, Macro sensed the eyes of the enemy upon him, sizing up his broad back and thinking what an easy target he would make. At the same time, he trusted that Boudica would not countenance such a cowardly and ignoble act. And if she acted with honour towards him at that moment, he resolved to do all in his power to fulfil her request when the time came. He would strive to save their daughter.

They reached the ditch, which had been mostly filled in the night before, and climbed through the gap in the palisade. On the far side, one of the Eighth Cohort's cavalry contingent stood ready by his mount.

'My compliments to Centurion Galerius,' Macro said. 'Tell him to light the signal beacon and send the ram forward.'

'What are they up to now?' Syphodubnus muttered as he stared at the column of smoke rising from a point between the Roman camp and the men at the fieldworks a short distance down the track. The latter had moved into action the moment the two officers had returned to their line. Now the auxiliaries were stripping away the palisade and shovelling the earth of the rampart into the ditch.

'They're going to attack,' said Bladocus. He turned to Boudica. 'Majesty, you should give the order to sound the alarm.'

Boudica was still watching Macro, his crest visible among the Roman soldiers. She tore her gaze away. 'Yes. Do so.'

Syphodubnus nodded to the two men with war horns at the rear of the tower. A moment later their braying notes blasted out, to be echoed shortly afterwards by the other war horns across Lyngomara. The men along the palisade stood to, staring towards the Romans as they waited for them to advance. Behind the outer gate, more men were spilling out of their huts to go to their appointed stations along the defences that lined the island.

'Something's moving over there!' One of the warriors raised his arm and pointed as a dull brown shape appeared above the reeds where the track rose slightly, then disappeared again. Now they could hear the crack of whips and a dull rumbling sound.

'What is that?' Syphodubnus asked.

There was a strained silence and stillness on top of the tower as the sounds increased in volume. The Romans had almost completed the demolition of the rampart and filled in the ditch, and were now pounding the loose soil with mattocks to render it more compact. Something appeared around the last bend in the track, and Boudica saw the first pair of mules struggle into sight, followed by more, until at least twenty could be seen. Behind them, the traces were attached to what looked like the end of a large tent. More of the structure emerged, with sturdy wheels on each side. Then she saw an object protruding from the opening at the front: a wooden beam with what looked like an iron cover at the end. The mules halted just short of the auxiliaries preparing the ground and the device rumbled to a stop in full view of the defenders.

'They have a ram,' Bladocus observed.

They could all make out the sturdy beams used to construct the mantle and the thick layers of leather that covered the roof and sides. Men were moving up through the interior to take their place on the bars that would be used to heave the siege weapon into position. Behind, a column of legionaries made ready to follow the ram as it approached the outer gate.

366

'Bring fire up to the gate,' Boudica commanded as the spell was broken. 'Bring kindling and flammable materials! Do it now!'

Several warriors hurried to do her bidding, racing towards the campsite in the sacred grove where cooking fires still burned.

It was at that moment that another warrior came rushing to the foot of the tower. 'Majesty, come! There are Romans to the north!'

Boudica leaned over to look down at him. 'What are they doing?'

'I don't know, but there are many of them. Hundreds, maybe.'

She hesitated, glancing back towards the ram. It had not moved, and the auxiliaries were still busy preparing the ground where the ditch and rampart had stood. There would be a brief delay before the ram began to move again, and it would be a while until it advanced into position to batter the gate. There was time to investigate the other Roman force that had materialised.

'Syphodubnus, take command here.'

She hurried down the ladder inside the tower, with Bladocus behind her, to join the warrior waiting at the bottom. He led the way back along the neck of land to the second gatehouse, and through that and on into the sacred grove. There they turned to the right and passed through the trees, making for the nearest of the watchtowers, a much smaller construction than the gatehouses, with scarcely enough room at the top for five or six people. The veteran who had sent the warrior to fetch Boudica pointed across the water. Her heart was beating quickly as she rested her hands on the rail of the tower. A few hundred paces away, she saw a stretch of embankment covered in Roman soldiers feverishly swinging picks as they broke up the ground and carried the spoil away. To one side stood a small group of officers overseeing the work. More men were in the water, clearing a wide path through the reeds.

'What are they doing?' She frowned. 'What are they constructing over there?'

'They don't appear to be constructing anything, majesty.' Bladocus squinted, his face crinkling as he strained to make out the details. 'They're clearing the ground. Perhaps they intend to place some of their catapults there.'

The first section of the bank collapsed, and then some more, and the spoil was hurriedly removed. Through the gap Boudica could see an open channel of water – and the unmistakable lines of the hull of a Roman warship, stripped of its mast and towers, with smaller vessels seemingly moored alongside. She could make out the catapults and bolt-throwers on the deck. Beyond she could see another warship being eased up behind the first. As more of the embankment was cut away and the water from the channel linked up with the broad surrounding Lyngomara, she at last understood the enemy's intentions. She understood too the stealth and great care that had been taken to bring the power of the warships to bear on her stronghold, and could not help admiring the speed with which the work had been done. The purpose of the smoke signal was now clear: the Romans were making ready to bombard her warriors with their deadly missiles at the same time as the ram battered a breach in their defences.

Boudica had seen Roman artillery in action and knew how deadly its impact could be. It took all her effort to conceal her dread from the others in the tower as the gap in the embankment opened still wider and the first of the floating batteries crept along the channel towards her stronghold.

CHAPTER THIRTY-ONE

As soon as the first liburnian was anchored in position on the flank of the outer gate, Cato gave the order for the floating battery to commence bombarding the rebel defences some two hundred paces away. In a loud, methodical voice, the marine optio in charge of the battery went through the procedure to load, aim and shoot. The iron ratchets on the winding gear of the catapults and bolt-throwers clanked as the crews strained on the lever bars. With the range estimated and ammunition loaded, everyone stood back save for the man operating the release gear.

The optio swept his arm forward. 'Release!'

Watching from the raised foredeck, Cato felt the vessel lurch as the throwing arms crashed against their restraining bars, transmitting the shock of the impact through every timber in the vessel. The trajectory of the bolts, low and fast, was difficult to follow as the dark shafts whipped across the water towards the enemy. He saw a burst of muddy soil as one bolt slammed into the bank at the foot of the palisade. A second bolt narrowly missed the rear of the tower, but the third struck home, skewering a group of men and tearing them off their feet. Their flailing bodies knocked down several others in a bloody heap of torn and bruised flesh. The two catapults on board were less successful, and both shots fell just short, showering the nearest rebels with spray.

The artillery crews cheered and were instantly silenced by their optio.

'What in bloody Hades are you lot celebrating? One bloody shot on target from five weapons. You can train monkeys to do better than that. Reload, you careless bastards! And adjust your elevation. Shoot at will! Watch the fall of your shot.'

The barrage continued, with more casualties inflicted on the men along the palisade as the catapults found their range and the first stones smashed into the timbers of the gatehouse. The marines were using small flint boulders from a beach along the coast. Largely regular in shape, hard and heavy, they dealt considerable damage to the enemy structures. They also had a tendency to shatter if they struck a hard enough surface, showering the defenders with razor-sharp fragments that cut through flesh like a knife. The rebels swiftly got over their surprise, and soon a party appeared from the second gatehouse, carrying wicker baskets filled with shingle and soil. They began to stack these up on the end of the palisade closest to the floating battery to shelter the men there. It was dangerous work as the optio directed the bolt-throwers to turn their aim on the rebel work party, who suffered a number of casualties as they built up the makeshift defences.

A loud splintering crack drew Cato's attention away from the enemy's brave efforts, and he saw that the arm of one of the bolt-throwers had shattered. A common enough occurrence for the weapons given the enormous stress placed on the timber limbs by torsion cords. The optio sprang towards it to oversee the replacement of the broken part and the removal of the casualty, who had been standing too close and been struck by the fragment still attached to the thick bowstring, knocking him off his feet. He was clutching his shoulder, and let out a sharp cry as he tried to push himself up.

'You stupid dozy bugger!' the optio bellowed. 'How often do

you have to be fucking told to stand back? You, and you! Get him aft. He can wait there until the surgeon comes.'

While the crew went about removing the shattered stump of the throwing arm and fitting a replacement, Cato made his way aft to inspect the progress of the second liburnian. The bows were just emerging through the gap in the bank, and he could see the prow of the empty barge bound alongside. The handful of crew on board were working the long sweeps to punt the combined vessels through into the mere. It was physically demanding work, as even with a much-reduced draught, the warship's keel touched the mud beneath the water and had to be heaved free before it could continue up the channel prepared by the engineers. It was going to take at least an hour to get each liburnian into position, Cato calculated. Long enough for the rebels to recover from their surprise and take counter-measures.

Leaning over the stern rail, he called down to the sailor in the skiff below. 'Go to the navarch. Tell him I want the last ship's bolt-throwers mounted on the bank to the right of the gap. As quickly as possible.'

The sailor knuckled his brow, then cast off and paddled back towards the gap and out of sight. Cato watched the liburnian's slow progress for a moment longer before he turned his attention back to the outer gatehouse. The catapults had inflicted considerable damage, smashing in the hoardings and battering the beams that held the tower up. Only a handful of figures could be seen on the tower now, and each time the catapult arms whipped forward, their faces lifted as they followed the arc of the missile coming towards them and then rushed to get out of the way. The men along the palisade were now screened from the bolt-throwers, and each impact caused the barricade of filled baskets to shudder. Some were split wide open, disgorging their contents, and replacements were hurriedly shoved into position.

The optio approached Cato. 'Sir, we could try incendiaries on that lot. Apart from the chance of setting the gatehouse alight, there's the damage it'll do to their morale.'

Cato had already considered this and shook his head. 'If we set fire to the gatehouse, we'll have to wait until it's burned down before Centurion Macro can get the ram over the ruins. It'll cost too much time. Time the rebels will put to good use. Our best chance of getting this done is to do it as swiftly as possible. No incendiaries.'

The optio looked disappointed, but saluted and returned to his position behind the battery. A few shots later, the crew of one of the catapults let out a fresh cheer, and this time the optio momentarily cheered along with them as the tower gave a lurch. One of the upright beams had shattered, and now the tower was canted over on one corner. The occupants were scrambling to keep their footing; then, realising the danger, they scurried down the ladder before the structure could collapse.

'Finish it off, boys!' the optio roared.

The two catapult crews threw their weight onto the ratchet levers with renewed enthusiasm as they competed to bring the structure down. Only a few shots later, the same crew that had shattered the upright scored another hit on the structure. The tower gave another lurch, then tipped back and to the side and collapsed on top of the rebels sheltering there, amid a dull rumble of falling debris and the crack of snapping timbers.

This time, all the artillery crews broke off from their efforts to give a wild cheer, and the optio indulged them for a moment before turning to Cato with an enquiring look. 'Cease shooting, sir?'

'No, I want you to keep their heads down until the ram reaches the causeway.'

As the optio directed his men to continue the barrage, Cato cast his gaze towards the track hidden by reeds in front of the outer gatehouse. Somewhere, out of view, Macro would be ordering the assault on the gate to begin.

★   ★   ★

'That's it, lads!' Macro grinned as he watched the tower collapse. The legionaries formed up within the mantle and behind it let out a cheer before their officers silenced them. Taking up their shields, Macro and Agricola strode over to the colour party of the leading century of legionaries and took their places just ahead of the standard-bearer.

'Here we go,' Macro said, before he breathed in and gave the order. 'Mantle! Advance!'

The men in the mantle threw their weight against the crossbars while a centurion called the time, but it took a moment before the heavy structure eased forward on the six large wheels that supported it. Once in motion, it moved across the remains of the rampart and the ditch and then continued down the track towards the enemy's outermost defences. The tower might have come down, but both gates still stood, undamaged. Macro was aware that the artillery had ceased their barrage, and now the enemy warriors were resuming their position on the palisade. As soon as the mantle came within range, they unleashed arrows and slingshot, but the missiles made no impact on the heavy leather curtain shielding the front of the mantle, nor the angled roof.

Behind the mantle, Macro gave the order for the leading century to form testudo, and the legionaries hefted their heavy rectangular shields overhead and overlapped them to provide cover for the men beneath as they followed the mantle towards the gates. The barrage from the defenders became increasingly ferocious as the gap closed, and then the centurion in charge was forced to slow the pace to ensure that the front was lined up with the causeway, with no danger of falling into the ditch. Easing the siege weapon forward, he gave the order to halt as soon as the tip of the ram came up against one of the gates with a thud. Inside the confined space of the mantle, the legionaries released their hold of the crossbars. Amid the cacophony of missiles striking the roof, they took their places along the ram suspended from the roof of the mantle by strong ropes, each man grasping one of the rope handles. When they were ready, their centurion had to bellow along the length of the mantle to be heard above the din overhead.

'On my order! Heave!'

The legionaries grunted with the effort of drawing the ram back, then they let it go and it swung forward a short distance. The heavy iron casing at the end of the ram slammed home against the solid timbers of the gate, splintering the surface and opening up splits in the grain and between the timbers. Blow by blow the gate weakened and gave under the impact until it finally split in two, only twisted splinters and rope holding the top together. Several more blows were required to shatter it completely before the centurion glanced through the leather curtains and decided that the breach was practicable for the assault.

'Release your handles and retire!'

The legionaries turned to the rear and filed out, breaking into a trot as they passed the testudo and made for safety further down the track, out of range of the defenders. Macro waited until the way was clear before he ordered the waiting century to enter the mantle. Man by man they moved forward, only lowering their shields as they entered shelter, and positioned themselves either side of the ram. As soon as they were ready, Macro turned to Agricola.

'These are your men. Give the order, Tribune.'

Agricola nodded grimly, then spat to clear his mouth and called back along the confined space. 'First Century, Fifth Cohort, Second Legion! Are you ready?'

His men, keyed up for action, roared back at him. 'Ready!'

Agricola swept the curtain aside, ducked out onto the causeway and drew his sword. Macro cleared the curtain on the other side and followed suit as legionaries poured out of the mantle and surged towards the shattered gate. The defenders stood their ground behind their kite and oval shields, axes and swords raised, faces fixed in determined expressions. The legionaries slammed their heavier shields into those of the rebels and pressed in behind them. There was a brief moment when weapons could be wielded before the bodies of both sides were so closely pressed together that it became a test of brute strength only. Neither side gave ground at first, and then the superior grip of the Roman boots handed the advantage to the attackers, and they began to edge forward, passing through the broken gate and shoving the fragments aside as they pressed on.

Agricola, being tall enough to see over the heads of the melee, spotted more rebels emerging from the sacred grove and rushing along the neck of land between the two gatehouses to join the fight. At once he turned and called back down the track for the rest of the cohort to double forward. The men of the First Century succeeded in pushing a short distance beyond the gates and formed a shallow arc amid the swelling numbers ranged against them. Now they could use their shields to punch their opponents back and create enough space to wield their short swords, stabbing at any rebel within easy reach.

Macro thrust his way past the ruined gate and moved over to the tangled debris of the fallen tower, climbing onto some timbers to get an overview as Agricola and the rest of the first unit fed into the fight. As more legionaries came through, the rebels were slowly pushed back a short distance before holding their ground. From his vantage point, Macro could see that most of them were also armed with short swords and were fighting using the Roman technique of leading with the shield and relying on the point rather the edge of their blades. He smiled ruefully. The enemy had profited from the lessons they had learned and applied over the winter. The fight was going to be more evenly balanced than the last time the two sides had met in battle. Men were being wounded on both sides, the fortunate ones able to pull back from the fight, the less lucky slumping down and falling under the feet of the combatants, where they were vulnerable to sword thrusts from above, or being clubbed with the bottom of a shield.

Macro was alerted by shouts and turned to see three rebels climbing over the splintered remains of the tower, eager to claim the head of a Roman centurion. The nearest was a bulky youth with a spear, who made a two-handed thrust that was easy for Macro to block with his shield as he braced his feet on a small clear patch of ground between two beams. The spearman kept up his attack, feinting and stabbing, as his comrades, also armed with spears, worked their way over the angled timbers to get at Macro's flank.

Macro smacked the first man's weapon aside and hacked at the shaft just beyond the leaf-shaped blade, but failed to break it. He managed a quick call over his shoulder.

'Some help here would be appreciated!'

The optio of the First Century ordered the closest men from the rear of the melee to come to his aid. They managed to negotiate the ruins just in time, as the spearman's comrades came in reach of Macro and he was hard pressed to keep the darting spear tips at bay. As the legionaries drew level with him, the spearmen could not get past the large Roman shields, and after a few more attempts they pulled back over the broken timbers to safer ground. The legionaries made to go after them, but Macro ordered them to hold their position.

'Stay with the formation! You go running after them and they'll turn round and have you like hounds taking down a stag. Stick to your training.' Even as he admonished them, he could not help admiring the keenness of their spirit, given that this was the first fight almost all of them had ever been in outside of the training ground.

As the Second Century poured through the gate and added their weight to the struggle, the rebels were forced back along the narrow neck of land that linked the two gatehouses. Macro could see an older Icenian standing atop the tower, observing the progress of the fight; then he turned to issue an instruction, and war horns sounded. The men at the rear of the fight peeled away and trotted back through the open gates of the second gatehouse. Their retreat was covered by one of their chiefs, taking command of fifty or so rebels still facing the legionaries. As he began to call the pace, the rebels stepped back, keeping their shield wall intact and their swords levelled, the Romans following them warily.

Macro saw the opportunity to rush the second gatehouse slipping from their grasp, and bellowed at the men of the First Century.

'What the fuck are you doing? Charge the bastards!'

'Charge!' Agricola repeated the command, pushing himself forward into the front rank and taking a quick step to slam his shield into that of the nearest rebel. The legionaries followed suit, forcing the pace that the Icenian chief was trying to maintain. The enemy line became uneven as they were pressed back on the open gates. Now a fresh danger presented itself to the Romans as archers on the tower and the second stretch of palisade began to shoot over the retreating rebels' heads into the ranks of the legionaries. It was an impossible target to miss at that range. Arrow shafts glanced off shields and helmets, but some men were struck on their exposed arms and some in the face.

As the enemy rearguard reached the open gates, they fell back in good order until only a handful were left to cover the gap. The attack was over, and the legionaries backed off, shields raised as they collected their wounded comrades and retreated towards Macro's position. The chief in command of the rearguard called his men in, brandishing his sword in a final defiant gesture before the gates closed.

Agricola fell back and stood by Macro, chest heaving. He had a flesh wound on his arm and his eyes were wide with exhilaration.

'Been enjoying yourself?'

Macro grinned. 'You're getting a taste for it. If you stick with the army, you'll be fine. Like the rest of these lads. They've done well for first-timers.'

Agricola grinned with pride, then nodded towards the enemy's second line of defence. 'What now?'

'We clear the gates and the wreckage of the tower away and get the ram ready for the next attack. Same as before. The navy artillery will soften them up and we let the ram do its work again.'

Macro became aware that the tribune was no longer looking at him, but over his shoulder, across the open water. He turned and saw that the second liburnian was in position and the sailors were hurriedly unlashing the barges. To the left of his field of vision, coming into view beyond the trees of the sacred grove, were several low-sided boats packed with rebel warriors, urging on their comrades with paddles as they surged towards the liburnians.

'Looks like the prefect might have his hands full before he can help us out with the next attack,' he said laconically.

'New target!' the marine centurion yelled. 'Aim for the boats!'

Cato clutched the stern rail tightly as he assessed the danger. The rebel boats must have been kept ashore. That was the only way they could have been missed during the reconnaissance trip. There had only been the one that they had seen at the time, the patrol boat out on the channel. He had assumed there might be a handful of smaller fishing boats, but nothing on the scale presented by the new threat.

They had appeared around the end of the strongpoint at the far end of the island, at least ten of them along with some smaller craft, paddling swiftly across the water towards the two warships already anchored and the third that was halfway through the excavated channel. The marines on the bank either side were gesticulating wildly as they raised the alarm. On the far side of

378

the gap Cato saw the navarch urging his men to complete their preparation of the artillery pieces Cato had ordered to be set up there earlier that morning. Only one of the catapults appeared to be fully assembled and the crew were desperately working the levers to draw back the throwing arm. The men on the second liburnian were similarly engaged in setting up their weapons. Apart from the artillery crews, only a handful of marines were on each vessel. The rest were busy preparing the remaining warships to enter the broad. By the time they could arm themselves and use the flotilla of smaller boats on the far side of the embankment to get through to the ships, the rebels would be on them.

The ballista crews trained their weapons round swiftly, but the catapult was a far heavier and more cumbersome affair and it would be a while longer before it could come into action.

'Aim for the leading boats!' Cato ordered in the hope that they might achieve a lucky shot on one of the nearer craft and discourage the others. The optio nodded and went to each weapon to aim it before standing back to release the trigger. The first bolt plunged into the water ahead of the leading boat, sending up a sheet of spray. The second passed between it and the next boat, while the third went a little too high but still plucked a man off the leading boat and sent him splashing over the side.

'You have to do better than that,' Cato snapped, then wished he hadn't. It would not help the optio's concentration.

The rebels were already halfway across the water, the men on the paddles straining to drive the vessels as fast as possible. A crack from the bank told Cato that the catapult crew had got their weapon into action. It was a hurried shot, but whoever had set the range was clearly a skilled individual. The heavy stone plunged into the water close to one of the small boats in the middle of the group, sending up a tall column of water. There was an instinctive recoil away from the spray by those on board, and the light craft tipped over, spilling them into the water.

379

'One down!' Cato thumped the side rail.

There was another ragged volley from the bolt-throwers, and this time two shots told. One pierced the fragile side of the nearest craft, striking down one of the men paddling and a warrior crouching next to him, then exited on the far side. Deprived of one of the paddles, the boat slewed round and came to a stop in the confusion. But order was quickly restored as a fresh pair of hands took over, and the vessel resumed its course. Cato's mind was racing as he calculated the speed of the boats and the time it took to load the bolt-throwers. There would be an opportunity for a few more quick shots. The marines would not be able to reach the warships before the rebels. It was down to those on board the liburnians to defend the ships and their valuable artillery pieces.

The catapult on the embankment released another shot. This time the stone plunged down close to the bows of one of the large boats, snapping the slender keel and shattering the bottom. The vessel lurched as if the bow had been pressed down by some giant invisible hand, and then it rapidly slowed and stopped as water poured in. The overladen boat began to sink almost at once. A handful of warriors managed to scramble aboard another that drew alongside briefly and then moved off, leaving the rest to fend for themselves. Others flailed in the water as the first began to go under and drown.

The bolt-throwers claimed more victims as three bolts targeted the largest of the enemy boats. All three were well aimed, and they cut down several of the rebels as well as scoring two hits on the side. The boat swayed, and men spilled into the water as it slowed to a stop.

Cato looked to the neighbouring liburnian and saw that the artillery crews were still trying to assemble their weapons. But it was already too late for that. Cupping his hands to his mouth, he called across, 'Leave the weapons! Prepare to defend the ship!'

The bulk of the boats were making for the nearest ship, and only three or four seemed to be steering towards the one Cato was aboard. The angle they were at was such that only one of the bolt-throwers could bear on them now.

'Leave the catapult! Bring in the stern anchor cable!' Cato ordered the nearest artillery crew as he grasped the coarse fibres of the cable that led over the side and down to the anchor. When the other six men had a firm grasp, he called the time and they heaved on the cable. At first nothing seemed to happen, and then it began to give, and the stern of the warship slowly shifted round to present more of its beam to the enemy boats as they drew close to the other liburnian.

'Make fast!' Cato called out, and they fastened the cable around a stern cleat. All the bolt-throwers could be brought to bear now, and they succeeded in sinking two more boats before the enemy reached the liburnian.

As soon as the first boat was alongside, rebels were hoisted up the side. The marines stood ready along the length of the ship, shields and spears raised. They managed to stab the first two men attempting to get aboard, but there were too few of them to hold the line for long as more and more of the enemy boats crowded along the hull.

'Keep shooting!' Cato yelled as he realised the ballista crews were making no attempt to do so.

'But sir,' the optio responded, 'we might hit our own.'

'Do it!'

The optio nodded and issued fresh orders to his crews, who heaved at the loading levers. The next shots were at close range, and cut through the tightly packed bodies alongside the other warship. One bolt struck the hull at an angle, and splinters exploded over the attackers, wounding more men. But now their numbers were beginning to tell, and several had gained the deck and hurled themselves at the marines as more of their comrades scrambled up the side and over the rail to join the struggle. The marine optio in command of the detachment on board recalled his men to the stern of the warship to make their stand there.

Meanwhile, four large boats filled with warriors were making for Cato's ship. There was time for one last volley. One shot went wide, while another flew straight down the line of the nearest boat, striking down several men, who collapsed over the men at the paddles so that the craft swung side-on as the victims cried out in agony. The third bolt smashed into the bows of the following boat and tore through the leg of the man urging his comrades on. He fell back among them with a brief cry before the impact drove the breath from his lungs. A moment later, the first of the boats bumped against the stern quarter, just below the catapult.

'All hands, repel boarders!' shouted the optio, and the crews abandoned their weapons at once to snatch up their shields and spears before rushing to the side. Cato was among them, and he saw a pair of hands grasp the rail directly in front of him. Drawing his sword, he slashed at one of them just as the rebel's head rose up between them. The blade cut at an angle across the hand, shattering bones and severing three fingers. The rebel's jaws opened in a howl of agony, and he released his grip and dropped down into the boat as his fingers rolled off the rail onto the deck.

Another warrior was hoisted up near the stern post, and Cato turned to engage the man as he scrambled onto the deck. He was the same age as Cato, armed with a two-handed axe which he whirled overhead as he made to attack the Roman officer. There was just time for Cato to raise his shield before the axe head smashed into the top of it, shattering the surface and ripping it from his grasp. He staggered but managed to thrust himself forward within the reach of the weapon, and fell against the warrior almost face to face. For the briefest instant he was aware of every detail of his opponent's facial tattoos, the piercing blue of his eyes and the sour odour of his expelled breath. Then he slammed his head forward, crushing the bridge of the man's nose with the reinforced rim of his helmet. At the same time, he thrust his sword up, the point piercing the soft flesh under the rebel's ribcage before tearing through his vital organs and piercing his heart. The man let out a groan and was blinking fitfully as Cato thrust him back with his left hand while he wrenched his sword free.

A quick glance along the deck was enough to see that the marines were holding their own for now as the men in the three boats alongside struggled to get aboard. Cato sheathed his sword and stepped over to the catapult's ammunition basket, picking up one of the rocks and hurrying back to the side. Raising it high, he took quick aim and hurled it down amid the faces looking up at him. They pushed aside to avoid it, and it smashed into the bottom of the boat, splintering the wood and letting the water gush in. He repeated the attack with the same result before the rebels grasped the danger and renewed their efforts to get aboard the warship. They were too few to overwhelm the defenders, though, and Cato and the marines were able to keep them at bay. At length, exasperated, the surviving warriors aboard the three remaining boats pulled back and paddled over to the other anchored ship, the craft that Cato had damaged limping behind the others.

The marines on the other liburnian had been reduced to a tight knot at the stern, fighting for their lives as the enemy swarmed before them. Some of the warriors had their wits about them and had heaved one of the bolt-throwers over the side and moved on to the second. Others were doing the same for ammunition and any other items aboard while another hacked at the bow anchor cable with his axe. Beyond the embattled warship, Cato could see the first of the boats loaded with marines paddling through the gap. They would not arrive in time to save the men on the other liburnian, Cato realised. Not unless something was done to shake the enemy's nerve. He turned to the artillery crews.

'Train the bolt-throwers on the other ship. Sweep the deck.'

The optio hesitated.

'We'll be dead if we don't do something now! Shoot the rebels down, Optio!'

The crews hurriedly adjusted the aim of their weapons, then reloaded and loosed the bolts at close range, an almost flat trajectory. The effect was devastating among the packed ranks of the enemy. The man with the axe had just parted the cable and sprang back, punching the air in triumph. He was caught in the chest and thrown backwards over the side. The rebels had managed to heave the two remaining bolt-throwers overboard and had hacked the torsion cables of the catapult to ribbons before their leader bellowed an order and his surviving men began to return to their boats and strike out for the island. They had spotted the approaching marines and rightly feared they might be trapped if they remained any longer. The crews on Cato's ship swung their weapons to bear on the enemy boats.

'Cease shooting!' he cried out. 'There are friendly boats out there too!'

The marines stood down and became bystanders for the final phase of the fight as a running battle developed between the rebel boats and those of the marines attempting to cut them off from Lyngomara. Cato could only watch as the bloody duel unfolded before him, like the spectacular gladiatorial naumachia he had once seen take place on a lake outside Rome during the reign of Claudius. The combatants stood and braced themselves in the unstable craft as they exchanged blows over the heads of those still at the paddles. Some boats had been boarded, and there were scenes of mayhem as weapons and limbs flailed. There were men in the water, dead, wounded and drowning, the latter carried under by the weight of their armour as they struggled in vain. It was by no means a one-sided fight, and the marines paid a high price for driving the enemy away. By the time the last of the rebel boats had escaped, the surface of the broad was littered with boats filled with bodies and the marines abandoned the chase to rescue their comrades who were still thrashing about in the water.

Cato's shoulders slumped as he surveyed the carnage on the deck of the other liburnian. Only six marines had survived the onslaught, and the battery had been destroyed, depriving him of a quarter of his artillery. He was furious with himself for not guarding against such an eventuality, but at the same time he could not help being in awe of the almost suicidal courage of the rebels.

Taking a deep breath, he indicated the aft anchor cable.

'Let that out, and get the battery trained on the second gatehouse. We've still got plenty of hot work to do today, lads.'

CHAPTER THIRTY-TWO

In the afternoon, the second gatehouse fell in the same way as the first, and Macro and Agricola led the legionaries pursuing the rebels past the burial mounds and into the sacred grove. A handful, marshalled by a Druid, made a last stand around the largest of the altars in the eerie atmosphere of the clearing ringed by oak trees. They were swiftly overwhelmed, the splashes of their blood bright red against the dark stains of that shed by sacrificial victims over countless generations. Small groups staged fighting withdrawals to cover the flight of their comrades and to keep open the causeway leading across the widened ditch to the gatehouse of Lyngomara itself. When the last of the surviving warriors had crossed into the settlement, the rearguard fell back in good order, using a shield wall to keep the eager Romans at bay. They heaved the gates into position in the faces of the legionaries, who were then driven back by a shower of arrows and javelins from the rebels on the tower and the palisade on each side.

Cato gave orders for the three remaining floating batteries to be moved opposite the settlement and the strongpoint. As he regarded the hall there, he wondered if Boudica had survived the day's fighting. Even as he found himself hoping that she had, the rational part of his mind realised it would be better if she had been killed. It would demoralise the rebels and spare her the indignity of being captured and paraded through the streets of

Rome before being subjected to a shameful execution in front of Nero. Once the warships were anchored in place, with their full complement of marines manning the decks to protect the artillery crews from any further assaults, Cato had a boat carry him over to the island.

He found Macro supervising the engineers as they levelled the ground through the sacred grove so that the ram could be brought forward to the last of the enemy's gatehouses. They exchanged relieved grins that they had come through the day unscathed before Macro reported on the actions to overwhelm the outer defences.

'They put up a game fight. Disciplined, brave and, I have to admit, well trained. Whoever has been drilling them has done a good job. Unfortunately for them, I did a better one. The new lads of the Second Legion performed like veterans. The boy Agricola acquitted himself admirably. He's got the makings of a fine leader one day, and maybe the brains to rise to high command. As long as he knows how to play politics as well as he fights. Reminds me of you, as it happens.'

'I'm not sure about that,' Cato replied. 'He has the advantage of being born into the patrician class. I've already been promoted as far as my origins allow. He can go further. Much further. Maybe one day he'll have Suetonius's position? Who knows?'

Macro removed his helmet and wiped his sweaty brow. 'If he rises that far, I hope for his sake they make him governor of a better province than this cold, damp shithole.'

Cato smiled. 'I'm sensing you don't have any plans to remain here once the job's done.'

'Not on your life. I've had it with Britannia. I've seen too many good people die here, and the place has taken everything I ever owned. Once we leave, I never want to set foot here again.'

'Let's go and see what we're up against now,' said Cato, and they left the engineers to their work and walked through the

387

glade and out of the trees to inspect the enemy's last line of defence. There was open, level ground for nearly a hundred paces before the land tapered in the approach to the ditch before the third gatehouse. Two lines of battered posts stood off to one side, along with leather bags bulging with pebbles. 'Looks like their training ground.'

Macro nodded. 'We're lucky it's taken them so long to get round to training their men properly. I wouldn't have given much for our chances of conquering Britannia if they had adopted such methods before we arrived.'

'Sometimes the adage "better late than never" loses its bite,' said Cato. 'Fortunately for us.'

The legionaries had pulled back out of effective range of the defences and were resting on their shields or sitting on the ground, clustered about their standards, as they waited for the mantle to be wheeled into position for the final assault. Macro looked up at the sky.

'We've perhaps three hours of light left. It'll take at least an hour to clear the way for the ram to get through the remains of the second gatehouse and another to get it through the grove and across the open ground. It's going to be tight timing if we're going to manage another attack before night comes.'

Cato nodded. 'Then give Agricola the order to bring forward the rest of the legionaries and have them prepare field defences across this open ground.'

'You think they might mount a counter-attack?'

'After what happened earlier, I'm not prepared to take any risks. If they're desperate enough to try something else, we'll be ready for them.'

Macro was silent before he spoke. 'I was watching that. We were lucky we got away as lightly as we did.'

'Lightly?' Cato recalled the sight of the bloody action fought across the water.

'It could have been much worse.'

'True ... We'll rest our men tonight. Meanwhile, they'll have plenty to keep them occupied once the warships begin to bombard the defences. When morning comes, we'll just have to deal with whatever exhausted remnants they have left to oppose us.'

As soon as the liburnians were anchored in line facing the settlement, smoke trailed from the braziers on board, ready to light the incendiaries. Heavy clay pots filled with glowing embers were loaded onto the catapults and launched towards the settlement, where they burst on and around the huts. Soon a number of fires had started and smoke billowed into the air. When darkness fell, the surrounding palisade was starkly delineated by the glow of flames within. As fast as one fire was extinguished, another broke out, and by midnight, half of the settlement, including the gatehouse, was an inferno. Only the round huts closest to the final strongpoint and the hall remained unscathed.

In the Roman camp, few men slept. Most were transfixed by the terrible spectacle of the inferno, their faces and armour gleaming red in the glow of the flames. Even Macro, who had long since mastered the veteran's skill of falling asleep on demand, remained awake, sitting at Cato's side as they watched the blaze, accompanied by the steady crack of the catapults unleashing their missiles from the illuminated decks of the three ships. The surface of the water gleamed and glittered with their reflections, each shot from the catapults causing the hull to tremble and send out ripples across the surface of the mere. Cato could only imagine the fear and despair of the rebels trapped within their ill-fated stronghold.

'We can't save the gatehouse,' Syphodubnus reported as he stood before his queen outside the hall, his face streaked with grime. Behind him loomed most of what was left of the rebels. A few

389

others were still fighting the fires to keep them spreading too close to the strongpoint and endangering their last refuge. 'It'll be burned out long before dawn. There will be nothing to stop the Romans breaking into the settlement. We've also lost men fighting the fires. Struck down by their catapults or bolt-throwers.'

'How many are left?' asked Boudica, her voice strained.

'Perhaps three hundred, majesty. No more than that. Aside from your personal bodyguard.'

'Three hundred and fifty in all,' she mused wearily. 'Enough to make another attack on their warships?'

'It would be suicide. Our boats would be lit up by the flames the moment they set off. Easy targets for the bolt-throwers. We'd be slaughtered.'

Boudica gestured towards the fire. 'It would appear that we will be dead anyway come the morning.'

Syphodubnus was still, and then nodded. 'Yes. All is lost. What matters now is the manner of our deaths. Or do we choose surrender?'

'No surrender,' Boudica replied. 'Not for me. I will not be taken alive. Not while I have the strength to fight. I will die with a blade in my hand and spitting curses at the Roman dogs. That is my choice, but you and the others must decide your own fates. You have earned that. If any wish to surrender, they must live with the shame of that for every day they endure as slaves until the Romans work them to death. If they choose to fight on, they will die as warriors. If they choose not to risk being taken alive, they will be honoured for their courage by their ancestors in the Otherworld.'

'Suicide?' Syphodubnus said slowly. 'Is that what you have chosen for yourself? There is a better option, my queen. I have spoken to the others.' He gestured to the dark shapes of the men behind him. 'The way is still clear to the last of the boats. We

390

can use them to escape into the marshes to the south. If we can reach the tribes of the far north, or those still fighting on in the mountains to the west, we can keep the rebellion alive.'

'I will not flee,' she replied firmly.

'Then we can use the boats to cross to the grove and attack the Romans. We would be honoured if you were to lead us in the last charge of the Iceni.'

She smiled sadly. 'I cannot lead a charge.'

She opened her cloak, and in the glow of the distant flames, all could see the shaft of the bolt that had pierced her side during the barrage of Roman missiles shot at the second gatehouse. She had tried to remove it, but the agony was unbearable and only caused further loss of blood. She could already feel herself weakening and did not want to collapse in front of her followers. There were gasps and groans as the warriors beheld their stricken queen.

She swallowed and summoned up the strength to speak clearly above the muted crackle of the flames. 'We have done all that can be asked of us in the name of liberty. We fought against the tyranny and injustice of the Romans. We brought them to within an inch of defeat. The people of this island will never forget us. Rome will never forget us. We have earned their respect and now we must make the final sacrifice to set the seal on a reputation that will echo down the centuries . . .' She swayed slightly, and Syphodubnus rushed forward to take her arm and steady her. She took a few breaths to recover enough to continue. 'It is time for us to die. All that is left for us is to make a good death. I wish it could have been different. I wish we could have won a famous victory and revelled together in its aftermath. But we have lost and we must pay the price. I thank you for your loyalty. It has been a privilege to serve as your queen.' Tears rolled down her cheeks so that she turned her face away from the others in shame. 'Take me away. Take me to my throne.'

The warriors looked on in silence as Boudica was helped away into the darkness of the hall. They knew it was the last time any of them would see her.

Out of sight of her followers, Syphodubnus picked her up as gently as he could and carried her to the oaken chair on the dais. He eased her into position, and she winced as the shaft moved slightly in her side.

'Where is Bardea?'

'I haven't seen her today, my queen. I can send men to find her.'

'No. Let her come to me, if she will. If you can't find her, maybe the Romans can't either. Maybe she has found a way to escape. I pray to Andraste it is so.'

Her voice was fading and her eyes fluttered, then she grimaced and her face twisted in agony for a while before the worst of it passed.

'I'm thirsty.'

Syphodubnus looked round and saw a jug and clay cups on the nearest of the trestle tables. He returned to her side with a cup and cradled her head as he raised it to her lips. She managed a few sips before turning away. 'Enough.'

He held her a moment longer before easing his arms away.

'Do you have a dagger, Syphodubnus? I lost mine earlier.'

'Yes, majesty.'

'Let me have it.'

When he hesitated, she forced a smile. 'You have been a loyal and obedient adviser and companion this last year. Will you deny me your obedience now, at the end? Very well, I ask you . . . as a friend.'

Swallowing his grief, he reached for the handle above the small scabbard hanging from his belt and drew the blade. He closed her fingers around the handle and laid the weapon in her lap. She nodded her thanks, then raised her other hand and waved him away. 'Go, Syphodubnus. Go and make your prayers to the gods before you die.'

He bowed his head and made to turn away, then came to her side and kissed her on the brow. As he strode back down the hall, he forced himself not to look back at the lone figure sitting in the high chair.

Boudica watched him leave, then let out a groan as she tried to find a less painful position to sit in. She kept a firm grip on the dagger, fearful that if it slipped from her grasp and fell to the floor, she would not have the strength to retrieve it. Her mind wandered, and powerful memories flowed through it in no seeming order. She saw Prasutagus as he had been before his illness, the powerful warrior with the hearty laugh who was loved by his people and his family; her daughters as children, breathless and flushed with unbridled joy after playing in the fields on a hot summer's day; her father and mother seated on stools by the hearth of the round hut she had grown up in; Macro grinning with delight as he looked down at her the first time they had made love, in a stable at Camulodunum; Bardea, her face contorted with rage after being told who her father really was.

The pain came again, and she clenched her muscles to fight it, the fingernails of the dagger hand biting into the palm as she shifted the blade across the upturned wrist of her left hand and closed her eyes. It was too bad that Bardea could not be there at the end, but there was little time left if she was to die by her own hand.

'Farewell, daughter . . . my love, my life. I go to join your sister and Prasutagus . . . Farewell.'

Outside the hall, Syphodubnus called the men together to explain his plan. None demurred, and when he left the strongpoint, he gathered up those fighting the fires and led the way around the interior of the stockade towards the small landing stage where the remaining boats were moored. The first wave climbed aboard in silence and followed his boat as they paddled as quietly as possible to the edge of the open ground across from the Roman field defences. He could see campfires blazing among the oak trees of the sacred grove and felt unfathomable rage over the Romans using the limbs of the trees for firewood. It took a while for the last of the men to be landed, and they crouched down by the water's edge to stay out of the light of the flames consuming the gatehouse and the settlement beyond.

Syphodubnus quietly called for all the surviving chiefs to join him to issue his final orders.

'We go along the shore, keeping out of the light. There's to be no noise. No war cries. We go in hard and fast before they realise what's happening. Tell your men to target their officers first. No prisoners, no surrender and fight until the end . . .'

He sent the first band off and then followed with the rest, crouching as they made their way along the line of posts marking the uncompleted palisade. As they drew closer to the Roman position, he could clearly hear the singing and cheerful banter of those still awake. The first band had almost reached the freshly dug ditch that stretched across the island when a sentry challenged them. They made no response, but rose up in a dark wave and swarmed across the ditch and up the far side before dragging the wooden stakes aside and pouring across the rampart.

'To arms! To arms!' the sentry managed to cry out before he was overwhelmed and cut down. The alarm was repeated by sentries further along the rampart and then picked up by those in the camp.

'Spread out!' Syphodubnus bellowed. 'Kill them! Kill them for Boudica and the Iceni!'

His men spread out, racing across the camp and slashing their long swords at the enemy. Their silence unnerved the Romans as they seemed to come from all directions, criss-crossing the tent lines and moving swiftly towards the centre of the camp in the heart of the sacred grove. Syphodubnus, who had trained alongside the other rebels over winter and was every bit as fit as them, followed two men as they sprinted between the rows of tents. Some of the legionaries were already standing outside and were cut down as the rebels raced through. Others spilled out, swords drawn, and managed to fight back, killing some of the raiders. Confusion consumed the camp – dark shapes running, fighting, stumbling amid the cacophony of Roman voices calling out in alarm, issuing orders, shouting warnings while blades clashed and scraped.

Despite the initial surprise and casualties inflicted, the legionaries recovered swiftly and struck down the outnumbered rebels. Syphodubnus saw one of the men ahead of him run straight into a group of legionaries forming up outside their tent, swords drawn. The rebel's sword hacked deep into a Roman skull before he was knocked down by two more and stabbed repeatedly. The second warrior charged in, slashing his sword wide so that it cut almost through the arm of a legionary. He too was felled by the man's comrades.

Syphodubnus swerved aside, keeping low as he ran, all the time heading in the direction of the cluster of command tents in the centre of the grove, illuminated from within by braziers. Outside, the Roman standards gleamed tawny gold in the firelight. Officers had emerged from the tents, roused by the cries of alarm and sounds of fighting. He saw one, tall, slender and dark-haired, with a scar across his face, turning to look in the other direction as another officer, shorter and more muscular, came running out of the darkness. With a flash of realisation Syphodubnus recognised the latter as the Roman who had called on Boudica to surrender the previous day.

All around him the sounds of fighting were diminishing, and he realised he had one last chance to make his mark before he died. Steeling himself, he increased his pace into a dead run and burst out between the tents, making for the taller of the officers.

Two legionaries stood in his way, but only one was looking in his direction. Syphodubnus shoulder-barged the other, sending him flying, before he swung his long sword at the first. The man instinctively raised his own sword to parry the blow, and at the last moment, Syphodubnus angled his blade up, knocking his opponent's weapon aside and slicing off the top of the man's scalp. Then he was through, with only ten paces to cover before he could reach the startled Roman officer he aimed to take into the Otherworld with him.

His face stretched into a savage, triumphant snarl as he leaped at the man, sword outstretched, the point aimed directly at the officer's throat. Then there was a blur of movement to his left as a figure slammed into his side and both men tumbled to the ground. The air had been driven from Syphodubnus's lungs, and he could not breathe as he wrestled to break free of the man's grip on the wrist of his sword arm. More figures were moving in around him, and he felt a blow on his shin as a blade cut through the bone.

'Hold him down, lad!' a voice cried.

More blows landed, cutting into Syphodubnus and piercing deeply into his body, which jerked under the impact. He felt a terrible sense of failure as his life bled out of him. Boudica was dead and his men had been killed, and now he was the last of the rebels, the last warrior of the Iceni, and the rebellion died with him. He felt a heavy blow land on his head and there was an explosion of light in his skull, and then nothing.

The Romans backed away from the body and Macro reached down to haul Tribune Agricola to his feet. In the light of the nearest campfire, the young officer looked shaken as he felt over his body checking for wounds. Finding none, he grinned in relief.

'Well done, lad!' Macro clapped him on the shoulder. 'If you hadn't acted so quickly, the bastard would have got our prefect.

That was a close escape, Cato. As close as it gets. He did all right, our Agricola!'

Cato had recovered his wits, and drew his sword as more men formed up to protect the command tent. There were still confused shouts from across the camp but no sounds of fighting as the legionaries stalked between the tents to hunt down and finish off the last of the wounded rebels. He looked around, still surprised by the daring of the enemy when all seemed lost. His men would have to tread carefully when they launched the final attack in the morning.

CHAPTER THIRTY-THREE

A handful of fires burned across the settlement as the sun rose, and a pall of smoke hung over the island in the still air. There was not even the faintest of breezes, and that added to the tension of the atmosphere. The legionary cohorts had been given the honour of completing the capture of the rebel stronghold and planting their standard outside the hut in Boudica's strongpoint. They stood formed up on either side of the enemy's training ground as the mantle slowly rumbled across the open ground towards the last of the gatehouses. It was the only sound, apart from the faint crackle of flames, and the eyes and ears of every Roman strained to detect any sign of the enemy.

'Some kind of trap, perhaps?' Tribune Agricola wondered as he stood with the other senior officers at Cato's side.

Cato shook his head. 'I don't know. It seems unlikely. What can they hope to gain by keeping out of sight.'

'Perhaps some escaped while we were attacked last night, sir.'

It was possible, Cato reflected. The Romans had been preoccupied by scouring the camp for the enemy and counting the cost of their surprise incursion. Over eighty men had been killed and twice as many wounded. Fortunately most were flesh wounds, and the walking wounded had insisted on forming up with their comrades this morning in order to take part in the final action of the rebellion.

The frame of the gatehouse was intact, but fire had burned away all the hoardings and ladders, and only the blackened structural timbers remained along with the scorched gate.

'We'll know what they're planning soon enough,' said Macro. 'Once the ram has done its work.'

The officers watched as the mantle made steady progress towards the causeway. Not a single face appeared on the palisade. No missiles arced over the defences to bombard the mantle as it slowed to a halt. A moment later, there was a thud as the ram struck. Then again and again in a steady rhythm. Each time the gates shuddered, gradually being pounded to pieces, until at length the locking bar broke and they swung inwards, one falling off its hinges. The final impact proved too much for the fragile skeleton of the tower, and the charred timbers collapsed in on themselves and tumbled down across the ruined gates and the front of the mantle as choking ash swirled into the air.

'Lead the First Century forward, Tribune Agricola,' Cato ordered. 'Take the gatehouse.'

The first formation of legionaries marched in column towards the rear of the mantle as those inside came out, the last of them coughing and spluttering as they supported the handful of men who had been injured by the debris that had collapsed the front of the structure. Agricola led his men along either side and they began to clear away the charred and broken timbers to gain access to the gates and pass through into the settlement. As the last of them disappeared from sight, Cato could hear occasional shouted orders, but no sounds of fighting.

'I don't like the look of this,' Macro said quietly.

'Take the next century forward and pull the mantle back, then clear the rest of the debris away.'

As Macro carried out his orders, Cato noticed that one of the legionaries had mounted the palisade and was waving an arm to attract attention. He trotted forward to the edge of the ditch.

'What's happening?'

'There's no one here, sir. The place seems to be deserted. Just ruins, a few fires and some undamaged huts. Nothing besides.'

'I'm coming in.' Cato turned to Macro. 'Bring up the rest of the legionaries. Close order.'

'Yes, sir.'

Cato strode across the causeway and through the gap where the gates and debris had been cleared away. Beyond, the settlement was in ruins as far as a section of undamaged huts close to the strongpoint, where the hall still stood proud above the line of the palisade. Some huts still burned, the thatch of the roofs in flames amid the charred remains of the wattle-and-daub walls. Others were blackened piles of ashes and timber. The acrid stink of burning caught in Cato's throat as he made his way through what was left of the place. Small groups of legionaries picked over the ruins or stood looking on with a mixture of puzzlement and vigilance in case the rebels had a final trick to play on their foe.

Behind Cato came the rest of the legionaries. Macro halted them just inside the settlement to wait for further orders before he moved forward to join his friend. They proceeded to the far end, where Agricola and two sections were sheltering behind an undamaged hut close to the narrow bridge that connected the settlement to the final strongpoint where Boudica's hall still stood, untouched by the fires.

'We've seen no sign of life, sir,' the tribune reported. 'Only a few bodies. And a mass grave over to the side there.' He pointed to the northern-facing palisade running along the water's edge.

Cato stepped out into the open to examine the single gate of the stronghold directly opposite and saw that it was slightly ajar. He filled his lungs and shouted across.

'In the name of Rome, I call on any still within to surrender!'

There was no reply. He waited for a while before he turned

to the others, drawing his sword. 'Let's go. Keep close and watch for any sign of danger.'

With Macro at his side and Agricola leading the small column of legionaries, he approached the bridge and crossed to the gate. He pushed it open slowly and looked round the perimeter of the stockade, but there was no movement. Entering, he stepped to the side, waving the others through, and the party stood, shields to the front, eyes sweeping their surroundings. Besides the hall there were some empty stables, a few store sheds and a handful of small round huts.

'Search the buildings,' Cato ordered.

The legionaries fanned out, kicking open doors and looking inside the buildings for any sign of the enemy.

'Sir! Over here!' One of the men who had made for the hall was standing on the threshold. 'We've found someone!'

Cato and Macro hurried forward as Agricola trotted across from the stables. The interior of the hall was gloomy, save for the angled shafts of light piercing the vents in the roof above the hearths. Another legionary stood halfway down the hall. Beyond him, on a raised platform, beside an ornately carved chair, were two figures. One was a woman lying on her back atop a low bier. She was formally posed, with her arms crossed and her hands covering the handle of a sword that lay on her chest, the blade resting between the thighs of her leggings. At her feet gleamed an eagle, the one that had been taken from the Ninth Legion, Cato realised. Another woman knelt beside her, facing the Romans as she held up a dagger, the dull point aimed in their direction. Macro and Cato recognised her at once. Bardea, the elder daughter of Boudica, who was surely the person lying on the bier.

'What are your orders, sir?' asked the legionary. 'Shall I kill the bitch?'

Macro felt his muscles flinch with rage, and he clenched his jaw as he snarled, 'Get out! Get out before I shove that shield so far up your arse you start spitting wood shavings. GET OUT!'

The legionary scurried back towards the entrance of the hall, ducking as he ran past Macro.

Cato turned to Agricola. 'You go with him and close the door. Make sure no one enters. Have the men continue to search the other buildings.'

The tribune gestured towards Bardea. 'She's armed, sir.'

'So she is. I think Centurion Macro and I can handle matters by ourselves. Go.'

Once the door was pulled to, Cato undid his chin strap and removed his helmet, setting it down on the nearest table. He glanced at Macro. 'Take off your helmet so she can see who you are.'

'I know who he is!' Bardea cried, jabbing her blade in Macro's direction. She looked down at her mother's body with an anguished expression. 'She told me . . . How can it be true? I am a princess of the Iceni. How can I have Roman blood in my veins?'

Macro had quietly removed his helmet as she spoke, and now he approached her. She spun back to him. 'Stop! I swear to Andraste that I will kill you before I turn this blade on myself.'

He did as she said, now no more than ten feet from her, and slowly extended his hand. 'Give me the blade, lass. I swear on my life that I mean you no harm.'

Her face twisted into a mask of despair and hatred. 'How can you be my father?'

Macro gave a simple shrug. 'Because we wanted each other. At the time, it was as simple as that. You were conceived out of affection, Bardea. That is something to be grateful for in this world, believe me.'

'Grateful? My world has been destroyed. Rome destroyed it. Romans raped me and my sister. Rome killed Merida, my mother and those who followed her. And now I find that Rome has even destroyed who I thought I was.'

Cato stayed where he was, sensing the danger of the situation. Any approach he made might cause her to turn the dagger on herself before she could be stopped.

'You are who you have always been,' Macro pointed out gently. 'Nothing has changed in you. And you can't blame your mother for something that happened many years ago. At the time, my people and your mother's were allies. You must know that we fought together then, and that she helped us face down the Londinium gangs only two years ago. If you know that, then you must know there was a strong bond between us. Why else would I have helped the three of you escape from the procurator who abused you all? If your mother had not been promised to Prasutagus, who knows what might have happened? I might have married her and raised you, and I would have been proud to be your father. I *am* your father.'

She shook her head slowly from side to side.

'I spoke to your mother only yesterday. In front of the gatehouse.'

'I saw you.'

'Then you will recall how we had a moment's exchange in private?'

She nodded.

'Your mother knew then that her cause was lost. And she knew that she would never be taken alive. She made me promise on my most sacred oath to find you and protect you. I gave her my word, freely. As I give it to you now. I swear that I will take care of you, Bardea. And we shall both always honour her memory. As long as you live, she lives on.'

He stepped towards her. 'Let me have the dagger.'

'No!' She sprang at him and thrust the dagger into his chest. The point caught on one of his medallions as he wrapped his arms around her and held her close. She tried again, limited by his embrace, and it stabbed into the ring links of the armour over his shoulder. Then it dropped from her fingers and she pressed her face into his chest.

'Easy does it,' Macro said softly. 'You're safe. No harm will come to you.'

Cato came forward slowly, passing them, and looked down on Boudica's body. He could see the stump of the bolt protruding from her side, and the self-inflicted wounds to her wrists, washed clean now. Her expression was peaceful. Someone had closed her eyes and combed out her hair so that it framed her face like flames frozen in the act.

He leaned down to retrieve the eagle.

'What now?' Macro asked over Bardea's head.

'The orders were to produce Boudica dead or alive.'

'But we're not going to do that, are we, brother?' There was a determined hardness to Macro's tone that would not brook disagreement. He sounded almost dangerous, thought Cato.

'No, we're not. She must be honoured like a queen, not treated like a slave or a criminal.'

'I agree,' said Macro. 'Give me a hand.'

He gently eased Bardea away and sat her down on a nearby bench before he indicated the bundles of kindling wood stacked at the side of the hall. 'That'll do to start with.'

Cato set the eagle down, and the two Roman officers silently built up the kindling around the bier, then surrounded it with benches and tables. Macro crossed to the nearest hearth and used the toe of his boot to shift the ashes aside until he saw the red glow of the embers. He took some dry rushes from the floor and twisted them into a taper before kneeling to present it to the embers and blowing gently. They flared red, then orange, before a tiny flame flickered. The flame spread to the taper, and he stood up and went to Bardea. 'Here. You should do this.'

Bardea's hand trembled as she approached the bier, and Macro stepped up beside her and steadied her hand with his own as she held the flame to the kindling at the foot of the bier. It took a moment for the brittle twigs and shavings to catch light. As soon

404

as the fire was lit, he took the taper and went to the side of the hall, thrusting it into the thatch. That caught quickly, and smoke swirled into the shaft of light above.

'Let's go,' said Cato, tucking the eagle under his arm. For a moment he was afraid that Bardea might leap onto her mother's pyre, but she bowed her head and turned away. Macro put his arm around her shoulder, and the three of them paced towards the far end of the hall and pushed the door aside.

Agricola glanced at the girl but said nothing as she and Macro walked past him towards the gate in the palisade.

Looking back into the hall, Cato could see that the pyre was alight and the flames were roaring softly as they began to consume the body. More flames were spreading rapidly across the thatch, and a wash of heat swept towards him.

'Who is she?' Agricola asked, nodding towards Macro and his daughter.

'A serving girl,' said Cato. 'She's the centurion's prisoner now.'

'And the body?'

'One of Boudica's daughters. The other died months ago. That one was killed in battle yesterday. Like her mother.'

'Boudica's dead?'

'Shortly after the first attack began, according to the girl. The rebels weighted her body and let her sink into the broad.'

'Did the girl say where?'

Cato shook his head.

'Too bad. We'll never find the body.'

Cato turned away. 'I want this place torched. Every building. Every boat. All that is left of the fortifications. No trace of Lyngomara is to remain. Understand?'

'Yes, sir.'

'Carry on, Tribune.' Cato exchanged a salute and set off after his friend.

CHAPTER THIRTY-FOUR

Londinium

'You did well to recover the Ninth's eagle,' said Julius Classicianus as he admired the gleaming ornament on his desk where Cato had placed it.

'We were lucky to find it, sir.'

'But not so lucky with respect to finding Boudica. No trace of her body, you say?' the procurator asked. 'Other than the story you were told about it being dumped in the water.'

'None, sir,' Cato replied. 'We searched through the enemy bodies. There were very few females. Some were too badly burned to be identified, but none of them had any jewellery on them, as you'd expect to find on their queen. But then again, such items might have been removed by her people. Either way, she died at Lyngomara and we weren't able to recover her body to return it to the governor.'

'The former governor,' Classicianus corrected him.

In the months since Cato had last been to Londinium, much had changed. Suetonius had gone and Classicianus had been appointed acting governor in his place. It had only taken Polyclitus a short time to conclude that Suetonius had been reckless to have taken so many men with him to conquer Mona, leaving the rest of the province dangerously short of troops to keep order among the tribes assumed to be friendly or pacified. The devastation of Londinium and other towns and settlements had shocked the freedman, as had Suetonius's vengeful policies after defeating the rebel army, which had smacked more of revenge than restoring order. Accordingly, Polyclitus had exercised the authority extended to him by Nero to relieve Suetonius and send him back to the capital to explain himself to the emperor.

'Yes, sir, the former governor.'

Classicianus sat back in the finely upholstered chair he had inherited from his predecessor and folded his hands. 'It's a pity you failed to persuade her to surrender. It might have helped rehabilitate Suetonius if he had been able to present her to Nero.'

Cato could see where the conversation was leading. The acting governor was trying to ascertain how far Cato had gone along with Suetonius's vengeful policies, and Cato was determined to defend his actions. 'Believe me, if I could have persuaded her, I would have. We gave her every chance, right down to the day of the final attack. She chose to die rather than surrender, sir. It's regrettable not only because it means there is no captive to parade through Rome's streets but also because it led to so many avoidable deaths once it was clear the rebellion had failed. Saving lives was uppermost in my mind when I set about putting an end to Iceni resistance.'

'Well, yes . . . quite. The pointless slaughter of barbarians has a deleterious impact on the taxes we could extract from them.'

'That was also on my mind, sir,' Cato responded drily.

'I can see that from the comments in your report about showing clemency to the Trinovantes and the Iceni. You are lucky that I'm the one reading your report and not Suetonius. I imagine he would not be impressed by your views.'

'Almost certainly.'

'In which case, you are either a rash individual or one who puts principle before personal progress.'

'Or one who has ceased caring about how his words are

received as long as they are accurate, sir. In my report I merely stated the truth. The people of the tribes have suffered enough. If they are pushed any further, we will only provoke more uprisings. More atrocities. More revenge. More bloodshed . . . Less tax revenue.'

Classicianus smiled. 'Indeed. It seems to me that I could use someone with your understanding of the province and its people on my staff. There's plenty to do to restore order and rebuild our relations with the people we rule. That requires men with the kind of qualities I see in you. If you are prepared to give up your military career and take on administrative duties, I am sure you will find that the work gives you ample scope to put your values into practice. It could also be quite lucrative. What do you say, Cato?'

'It's a generous offer, sir. I appreciate it, truly.'

'But . . .'

Now it was Cato's turn to smile. 'But I am exhausted, sir. In truth, I have had enough of this island. And . . . There was a moment, during their last attack, when I was sure I was done for. One of their warriors broke through to the headquarters tent and came at me. I have never seen such inchoate rage and hatred on a man's face. I was terrified. The man was feral. These people are barbarians.' He shuddered at the memory before he managed to push it aside. 'Much as I admire many of the qualities of the Britons, I am tired of their petty tribal rivalries and arrogant belligerence. You may not have been here long enough to understand it, but you will find out soon enough that though we rule them, they still consider themselves superior to us.'

'Superior?' Classicianus scoffed. 'By all the gods! They live in crude huts. They have no written language. No appreciation of culture, civilisation or the rule of law. Every army they have sent against us has been soundly beaten and every fortification stormed and destroyed. They are the very essence of all that we subjugated.'

'Every word of that is true. But they lack the intellect to

understand it. They have an arrogance about them that is only matched by our own. The difference is we can justify ours rather more convincingly. They are a defeated people. They should understand that and accept it, but they won't. You will find that something of a challenge to deal with, sir. I'd begin with Vellocatus. He will need some taming. It was fortunate for us that Boudica made an enemy out of him. His scouts proved of use to us, but I had to ensure that he was kept out of Icenian territory as far as possible for fear of what he might do to them. Now that Boudica is dead and the rebellion is over, he may be an obstacle to restoring peace in the region.'

Classicianus sighed. 'We seem to be good at making alliances with those we have to subsequently destroy in order to get the kind of peace we want.'

'It's an old story, sir. I don't suppose that will ever change for any empire in the future.'

'I expect not.'

'I wish you well,' Cato continued. 'If I was ten years younger, I might take you up on your offer. But I have served Rome as a soldier for nearly twenty years without pause. I have earned a rest. That is why I am requesting that my resignation from active service is accepted with immediate effect.'

Surprise contested irritation in Classicianus's expression before he responded. 'You are needed here, Prefect. That is your duty.'

'With respect, sir, I am no longer needed. The rebellion has been crushed. The legionaries and the other units have returned to their bases, and I have left the Eighth Illyrian at Camulodunum under the command of Centurion Galerius. He's a good officer. Perfectly capable of keeping order in that part of the province. There are plenty of men in Rome awaiting the chance to command an auxiliary cohort, so you will replace me easily enough. All I ask of you is that you give me permission to leave Britannia and return to Rome.'

The procurator stared at Cato for a while before he sighed. 'Very well. I'll have the travel warrant drawn up for you. I hope you understand what you are doing. A man who chooses to give up his command is unlikely to be offered another any time soon. You'll get your rest, Prefect Cato, but it may last longer than you find comfortable. I don't get the impression that you are cut out for a peaceful civilian existence.'

'I'll have to discover for myself if that's true, sir.'

'Very well. I have to say I am disappointed by your decision. At the same time, you have surely earned a break and I wish you well on that account. For the sake of the Empire, I hope that once you have rested enough, there will be another command waiting for you. I suspect you will be needed again at some point.'

'I am sure the Empire can get along without me until then, sir.'

They shared a smile before Classicianus gestured towards the door of the office. 'Dismissed. May the gods grant you a swift and safe journey home.'

'Rome?' Claudia responded anxiously once Cato had related the details of his meeting with the procurator.

'Not Rome,' said Cato. 'We'll live on the farming estate. We'll keep to ourselves and enjoy some peace for a change. I can visit the house in Rome from time to time. If only to check in on Macro and Petronella. I've said that they can live there as long as they want.'

His friend smiled. 'Are you sure about that? It's a big place for the three of us.'

'It'll give Bardea a chance to get used to her new life. What better place to begin than Rome? Where is she, by the way?'

'With Lucius, in the other room,' Petronella answered.

Cato felt a surge of alarm. Ever since they had left Lyngomara, Bardea had been quiet and moody, sometimes grieving for her lost family and her lost people, sometimes bitter and angry and

410

full of hatred towards Rome. That had moderated a little over the month that had passed, but he still retained a degree of concern about her uncertain behaviour, and the thought of her being left alone with Lucius set his heart racing. He rose from the table in the cramped quarters they were sharing and went to the door of the room assigned to him, Claudia and Lucius, opening it quietly and peeking in.

Lucius was sitting on the camp bed on his side of the room and Bardea was next to him. The boy was reading from a scroll, enunciating words clearly before he spelled them out letter by letter, pointing them out on the scroll for Bardea to repeat. The door creaked on the hinges and both stopped to look up at Cato.

'Is anything the matter, Father?'

The relief in Cato's heart gave way to pride that his son was helping the girl to take her first steps into a new life. When Bardea smiled shyly, he felt a spark of hope. After all that had happened, this small scene held promise of a better future for all of them.